"YOU KNOW, I'VE WATCHED THAT MAYBE TWO DOZEN TIMES NOW, AND LET ME TELL YOU IT NEVER GETS ANY BETTER."

"It only ever gets worse. Life, huh? Only ever gets worse. Let me show you the best-case scenario."

This, Picard thought, as he watched the rings spread out again, was stretching the definition of the word *best* beyond reason.

"Our best estimate?" said Raffi, to the question Picard was posing in his mind. *"The impact is likely to be felt within 9.7 light-years of the Romulan star. Whichever way we model this—and trust me, we've run a lot of models—the threat to the stability of the Romulan Star Empire is catastrophic. Shall I go into the specific ramifications of this, or are the broad lines pretty clear?"*

Quite clear, Picard thought. Trillions would be affected, not only in the home system, but well beyond. He leaned forward in his chair and watched the presentation to the unhappy end. Beside him, his tea, forgotten, cooled. *Nothing will ever be the same again. . . .*

… **STAR TREK®**
PICARD
THE LAST BEST HOPE

Una McCormack

Based upon *Star Trek*®
created by Gene Roddenberry
and
Star Trek: Picard®
created by
Akiva Goldsman & Michael Chabon
&
Kirsten Beyer & Alex Kurtzman

GALLERY BOOKS

New York   London   Toronto   Sydney   New Delhi   Stardust City

Gallery Books
An Imprint of Simon & Schuster, Inc.
1230 Avenue of the Americas
New York, NY 10020

This book is a work of fiction. Any references to historical events, real people, or real places are used fictitiously. Other names, characters, places, and events are products of the author's imagination, and any resemblance to actual events or places or persons, living or dead, is entirely coincidental.

™, ® and © 2020 by CBS Studios Inc. All Rights Reserved.
STAR TREK and related marks are trademarks of CBS Studios Inc.

This book is published by Gallery Books, a division of Simon & Schuster, Inc., under exclusive license from CBS Studios Inc.

All rights reserved, including the right to reproduce this book or portions thereof in any form whatsoever. For information, address Gallery Books Subsidiary Rights Department, 1230 Avenue of the Americas, New York, NY 10020.

First Gallery Books trade paperback edition September 2020

GALLERY BOOKS and colophon are registered trademarks of Simon & Schuster, Inc.

For information about special discounts for bulk purchases, please contact Simon & Schuster Special Sales at 1-866-506-1949 or business@simonandschuster.com.

The Simon & Schuster Speakers Bureau can bring authors to your live event. For more information or to book an event, contact the Simon & Schuster Speakers Bureau at 1-866-248-3049 or visit our website at www.simonspeakers.com.

Manufactured in the United States of America

10 9 8 7 6 5 4 3 2 1

Library of Congress Cataloging-in-Publication Data is available.

ISBN 978-1-9821-3944-5
ISBN 978-1-9821-4218-6 (pbk)
ISBN 978-1-9821-3945-2 (ebook)

For Kirsten Beyer, with love

Fellow citizens, we cannot escape history. We of this Congress and this administration, will be remembered in spite of ourselves. No personal significance, or insignificance, can spare one or another of us. The fiery trial through which we pass, will light us down, in honor or dishonor, to the latest generation. We say we are for the Union. The world will not forget that we say this. We know how to save the Union. The world knows we do know how to save it. We—even we here—hold the power and bear the responsibility. In giving freedom to the slave, we assure freedom to the free—honorable alike in what we give, and what we preserve. We shall nobly save, or meanly lose, the last best hope of earth. Other means may succeed; this could not fail. The way is plain, peaceful, generous, just—a way which, if followed, the world will forever applaud, and God must forever bless.

—Abraham Lincoln
State of the Union 1862

It is possible to commit no mistakes and still lose. That is not a weakness. That is life.

—Jean-Luc Picard

Give me your tired, your poor,
Your huddled masses yearning to breathe free,
The wretched refuse of your teeming shore.
Send these, the homeless, tempest-tost to me,
I lift my lamp beside the golden door!

—Emma Lazarus
"The New Colossus"

Part 1

THE HOPE

2381-2382

1

LA BARRE, FRANCE
MANY YEARS AFTER

In latter days, sitting alone in his manor, pondering the events of the years that preceded this self-imposed exile, trying to understand where and how it had all gone wrong, M. Jean-Luc Picard (formerly of Starfleet) would often come back to one moment. Sitting on the bridge of the *Enterprise*, in command, listening to the gentle rhythms and pulses of his ship . . .

Playing back the memory, he would slow down time, as if instructing the visuals to move at half speed, at quarter speed, and he would observe himself, sitting in his chair, and he would marvel at the sight of the man he had once been: calm, assured, fully in command of himself and all around him. This, he would think, was the moment before the storm began, the split second before the end of his old life, when he took the first step down the path to here—the house that had never been the home, the land that he had longed to swap for strange and distant lands, the quiet, the immobility. The knowledge that nothing that he did now with his days mattered in the slightest. One more outcast, cast adrift. Prospero, on his island. An old conjurer, his magic spent, nursing old grievances.

Here, now; this was the moment when everything changed. It was nothing that anyone noticed at the time. His ship, the *Enterprise*, his home, from which he had been banished, was sailing close to the Neutral Zone. The old order. A quiet chime on the comm, and La Forge's voice coming through.

"Captain, we're picking up some very strange readings here . . ."

And he had said—Incredible, now he thought of it! How blind can a man be!—he had indeed said, "Anything for us to worry about, Commander?"

Yes, thought Picard, years later, *yes, more than you could have ever known. Watch out. Beware. Choose your course wisely now . . .*

"Let me get back to you on that one."

Another chime, this one signifying an incoming message from Starfleet Command. Picard stood up, smoothed imagined imperfections from his uniform, and went into his ready room, where he received a summons back to Earth.

And all that was to follow had followed. He had not, now that he thought about it, seen the *Enterprise* since.

Clouds flecked across the hillside. The vines hung heavy. The old clock ticked in the hall. Time yawned ahead: empty time. Picard, in limbo, pondered the past, and continued to fail to find answers there. Such were his mornings, his afternoons, his evenings. Such passed the days, for M. Jean-Luc Picard (formerly of Starfleet), the most disillusioned man in two quadrants.

At this point, usually, Picard would sigh, and raise his eyes, and look around his beautiful, too-quiet land, and he would catch sight of either Laris or Zhaban looking back at him, shaking a head, as if to say: *He thinks too much, and it does no good.*

No, he thought. None of it had ever done any damn good.

STARFLEET COMMAND
SAN FRANCISCO, EARTH

It was a fine morning for the start of the end of everything. San Francisco gleamed in the sunshine, brash and confident, the sleek and rhythmic pulse at the heart of a great power. The kind of morning in spring that makes the world seem full of possibility. A sea breeze freshened the air when Picard stepped out of the transporter and walked with purpose across the plaza to the headquarters building. Waved through at once by a young ensign who purpled at the sight of the great man. Ushered with some ceremony up to the commander-in-chief's meeting room. Earl Grey tea ready when he took his seat, steam rising in wisps from the cup.

A room that spoke of power, of duty, honor, and responsibility. Seated already: two colleagues, about to change everything, forever.

"What we are about to tell you, Jean-Luc," said the C-in-C, "is almost unbelievable."

Captain Jean-Luc Picard of the *Enterprise*, accustomed to believing many impossible things before breakfast, nodded at his commander-in-chief, folded his hands, and made himself more comfortable in his chair.

"I need hardly add that it is highly classified," said the C-in-C.

Picard, hardly unused to being privy to such information, gave a noncommittal smile. Inwardly, he felt himself tighten, shift onto alert. He gave his C-in-C a more careful look.

Admiral Victor Bordson, several years his junior, was, in Picard's estimation, a careful man. Picard did not mean this pejoratively; quite the contrary. Rather, he considered Bordson to be a man who took care: measured, disinclined to make rash decisions, somewhat impersonal, and lacking the common touch. Picard had often tried to place him—not German, not Austrian, not Swiss, not Belgian . . . What, then? (He had been amused, at a formal dinner one evening, seated next to the man's husband, to discover that Bordson was from Luxembourg. He had only just stopped himself from slamming his palm onto the table and exclaiming, "Of course!") Bordson was not averse to taking action, but considered action; he was decorated, as one would expect of his generation and seniority, multiply so—a veteran of some of the grimmer arenas of the Dominion War. One did not come through repeat engagements with the Jem'Hadar without a mark being left, some bruise, whether visible or not. Typically, in Picard's observation, such officers were dogged, implacable, and more than a little haunted. Northern courage, he believed it was called in the sagas, the determination to carry on even when all hope was gone. Yes, Bordson brought to mind the Saxon warrior, shaking his spear at his enemies, sure only of defeat:

"Thought must be the harder, heart be the keener,
mind must be the greater, while our strength lessens."

A careful man; a man of cares. Gently, Picard said, "What's going on, Victor?"

"Everything," said Bordson, "is about to change."

He turned to his second. Captain Kirsten Clancy, sitting at his right hand, nodded. Leaning forward, she whispered, "The Romulan star is about to go supernova."

Picard took a moment to consider some of the implications of this statement. As these became overwhelming, truly and terrifyingly all-encompassing, he lifted his hand to press his fingertips against the right side of his face. An instinctive action that he had never quite suppressed, to protect where he felt most vulnerable. Where he had been most harmed.

"*Merde.*"

"Quite," said Bordson. "Kirsten, shall we look at the presentation?"

Clancy reached out and activated a padd. A huge screen, on the opposite wall, glowed into life. The room began to darken. Before the presentation began, and under cover of the dimming light, Picard stole a rapid look at Clancy. A crisp woman in her middle years, hair short and turning white, she had considerable poise. One also sensed steel. Not someone to suffer fools. They had met only once or twice, briefly, in passing, at some function or other. Picard knew her chiefly by reputation, which was, as befitted someone this high up in Starfleet Command, exemplary. She also plainly had her eye, ultimately, on Bordson's post. Picard did not covet that role, far from it. The commander-in-chief was the person in whom the military functions of Starfleet and the political concerns of the Federation met. A great deal of Bordson's time, Picard suspected, was spent setting councilors at ease, appearing in front of committees, listening rather than acting. No, Picard would not willingly take on that role.

Give him a ship, heading into the unknown, the chance to explore, to make a difference . . .

On the screen, an officer in a gold ship's service uniform was getting ready to deliver a presentation to a small audience. Picard, leaning over to Bordson, murmured, "Who has seen this already? Who was there?"

"Me, Clancy, the president, the chief of security. The officer giving the briefing, of course, and her immediate superior." Bordson gave a wan smile. "You're seventh to know, if that's part of what you're asking."

Seventh. A not-insignificant part of Picard's mind shifted toward sketching out what the mission was going to be and computing how quickly he could be back on the *Enterprise* to begin the undertaking.

On-screen, the woman said, *"My name is Lieutenant Commander Raffi Musiker, and I'm an intelligence specialist at Romulan Affairs. As you're aware, we've been tracking some odd communications from Romulan space in recent weeks—odd even by Romulan standards."*

Listening to Musiker, Picard found himself taking a liking to her. She had a faintly disreputable air, a pleasant change from the smooth operatives that Starfleet Intelligence usually fielded. Her frankness was refreshing, as was the fact that she was clearly not daunted by the grandeur of her audience. Most of all, she was on top of her briefing. A question came about the reliability of their sources, which was dispatched with confidence and ease. Then another question came about the range of the blast from the supernova, and here she stopped and took a moment to collect herself.

"What I want to say is that these calculations are a worst-case scenario. This implies that effects in climate change are already being felt. Sometime in 2387. I'll show you that first. Because it might make the best-case scenario less damn frightening."

Picard leaned over to Clancy. "What was her name again?"

"Raffi Musiker," said Clancy. "Lieutenant Commander Raffi Musiker." Picard filed the information away for future reference.

On the screen behind Musiker, a simulated model of the Romulan system appeared. Its wounded star lay in the center. As Picard watched, the star imploded, and concentric circles spread out from its death throes. They fanned out, and out, and out, on and on . . . Someone in Musiker's audience, said, *"Holy fucking shit."* Picard could not be sure, but he thought it might be the president.

"Yeah," said Raffi. *"You know, I've watched that maybe two dozen times now, and let me tell you it never gets any better. It only ever gets worse. Life, huh? Only ever gets worse. Let me show you the best-case scenario."*

This, Picard thought, as he watched the rings spread out again, was stretching the definition of the word *best* beyond reason.

"Our best estimate?" said Raffi, to the question Picard was posing in his mind. *"The impact is likely to be felt within 9.7 light-years of the Romulan star. Whichever way we model this—and trust me, we've run a lot of models—the threat to the stability of the Romulan Star Empire is catastrophic. Shall I go into the specific ramifications of this, or are the broad lines pretty clear?"*

Quite clear, Picard thought. Trillions would be affected, not only in the home system, but well beyond. He leaned forward in his chair and watched the presentation to the unhappy end. Beside him, his tea, forgotten, cooled. *Nothing will ever be the same again . . .*

(M. Jean-Luc Picard, recalling himself thinking this, almost laughed out loud at the naivety.)

The presentation ended. Raffi Musiker was held freeze-framed on screen for a split second, and then her image was replaced by the symbol of Starfleet Command. Clancy raised the lights.

"Well?" said Bordson.

"We must help," Picard said simply.

"Indeed," said Bordson.

There was a pause, as the thought of what that might involve seeped through the room.

"Whatever happens, Victor," said Picard, "saying that is worthwhile, and will also be worth remembering whenever we face doubts or obstacles, as we surely shall. But we *must* help."

"Yes," Bordson said. "But how?"

Clancy stirred. "There are significant complications. Not least that the Romulans are not entirely keen on Federation involvement."

No, thought Picard, *they would not be.* "Have they asked for help yet?"

"They've only just admitted to us that the star is going supernova," Clancy said, "and then only because we sent them some of Musiker's reports. And their own secure communications, back at them." She gave a grim smile. "They didn't like that much."

"I imagine not," said Picard.

"The good news," said Clancy, "is that after . . ." She pushed out a breath. "Well. Let's say that after a few *intense* days of negotiation, the Romulans have agreed to some limited involvement on our part. But we need to play our hand carefully if we want to ensure that agreement holds." She shook her head impatiently. "We're trying to help! And they're playing hard to get."

"Secrecy is hardwired into the Romulan psyche," Picard said. "What have they said?"

"They won't allow us into the home system," Bordson said. "No surprise. But we are being allowed limited access to some of the systems beyond. The environmental impact won't be felt as badly there, but the stress on infrastructure most certainly will. If we are successful there, and keep the Romulans on board, then we might be allowed to help further."

"How many people?" said Picard.

"Across the worlds to which we have access?" said Bordson. "Nine hundred million."

A massive undertaking in itself. Picard rose from his seat and walked over to the window. The view from Bordson's briefing room was marvelous, of course. The complex of buildings around HQ. The vast ocean. The blue sky. One could become overly familiar with such a view, he thought. One could begin to take it for granted. How safe Earth was, how beautiful. Impregnable, like a castle that had never fallen. How would one feel to learn that one's home was going to be destroyed? To know that you would have to leave all that was familiar, and safe, and loved, and never return? It would be like . . .

Like being forced to leave the stars behind, reduce one's vision to a limited horizon or, worse, to nothing. It would be terrible.

Behind him, Clancy was talking about the need for diplomacy, for building consensus not only with the Romulans but here at home, for ensuring that the will was found to act . . .

"It will mean ships," Picard said. "A great number of ships. And the people to crew them. Thousands of ships, in time, given the numbers of refugees. The capacity to take many people to many different places. And then, when they arrive at their destination—the capacity to aid them. Food and shelter. Homes, schools, doctors. Work—fulfilling work. Good facilities, places where we would be happy to live. Not haphazard and temporary camps." He shuddered at the thought, as anyone in their right mind should. No, he would not allow that. He would not see people treated as no better than garbage, to be disposed of, thrown away. Piled high. "These should be places that encourage hope, not despair. That bring relief, not disappointment—"

Turning, he saw that Clancy was alarmed. "Now, let's not start over-reaching!" she said. "We don't have much information about what the Romulans are doing themselves—we only know that they've agreed that we can help. They've not yet said exactly how much help they'll eventually allow, and we don't know how much relocation work they're carrying out themselves. This might be a matter of a small fleet of refitted ships, removing a relatively small number of people to safe locations—"

"No," said Picard firmly. "In the face of such a calamity, there can be no half measures. We have to be ready to scale this mission up."

Clancy appealed to Bordson. "A relief effort like that would be . . . unheard of!"

"A disaster such as this is unheard of," said Picard.

"But *thousands* of ships?"

"If necessary."

"That would significantly change what Starfleet does," Clancy said. "That's going to affect what we can do, going forward. We would be changing our core mission for . . . what? The best part of a decade?"

"If that's what's needed," said Picard, "then that is what must be done."

"Well, I'm not sure the political will is there—"

Picard was sure that it was not.

Clancy pointed out, "Without the support of the Federation Council, we won't get the resources, and without the resources we have nothing more than castles in the air."

"I agree that this is unprecedented. So is the disaster," said Picard. "It will demand the very best of us: the best engineers, the best administrators, the best ships—"

"But for how long?" said Clancy. "Are we willing to sacrifice to get it done on that scale? All the planned exploration? What if they're canceled now? Are there enough ships that can be diverted to this? What else gets cut? Reclamation work on frontier worlds? Terraforming projects? How do you think that will go over with the citizens of the Federation? How do we choose? What goes? What stays? And even if we can get everyone behind this, how do you persuade people that helping the Romulans is in their interests? How do you persuade the *Romulans*?"

"Nine hundred million people, Captain," Picard said softly. "Maybe many, many more."

Bordson raised his hand. "Thank you both." He rested his head upon his hands and closed his eyes. After a moment, he said, "Political will, yes. Never easily achieved, not even from our own people. And the Romulans? I'm doubtful, very doubtful. But you see . . . I keep thinking of those rings, spreading outward."

Picard nodded; yes, yes, Bordson understood. He had grasped what Musiker had shown them.

"All the truly great emergencies we have faced," Bordson said, "the climate crisis, global wars, interstellar wars—it is too easy to forget what the cost was to the individuals who suffered through these events. I keep remembering what those rings mean—on the ground, you understand. For the people there. What those rings signify. Loss of home, of all that matters, all that is familiar . . . I keep thinking of this." He opened his eyes and he glanced at Picard. "It is clear that we must help and in a serious and committed manner." His gaze fell on Clancy. "How will we achieve that—that is what we shall learn over the coming weeks."

"The problem is that this won't be a matter of weeks, sir," Clancy said. "Starfleet will be in this for *years*. As long as we understand what we're getting ourselves into."

"I believe we do." Bordson sat back in his chair. "Who should lead such a mission?" He turned to Picard. "Jean-Luc—"

"A moment or two while I consider who might be suited—"

"No need," said Bordson. "The job is yours . . . if you want it."

Clancy gave a short laugh. "Fools rush in . . ."

Picard did not reply. He turned back to the window. He stood and watched the ocean ripple. Bordson's words about the people who must live through this disaster had moved him, profoundly. Still, some part of him shrank back from the horror—the enormity—of what this calamity meant. Hundreds of millions of people, to be removed from their homes—some unwillingly, surely—and transplanted . . . Where? Where would they live? What would they do after this? What would the Romulan Empire do? Would their culture survive? *Could* it? These were the fears of one part of him. But the other part—the best part of Jean-Luc Picard—was already mobilizing for the work that lay ahead and had been even before Bordson's offer. Standing there, looking across the Pacific, it suddenly felt to Picard as if history was aligning correctly, such as when, in a game of chess, check is declared, and the soon-to-be winner sees precisely how well their moves have been laid. For one bright and joyous moment, Picard knew he was the right man at the right time, a man presented with a serious task for which his life, his experience, and his temperament made him uniquely suited.

He could do this. He *would* do this.

(In the future, M. Picard gave a hollow laugh that echoed back down to the past.)

He turned back to Bordson and Clancy. His voice was far steadier than he imagined it would be. "Very well."

Bordson and Clancy exchanged a look.

"Very good," Bordson said. "Congratulations, Admiral Picard."

"I beg your pardon?"

"You said it yourself," said Bordson. "An unprecedented project. We can at least acknowledge that formally. Besides," he said, "it's long overdue."

Picard, oddly moved, merely tilted his head.

Bordson wasn't finished. "You understand this means saying goodbye to the *Enterprise*?"

"Ah," said Picard. He walked back over to the table and sat down heavily. He picked up his cup. The tea was stone cold. "And there I was thinking that there would be no catch."

"Oh, there's always a catch," said Bordson. "Kirsten, will you explain?"

"We know you'd rather go in with your own ship and your own crew," Clancy said. "But the reality is that *Enterprise* is a red flag to the Romulans. The flagship. The symbol of our enmity. *Enterprise* has been their foe far too often. We don't want to remind them. We need to be extremely diplomatic right now. Do you see?"

"Can you do this, Jean-Luc," asked Bordson, "without the *Enterprise*?"

Picard hesitated. Yes, they were right; to the Romulans the *Enterprise* was hardly a signal of amity . . . But do this without *his people*? His crew? Those that he knew so well, trusted so completely? To try to do this vast and unparalleled task while learning the ways of a new crew, a new ship?

"You don't have to decide immediately," Bordson said with compassion. "Take a day or two. Consult your senior staff. Kirsten's already arranged the security clearances—"

"No need," said Picard. "I'll do it."

The belief was profound; he was the right person. The one with the vision, the one with the ability. He must not let this pass. No, not that, which sounded like vanity. It would be *wrong*, to let this pass. There was no task in the universe more important than this. Starfleet *must* help. He *must* help.

"Good," said Bordson. "Then let us deal with the simplest question first. Who takes command of the *Enterprise*?"

"Worf," said Picard, as Clancy said, "Not Worf."

"First check, I see," said Bordson dryly. "Let us practice what we preach and build consensus. Kirsten—what is your objection? Is this about what happened on Soukara?"

A bad decision, made almost a decade ago, in the kind of situation where nine out of ten officers would have done the same thing. Worf had been on an undercover mission inside Dominion-controlled space with Jadzia Dax, his wife. Dax had been badly wounded, but Worf had chosen to go back and save her life rather than continue with the mission. The Dominion agent they had been sent to extract had died as a result.

"He made a bad call on Soukara," Clancy said. "An agent *died*. Who knows how long we could have staved off the Dominion War with his information! Worf knew that when he made the call. He was choosing to save her."

"This was almost ten years ago," said Picard. "Surely his faultless record since must count for something?"

"But it goes to his judgment," said Clancy. "Would he make a call like that again?"

Hardly likely, thought Picard, jaw tightening, given that Jadzia was dead. "On the other hand, given what happened last time, Worf may be even more considered about his decisions. I must protest the idea that a question mark hangs over my XO's judgment. Do you honestly think, Captain Clancy, that I would select a first officer who I did not think was both worthy and capable of commanding a ship of their own?"

A slight flush rose on Clancy's cheeks. "You know him better than I do; you've worked alongside him for many years—"

"Yes indeed."

"But this is the *flagship* we're talking about!" She turned to Bordson. "He received a formal reprimand. Sir, for the good of the service, I have to bring this up."

Picard glanced at Bordson; he was giving nothing away.

"Let me make another point," said Picard. "A century ago, one of the moons of Qo'noS exploded. The Klingons were unwilling to take our help at first—but they did, and, in time, our interactions led to the Khitomer Accords. Our relations are now so cordial that we are considering whether a Klingon might be suitable to assume command of our flagship. Imagine the impact of this! Imagine what we would be saying. We would remind people not only of the help we gave then, but of how far our friendship with the Klingons has come *since* then. And in so doing we suggest how far our friendship with the Romulans might evolve."

Bordson said, "He has a point, Kirsten."

She was looking less certain. "The optics are good . . ."

"He's a fine officer," Picard said, with quiet resolve. "He will make a fine captain."

Bordson looked at his second. "Well? Any other objections?"

She glanced at Picard. "I thought someone should raise the issue, that's all."

Picard acknowledged what he assumed was an apology.

"Then we're agreed," said Bordson. "Worf takes command of the *Enterprise*. Good. Two promotions in one morning. I feel quite dizzy with power." He studied Picard. "I imagine you'll want to speak to your crew immediately; let them know what's happening. We've set an office aside for your use . . ." He rose from his seat. "Mission command, for the moment. Until your new ship is found."

Picard, standing, looked at him curiously. "An office in place already. You didn't doubt that I'd say yes?"

Bordson smiled. "No, Jean-Luc—I didn't doubt that for a second."

They shook hands. Clancy, too, reached over to shake hands with him. "We're all behind you," she said. "We're going to do our damn best to make this work. Please remember that."

And he did remember—or tried to.

Outside Bordson's office, Picard took a moment to collect himself, standing still with his hands clasped together, his eyes closed. In another man such a stance might be mistaken for prayer, but Picard was thinking yet again about those concentric rings, fanning outward, and the worlds upon which this disaster was going to fall. An hour, he thought, and his whole universe had changed utterly. A lesser man might panic, but Picard was decisive, and hardly careless. He should, he thought, get to work. He opened his eyes and wondered where he might find his office. His eyes fell on a young Trill officer, hovering at a polite distance. When she saw him move, she stepped forward to speak to him.

"Admiral Picard, sir—"

News traveled fast, thought Picard. "I am he."

"I'm Lieutenant Vianu Kaul, sir. Admiral Bordson has assigned me as your aide-de-camp while you're here on Earth. May I take you to your office, sir?"

Picard, open palmed, gestured along the corridor. "By all means, Lieutenant."

They walked along together. Picard waited for the inevitable.

"May I say what a privilege it is to meet you, Admiral, sir?"

Picard gave the gentle, generic smile he had perfected for these moments. Young officers, astonished to be in the company of a "legend," were often left breathless and stammering. One reason he favored his crew. There would be a great deal made over his mission in the coming days, he thought, regretfully. He would have to be on his best behavior.

The senior staff on the *Enterprise* were used to his moods and did not mind when he was irritable. He would not be able to permit himself such indulgences for a while. He did not wish to disappoint young and earnest officers such as this. But he would need an outlet. Who would be a good foil for him? Who could he bring with him, on his ship, once the mission was underway? Data would have been his first choice, of course, but . . .

Kaul led him briskly into the elevator, down a level, and then out again into a large and airy space that was currently almost empty. One or two people were there, busy at their desks; they jumped up as Picard sailed past. "Your staff as it currently stands, sir," Kaul said, almost apologetically. "Procurement specialists, mostly. Those people are magicians."

"We'll soon fill the space," Picard said calmly. There was room for a dozen more; that would do for a start. But the operation would expand, and rapidly. He would need experts in this kind of work. He nodded across the room to a private office. "Is that for me?"

"Yes, sir—sorry your name isn't on the door yet, sir."

"That would have been a significant piece of sorcery. I didn't know I was taking on the mission until half an hour ago."

Kaul, momentarily wrong-footed, took on a panicked air. Then she saw the twitch of Picard's lips, and relaxed, ever so slightly. Picard, too, eased. The sooner they could get past this stage, the better. "Of course, sir." Kaul opened the office door. "Well, this is your space. Fairly basic, but enough to get things underway, I hope."

A desk, a chair, a computer. Sufficient, for now. Picard went to stand behind the desk.

"Can I get you some tea, sir? Earl Grey tea? Hot? Is that correct?"

Picard smiled, this time completely freely. "Exactly correct, Lieutenant. Thank you. That would be most welcome."

The tea arrived quickly, and not replicated. He drank a little, and then ran his hands over his desk. There could be no more delays. There must be a new ship, a new crew, a new fleet . . . A new mission, and a new way of life. But first things first. He composed himself and opened a channel to the *Enterprise*.

"Worf," he said. "My dear friend."

When the door closed behind the new-minted admiral, Clancy fell back in her chair and gave a sigh of relief. "I'll be honest, Victor, I wasn't sure we'd pry him from his ship."

Bordson smiled wanly. "Neither was I."

Clancy gave him a sharp look. "Didn't doubt for a second, huh?"

"The occasional judicious white lie never harmed a soul."

Clancy stood and stretched. "Well, at least we keep the flagship dealing with something other than all this." She held her hands out, as if to try to grasp the enormity of the operation. "Something will still be out there, reminding us of our mission. And what better than the *Enterprise*. The heart and soul of Starfleet . . ."

Bordson eyed his second shrewdly. "Tell me what worries you, Kirsten."

Again, she gestured outward. "This mission—it's massive, unprecedented. The scale of it! It could consume Starfleet for a generation."

"But it has to be done. The alternative is unimaginable."

"So you and Picard say. But *can* it be done, Victor? Can we sustain the will for this? We've only just managed to get the Romulans to agree to let us help. Sometimes I think they'd rather their people died than reveal anything to us." She shook her head. "And if the Romulans don't want us, how can we persuade our leaders that we should be involved? How can we justify it?"

"That, I must admit, is my chief concern," said Bordson. "That we overreach."

"One misstep and the Romulans will be arguing that this is invasion by stealth. Like the Cardassians on Bajor, offering aid as a prelude to conquest."

"We helped Bajor," said Bordson.

"And then Bajor joined the Federation. The Romulans must be looking at that and thinking, 'Is this how their aid works? Is it all conditional? Will we escape intact?'"

"The Romulans," said Bordson, "must take care of their own paranoia. In the meantime, let us do all that we can while we can. And hope that we carry the day for long enough to make a real difference."

The afternoon turned softly into evening. The sun lowered majestically over the darkening water, setting the sky aflame. The rich warm light of a nonhostile star. As the day lengthened, Picard continued to inform his senior staff one by one—his trusted advisors, his friends—that he was not returning to the *Enterprise*.

It took longer than he would have liked to reach Beverly. She was in surgery, it transpired; not an emergency, but a long-overdue operation on a junior officer who, he recalled, had found excuse after excuse to delay the procedure. Such intimate knowledge of the crew of his ship: he would no longer have this. He would not know the people around him as well as he knew this crew. As well as he knew Beverly Crusher.

At last she appeared on screen. She was tired.

"Hi, Jean-Luc. Is this urgent?"

The wind was taken out of his sails. "Not urgent, no."

"It's been a long day, that's all—"

"Beverly, I'm leaving the ship."

She leaned back in her seat. *"You do yourself an injustice, Jean-Luc. That's the very definition of urgent. What's going on?"*

Quickly, he sketched the situation; the dire need; the mission. She listened calmly—she was always calm—as he explained why the *Enterprise* could not go to Romulan space, and why he was leaving. When she heard his full news, a puckish smile crossed her lips.

"Admiral, hey? I always knew you'd make it eventually. I used to say to Jack—that one will go far—"

"Beverly . . . I'm going to miss you terribly."

"Oh, Jean-Luc—"

"No, listen to me, please." *Before I lose confidence.* "You have been my friend for almost my entire career. I have not had a better one. The gifts of your friendship have been infinite—"

"Jean-Luc, you're talking as if you're never coming back!"

"I'm going a very long way."

"I know."

She looked at him, almost expectantly. Would she come with him, if he asked? She would be a great asset, of course; a vastly experienced doctor on a relief mission like this.

Did he dare ask?

She sat watching (*waiting?*), and then she sighed.

The moment had passed. He had never quite summoned up his courage, when it came to Beverly Crusher.

"Can I offer you some free advice?" she said.

"Of course, Beverly. Of course."

"Put someone right next to you who isn't scared of you."

"Scared—?"

"You're quite . . . now, let me get this right. Not intimidating . . . not severe . . . huh. That's it. You can be quite certain *of yourself. And that can stop people from telling you things that you need to know."*

"Certain of myself?"

That half-smile again. *"Don't get me wrong! With good reason. Most of the time. But you're only human like the rest of us. You make mistakes. And you need someone there who's able to tell you when that's happening."* Her face fell. *"Particularly with a mission like this. So much at stake."*

"I'll find somebody."

"Good. I won't worry so much in that case."

"Thank you for worrying nonetheless."

She gave him a full, sweet smile. *"Oh, Jean-Luc. I'll never stop."*

He nodded. Could not quite trust his voice.

"Are you coming back to say goodbye?"

"I'm afraid not."

"I see. All right, then. Well . . . I'll make sure everything is packed up safely. Do you have a forwarding address yet?"

That question caught him; where, right now, was home? "Here to Earth, I suppose . . . until I know my new ship."

"Consider it done." She shook her head. *"Captain Worf. Did any of us see that, all those long years ago?"*

All those long years. "I certainly didn't."

"I guess we couldn't keep you forever."

"I hope I've made the right choice, Beverly."

"It's what you were born for. Congratulations, Admiral. It's long overdue."

"Thank you, Beverly. For everything."

And he let her go.

Before what would be his final call for the day, another cup of tea appeared, which Picard gratefully received. Kaul hovered at his shoulder, carrying a padd.

"Go home," said Picard gently. He pointed to the padd. "Leave that. I'll read through it before I go."

Kaul hesitated but was clearly loath to disobey an order. "Are you sure there's nothing else I can do, sir?"

"You can get a good night's sleep. Be back here in the morning ready to work like you've never worked before."

The Trill's eyes shone. "Of course, sir!" She put down the padd and made to leave. At the door, she hesitated again. "This really is an honor, sir."

"This mission," said Picard, reaching for his cup of tea, "will be enough honor for all of us."

Kaul left, the door closing behind her. Picard opened a channel once again to the *Enterprise*. The familiar face of his chief engineer appeared on screen.

"Geordi," he said warmly.

"Sir, what time is it there?"

Picard shrugged. "Twenty hundred?"

"I thought it would be getting late. I figured I might not hear from you until the morning. But big news, hey? Admiral."

Picard's lips twitched. "You've heard?"

"Well, you know Worf. Can't keep his mouth shut."

Picard laughed for the first time in what seemed an age. "That certainly sounds like Worf."

La Forge smiled. *"You know it was clear something was up. He did me the courtesy of looping me in rather than leaving me hanging."*

"He gave you the reason why?"

"He did." La Forge whistled. *"I've got to say, sir, you've got your work cut out for you."*

"Speaking confidentially, Geordi, I fear I may have underestimated the sheer scale of the task ahead—"

"I bet you have, because I've been thinking about it all day and I'm raising my estimate of the size of fleet you'll need by the minute."

"Nine hundred million people, by the most conservative estimate. How does one go about moving that many people? Do we even have the capacity? How do we move them? Where do we move them to? What do we need in place for them when they arrive?"

"Well, I'm going to leave the touchy-feely people-handling stuff to the kind of folks who excel at that kind of thing, but I've got plenty of ideas about hardware. We can talk them through when I arrive."

Picard looked at him with sudden hope. "You're coming here?"

"You're gonna ask me to come, aren't you?"

He'd thought of asking, yes; but then thought better, for La Forge's sake. "But the *Enterprise*. I couldn't ask—"

"The greatest engineering project our generation will ever undertake, and you weren't going to ask me to come on board? How long have we served together now? Jeez, I could be offended if I thought about this for too long!"

Relief rushed through Picard. Of course it must be Geordi La Forge. Who else? And, even more, to have one old comrade on this new voyage, wherever this mission should take him—that was a great blessing. "Thank you, Geordi," he said. "I mean that from the heart."

"Admiral, I've been packing since this morning. Got my passage to Mars all fixed."

Mars: The home of the Utopia Planitia shipyards. Starfleet's main vessel design and construction site. The number of ships this mission would eventually require was going to have significant impact on the facility.

"I'll be frank," said La Forge. *"You're gonna have to give me some fairly serious executive authority there, because we are looking at a major retooling if we're going to get enough ships off the production lines quickly enough. I bet you dollars to doughnuts there'll be complaints."* He pushed out a breath. *"This is gonna be serious work—and it's not so much the raw material as the labor. Who's gonna build these ships? Can we find enough people? Are there enough people?"*

"I had barely begun to think about that," Picard said.

"In the end, you see, it always comes down to labor. Anyway, I'm working on it. I'll speak to the engineers at Utopia Planitia, see what they suggest. And I'm sure to have ideas of my own once I'm there and have a look around. Well, the good news is there's gonna have to be some major innovations in shipbuilding technology over the next couple of years. Gonna have to be!"

Problems Picard was only beginning even to conceptualize, and La Forge was already working on them. He was glad he had not deferred this call. He already felt better, more optimistic about the prospects of success.

"Congratulations on the promotion, by the way," said La Forge.

"Thanks," said Picard, and gave a short laugh. He had more or less forgotten about that. How odd. After all this time, and it barely figured.

"All right. I'm gonna get back to my packing. I'll see you when I'm done on Mars—"

"Geordi," Picard said abruptly. "Are you quite sure? This mission—it might require everything. The rest of your career—"

"Somebody has to help these people, sir. I think I can help. That's sure enough for me. Is it sure enough for you?"

"Yes," said Picard. "More than enough. Thank you," he added, with great feeling. "You give me courage."

"No problem, Captain. Admiral. Whatever! All right—you get back to what you need to do; I'll get on my way."

La Forge closed the channel. Picard sat back in his chair. So now his last link with the *Enterprise* had been severed, for better or worse. He was, for the moment, a captain with no ship, a handful of staff, and a major operation to mobilize.

What, he thought, as he picked up the padd that Kaul had left for him, would that involve? He anticipated leading from the front, as ever, on board a ship, directing operations from inside Romulan space. That meant he would need someone to run this office on Earth while he was away. A starbase on the Romulan border needed to be a forward command, and there would have to be someone to run the show there.

Most of all, and perhaps most pressingly, he lacked a second. Someone to take on the task of ensuring his orders were carried out. He was grateful beyond measure to have La Forge working with him, but he had a vital job, one that would keep him near Mars. Picard needed someone at his side, someone to travel with him as these rescue and relief missions got underway. Someone who understood in full the difficult and charged situation into which they were flying. Someone who could handle not only all kinds of Romulans, and Starfleet admirals, and Federation politicians, but someone who could handle Jean-Luc Picard: an XO he could trust to tell him the truth. Not somebody cowed by the name, the rank, the legend that surrounded Jean-Luc Picard.

Did such a person exist?

Data, of course, would have been the perfect fit. But . . .

But.

No, thought Picard firmly; one could not dwell on what could not be. Clearing his throat, he turned his attention to Kaul's report. The first seven ships had been reassigned to his fleet. Seven. That was a start, he supposed. Nearly a billion people. Seven ships would barely scratch the surface.

A man could be daunted by a task like that, but Jean-Luc Picard was a man of great wisdom and experience, and not least among his talents was the ability to know when to worry and when to delegate. There was very little that he could do—alone at twenty hundred in an office that had been operating for no more than a day—about his lack of ships, and he already had someone working on that. For the next ten hours, this could be La Forge's problem, and his alone. Picard was tired now, and hungry. He put down the padd, rose from his chair, and walked across the room to look at the bullpen space beyond. The lights were dim; his staff of three had all left for the day. Tomorrow, according to Kaul, there would be ten people there, and the next day there would be fifteen, and so it would continue, the mission expanding as the huge starship that was Starfleet slowed down and switched course, turning its considerable skills and capacity toward this vast and vital work. The work of a lifetime.

Picard left his office and turned to face the door.

There, fixed in place, was his name, gleaming in what remained of the light.

Admiral Jean-Luc Picard.

He tapped his fingertip against it lightly. "Procurement," he murmured as he went in search of dinner. "Truly they are magicians."

2

Admiral's Log: A week, and thus far no Romulan lives have been saved, yet I'm pleased with the progress we have made. Whatever orders Victor Bordson has given, every request has been met. Personnel, offices, equipment, and the promise of fifteen *Wallenberg*-class transport ships within four to six weeks. I have the makings of a solid team here at Command—with more expertise being brought over from various agencies such as the Colonization Bureau. I shall soon be able to leave Earth and begin to take the first fleet of ships into Romulan space. It is a great relief to know that I can leave advocacy for this mission in Bordson's careful hands and get on with the work that needs to be done.

I must also acknowledge the efforts of Captain Kirsten Clancy, who has been chiefly responsible for liaising with the Romulan military. She has had considerable success in negotiating Starfleet access to the planets most in need. We have, remarkably, been permitted to travel into Romulan space unaccompanied: provided we follow precise and pre-agreed routes. I assume this means that their resources are already stretched thin. I am prepared to discover an occasional cloaked ship monitoring our progress once we go beyond the Neutral Zone.

Our first mission has been narrowed down to three worlds: Tavaris IV, Ectis II, and Insitor V. These three worlds are of course beyond the Romulan home system, but are likely to be among the first affected by the internal changes happening within the Empire. My instincts tell me that the Romulans will ask us to proceed first to Ectis. A small mining colony, Ectis is completely reliant for essential supplies such as food on imports from the home system. As well as transporting the colonists, we have offered to assist in settling them at their destination (when that is decided), but the Romulan authorities have assured Starfleet that everything in that respect is under control. The residents of Ectis II are, in the main, relatively well off: the mining operations there are, as I understand it, largely automated, and the engineers and technicians who maintain the systems enjoy a comparatively high standard of living. I suspect that this will bring its own problems: however comfortable we make the quarters on our ships we cannot replace the homes that they must leave behind. I have tasked a small team to consider what can be done to make our ships more agreeable to our guests in terms of design and layout. I can by no means justify expending a large amount of resources on this, but it seems that some simple consideration of this issue will go a long way to helping our guests adjust to their change in circumstances.

In the meantime, I too must adjust to my own change in circumstances. I receive regular missives from Deanna instructing me not to underestimate the impact upon my own well-being of leaving behind the ship and crew that have been my home and—I must say it—my family, for so long. The enormity of this task—and the rapidity with which the number of staff assigned to the mission grows—does not leave me a great deal of time to reflect on what I have left behind, but I confess that I do find the absence of someone in whom I can confide somewhat trying.

Our first mission will be ready to commence in six weeks, by which time I hope to have my own ship, and I must make a decision about an XO very soon. I do, at least, have some potential candidates in mind.

STARFLEET COMMAND
SAN FRANCISCO, EARTH

Lieutenant Commander Raffi Musiker, when asked to wait for a senior officer, did not generally sit patiently in a chair, and she saw no reason to do so for a legend either. She stood outside the admiral's office, bouncing up and down ever so slightly on her heels, ready for action.

All around her, the office was bustling. Only six days since the admiral had been appointed, and there were two dozen people here, busy with the preliminary tasks involved in getting the mission up and running. A huge interactive map of the Romulan Star Empire was displayed at the far end; likely relocation sites were marked in green, other secondary possibilities in amber. There were six people standing in front of the map, talking rapidly, highlighting worlds and getting full data up on screen as they needed it. Information and colors updated as they conferred and made decisions. At the workstation near where she was standing, a painfully young ensign was studying a running update from the *U.S.S. Nightingale*, which was being refitted as a people carrier. *Wallenberg*-class—good choice, that's what Raffi would have picked too. They were often used to ferry colonists, so they were capacious and able to cope with a large number of civilians. At the next workstation, someone was talking via comm about temporary shelters. *Well, can we replicate them? No, I'm not sure yet what the weather conditions will be like on the ground. Well, what* are *the resettlement parameters? Hey, don't worry, it'll all be good—we got these things to work on Cardassia Prime and that was a freakin' hellhole . . .*

Raffi smiled. Everyone here was keen, and they were going to have to be. Many were in Starfleet uniforms, but not everyone: there were some civilians, wearing the logo of the United Federation of Planets High Commission on Refugees. This was going to be an interesting mission, Raffi thought, combining the political clout of the UFPHCR with the personnel and matériel of Starfleet. She guessed it could go one of two ways: the two organizations working in harmony, pulled together by the enormity of the task, or else there would be a tug-of-war, each side trying to press their priorities and working practices. And that was only within the Federation. The admiral was going to have to juggle Romulan requirements. Someone hurried by, apologizing as they brushed past, carrying a stack of padds. Paperwork. If there was one thing you could rely on, whether civilian or military, it was the rapid expansion of paperwork.

Raffi mentally ran through her presentation one more time. The instruction to see the admiral had been brief, courteous, and not particularly informative as to the purpose of the meeting. She knew, from superiors and colleagues, the impact of her presentation and so she assumed she was here to give a direct one to the man himself and answer any questions he might have. Then back to her desk at Romulan Affairs. Only now she would have met a legend. Gabe, her son, was dying to hear about him. Mom's job was mostly that thing that meant she didn't always make his soccer matches, but every so often she managed to deliver something incredibly cool, like this.

The door to the admiral's office opened. Raffi snapped back to the present. A young Trill officer came out. "He's ready for you now, Commander."

Raffi walked inside. The admiral was sitting behind his desk, eyes intent on the screen there. "Thank you, Kaul," he said, slightly absently, attention elsewhere, but still polite.

The door closed, leaving the two of them alone. Raffi stood patiently, used to senior officers who were always completing some task before turning to the next one. She took the opportunity to appraise the Great Man. Calm, focused, looked like he kept very fit. She surveyed the room. Remarkably tidy for the office of the person heading what might well be the biggest mission ever attempted by Starfleet. The only hint of disorder was the vase of flowers at one end of the desk: a stunning bunch of riotously bright chrysanthemums, yellows, pinks, oranges, and a deep shade of vivid crimson. Some of the petals had fallen and lay like lost souls on the desktop. She wondered who had sent them, or whether this was the kind of thing that came as standard in your office when you reached these dizzying heights.

The admiral closed the screen, rose from his chair, and came to greet her. The legend, come to life. She had the edge on him when it came to height, but he moved with a commanding grace. "Commander," he said, "thank you for making the time to see me today." His voice was measured, cadenced; the kind of voice, she suspected, that you could not help but listen to, and then do exactly what was requested.

"Happy to supply whatever you need, sir." She looked around the room for an audience that wasn't there. Didn't he have a senior staff in place yet? "Are we meeting here?"

He gestured to two comfortable seats in the corner of the room, where teapot and cups stood waiting on a low table. "Take a seat. Tea?"

"Sure, thanks." Raffi sat, uneasy in the easy chair, putting padds on the floor beside her, and then leaning forward, palms on her knees. He took the chair opposite, smiled disarmingly, and poured tea. "I assumed I was giving a presentation this morning, sir." She sipped her tea. What the hell *was* this stuff? It tasted of goddamned perfume. Was it too late to ask for coffee?

"I've watched your presentation half a dozen times now," he said. "It's insightful, informative, and precise. I was very impressed."

Hey Gabe, wait till you hear what the Great Man said about Mom. "Thank you, sir."

"Could you tell me, please, from your perspective as an expert on Romulan affairs, what you believe our chief difficulty will be in Starfleet's dealings with them?"

He didn't waste time, did he? Raffi took a breath. "Opposition, sir," she said. "Believe it or not, they are *not* happy that Starfleet is devoting so much time, energy, and resources to helping them. They are *hating* all this. They hate that we know they're in trouble, and they hate accepting help. They won't want to lose face."

"I understand. What else?"

"And even if they're united on this, they'll be divided among themselves about what to do with us. Some will want to accept our help for a while. Some will try to make it impossible for us to function. Others might try to get rid of us—"

"By force?"

"By subterfuge, more likely. Secretly, so that half of them won't know whether it's a sanctioned operation or not. The saying in our office goes that Romulans don't tell their left hand what their right hand is doing."

The admiral nodded. Yes, he recognized that.

"That makes them inconsistent and unpredictable," Raffi said. "Not to mention damn annoying. They'll say one thing and do another, and they won't even know themselves what their real policy is toward us. Expect the unexpected, sir."

"I see. Would it help at all, Commander, if I approached Ambassador Spock and had him petition the Senate to instruct cooperation with this mission?"

"Excuse me, sir? How would that help?"

He looked surprised. "The ambassador surely commands considerable respect—"

Raffi laughed out loud. "*Spock?* They think he's a nutcase!"

His eyes opened wide. *Shit*, she thought, *me and my big mouth*. She had a vision of herself, explaining to Gabe: *No, the admiral hated me, and that's why I'm being court-martialed . . .*

Hold on. Was he . . . *smiling*?

"Sorry, sir," she said quickly. "No, I wouldn't advise that. Ambassador Spock's mission to Romulus may look very laudable to us, but from the Romulan perspective he and his supporters are outliers. Reunification of Romulus and Vulcan? Hey, when I was a kid, I wanted a unicorn. With wings. I didn't get one. I didn't even get a damn *pony*—"

"A personal mission of peace, the ambassador calls it."

"Well, the Romulans consider it very personal. Almost . . ." She scraped around for a word that wouldn't offend. "Um. *Idiosyncratic?*"

"In other words, they think he's a crank." He was most definitely smiling. "Carry on talking so frankly to me, Commander," he said, "and we shall get along very well. Very well indeed."

The door buzzer sounded. He called out, "Come."

Kaul came in. "Apologies for the interruption, sir, but you asked me to let you know immediately when the ship was ready for you."

"Ah, yes, thank you, Kaul! Yes, I'll be on my way shortly." He turned back to Raffi. "The *Starship Verity* has been assigned to lead the first fleet out to Romulan space. A nice name, don't you think?"

"Sure . . . ?"

"'A true principle, especially one of fundamental significance.'" He looked pleased. "I believe that remembering such things will be crucial to the success of our undertaking. Above all, we are on a mission to protect, preserve, and save lives."

Raffi nodded, faintly. This meeting was not going in the slightest how she had anticipated. No presentation. He said he'd already watched it half a dozen times. He clearly didn't want it in person. For some reason they were now discussing eternal verities. She was a simple intelligence officer, maybe turned a mite suspicious by having to think like a Romulan twenty-four hours a day. She wasn't any kind of philosopher. Why was she here?

"Lieutenant Kaul," added Picard conversationally, "was on staff here before even I was. Seconded from Admiral Bordson's office. Their loss has been my gain. She'll be vital to operations here on Earth."

There it was again, that extraneous information, as if giving her a picture of the setup here.

"Sir," said Raffi, "may I ask you something?"

"By all means," said the Great Man. "You must always feel you can speak freely to me."

She'd never had any superior officer say that to her. Sometimes quite the contrary.

"This isn't a briefing, is it?" said Raffi. "This is an interview."

"That's correct, Commander. My apologies if I kept my cards close to my chest, but I wanted to see how you answered my questions face-to-face." He sipped some of his revolting tea. "You've answered them most satisfactorily."

"Which means . . . ?"

"Which means I'd like you as my XO."

She put down her cup with a rattle. Tea spilled. "Shit!"

His mouth twitched. "I sincerely hope not. Most certainly we have some difficult times ahead. More difficult than either of us can imagine."

She turned and looked out through the transparent aluminum partition into the busy office. All those people, dashing about, putting the nuts and bolts of this mission together, building this operation from data, information, decisions, actions. Sure, it was easy to take the piss out of the padd pushers, but nothing could happen without them. Working out what was needed, where it could be found, how to get it all to the right place at the right time. She had no idea how to do this . . . She took a breath. How do you say "no" to a legend?

"Sir," she said, "I'm not an administrator."

He blinked. "I beg your pardon?"

"I mean, this is a flattering offer, sir, I hope you understand that. Truly flattering. But an operation like this?" She gestured to the room beyond. "I'm not cut out for this kind of work. I wouldn't know where to start."

She saw understanding dawn in his eyes. "Ah, there has been a misunderstanding. I have a very able administrator arriving to head up the office here on Earth, Commander Crystal Gbowee. She's on her way from Starbase 192 as we speak. She's worked with the UFPHCR coordinating numerous missions—she was on Bajor for a while after the Occupation, and on Cardassia Prime during the reconstruction effort there. Once she arrives, I shall move over to the fleet. This mission must get underway, and soon." He glanced out across the busy room. "No, the appointment here is filled, I'm afraid. I'm sorry if that's a disappointment."

His eyes were quietly twinkling with suppressed mirth. No, of course he didn't want her here. She'd be no damn good here, would she?

"Then—"

He leaned forward in his seat, held her eye, very serious now. "I'm asking you to come aboard my ship, Commander. Be my first officer on the *Verity*. But I'm asking more than that, and I think you know it. I have left my crew behind on the *Enterprise*. I must replace them, and if I am to succeed, I need an excellent XO. And what I require above all from my XOs is honesty. I shall need you always to tell me the truth. What do you say? Is that something you believe that you could do?"

Shit, she thought, and managed not to say it out loud this time. No, this was *not* what she'd been expecting when she'd walked into this room.

"It's a big decision," he was saying. "There may be all manner of ties keeping you here on Earth . . ."

Gabe had a soccer match next week. She'd missed the last one putting together that damn presentation. "When does the ship leave?"

"Six days."

So she *could* make Gabe's match. But there would be the next match, or the match after, the long months away, the individual seconds and moments of simply being present that were tiny for her, but that constituted the whole of Gabe's life, his childhood.

"I . . ."

Damn, she wanted this post. She could do this job. She was *made* to do this job. She'd known the second she walked into this room that she wanted to work with this man in some way. But she'd never imagined she would be offered this.

Right hand to a legend. Right in the middle of the greatest operation that Starfleet would ever mount.

He was smiling at her. "Would you like to see the ship, Commander? The *Verity*? You'd be spending a lot of time there, after all. You can make your decision after that."

"Yes," she said, already knowing what her decision would be. "I'd love to see the ship."

Utopia Planitia Shipyards
Mars

The construction sites, and the skeletons of half-built ships, obscured the view of the red planet below. La Forge watched the production drones zipping to and fro, the supply shuttles bringing out components and subassemblies. His own shuttle sped past the main shipyard and began its descent into a low orbit. With the bulk of the shipyards behind, the factory complex on the surface was now clearly visible: a huge domed structure at least two miles in diameter, a jewel set into the sandstone. Under the cover of the dome, La Forge knew, tucked into a deep crater, was the warren of offices, labs, and habitations that comprised the working and living spaces of the people who kept this whole vast operation up and running.

A communication exchange with the folks on the ground, and he was ready to be transported down to the complex. There he was met by T'sath, the Vulcan chief operating officer. They had never served together directly, but naturally the overseer of the Federation's main shipyards and the chief engineer of Starfleet's flagship were in regular communication. Plus meetings at the odd conference here and there over the years. La Forge had always found T'sath reliable, knowledgeable, resourceful, and—perhaps inevitably—calm. Today she greeted him with what he guessed passed for a significant emotional display: a slight furrow of the brows, some tightness in the lips.

"Is what we're hearing true?" she said.

The embargo on the news about the supernova had been lifted, although Starfleet officers were being requested to use discretion, particularly those directly involved in the project. Still, one could not promote and reassign Jean-Luc Picard, put a Klingon in charge of the *Enterprise*, commandeer more than a dozen ships, and begin to establish the base of operations for what was plainly going to be a major mission without attracting some attention. Besides, secrecy was more the Romulan way.

"Uh-huh," said La Forge. "And we're going to need ships."

"Ships?" said T'sath.

"There's going to be a major relief mission. They've asked us to help—"

That almost startled her. "The Romulans have asked for Federation help?"

"Can you believe it? Only limited, but we're going to need ships."

"Ships. To carry Romulan refugees . . ." Her eyes narrowed, briefly. "How many people to transport?"

He lowered his voice. "A lot."

"Precision would be more helpful, Commander."

"Not quite a billion."

"Again, somewhat imprecise, but slightly more informative." She gestured to him to follow her. "You should speak to the senior staff. I've asked them to come and join us at fifteen hundred hours."

That gave La Forge about an hour to get to his assigned quarters, change, pull out his presentation, and check he had everything he needed. Exactly enough time before T'sath was back at his door to take him to one of the main conference rooms.

There were about two dozen people there: various heads of departments from across the operation, such as the director of the research lab and several of the principal investigators on the main development programs underway at the base. Production managers, operations managers, quality managers, construction specialists, senior process engineers. He started with a segment from Raffi Musiker's presentation: the section that had blown his mind when he had seen it, showing the blast radius fanning outward from the Romulan star, sucking in world after world . . . Then he explained Starfleet's mission: to proceed to the outer systems and save as many as possible of the millions of lives at risk there. He described, in broad brush strokes, what that meant for Utopia Planitia. First, a round of refitting existing ships. Then, a serious commitment to building the number of ships that would be needed to carry out this task, as quickly as possible. He was no more than a few minutes in when he sensed that he was not carrying the crowd with him. He finished, and said, "Any questions?"

There was a silence. Then one of the people at the back said, "This can't be done."

"It's going to have to be," said La Forge.

"We're not *magicians*," someone else said. "We can't pull thousands of ships out of a hat. This is going to mean a major restructure—"

After that, the questions—and comments—started coming in thick and fast. "Which projects are we supposed to stop? Which lines of research are we supposed to be dropping? Whose damned stupid idea was all this in the first place?"

Wow, thought La Forge in dismay, *this was not what I expected . . .* He held up his hands. "Hey now, hold on a minute! Try to remember, please, exactly what's at stake here. We've been asked to take on responsibility for saving hundreds of millions of people at risk from the effects of this star going supernova—"

"The Romulan star," someone called out.

That was enough. "I don't know what the hell is going on here," La Forge snapped, "but I don't expect crap like that from anyone in Starfleet, and I'm telling you now, if I hear anything like it again, there'll be consequences for the people concerned! This mission is happening, whether you like it or not. It's happening, and it needs ships. We have a fleet to build, in record time, and this is where it's going to happen. You can be a part of it, or else I'll expect your request for separation from the service on my desk within the week."

The room was silent. La Forge looked around. Some people glared back; others were studying the ground. "Okay," he said. "I'm going to meet each of you one-to-one. In the meantime, I expect preliminary reports from each division as to how they intend to meet this challenge. Dismissed."

They made their way out, leaving only La Forge and T'sath behind.

"What the *hell* was all that about?" said La Forge.

T'sath looked unperturbed. "I expected some resistance."

"Resistance? That was nearly a goddamn mutiny!"

"I believe that people do not enjoy being asked to put aside their life's work to turn their attention fully to somebody else's project."

"Somebody else's . . . We're going to be saving lives! It's what Starfleet is all about!"

"Romulan lives."

"Now wait a moment, Lieutenant—"

She turned away from him and walked toward the door. "Strange as this may seem, Commander La Forge, Romulans are not popular. The people here will do what you order, and they will do their best, but do not expect them to be happy. Again, I say—you are asking people to put aside their life's work, and to assist people they have been accustomed to thinking of as their enemy. I suggest you find a reason to persuade them of the benefits."

"If you feel that way, Lieutenant T'sath, should I expect your resignation?"

She gave a small smile. "Certainly not. Where else could I practice my trade? As you have made clear—this is the only business in town."

She left. He stood for a while, alone in the empty room. It was not the most auspicious start to the task of a lifetime.

STARFLEET INTELLIGENCE
OFFICE OF ROMULAN AFFAIRS

Raffi Musiker, reeling slightly from the last few hours, walked back into her office, sat down at her desk, and tried to collect her thoughts.

The *Verity* was beautiful. Not the *Enterprise*, no, but then nothing was, and this was the ship needed for this mission. As they took the tour, the admiral looked increasingly pleased. He made a point of checking the passenger facilities. They were not spacious—they had a lot of people to move, and only a limited number of ships, for the moment—but they were comfortable.

"There's some real thought gone into this," Raffi said as they went into a cabin designed for a family unit.

"We must remember how frightening this must be for the people we shall be carrying," Picard said. "They are leaving behind their homes and many of their possessions. We cannot carry them as if they were cargo. As far as possible, these spaces must make them feel secure and, most of all, they must feel *hope*. That even though they are forced to leave their old lives, the possibility of a new life lies ahead. Fear, uncertainty, dislocation—all these will lead to trouble. We must prevent that from arising."

"Close quarters won't come naturally to many Romulans," she said. "Too little privacy. Whatever we can do to lessen the impact of that will make a big difference."

He walked on beside her. " 'We'?"

"Starfleet, I mean," she fudged.

He carried on down the corridor. "Of course." That charade had lasted, oh, another fifteen minutes, max. By the time they had taken a quick look at the day-care area and were kneeling in front of a crate of essential supplies to be issued to each group—checking the quality and durability of the blankets, the hygiene kits, the spare clothes, the padds—they both knew she was accepting. As they walked back to the transporter, he started describing what he believed was the most likely first mission—a small colony on Ectis II—and she pointed out some strategic sensitivities associated with the world's defense grid. And then it was time for her to leave. He reached out and shook her hand.

"Welcome to the mission, Commander," he said. "I am extremely glad to have you on board."

"I'm glad to be able to help, sir."

His grip on her hand tightened, and he looked straight into her eyes. Quietly, he said, "This mission is unprecedented, Raffi. It is going to require as much as you are able to give."

I've become "Raffi" . . . "I won't let you down, sir."

"You have my complete confidence and trust."

Dammit, she thought, sitting back at her desk, *that voice*. She'd suspected, when she'd first heard him speak at the start of their meeting, that she would be persuaded to do whatever he asked. And now, here she was, about to contact her husband, and her son, and tell them that Mommy was going away, for who knew how long. She put her hands flat down on her desk, and thought: *Do I really want this?* And the answer was plain: *Yes. Yes, I do.*

She thought about what she would be leaving on Earth. Gabe, her not-so-little-anymore boy. Jae, who did most of the quiet, steady, constant work that kept an eleven-year-old moving around from meal to school to soccer games to sleepovers, and still managed to produce his holo-sculptures. The ramshackle house on the outskirts of Santa Fe; the mess that came from a smart, active kid, an artist, and a busy Starfleet officer. The studio that they had been kind-of-nearly-not-quite building for Jae for nearly five years; the half-dug vegetable patch. Her office, where she pored over reports late into the night, where she had been sealed for nearly two weeks writing the presentation that had landed her this post, coming up every so often to say: *This'll be done soon, Jae, I promise, and then I'll be back . . .* Her home . . .

But thinking of home made her think of all she had seen on the *Verity*. Those little quarters, where whole families would soon be housed. What that must mean for them, to lose everything. She thought, *Is there something wrong with me, that I think I should be spending my time with some abstract Romulan kids rather than with my own child?* But the truth was, she knew she had to help.

She opened a comm channel.

And there was Gabe, gorgeous Gabe, her baby boy. He was eating. He was always eating. Just walking around, eating. Any day now, the growth spurt would happen, and the last vestiges of the little boy he had once been would be gone, replaced by the makings of a man . . .

"Hey Gabe!" she said. "How are you doing? What have you been up to?"

He looked at her like she was entering her dotage. *"Er, Mom, we saw each other at breakfast."*

"I know, I know . . . How was school? What did you do today?"

"Oh, you know, stuff . . . Do you want to talk to Dad?"

"Sure, honey bunny."

He pretended to be throwing up. *"Don't call me that,"* he said, and stepped out of view. *"Dad!"* he yelled. *"It's Mom! She wants to talk to you!"* He looked back over his shoulder and grinned, his lopsided, half-toothed, still-a-boy grin. *"See ya later!"*

And he was off, back to whatever he'd been up to before she interrupted him. She felt that sharp sense of loss every parent feels, watching their baby move away from them. She wanted to reach out, scoop him up into her arms, and press her face into his hair, capture and savor these brief moments of his childhood, before he was gone for good. She thought: *What am I doing?* and answered herself at once: *The job I'm supposed to do. Making a difference.*

She blinked, twice, and rubbed her eyes.

"Hey, Raffi," said Jae. *"You don't usually call at this time. What's up?"*

"Honey," she said. "I have news."

"Oh yeah?" He was fiddling with something on the desk, not quite looking at her. *"Good news?"*

"Big news."

He looked up properly, and they embarked on what she had correctly predicted would be one of the most difficult conversations of her life so far.

Nine days later, unpacking in her new quarters on the *Verity*, she lifted out a holopicture of the three of them, out in the Grand Canyon, all happiness. Her little family. For a brief and terrifying moment, she thought of the vast distance that was about to open between them all. But then she pulled herself together. "Six months, Jae. We'll give it six months, and then we'll see whether or not it's working. And if it's not—I'll come right back. I promise." There were so many promises. This one she meant to keep.

UTOPIA PLANITIA SHIPYARDS
MARS

La Forge, filing his daily report to Picard, wasn't sure how long he would be able to keep the upbeat tone going. His first weeks on Mars had not been the success he had expected. The pushback against the mission that had been expressed in that first meeting was still ongoing, and he was struggling to think of ways to break through. There were folks here who, even after hearing what the Romulans were facing, were willing to shrug and look the other way. How did you persuade them? If you could look at desperate people, refugees who were fleeing their homes and could never return, and simply turn away, then there was, in La Forge's opinion, something not quite right about you.

La Forge knew that some people found engineers odd. The specialist knowledge and language, the fixation on detail, the ability to focus on a problem that meant thirty-six hours could go by without anyone noticing as long as the coffee and the snacks kept coming . . . Not to mention the goofy sense of humor, the penchant for terrible puns, and the fondness for science fiction. Yep, the wider world, in general, thought engineers were, to put it frankly, weird. Hey, he wasn't disagreeing. He liked himself exactly the way he was.

Every so often, though, there was someone who got it. Someone who saw that these smart goofballs were something special: curious, open-minded, flexible, and practical. Picard was one. Picard understood. And within the tribe, of course, you knew the truth. You knew that what you brought to the table was the ability to change the world: to take the material stuff of the universe and, from it, build tools and machines and processes and systems that transformed lives. That was what this mission was all about, wasn't it? To gather together a group of the smartest people alive, and, through their dedication, intelligence, imagination, and sound understanding of the physical properties of the universe, build tools and machines and processes and systems that would save millions of lives.

When La Forge had set out for Mars, he had assumed that his people—his tribe of offbeat pun-loving geniuses—would also understand. An incredible, daunting opportunity to do what they did best, on a scale that they could barely imagine—and not for the purposes of war, but for the purposes of peace and cooperation. An offer of friendship. It seemed to La Forge to be exactly what Starfleet was meant to do. A simple, magnificent equation: ingenuity plus hope equals change. He thought he would arrive at the shipyards explaining what they had to do, and be met with the immediate enthusiasm of the engineer who, presented with what everyone was saying was an insurmountable problem, replied, "Yeah, you say that, but has anyone thought about trying *this* . . . ?" But that was not how things were panning out.

The door chime sounded. "Come in," he called out. Yet another department head, he guessed, about to explain to him in no uncertain terms that his latest request was not achievable.

A woman in uniform trimmed in engineering gold marched in. She was small, not much more than five feet, solid, short curly hair, fifty-something. Commander's pips. Her eyes were flashing. His heart sank. She walked right over to his desk, dropped a pile of padds there, and stood with her hands upon her hips. Had they met? He had a feeling he would have remembered meeting a hobbit. He pulled one of the padds over and started a quiet search for her name and file. *Commander Estella Mackenzie.*

"Hey!" he said, trying his best to sound upbeat. "How can I help?"

"Physically manufacturing the components," she said. "Have you even *begun* to think about that?"

La Forge blinked. "Excuse me?"

"We want an accelerated program of shipbuilding and that's great. Up to ten thousand ships, you said, within the next few years. And why not? We're the best engineers in the quadrant, possibly two quadrants. But there are limits to what we can replicate, and to what we can automate. Do you understand what that means?"

She glared at him, which he took to be a signal that he was now allowed to speak. "I guess I think it means—"

She blew out a breath that made her sound like a pissed-off camel. "No, no, you don't understand. Let me show you."

To his bewilderment, she began pulling ship components out from her pocket, dumping them onto the desk in front of him. "Hey," he said. "Do you mind not—"

She cut him off. "These two here are components used in the forward sensors." She rummaged in another pocket. "This one is used to monitor and regulate temperatures in the warp plasma conduits. This one goes in the air filtration—"

His desk was starting to look like a junkyard. "I know what they are, Commander," he said, allowing some of the irritation he was feeling to creep into his voice.

"Bravo, so you *do* know your stuff. So—tell me, what do they have in common?"

La Forge stared down at the heap in front of him. Engineers were good at patterns. There was no discernible pattern to these that he could see.

"I'll give you a clue," she said, "since you're looking clueless. It's nothing to do with function. Think about how—"

"How they're made," La Forge said. "They're made by hand. Each one of these is individually manufactured."

"That's right. And now we hit a wall. Because we don't have enough people."

"People?"

"To make the components."

A manufacturing issue . . . a personnel issue . . . La Forge began to do what he always did when faced with a problem, which was to try to break it down into its simplest terms. If there were not enough people, what could be done about that? How could you make more people available? How could you bolster the workforce? Perhaps some kind of stint that would count as credit at the Academy? What sort of numbers was she even talking about?

"If we need more people," he said, "we can get more people."

Mackenzie stared at him. "The average human takes roughly eighteen years to reach maturity. I assume you're not prepared to wait that long, and that you're not envisaging a workforce based on child labor?"

"I am not," said La Forge. "I'm not keen on either of those options. Can we draft people over from across Starfleet?"

Again, that camel-like *harrumph*. Yeah, she was *really* pissed off . . . "This is specialist work we're talking about, not whacking a nail into a piece of timber!" she snapped. "It's skilled work! It takes time to learn! There aren't the people. There aren't the *bodies*."

La Forge's heart felt like a stone in his chest. Yet again, resistance. People telling him that what had to be done couldn't be done. "So what you're telling me is that what I want to do is physically impossible? That I can't speed up manufacture the way we need—?"

Mackenzie looked at him in absolute fury. "What? No, no, no! *Of course* I'm not saying that! For goodness' sake! Do you think I'd come in here with a problem and not have the solution?"

"No," said La Forge humbly. "I'm sorry. Please go on."

She took a deep breath. "What do you know about bio-neural circuitry?"

"I know . . . a little."

"Yes, well, I know a lot."

La Forge glanced down at her file. She wasn't lying. She was the Federation's foremost authority on the damn stuff, specializing in its practical applications for starship design.

"Don't look at your padd," she said sternly, as if addressing a freshman class. "Look at what I'm showing you."

"Yes, sir," he muttered, and obeyed.

"You'll recall—or will have informed yourself from my file, open in front of you—that my recent work on bio-neural circuitry has been concerned with seeing how far we can push the smart elements of the manufacturing systems. How far they can learn. Because looking at these components and thinking how much we rely on *handcrafting the damn things* seems to me to be insane. Ideally, I want the things to be as self-replicating as possible."

"How far have you come with that?"

"Huh? Oh, nowhere. I've persuaded a couple of simpler components to self-replicate, but they degrade far too quickly. You've barely installed them and you're ripping them out. No, there's a decade's work in that yet. And we don't have a decade, do we?"

"You said you had a solution, Commander. Am I about to hear it?"

"You are. Because after a month tearing my hair out, I realized I was coming to this problem the wrong way. These complex components need to be individually assembled. But we need to mass produce. Which means more people."

"Like you said—eighteen years to grow a person—"

"Not an artificial one."

He sat back in his chair. "Say what?"

"Androids, Commander. Synthetics. They're fast, smart, they can be trained to perform specific tasks."

Disappointment washed over La Forge. This stocky, blunt woman had, for a moment, made him think that she was onto something. But she wasn't. "They're nowhere near this at the Daystrom Institute, surely—"

"I don't know about that, because I'm not an expert. But I will bet you every single day of my accumulated leave that those clever people at the Daystrom Institute have never looked at my work. Why should they? What have self-replicating ship components got to do with creating artificial life? But something like this project has never been attempted before, and we need bold ideas. Bio-neural circuitry is smart—for certain definitions of smart. Androids, synthetics—they're smart too. Let's put this work together and see what comes out the other end."

La Forge stared down at the components in front of him. He had watched some of them being manufactured, had seen the careful and precise work involved. They needed to speed this process up somehow . . .

"Do you understand what I'm saying?" Mackenzie said.

"Yes," said La Forge. "You're talking about . . . you're talking about a new kind of synthetic life . . ."

He looked over at her. She was smiling, her face lit up and transformed: a brilliant professor seeing her brightest student make a breakthrough. "That's right. A new kind of synthetic life. One not based on current positronic models, but on what we know about bio-neural circuitry."

Suddenly, in his mind's eye, he had an image of these synthetics, working crisply and quickly and efficiently, around the clock, providing him with everything he needed to make this rapid expansion of the fleet possible. For the first time since he had arrived on Mars, he felt cautiously optimistic. *Synthetics . . .* He fell back in his chair. This was amazing. This was *brilliant*.

"I didn't even know that non-Soong-type androids were *possible . . .*"

Mackenzie cleared her throat. "Well, don't get too excited," she said gruffly. "We're not there yet. We need an expert on androids for one thing."

"I'll get onto the Daystrom Institute immediately." He turned to the computer on his desk and sent a message to the one man who, he knew, could do this. Bruce Maddox. *Bruce. I'm on Mars. I need to see you as quickly as possible.* As he sent the message, he thought of Data, and a pang of loss went through him. He longed, suddenly, for his friend. These new synthetics—they would not be Data. Nothing could replace Data. They would be something else. They would be exactly what was needed . . . but not entirely what was wanted.

He glanced up again at Mackenzie. She was standing stock-still, staring down at the components she had brought. She looked tired and deflated suddenly, as if she had given everything that she had to give. He felt a sudden rush of affection for her.

"Hey," he said softly. "You know, you're the first person here on Mars who has made me think that what we have to do can be done. You are without doubt my favorite person on Mars, and right now you are possibly my favorite person in known space."

She smiled. Rather sweetly, her cheeks dimpled.

"Have I?" she said. "Am I? Oh, I'm glad. I'm so, so glad." Suddenly, her eyes filled with tears. "I can't stop thinking about those poor people," she said. "Having to leave their homes behind. The absolute terror of it all . . . I haven't slept since your presentation, Commander. I had to think of something I could do. I had to *help . . .*"

He came around his desk to join her. He put his arm around her shoulder and gave her a quick hug. She sniffled, and rallied, and cleared her throat. "Yes, well," she said. "Like I said, I don't come into a room to tell someone about a problem without having a solution in my pocket."

"You sure don't," he said. He picked up one of her padds and handed it to her. "Okay," he said. "Bio-neural circuitry. Run me through the basics."

As he listened to her speak, his heart rose. *The best of Starfleet*, he thought. Ingenuity. Hope. Change.

We can do this.

3

Admiral's Log: Our first mission has been confirmed. As expected, we have been formally requested by the Romulan government to remove the population of the mining colony on Ectis II to Arnath IV. This is of course very easy to say, when the reality is that we shall be facilitating the removal of nearly ten thousand souls from their homes, carrying them for slightly over two months to their new world, and then assisting—to a small degree—in their settlement there. I believe, however, that we have done the very best that we can to prepare for this mission. Now we must act, in good faith, and learn all we can from this operation to make the next expedition even more successful.

During this brief pause, this hiatus before the whirl of activity that is about to follow, I must take a moment to remind myself how profoundly grateful I am to everyone who has willingly put aside everything to commit themselves to this mission. Above all, I thank the stars for the work done behind the scenes by my new XO, Commander Raffi Musiker. I am aware that through her efforts what should be problems are presented to me as wholly solved. Captain Kirsten Clancy has been liaising with the Romulans, and Raffi is of course a specialist in Romulan affairs. I have the distinct impression that Clancy's tendency toward micromanagement has been a burden that my XO has also borne on my account, and I am greatly appreciative. This has left me with the time to fully concentrate on staffing, coordinating, and directing the fleet. On Earth, Commander Gbowee has rapidly constructed an organization and processes to respond to our requirements for matériel and staff; she and Lieutenant Kaul are masters of the concise briefing. Messages from Commander Geordi La Forge are proving an interesting read: I sense behind his words some resistance from the yard's engineers at these new and overwhelming demands that are being placed upon them. I understand too that for many, this will mean setting aside research for many years that may well have been the chief concern. But if any officer can corral them toward a common goal, it is surely Geordi, among the most optimistic, practical, and sincere officers of my acquaintance.

Tomorrow, it begins: the most complex project ever mounted by Starfleet and the Federation. In between the briefings, duty rosters, charts, files, data, and all the necessary bureaucracy, let us not forget our goal: to protect and save life.

STARSHIP VERITY

Picard sat in his chair on the bridge, ostensibly at ease; in fact, he was taut as a wire. The fleet—fifteen ships in total, with the *Starship Verity* front and center—was fifteen minutes away from setting out on its first mission of mercy. All around, the bridge crew was busy with last-minute systems' checks, engineering reports, all the vital preparations for the voyage. They were a fine crew. He knew that he should say something to them—in fact, to the whole fleet embarking on this journey—to mark the occasion, but he could not quite decide on the appropriate words. Not for the first time in his life he felt the terrible isolation of command; not for the first time in his life he reminded himself that this melancholy always settled upon him before any major voyage. That this might prove to be the voyage that would define him.

Raffi, beside him, touched his arm. "Penny for your thoughts, sir?"

He straightened up and cleared his throat. "Contemplating our mission, that's all."

"That's all, eh?"

"That's all."

"Huh. Big thoughts. I'll need to give you more than a penny for them. Hey, you know how the advice goes about how to eat an elephant?"

This should be good, he thought. "Do tell, Commander."

"One bite at a time, Admiral. How else d'you think you eat a damn elephant? One bite at a time. How about we get the ship out of dock before we worry about anything else?"

He relaxed. From the corner of his eye, he saw her nod, satisfied that her intervention had had the desired effect, and turn her attention back to proceedings.

One bite at a time...

Yes, these were simple maneuvers, performed thousands of times. He need not worry for the moment.

Lieutenant Marshall, handling comms, turned to him. "Admiral, incoming message from Starfleet Command. It's Captain Clancy."

"*Chrissakes*," muttered Raffi, "what now? Probably checking we've packed our lunches." She caught his eye. "Sorry, sir."

Picard, smile firmly suppressed, rose from his seat. "In my ready room, please, Lieutenant." His eyes twinkled at Raffi. "The bridge is yours, Commander."

In the quiet of his ready room, he took the message. Clancy appeared on screen. *"Admiral Picard, I wanted to wish you the best of luck."*

"Thank you, Kirsten."

"Also, before you leave—I'm sending someone over to join your team. Her name is Koli Jocan. She's a specialist on refugee relocation."

This, thought Picard, was typical Clancy: to decide, without consultation, that there was a problem and to provide, without asking, some kind of solution. He bit back his instinctive response, which was to say that he was perfectly capable of crewing his own damn ship, and said, "The name sounds Bajoran."

"That's right. Born in a Rankath refugee camp at the end of the Occupation. She knows her business."

He was taking along numerous experts on refugee resettlement. Why was Clancy so keen on this one? "I'm sure she'll be an asset."

"She's wholly committed. Very focused. I think you'll get along with her."

She sounded as if she might be hard work. "Indubitably."

There was a pause. Clancy looked about to say more, then clearly thought better. *"Well, good luck. You go with all of Starfleet's well wishes for the success of this mission."*

"Thank you, Kirsten. *Verity* out."

Picard sat for a moment or two, contemplating the screen. He always sensed, in his dealings with Clancy, some . . . What would the word be? He hesitated to call it mistrust. Misalignment? That was fairer. Despite the same training, the same uniform, and the same stated ideals and values, he felt . . . at odds with her, in some undefined but crucial way. Picard filed this away for future consideration. He had a mission to get underway, and, besides, none of this was the fault of Koli Jocan. He must welcome her with good grace and accept her services in a similar fashion.

When he went back out onto the bridge, he saw a young Bajoran woman, neat in a blue Starfleet uniform, lieutenant pips, who started at the sight of him. Raffi, behind her, was pointing and mouthing: *Who the hell is this?*

He stepped forward to greet her. She was slightly built, below average height—common for a Bajoran of her generation, the usual if sad effect of a malnourished childhood. "Lieutenant Koli, I presume?"

"Yes, Admiral."

"Welcome aboard. You arrive in the nick of time."

"I'm very glad about that." In a quiet voice, she added, "I'm aware you didn't request me, sir. I approached Captain Clancy and asked to be assigned to this mission. I am extremely grateful to you for allowing me this opportunity. I cannot think of any more important work to be done right now than this."

He smiled gently. She was young, sincere, and Clancy's *faux pas* was not her fault. "We are in full accord. I look forward to serving alongside you."

He took his seat, collected himself. Clancy, it turned out, had inadvertently done him a favor. Rather than sitting and brooding over what to say, he had been distracted. And now the words came easily. He directed Lieutenant Marshall to patch his voice throughout the fleet and spoke.

"This is Admiral Jean-Luc Picard, speaking to you from the *Starship Verity*. Across this fleet, our combined experience encompasses many hundreds of years, thousands of worlds, and hundreds of thousands of missions. Today we embark upon Starfleet's greatest mission. The most honest, the most heartfelt, and the most necessary of tasks. To put aside centuries of doubt, fear, and mistrust, and to offer to our neighbors, in their hour of need, the unconditional hand of friendship."

He saw Koli nodding. Taking heart, he continued.

"I am grateful to each one of you for your decision to join me. You have left families, posts, and homes that you love dearly, in order to commit to saving lives. I say to you that there is no higher duty than the preservation of life. Let us take up our duties with courage, and with hope. With our talents and resources, we will achieve success, not for plaudits or medals or gratitude, but because it is the right thing to do, and because we are able to do it."

He finished. Koli began to clap, and soon a ripple of applause went around the bridge. Lieutenant Marshall patched in comms from the bridges of the other fourteen ships, and he heard the reaction there. Resolute. Determined. He turned to the helm.

"Lieutenant Miller . . ."

"Go on," Raffi whispered. "They're dying for you to say it."

And why not?

"Engage!"

He felt the delight from around his own bridge, and whoops and cheers from the other ships. His own full smile came naturally, and without inhibition. The *Verity* moved forward. Raffi, in the seat beside him, put two thumbs up. Then she quirked an eyebrow up and flicked a glance toward Koli. *Well?*

He gave a curt nod.

The fleet—sleek, beautiful, hopeful, the best of Starfleet—departed. So it began.

DAYSTROM INSTITUTE
OKINAWA, EARTH

Estella Mackenzie turned out to be exactly the ally that La Forge needed. She had fired up engines that he hadn't even known were present. Some people were willing to stand up to everyone no matter what, and Mackenzie was one of them. There were of course some requests for transfer, all of which were allowed. But even T'sath cautiously changed sides. Once she was on board, the rest fell into line.

Slowly, as the weeks passed, the work began to move forward. The briefings became less combative and agonizing. More and more, people started to wander past La Forge's office saying, "Hey, I had this idea . . ." Soon enough, he was confident that he could leave for the Daystrom Institute without everything coming crashing to a halt.

The campus of the Daystrom Institute, where the Division of Advanced Synthetic Research was housed, was set high on a clifftop overlooking the Pacific. La Forge passed through security. As he walked along the white corridors, he pondered his meeting with Bruce Maddox. It was not easy to feel goodwill toward someone who had tried to turn one of your best friends into a box of spare parts. Data had forgiven Maddox, and La Forge had to honor that, even if he struggled with it. Not for the first time, La Forge thought, Data had turned out to be the fullest, the best, the most human of them all. Measured, thoughtful, forgiving. *I try to live up to your example, Data. But some people sure make it hard.*

Doctor Bruce Maddox, tall and lean, welcomed him offhandedly. "I've heard of Mackenzie's work, of course," he said, his eyes drifting to the open files on his desk, "but it's nothing like my research. She's making . . ." He gave a slight smile. "Well, what does it amount to? Machines. Complex, and organic, but not life."

"I'm sure she'd be interested to hear your take on her work," La Forge said dryly. In fact, he'd like to sit ringside for that. Hell, he'd sell tickets. Mackenzie would make mincemeat of Maddox.

Maddox had the grace to look embarrassed. "I don't mean that what she's doing isn't difficult, or, indeed, laudable. And obviously there are a huge number of practical applications. But it isn't what I'm doing. They're two very different approaches. But I think you know that already, La Forge. I have to confess I'm pretty puzzled as to why you're here."

He didn't look puzzled at all; in fact, he looked not in the least bit interested. His eyes were already turning back to the file on his desk. La Forge said, "What have you heard about the Romulan supernova?"

"The what?"

How had he not heard? *Jeez*, thought La Forge. *This guy . . .* "The Romulan sun is going supernova—"

Light dawned in Maddox's eyes. "Oh yes! The refugee mission! Sorry, I'm teaching a graduate class at the moment, and if you could see the state of some their papers you'd understand my distraction. Yes, of course. What has that got to do with bio-neural circuitry?"

Do I have to spell this out? "We're helping to relocate hundreds of millions of Romulans," La Forge said. "It's demanding significant breakthroughs in starship construction in order to be able to supply enough ships to get the job done. Most of the research facilities at Utopia Planitia have been turned toward the problem."

"I bet *they're* pleased."

"Excuse me?" said La Forge frostily.

"Well, who wants to stop their research?" said Maddox. "I can see it's for a good cause, but . . ."

You're gonna love what's coming next, thought La Forge.

"So you're working on advancing starship construction technology," said Maddox. "That's going to cause some significant engineering problems, but those guys are great. What do you need from me today?"

"There are some insurmountable problems when it comes to the manufacture of certain components," said La Forge. "It's skilled work, but we can't train enough people quickly enough to meet demand. We need another solution."

"I suppose there might be a bio-neural solution there," said Maddox. "Intelligent circuitry—well, I say intelligent. Considerable learning capability. But not sentience."

"It's more complicated than that, but you've got the general idea," said La Forge.

"Great for Mackenzie and her work."

"Yep. But the reality is . . ." La Forge leaned forward in his seat. "Listen, Bruce. The tasks are so complicated. We're thinking about a range of nonsentient androids, based on bio-neural circuitry, to do the assembly work."

Maddox looked vaguely interested. "I guess that might work. Good job you've got Mackenzie. If anyone could do it, it'll be her. From what I've heard, she's dogged."

Okay, thought La Forge, *I am going to have to spell this out.* "I want you to work on this with Mackenzie."

Maddox stared at him. "Why on earth would I do that?"

La Forge was startled. He hadn't anticipated that question.

"I mean," said Maddox, "I've read her work, sure; it has very little in common with what I do. Like I said—they're two very different approaches."

He looked at La Forge. La Forge looked back.

"That's not what you're saying, is it, Geordi?"

La Forge shook his head.

"No," said Maddox.

"Bruce," said La Forge, seeing the explosion coming. "It's what's needed right now—"

"You want me to stop work—stop my work, my *life's* work—and start building . . ." He grasped around for the right word. "*Toys?*"

"Yes," said La Forge simply. "And before you say anything else, I'm asking because we have millions of lives to save. Can you understand that? Sure, this will mean stopping your work, but for a *good* purpose! What use," he said, "is the potential of artificial sentient life, if it comes at the cost of all these lives—these *real* lives—that right now are in desperate trouble? I need you, Bruce. I need your expertise, and you can do good work, *real* good, right now—"

"As opposed to the work I've been doing up to now? What's that been?" Maddox looked petulant; it was the only word for it. "Nobody has *ever* taken my work seriously."

La Forge, thinking of Data, didn't take a swing at him.

"This is what we need, Bruce," he said. "Hey, I can't compel you to do anything, but I can put it to you plainly. This is what Admiral Picard needs, what the mission needs, what Starfleet needs and, most of all, it's what millions of desperate people need. I'm asking you, to give a little—"

"A little? You're asking for . . . what? Five years of my life? A decade? More?"

La Forge struggled to answer. "Could be two . . . could be five . . ."

"I see," said Maddox.

"I'm asking you to give what's needed," said La Forge. "To help save all these lives."

Maddox sat back in his chair, arms folded, and stared bitterly at La Forge. "So no compulsion, then?"

"Like I said, I can't force you do anything. But this is where the resources are going."

"So no compulsion, other than soon I'll be able to do next to nothing. I guess it's only a matter of time before the lab space gets reassigned. Then the damn desk itself." A silence fell on the room. Maddox glared at the wall. "Nonsentient synthetics," he said at last. "What a waste. What a goddamn waste."

"You're on board?" said La Forge cautiously.

"For god's sake, Geordi, what choice do I have?" Maddox pulled up the latest file Mackenzie had sent over. "All right. Talk me through the basics."

Well, thought La Forge, *I'm glad to have you on board. I think.*

INSTITUTE OF ASTRONOMY
CAMBRIDGE, EARTH

Cambridge in autumn, early in the morning, had a special magic. Light mist curled around the fens; in the distance the colleges were hazy and mysterious. Doctor Amal Safadi finished her run with a sprint, reaching the gate a little below the twenty-minute mark. Not bad. She rested on the black-painted metal, getting her breath back, sipping water. A big reddish-brown cow, munching at the thick grass, pondered her. A heron flew past. This, she thought, was not a bad life.

She showered, changed, and breakfasted, but took her time getting on her bike to head over to work. The Institute of Astronomy was a little way out of town, to the north and west, and usually she liked to be at her desk early. This morning, she found all manner of small things to do at home. Check the power source on the replicator. Fiddle with the light settings. Stare at the empty bird boxes. At last she could find nothing else to do and she made herself start the day: leave the house, unlock the bike, push off on the pedals. Arriving at the cycle park, she fiddled around with the lock for a while.

This is ridiculous. Go and make sure. You can't put this off any longer.

Elena Richter, another astronomer with whom she shared her office, looked up when she walked in. Elena was just back from a conference in Hawaii and seemed very relaxed. "Hey! You're late this morning."

They had a chat about the conference. The keynote had gone over brilliantly. They tapped coffee mugs and toasted Elena's success. After that, Safadi had to sit down at her desk. The screen came on at her touch. She stared at the model she had run the previous evening. Her results hadn't gone away, and she was going to have to admit that they weren't going to go away.

"Elena," she said, at last. "Can you take a look at this?"

Seeing her friend's face, Elena came right over. "What's the matter?"

"The datasets came in while you were away," Safadi said, turning the screen around for Elena to see. "I started modeling the rate of expansion of the Romulan supernova based on them. And . . . well. Take a look."

Safadi watched as Elena went through the model. She watched her frown turn into concentration, watched her concentration turn into outright alarm. "This can't be right," Elena said. "Amal, have you checked this? Stupid question, sorry."

"I can't find a mistake . . ." The two women sat and watched the model for a while; watched the concentric rings move outward, faster than ever before. "If I'm correct . . . the rate of expansion is much faster, and the blast radius is going to be much bigger, than anything we thought was going to happen . . ."

"Holy shit," muttered Elena. She started to look through the figures again. "That's another ten worlds . . . Holy *shit* . . . Okay. Let's go through this again, step by step."

By midmorning, two more colleagues, including their group director, Durnyam Bekri, had come past Safadi's desk, and looked through both model and calculations. Others, sensing that something was up, wandered past and peered into the office, but didn't interrupt, particularly when the door closed, and the four of them held a conference, deciding what to do next.

Durnyam, sitting in Safadi's chair and studying the model yet again, said, "If it's any consolation, it's a beautiful piece of work."

"Thank you," said Safadi. "But problematic, I think . . ."

"I'd say," muttered Graish, a talented but rather anxious Bolian. "This is a drastic change from the previous model. Romulus hit sooner, more worlds coming within the blast range . . ."

"I know," said Safadi. "That was based on data supplied to us by the

Romulan Space Authority. This is the first model that's based completely on datasets taken from our own readings. Which suggests . . ."

"That the data supplied by the Romulans is in some way flawed," said Durnyam.

"Do you mean flawed," said Elena, "or false?"

There was a short pause. Graish started twisting his fingers around.

"I have no evidence," said Durnyam calmly, "that the Romulans have supplied us with false data. We have a model based on what they sent us, and a model based on what we ourselves have observed. Perhaps their scientists simply aren't as good as Amal."

"But surely they wouldn't lie about their data?" Graish said.

"It seems to me," said Elena, "that that is *exactly* what they would lie about."

"But *why*?" said Graish. "Why would they do that, with so many lives at stake? This takes months off their time to evacuate the homeworld. Years, possibly. They should have started yesterday! Why would they lie?"

"Why indeed," said Durnyam. She turned to Safadi. "Amal, if I'm struggling with anything, it's getting these figures to make sense given what we would expect from a nova of this type. Why is *this* one expanding so rapidly?"

Safadi looked back at her unhappily. "I don't know. It's hard to find a natural explanation that works with the data—"

"So a nonnatural one?" Elena frowned. "A deliberate attack?"

"On the Romulan *star*?" Durnyam looked horrified.

"Well, it's certainly thrown a major power into complete disarray," Elena pointed out.

"That would be monstrous!" Durnyam said. "No, I can't believe that—"

Safadi cut through. "I'm not going to speculate on anything that I don't have hard data to support, and I don't think any of us should. Not least because of the politics. What matters right now is the lives that are at stake. We're dealing with a much bigger phenomenon than we originally believed. Hitting harder, hitting faster. And that's going to have an impact on the relief mission." She looked again at her figures. "If I could visit the

Romulan home system . . . get some better readings closer to their sun." There was another short silence. They all knew how much secrecy had surrounded the Romulan datasets. All four of them had been asked by Starfleet Intelligence to carry out extra security checks, fill in extra non-disclosure forms, and so on and so on. ("As if I was going to sell Romulan data," Elena had muttered. "Who the hell would I sell it to?") And, of course, there was a series of carefully outlined protocols surrounding what they could do with the data, and who could and should be informed.

"We're obliged," said Durnyam, "to notify Romulan Affairs if anything significant arises in our work here. What I want to do is make absolutely sure that these figures are rock solid—"

"Amal doesn't get things wrong," said Elena.

"No, she doesn't," said Durnyam. "But Romulan Affairs doesn't know that, and their opposite numbers in the Star Empire . . . I want every single piece of this code scrutinized, every line, every formula, every function. When we are sure—absolutely sure—as a group that this is unassailable, that's when we contact Romulan Affairs. But we need to be quick. Because if this is true . . ."

They all watched once again as ten more worlds came within the blast radius and were consumed by its implacable force.

"Well," said Durnyam. "We can see what that means."

They went back to work, except Safadi, who followed Durnyam to her office, closing the door behind her. "I'm sorry," she said. "I know this is going to cause problems."

Durnyam peered at her over her glasses. "You're not responsible for a supernova," she said. "You're only responsible for studying and interpreting the data. If that data means bad news there are other people responsible for acting on it."

As ever, Safadi felt safe in this woman's hands, supported and secure. "I did have one suggestion to make. . . . I can't get over how different our model is from the Romulan model."

"It is a puzzle," said Durnyam dryly.

"I've used a lot of Nokim Vritet's work in the past. I even heard him speak once, that time he was allowed to uplink to the Delta IV conference. He's an exemplary space scientist. I can't believe the discrepancies."

"We have the best of all possible worlds here," Durnyam said. "Science that—even if it's not entirely understood, is respected. Our expertise—respected. Politicians, Starfleet officers—they give us the resources to be able to do our work, and they trust our results when we deliver them. They may not like what we have to say, but they don't try to deny it. Do you imagine that's the case for Doctor Vritet?"

Safadi shivered. No, she wouldn't like to be trying to do science on Romulus, not even before this. Science depended on being open: on sharing results and being willing to accept when you had made mistakes. Were Romulan scientists allowed to work that way? Were they allowed to make mistakes? Particularly when their work was as politically sensitive as this field had so suddenly become?

"Do you think," Safadi said thoughtfully, "that if I requested it, there'd be any chance of going to see Vritet? To work with him and his people on their modeling? See if they've missed something, or we've missed something . . . Even to have a means to correspond with him regularly—"

But Durnyam was shaking her head. "*You* know it makes sense, and *I* know it makes sense, but the reality is it's not going to happen. The politics of it . . ." She held up her hands. "There'll be conversations at Starfleet Intelligence, you know, about whether these figures should even be released to the Romulans."

"What?" Safadi was shocked. "That can't be right—they have to know!"

"I know. But at the same time, someone will be making a calculation: What's the impact of passing this on? Will the Romulans accept the new figures? Will they lose face? Will they pull down the shutters, refuse to allow us to continue with the help we're giving them?"

"It's math," said Safadi simply. "You can't argue with it. It's . . . how it is."

"And all we can do is be sure that our facts are straight. What other people do with those facts? That's something we can't control." She looked steadily at the younger woman. "You're sure about these figures, aren't you?"

"I am absolutely sure," said Safadi.

"Then don't worry about what comes next. You have done your best—and if everyone acts as they should, you'll have saved lives, Amal. How often, in our field, do we get to say that?"

DAYSTROM INSTITUTE
OKINAWA, EARTH

Bruce Maddox couldn't ever remember a time when he enjoyed teaching. He had never imagined himself as a teacher; his desire had always been to lose himself in the lab, immerse himself in the theoretical work. What he wanted was to be left alone, to work on what he had dreamed of since he was a boy, when he read and watched everything he could about androids, marveling at the idea that something could look alive and yet not *be* alive. Then, later, hearing about Data, and *seeing* Data . . . He was sure that he could build a machine like that. All he wanted was his chance. But so many things interfered: committee meetings, peer review, examining . . . No wonder Noonian Soong had hidden himself away. Sometimes Maddox dreamed of leaving everything behind, dashing off into the unknown where he would be left in peace to make his breakthrough.

Teaching was the worst for sucking up time and energy. Over the years, he'd done his best to limit how much time he was obliged to devote to the task, and yet here he was, as the afternoon wore on, taking a group of ten graduate students through advanced positronics. They didn't understand most of what he was saying. Of course they didn't: Maddox wasn't sure that he entirely understood himself. Only Soong had fully understood positronics; only Soong had created a sentient android, a scientific marvel. Maddox had intended to be next—but here he was, stuck in the classroom, and as soon as he got away, he would be stuck working for La Forge.

Life was short, and as the years passed, Maddox seemed to hear the clock ticking louder and louder. Sometimes he worried that his best years had gone, that his creativity was spent. Sometimes he was afraid that he had missed his chance completely. That he would never see the dream realized, see the spark of life come into the eyes of one of his creations.

Other colleagues, he knew, found teaching exhilarating. Working with energetic and unformed young minds kept their own work and passion fresh and vital. But Maddox found it exhausting constantly having to explain basic principles. Even at postgraduate level, where students had deeper understanding, he struggled to find a like mind. Sure, the kids here this afternoon were bright, but they weren't committed. They were checking off a box before being allowed to move into their specialisms. They might grasp the basics, but they didn't grasp what mattered. They didn't *care* . . . and that made this yet another monumental waste of his precious and rapidly disappearing time.

But academic protocol—not to mention ethics—required that junior colleagues did not bear the burden of teaching, especially while trying to establish themselves as serious researchers. However much Maddox argued that senior staff needed this time and space in order to be able to conduct top-level research, he still ended up teaching for hours beyond what he preferred. But once the classes were over, he had always been able to go back to his desk—to his work. With relief, he would return to the intricacies and puzzles of his studies, to the elusive promise of creating synthetic sentient life. Now even that was to be taken away. And for what? To build robots. Machines. Toys. It was weeks now since La Forge's visit, and between demands from him and classroom duties, Maddox had more or less given up on his research.

He looked without interest at his class. They looked indifferently back.

"Okay," he said. "That's enough for today."

They were up from their chairs and out of the door within seconds. Maddox shoved his notes into his briefcase. Back in his office, there would be questions from La Forge, messages from that damned Mackenzie. If he was lucky, he would find some time after hours to look at his own research.

"Doctor Maddox?"

One of the students was still hanging around. A young woman. He couldn't remember her name; he hadn't yet committed the names of all the class to memory, and he wasn't sure he would manage it before the end of the semester. He did recognize her, though. She had been sitting up front for every one of these seminars. Long, fair hair pulled back into a ponytail, wisps escaping from both sides, as if she hadn't quite remembered to fix it properly. Chewing her bottom lip. Eyes wide set and eager. Altogether, there was a freshness and energy about her that made him feel exhausted.

"Yes, Ms., er . . ."

"Jurati. Agnes Jurati. It's Doctor, actually. I'm a medical doctor."

"Doctor Jurati, of course." Now he recalled the name. Starfleet. She'd been seconded here, part of some interdisciplinary program or other, yet another Starfleet interference . . . She had sent him a message (titled "Potential dissertation subjects?") that he hadn't yet opened. He picked up his briefcase and began to move toward the door. "How may I help?"

She followed him. "I was wondering whether you'd seen my message?"

"I've seen it," he said.

"And I was hoping you had some thoughts? About the final project, I mean?" She looked anxious and keen to please. He was keen to get away. He felt so damn tired by the end of the day . . .

"I'm afraid I haven't had a chance to read in detail." She looked so crestfallen that he was faintly embarrassed. He gestured around the room. "Once teaching starts, you never seem to get on top of things."

She made a rather ineffective attempt to cover her obvious deep disappointment. "Sure, yes, of course . . ." She brightened and gave a wide, sweet smile. "Are you walking back to your office? I'm heading that way. Perhaps I could sketch my ideas out to you now?"

"Um, might be better if you set up a meeting?"

"Meetings take time, Doctor Maddox. This is time you're already spending walking."

Yes, he thought, *but walking time is thinking time, and once I'm at my desk I'm stuck thinking about the damned toys.*

She trotted alongside him, still bright and hopeful. She wasn't going to take no for an answer, was she?

"Doctor Maddox," she said, "I hope this doesn't sound weird—"

Why me? he thought.

"But I came to the Daystrom Institute to study with you. Nobody else will do. Nobody else is doing anything else worth studying. That's why I came here." She was gazing up at him with something close to devotion. "I've been reading your work on Soong-type androids. It's brilliant. It's what I want to do. You're the reason I'm here . . ." She held out her hands. "Please. Hear me out. While you walk back to your office."

Brilliant, gifted people are no different from the rest of us: subject to doubt, susceptible to flattery. Bruce Maddox was, after all, only human, and hardly the perfect creation of his imagination. He ushered the young woman out of the lecture room ahead of him, turned off the lights, and closed the door. He stood in the corridor and looked at the hope in her eyes.

"I've been talking for a while now," he said. "How about we go and get a coffee?"

Her eyes shone. "Oh, I'd love that!"

It was past five o'clock. Outside, the day was darkening, though it was still warm enough for him to carry his jacket. They ended up, inevitably, in the campus coffee house. She got iced coffee in a tall glass; he got green tea. As they were heading to the table, she suddenly backed up and ran to the counter, to replicate a pile of chocolate chip cookies.

"Sorry," she said, already biting into one as she sat down opposite him. "Your class bends my brain and I get so *hungry* afterward! You want anything?"

She hadn't stopped talking since the classroom, and the cookies weren't slowing her down. She explained how she had read nearly everything he had written, and he realized that she spoke with real understanding. She also spoke with her hands. She almost knocked over her tall glass of iced coffee as she talked about his last article. When they both reached out to steady the glass their hands brushed against each other. She laughed, and so did he. She was cute. But he had to put a stop to this, and now. If only she had walked in five years ago; ten . . .

"Doctor Jurati."

"I'm okay with first names, you know." She flushed. "I mean, as long as you are—"

"Agnes," he said. "I've enjoyed hearing you speak. It's been . . ." He laughed again. "It's been a joy, to be honest."

She grinned; she had a small smear of chocolate on her left cheek. "Hey, me too!"

"But I'm afraid I'm not taking on any students right now."

Her face fell. He felt like he'd kicked a puppy. Was she capable of concealing any emotion? Everything was immediately out there. "Excuse me?"

"I'm not taking on any students right now."

For a moment he was afraid she was going to cry. "But it's not as if I was talking about doctoral work . . . This is the final project for this semester and there's nobody else that I would want, I mean, I'm not even going to be *here* next semester, I'm going back to *Starfleet*—"

"Agnes—"

"*Why?* Why *not?*"

Ten years ago, he thought. Five. They could have worked together, blissfully, without disturbance. He imagined what it might have been like, having a student who truly understood his work and didn't treat him as nothing more than a gateway to a necessary credit. Would it have made the difference, having someone to discuss his work with? Maybe they would have made the breakthrough, the elusive breakthrough. All this time, working alone . . . And now here she was, and the damn Romulan sun had chosen one *hell* of a time to go supernova.

His tea had gone cold. He pushed the cup away; he hadn't wanted it in the first place. "Because I'm not working in that field any longer."

"What do you mean?"

"I'm not working on positronics any longer."

Her mouth fell open into a shocked O . . . "You've not given up, have you? You can't! I can't believe you'd give up—"

"Yes," he said bitterly; then: "No. I've not given up. I've been *made* to give up."

"Who?" she said. "Who's making you give up? You can't be made to give up your life's work!"

"I'm afraid I can," he said. "Or, to be fair, I can be asked by someone I admire and respect to do something so time-consuming and so necessary that I won't be able to carry on with my own research."

"What can be more important than what you're doing? Dammit, you're trying to create *life*!"

He began to laugh, not unkindly, but from the simple pleasure of hearing someone else say what he had only ever heard inside his own head. He fell back in his chair. "Oh, Agnes," he said. "I wish you'd turned up years ago. We could have done something special—"

"We still *can*!" Did she know how cute she looked? Her face covered in chocolate chip cookie; her eyes bright with indignation. No, of course she didn't. The obliviousness was part of the charm. "What are you being made to do?"

He glanced around the room. "You know, some of the things we do here don't need to be widely broadcast . . ."

She went scarlet. She put her hand over her mouth. "Oh, I am so sorry . . ."

"Don't worry. But . . . No. I'm the one who is sorry. I wish I could, but I can't. It's not possible." He drank the rest of his cold tea and stood up. "I'm sorry."

She jumped up, grabbing her padd from the table. "But I hadn't even started to explain my idea!"

He put up his hands to stop her. He didn't want to hear what she had to say. What if it turned out to make sense? What if it turned out to be the one thing that could have made a difference? "I can't work with you, Doctor Jurati."

"Look," she said, "have you ever considered the capabilities of a single positronic neuron?"

He wavered. But no, he couldn't allow this . . . "I'm shifting focus now," he said. "I'm working on bio-neural circuitry—"

She looked baffled. "Um, *that's* a big shift. Why would you be working on something like that all of a sudden?"

"I told you. It's what's needed right now."

He saw her brow furrow, watched the cogwheels of her brain shift and turn. "Hey, they've been working on that on Mars, haven't they? For shipbuilding?" He saw her come to an understanding. Jeez, she was sharp! "Oh. I see . . ."

"Yes, well, can you remember that it's not to be discussed widely and we're in a campus coffee house?"

"Oh, of course . . ." She took a step toward him. "But that doesn't make any difference, does it?"

"It's an entirely different field!"

"So?"

"So!"

"So you can work on both at once."

He stopped dead. "Excuse me?"

"Excuse *me*! You—you're Bruce Maddox! You're the galaxy's living expert on synthetic life! You can work on both at once." Her excitement was gathering momentum. "Why not? Maybe they come down to the same thing? Maybe there's something that will unify these technologies?" She began to laugh. "I don't know! You're the expert! You're the *genius*!"

Genius? he thought; then, *Hey, why the hell not?*

"You're the person to find out, though, aren't you?" She reached over to touch him, very gently, on the wrist. "Aren't you, Bruce?"

Yes, he thought. *I am.* He reached out to touch her cheek, to wipe the smear of chocolate away. She blushed when she realized what he was doing.

They met the following day, midmorning, at the same place. He watched in awe as she demolished two slices of carrot cake with cream cheese frosting. She talked about her project. The next day she came to his office and she talked about his last paper. The day after that she came to his home. This time he even got to do some talking. He explained more about the work he was doing with Mackenzie, and why. She was enthralled. He thought, *Perhaps it's worth doing after all.* And then she said: "But it's not your life's work, is it? Never mind. I promise you, Bruce— you can have it all."

He didn't take her seriously, not really. He knew she was going back to Starfleet soon, and he would go back to the damned toys. He asked her to go for coffee again after the next seminar. He watched her put away a giant slice of cake and found himself smiling at her enthusiasm. She was leaving soon. Surely they could simply enjoy each other's company—each other's *intelligence*—in the meantime? What harm was there in keeping each other company? No harm.

4

Admiral's Log: We are thirty-six hours out from Ectis II, when the process of relocating its population can at last get underway. All the advice given me by experts in the field of refugee relocation has indicated one thing: that after months of planning, our preparations, however meticulous, will most likely still not be sufficient for the specific task at hand. We shall see what happens two days from now. Certainly, we have done all that we can. The journey here has not been wasted, and the accommodations for our guests are in excellent order.

We have brought the full fleet of fifteen ships to Ectis. Commander La Forge reports to me that the refitting of an additional eight ships will be ready in six days, and these can proceed to Tavaris VI. That mission, commanded by Captain Nangala on the *Patience*, is becoming increasingly urgent. Tavaris is a partially terraformed world just outside the Romulan system; the terraforming process there was at a critical stage, and with the withdrawal of the resources, there have been severe and unanticipated effects. Raffi—through whatever official or unofficial channels she receives this information—has obtained footage of flash flooding in several towns, leaving thousands homeless and dispossessed. These images bring home to me the urgency of our mission and give immediacy to what might otherwise seem too vast and impossible a task. Briefings from my science officers tell me that we can expect these effects to become more marked as the months pass. Our aim is to remove populations from their homeworlds before such calamities strike: combining relocation efforts with on-the-ground disaster relief adds significant layers of complexity to our work. Nevertheless, I have asked Commander Gbowee to set up a task force to explore and model such scenarios, to see what special equipment and personnel would be needed. Starfleet Command continues to provide whatever is needed. In my last conversation with the C-in-C, he asked for some positive news to take back to the Federation Council.

We have retrofitted our ships to serve as people carriers. Geordi informs me that retrofitting of further ships is now well underway, and they should join our fleet within the next four months. The problem of rapidly expanding the capacity of the shipyards has not yet been solved. Nevertheless, I note that Geordi's reports have, of late, become more effusive, and my sense is that whatever resistance he had been facing on Mars is starting to break down. Perhaps the technical challenge of this mission begins to grip the imaginations (and consciences) of the engineers there. If ever there was a time to set aside personal goals for a greater good, this is it.

Here on the *Verity*, we wait for our mission to begin. We have relied upon the Romulan authorities to organize our guests. This is, according to Lieutenant Koli, precisely the kind of matter where Federation and Romulan sensibilities might not be in alignment, and offense may inadvertently be given. Left to our own devices, we would have taken the vulnerable first: children, the infirm, the elderly, and caregivers. I note from the lists that several of these groups are among the first to board. I note also the names of a large number of prominent politicians and officials. I am aware that Romulan culture is hierarchical in ways that the Federation is not. Nevertheless, I do feel some unease about the priorities implied by this order of arrival. I remain prepared for the unexpected, and I am glad of the presence of Lieutenant Koli, whose experience and outlook are proving to be most useful . . .

Verity
Approaching Ectis II

The first weeks on board ship had passed in a blur. Picard had found himself confronted with so many decisions that he was barely able to distinguish what was crucial, what was necessary, what could be deferred, and what was moot. Raffi proved his savior. She made him work out the system by which more mundane decisions were detoured to her and the various department heads, and the more crucial information filtered up to him. By the end of the first month, they had shifted from hourly briefings to four times daily. He was pleased with her, very pleased. The commander was confident, on top of detail, and she had a way with people that always seemed to elude him. She knew how to put them at ease. She knew how to put *him* at ease.

"How much of the elephant did we get through today, Raffi?" he would ask her at their end-of-day briefing. *"A fair chunk,"* she would reply. *"But there's another herd of the bastards arriving tomorrow."*

Still, the night before they were due to begin their work on Ectis, he lay in his cabin restless, sleep impossible. For the first time, he found himself missing the *Enterprise*. He listened to the gentle pulses of his new ship. The darkness of his room expanded in his thoughts to encompass all the empty decks of the vessel, soon to be temporary home to so many people. Doubt suddenly assailed him. This mission—so vast, so complex—was it in fact possible? To turn around the great vessel of Starfleet, to ask people to set aside their work, their lives, their goals, and sublimate everything to help not friends but long-term enemies? How had he actually believed that he could do this? Was this not the very definition of hubris? Was Nemesis lying in wait? He longed for his old ship, the familiar routines, officers who were also friends. Had he made the worst decision of his life?

"Stop this," he chided himself. There were others who were sacrificing more. Raffi, he knew, although she never mentioned him, had a husband and son, whom she was presumably missing greatly. La Forge had also left the *Enterprise* and was trying to do a difficult task in a less than supportive environment. He should not be brooding; he should be grateful of the people he had around him. What did Raffi say? *One bite at a time.* Quite. He rolled over, listened to his XO, and finally went to sleep.

In the morning, he was refreshed and calm. The senior staff from the *Verity* had gathered in the ship's conference room, and the captains of the other fourteen ships were patched in. Top of the agenda was, naturally, the mission to Ectis II. Ten of the ships were to position themselves around the more populated southern hemisphere, the remaining five to the north; each ship was assigned a particular urban center to which the local population had been gathered prior to Starfleet's arrival. This task had been performed by the authorities on the ground. Raffi, when she had broached his concerns about this part of the operation, had said, "If anyone can force-march large numbers of people into camps, it's the Tal Shiar." He hadn't been sure whether this had been meant to make him feel better.

As they ran through the mission, he saw that Koli Jocan was trying to catch his eye. She had asked to speak in this meeting. He nodded; *yes, yes, when we are ready.* She was a good advisor, although very reserved. He understood that Raffi—in between everything else—had made friendly overtures, which, while not exactly rebuffed, had not brought the two women much closer than arm's length.

The briefing drew to a close. Everyone seemed in good spirits, ready now for the work to begin. Some of them looked genuinely excited. "Very good," said Picard. "Before we conclude, however, I've asked Lieutenant Koli to give us a short overview of what our mission might mean to the Romulans whom we shall be relocating. All of us, I know, have signed up for this mission out of the desire to help, out of the desire to make a difference in the face of what could be one of the greatest calamities ever to overcome a sentient species. But the desire to aid is one thing, and the efficacy of that aid is another. Lieutenant Koli, could you explain?"

Koli took her place at the head of the table. When she knew she had everyone's attention, she reached up and gently touched the long earring, a symbol of her Bajoran heritage.

"When the Cardassians arrived on Bajor," Koli said, "they came under the guise of friendship. They said they were there to offer us aid. Well, that struck some of us as odd—we were interested in friendship, yes, although we didn't recall asking for aid . . . but it turned out we were going to get it, whatever our opinion on the matter."

Picard saw a couple of people stir around the table. Koli continued.

"I know—there's no direct comparison between this situation and the Occupation. The Cardassians imposed their rule over Bajor by superior force. We've been invited by the Romulans to give specific assistance. Starfleet comes with open hands, offering that assistance. But we should be careful. We should be conscious of our limits, and of the point where aid turns into . . . well, assimilation. What might seem to us like a gesture of friendship might well be perceived as overstepping the mark, particularly when dealing with a culture as closed as the Romulans. We come offering help to a longstanding enemy at a time of their weakness. They are afraid, not only of what is happening, but of what this offer of help might be concealing. What do we want in return? Do we ever intend to leave?"

Again, there was muttering around the table. She carried on, her voice clear and insistent. Picard found that he rather admired her. She was the only one here, he thought, with direct experience of living through a remotely comparable set of events.

"Above all," she said, "we must remember that this calamity *belongs to the Romulans*. I say this not to give us the excuse to turn our backs—quite the contrary. But Romulan self-determination *must* be at the forefront of your mind. However tempting it seems, whatever heart-wrenching situations you find yourself facing over the coming days, remember, please—the Romulans must lead. We do no good if we assert our authority over theirs. We do no good if we undermine them. Work such as this is *hard*, my friends. The line between help and colonization is very fine, and one that we will have to walk constantly. But we serve nobody—not us, certainly not the Romulans—if we make them the beggars of two quadrants."

The room was quiet. The excitement about the mission had been replaced now, not with disillusionment, but something more tempered, more considered. *Resolve*, thought Picard. *We are resolved to do this.*

"Thank you, Lieutenant," he said. As she took her seat, he addressed his staff. "Words of caution are not easy to hear, but, as Lieutenant Koli reminds us, nobody is served if we do not heed them." He caught Raffi's eye. *Lift the mood*, he told her.

Raffi, as ever, delivered the goods. "You heard them. Now get out there and bust your damn guts."

Laughing, inspired, motivated—and brilliant—his new team embarked upon their task.

VERITY
IN ORBIT OF ECTIS II

The first day was nearly done. Picard made his way toward deck twenty-nine, summoned there by Raffi. In the turbolift, briefly alone, he closed his eyes to gather his resources for the confrontation that he suspected was about to ensue.

All had proceeded more or less as expected. No access to the planet's surface, no sight of the accommodations on the ground. Settlers, transported in groups of twenty, each party accompanied by at least one Tal Shiar officer, at fifteen-minute intervals. Handed over to two Starfleet officers, who took them to their quarters, and returned within the hour to take their next assigned group. He watched them arrive, party after party, frightened and silent people, clutching bags to themselves, staring around this Starfleet vessel. Some were apprehensive, some fearful, some hostile. A considerable number seemed to him to look blank, as if all emotion had already been spent. To his private grief and shame, he realized that after an hour or two, the faces had begun to blur. Still they came. He left his staff to continue their work, returning briefly to his ready room to ask the ship's counselor to make sessions available for all staff involved. He then began his rounds of each deck, to see how well their guests were settling in, and to make sure that the various dignitaries felt they had been paid their due. Then the message had come from Raffi: "Deck twenty-nine, please, as soon as you can. We've got a live one."

The turbolift stopped. Picard opened his eyes. Even before the doors opened, he could hear the raised voices. He saw Raffi, lurking in the corridor, and went to greet her.

"Hi, JL," she said. She had found this nickname somewhere. Nobody else would get away with it; nobody on the *Enterprise* would have dared. Neither dismissive nor insubordinate, and yet somehow extremely familiar and disarming. Pure Raffi.

"Rather noisy," Picard said. "I could hear the fracas from inside the turbolift."

"Guess who," she said, and made a face.

"Suvim?"

"You bet."

Picard frowned. Subpraetor Suvim had already made his presence felt from the ground via a series of self-important communiques sent directly to Picard, which had consisted of a list of requirements for the journey, and which had made clear his expectation that the admiral would be present on his arrival. Picard's reply, polite and brief, had advised him to address his specific needs to Lieutenant Koli, and noted that he feared he would be unfortunately absent from the ship at the precise time of Suvim's arrival, being at a meeting with the governor. Picard had been inclined simply to meet the subpraetor, but both Raffi and Koli had advised not: it was chiefly posturing on Suvim's part, and any ground given now would not be won back later. The subpraetor had been on board now for slightly over an hour, and already there was trouble.

"What's his issue?" Picard said to Raffi as they made their way slowly down the corridor.

"You'll not believe this—the size of his quarters."

"They're standard—"

"I think that might be the issue."

"I see."

"Also—we smell."

Picard turned to stare at his XO. "I beg your pardon, Commander?"

"Apparently humans smell sour," said Raffi. "Of milk. Who would have known? All these years as part of a diverse federation of planets, and everybody has been too polite to mention that we reek of sour milk."

"I take my tea black," Picard murmured, and went to meet his guest.

Koli was there already, standing her ground in the face of a tall, elderly Romulan. Suvim, presumably. He was looming over Koli, shoulders squared, clearly trying to intimidate. Koli, to her credit, appeared not in the least daunted. Picard imagined she had faced Cardassians, with the power of life and death over her. Suvim's aggression would be small change in comparison.

Koli's gaze flicked from Suvim to Picard, coming along the corridor toward them. Suvim, alerted—as Koli intended—turned, and snarled, "Are you Picard?"

Picard came to stand beside Koli. A united front. "Yes, I am Admiral Picard. A pleasure to meet you at last, Subpraetor."

Suvim growled, "I doubt that. I'm not in the habit of pleasing Starfleet officers."

Picard looked back at him, blandly. "Is there a problem?"

"Aside from your absence on my arrival?"

"As was explained, I was meeting the governor. She sends her greetings, by the way, and hopes to hear that your journey to Arnath goes well."

That halted Suvim briefly. The governor of Ectis II was further up the food chain from him, and he would not want to think that a bad word would get back to her.

"Well," said Suvim, his voice slightly moderated, "having now seen the quarters you expect me to use, I cannot see how that could possibly be the case."

Picard, catching sight of Raffi's face, raised an eyebrow to prevent her from saying anything. Hours had been spent on precisely this, of course, making sure that the space available to each person was comfortable while still taking into account the sheer number of bodies to be transported. And then there was the intense Romulan need for privacy, bordering on the paranoid, which, it turned out, was paramount in their domestic living spaces, and made the open-plan arrangements generally favored by Starfleet on their ships out of the question. Each new internal wall took away precious centimeters of space that could be devoted to saving one more life . . .

"I'm sorry to hear these are unsatisfactory," said Picard, in his calmest, most measured tone, the voice he used to placate the ruffled feathers of the most aggrieved visitor, respond to threats from the captains of hostile ships, quell uprisings, and so on. The trick was to make the other person sound loud in comparison. Even if they didn't consciously register, they subconsciously got the impression that they were being noisy and unreasonable. "We're aware, of course, that the corridors will need considerable work before we take on board more guests."

Suvim, wrong-footed, blinked. Koli had already raised the issue of the corridors, and this had been passed along to the designers at Utopia Planitia. The internal walls of the decks on ships not yet in production could certainly be redesigned along more agreeable lines. It was a known issue, and therefore could be offered as a face-saving point in their conversation.

"Yes, the corridors," said Suvim, gesturing toward the corner that led back to the turbolift. "I have *no idea* who might be coming that way—"

"There are no known hostiles on board," said Picard.

"I am on a Starfleet vessel, Admiral," said Suvim.

Picard was prepared to concede, inwardly at least, that Suvim had a point. "It would be easy for us to arrange a security device there, Subpraetor, operated from within your quarters so that you could check regularly on foot traffic along the corridor outside. Not that there is likely to be much. We have, as requested, assigned you quarters in a quieter area of the ship—"

"And then there are the quarters themselves!" said Suvim.

Raffi whispered in Picard's ear, "Oh, this should be good."

"Subpraetor Suvim," said Koli, "believes that his quarters are too small."

Suvim turned back toward the door of his quarters.

"Well, of course he does," muttered Raffi, traipsing behind, earning warning glances from both Koli and Picard.

Picard stood in the middle of the room and looked around. He could see nothing wrong. The additional partitions made the space rather claustrophobic, yes, and he himself would certainly prefer something that gave as much illusion of space as possible, but otherwise all was clean, neat, and comfortable.

"As I understand it," Picard said, "you are the sole occupant of these rooms."

"What difference does that make?"

"You do know," said Raffi, "that we have a lot of people to move?"

Suvim turned to her, eyes flashing. But Koli, who had moved farther into the quarters, and was now standing by a small cabinet, said, "Excuse me, Subpraetor, but may I ask you a question?"

Distracted, he turned to her. "What is it?"

"Isn't this the Star Medal? Given for conspicuous bravery during the defense of Alaia?"

Picard, watching Suvim melt, thanked Koli's Prophets for her presence.

"Yes," said Suvim, reaching for his honor. "It is."

"You know," said Koli, "the Bajoran people have always been grateful for the support the Romulans gave during the Dominion War. What was your involvement at the Battle of Alaia?"

Raffi's combadge sounded, and she went outside to take the message. When she returned, she said, "Admiral, Governor Menima would like to speak to you at your earliest availability."

Picard turned back to Suvim. "If you'll excuse me, Subpraetor, I shall leave you in Lieutenant Koli's capable hands."

Suvim, absently, waved a hand in dismissal. Picard and Raffi beat a hasty retreat. As they walked together back to the turbolift, Picard pushed out a breath. "Thank you for the rescue."

"Thank Koli," she said. "Menima does want to talk to you, though. I gather there's a problem with her replicator."

They entered the turbolift. "Deck twenty-four," said Raffi. "Do you think all our problems will be this mundane?"

"Let us hope so."

"I mean—what do they expect from a refugee ship?"

Picard pondered how it must feel to have to leave one's home, to be forced to fit the meager possessions allowed into a few small rooms.

"I mean, we're not a hotel . . ." Raffi grumbled.

"I think that perhaps they have not entirely come to terms with their status, Raffi."

"I think that in Suvim's case, that's very charitable of you, JL." She shook her head. "We'll be choosing cushion covers next."

INSTITUTE OF ASTRONOMY
CAMBRIDGE, EARTH

Durnyam offered to lead the meeting with Starfleet Intelligence, but Safadi said no. The figures were hers; she should be the one to defend. But she was glad of Durnyam's presence beside her, the introduction of "My excellent colleague, Doctor Safadi," and then the encouraging look as Safadi rose to her feet and began her presentation. Durnyam nodded throughout, too, signaling her confidence in the figures being presented and that the underlying datasets were sound, and the modeling and analysis were solid.

At the table, a specialist from Romulan Affairs, Lieutenant Haig, sat scribbling detailed notes, looking up every so often to frown at the display. On the viewscreen at one end of the room, patched in from the relief mission's flagship, the *Starship Verity*, Commander Raffi Musiker sat chin in hand and eyes half-closed. She looked exhausted. For a brief moment, Safadi thought the commander had fallen asleep. No. The commander might be tired but was listening to every single word.

Safadi wound up her presentation with three key points: based on these figures, the speed with which the star was progressing toward its explosive end was greatly accelerated, and that the impact on the blast radius needed to be increased accordingly. And last of all . . . well, Safadi had saved the worst until last. "And this has serious implications for the relief mission as currently planned." She glanced over at Musiker. "This isn't only math, you see. It has direct consequences for your mission, Commander. Some of the worlds we previously thought were safe—they're now within the blast range. You can't relocate people to them. Worse than that. You now have to shift anyone already there."

Musiker lifted her head from her hand. *"I'm not even going to pretend I understand the calculations underneath all of this, and I don't want to imply anything improper, but—"*

"But how do I know I haven't made a mistake?"

Musiker smiled. *"You took the words right out of my mouth."*

"Well, anything's possible, of course," said Safadi. "We're flawed human beings after all. And one impeccable Bolian. But we are *very* good at what we do."

"I don't understand why the figures have been revised upward so significantly—"

"Because our previous model was based on figures supplied by the Romulans," said Durnyam. "This is based on our own readings."

"In which case, I do understand," said Musiker. *"All right. I'll take these figures to the admiral. Looks like we're going to have to do some reprioritizing. But in the meantime—is there anything else we can do to bridge this gap between their figures and ours? Haig? Are the Romulans giving us anything?"*

Haig said, "We can't force them to give us information, Raffi. You know that as well as anyone. They're Romulans. Their left hands—"

"Yeah, yeah, I know. But this discrepancy is going to cause us major problems—I can guarantee you—and we need as much evidence as we can get."

Durnyam caught Safadi's eye. *Quick! Ask!*

"There is one thing," said Safadi.

"Oh yeah?"

"The expert on this, on Romulus, is a scientist called Nokim Vritet. If I could speak to him, somehow. Show him my data, my modeling..."

Haig said, "As if that's ever going to happen!"

Musiker, too, looked skeptical. "*They're not exactly issuing visas these days, Doctor Safadi.*"

"No, so I'd like to issue him an invitation to come and visit us here at Cambridge. In the spirit of cross-cultural communication, that kind of thing."

Musiker and Haig exchanged glances. "A Romulan scientist on Earth?"

"*And his half dozen Tal Shiar handlers.*"

Haig shrugged. "I suppose we can issue an invitation. Is there any way we can make it less obvious?"

Durnyam, leaning forward, said, "Symposium."

"*What's that?*" said Musiker.

"It's a small gathering," said Safadi. "Usually experts in a specific field, addressing a particular topic—"

"Like a conference," said Durnyam bluntly, "but less hassle."

"*Do you think they'd let him come?*"

"If I'm being honest?" Haig shook his head. "Probably not. But if we issue the invitation in such a way that they would lose face to refuse, we might get someone sent. Probably Tal Shiar, but at the very least, informed enough to be able to sound like they know what they're talking about. Of course, they'll be trying to get information from us."

"It's scientific data," said Safadi. "Freely available. Open access. All they have to do is ask. Once I publish, they won't even have to do that."

Safadi became aware that Musiker was studying her closely. "Was there something you wanted to ask me, Commander?"

"*Yeah, actually. Do you mind, Doctor Safadi, having your research used in this way?*"

Safadi glanced at Durnyam, who shrugged. "You mean to form policy about the mission? No, of course not, that's one of the reasons we do the work we do—"

"*Actually, I meant—used as an excuse to invite the Tal Shiar to Earth and have Haig here and his team follow them around.*"

"Hey, Raffi . . ." said Haig. "That isn't fair!"

"*Honest question. I don't wanna piss them off. We need them on our side.*"

Safadi thought about that. The work they did here—it was so arcane. Watching her mother try to explain to her friends what her daughter did was hilarious: "*Whatever it is she does, she's doing it now in Cambridge,*" Mama would say firmly, closing down any further questioning. Safadi didn't pretend she was wise in the ways of intelligence agencies—but she wanted to help.

"I'm thinking about Nokim Vritet," she said, at last. "Science is about communication, the free exchange of ideas. It must be lonely, working the way he does. Must have got lonelier ever since his work became so critical. I'd like him to be able to come. I'd like to be able to meet him, talk to him." She smiled. "Besides, Cambridge is nice in the spring."

"*Then let's try it. The Tal Shiar will definitely want to come too though. I hear they like visiting ancient cultural centers. I know that's why I joined the intelligence services. Okay, I've got yet another meeting that started twenty minutes ago, and I want to brief the admiral on this first. Haig, let's catch up later. Verity out.*"

"Well," said Durnyam. "It seems we have a symposium to arrange."

"With spies," said Safadi. "That's very Cambridge."

"Yes, well, let's leave all that to the people who know what they're doing." Durnyam gave her a faint smile. "Did you ever think, Amal, that what we did would suddenly become the most politically charged field of study in two quadrants?"

Safadi smiled back. "As long as my mother sees me on the holonews," said Safadi, "it'll be worth it."

VERITY

Picard took Raffi's news with equanimity. "People told me," he said, when she finished, "to plan for the unexpected. And here it is. How is the discrepancy between figures explained?"

"Original estimates were based on datasets supplied by the Romulans."

"You need say no more."

"It must have killed them to give us even that much."

Picard said, "Do you think they know already?"

Raffi sighed. "If they didn't, they will when Safadi publishes her paper." She leaned forward to speak more quietly. "I think they must have known, JL. There's been spotty but steady intelligence suggesting they've been understating the effects of the blast. I'd taken it to mean that they were downplaying the impact of relocation so that people would move willingly. Well, perhaps it meant something else all along. Either way, our people at Romulan Affairs are informing Federation Affairs before Safadi goes public."

"Speaking about the impact of the news," Picard asked, "are we concerned about this information reaching the Romulan on the street, as it were? This news is likely to be a significant blow to morale—"

"Koli would tell you that that's an internal Romulan affair. And she'd be right."

Picard was content to concede that point: one less thing to worry about.

"Besides," said Raffi, "the average Romulan isn't going to hear the first thing about it."

"How can they prepare themselves," Picard said, "if they have no idea?"

"Typical Romulan secrecy. Riddles wrapped in enigmas . . ."

"But at the cost of saving lives, Raffi?"

Raffi shrugged. "Not much about the Romulans makes sense, JL. They're working from different fundamental principles from us. They're *bizarre*. And sneaky . . . Given the choice between what's coming from our astronomers, and what the Tal Shiar is telling us, I know which I'd pick. And that means we need to think through the ramifications for the mission. The difference between 9.7 and 10 may sound small, but not when you're talking light-years. Ten more worlds . . ."

Those concentric rings, Picard thought as they looked through Safadi's new model; they seemed to fan out farther every time he looked at them, each new wave bringing a host of implications—social, political, cultural, and of course the ramifications for the resources they would need to commandeer. More worlds affected—some of which they had assumed would be safe havens—more people affected. That would mean more ships, which meant more of . . .

More of everything; more of everyone. Grimly, he said, "I have no idea whether we can do this, Raffi."

"Sure we can. Think of it this way—nobody else is going to do it."

He smiled. "All right. I should speak to Geordi. And then to Bordson."

"In that order, sir?"

"When presenting a problem to your superiors, always present your preferred solution."

"That's good advice, JL. I'm going to try that on you."

"I thought you already did." He watched her stand and leave. "Oh, could you speak to Koli? Let her know what's going on and ask her to come up with some scenarios for how we handle this. Foremost, where the *hell* are we now supposed to take all these people?"

She gave him two thumbs up. "On it, JL."

Utopia Planitia shipyards
Mars

La Forge was out on the upper orbit production line when he got the call from the admiral. He slipped into one of the shuttles to take the call privately.

"Shit," he said, when Picard explained the new estimates for the supernova blast radius.

"And before you ask—yes, we are sure of the figures."

"Federation data rather than Romulan, huh? We should have seen that coming."

"It's going to mean more ships, Geordi . . ." Picard said apologetically.

He should have seen that coming too. "We're maxed out here, sir. Everything has been turned over to expanding the fleet. The new construction facilities are underway, but there's nothing coming off those lines until we can staff them properly, and that means waiting until Bruce Maddox makes a breakthrough." La Forge sighed. Maddox's lack of progress and enthusiasm was a concern.

"You're usually positive, Geordi. Is there a problem?"

The last thing Jean-Luc Picard needed to worry about right now was Bruce Maddox's sense of his own importance. "Oh, the usual problems you associate with pushing the boundaries of advanced synthetic research, sir—"

"Quite."

"But I've got a genius working on it, or so he tells me, and he's been given the lab space he always wanted, and the team he always wanted . . ."

"Anything else you can do to push him in the direction we need will be most appreciated. We need those ships."

"You'll get them, Admiral."

"Thank you, Commander. Picard out."

La Forge sat and watched Safadi's new model for the blast radius and whistled through his teeth. "Bruce Maddox," he muttered, "I am *throwing* resources at you. What more do you need?" Then a slow smile crossed his face. Maybe he could send Maddox something special. Or, rather, *someone* special. He opened a channel to the complex below. "Put me through to Commander Mackenzie." When she appeared on the screen, he said, "Estella. I have a job for you."

STARFLEET COMMAND
SAN FRANCISCO, EARTH

Captain Kirsten Clancy was fresh from a meeting with a deputation from Alaris IV, who wanted to know why the replacement industrial replicators they had been promised were no longer materializing and had not been pleased to hear it was because they had been sent to Romulan space. She was in no mood to hear bad news—but that was all there was.

"First check," she said as Picard briefed her and Bordson on Safadi's work, and ran through the ramifications.

"With a mission on this scale," Picard said, *"we always knew that there would be complications—"*

"There's complications," said Clancy, "and there's stretching our resources beyond limits—"

Bordson lifted his hand to stop the inevitable argument getting underway. "My immediate concern is how the Romulans receive this news. Are we assuming that they knew already?"

"My understanding is that it's impossible to tell. Starfleet Intelligence will be informing their opposites quietly. Whether they receive any response will have to be seen. I think we should assume that they knew already, but have chosen not to inform us."

"No," said Bordson. "One would hardly tell one's oldest enemies that news."

Clancy was looking through the rest of the briefing. "This space scientist, Safadi—has she published yet? Does she intend to publish?"

"She's agreed to organize a symposium where she will present her work. Starfleet Intelligence have asked her to invite Romulan scientists to the occasion—"

"She'll get Tal Shiar."

"I don't think Starfleet Intelligence minded, Kirsten."

Again, Bordson intervened. "We should not interfere with the process of open science. Safadi should and must publish her research. The Romulans can decide for themselves what to do about it." He nodded at Picard. "Clancy and I will discuss if ships can be temporarily reassigned if the call comes. In the meantime—perhaps our engineers might start offering solutions?"

"I shall endeavor to accelerate that process, Victor."

The comm cut. Picard was gone. "Kirsten," said the C-in-C, "you are not happy."

She threw her hands up. "You know what worries me. Each time we stretch ourselves a little further, some more cracks begin to show. Eventually, something will give."

INSTITUTE OF ASTRONOMY
CAMBRIDGE, EARTH

Safadi sent her invitation to Nokim Vritet to speak at her symposium expecting no response—and, indeed, none came. And then, after a week or two, she burst into Durnyam's office, crying out, "I don't believe this! Vritet has replied!"

He was declining the invitation, citing "the impossibility of leaving Romulus at the moment." He was sending two talented young researchers, who he hoped would be made welcome. And that was all.

"Get this over to Haig at Romulan Affairs straightaway," Durnyam advised. "He's going to want to know."

Moments later, back in her own office, Safadi watched Haig on a comm screen as he pored over the details of the two researchers. *"Nothing on our files, but then that isn't everything . . ."* He glanced at Amal. *"You realize they'll be Tal Shiar."*

"Should I say no?" said Safadi.

"What? No, invite them! We can get a good look at them!"

"Will they be scientists?"

"I hope not," said Haig. *"It will be fun watching them try to keep up."*

"But what's the point of having them here? What will we learn from them?"

Haig smiled. *"I won't know that,"* he said, *"until I have them right in front of me."*

VERITY

Raffi, sitting in a meeting with Picard and Koli, had stopped listening some time earlier. She was particularly good at keeping her personal business out of her working life, but her last conversation with Jae had not gone well. It had become clear to him as they spoke that she would not be returning after the promised six months. Worse, she was not offering another end date to replace it.

"Your son misses you," Jae said. *"If that's not enough to bring you back—"*

"That isn't fair, Jae! But I can't leave the mission now—"

"No?"

"No," she said. "Dammit, Jae, I'm the XO to the mission commander—"

"I know. It's a great job and I'm proud of you. But nobody's indispensable, Raffi. I hope you don't discover that too late."

They'd tried to make up before having to end the call—neither of them liked to leave a quarrel unresolved—but the breach was not healed. She didn't think for a moment, though, that they could not heal it. They always had in the past.

"He misses you, Raffi. Sometimes he wants Mom."

"You seem preoccupied this morning, Raffi," said Picard in a quiet voice. "Is there something wrong?"

Dammit, she thought. JL had enough to worry about without his XO turning flaky. With an effort, Raffi turned her mind away from domestic problems and back to galactic problems. "Everything's fine, JL." She glanced at Koli. "Sorry, both of you. You know how it is some days. I'm all yours now."

"Jocan was explaining that there are a number of habitable worlds suitable for refugee relocation that we have not yet considered."

"That's great news!" said Raffi, and then worried that she'd said it slightly too brightly. Never mind; focus on the job at hand.

"There's no such thing as great news," Koli said, showing glimpses of a sense of humor that Raffi had never previously suspected of her. "There's only mixed news. It's complicated."

"Our work seems to consist almost entirely of complications," said Picard. "Go on."

"The worlds are just beyond the Neutral Zone, in Federation space."

"Oh," said Raffi, "and I thought you were going to give us bad news."

"It's not an option, Jocan," Picard said. "The Romulans would never agree to it."

Raffi, staring at the scenario, said, "Would they become Federation citizens?" Both Picard and Koli turned to stare at her, and she shrugged. "I'm curious, that's all."

"I assume that the usual requirements for long-term residency would apply," said Picard.

"What I mean is, would the Romulan authorities allow it? Allow them to apply for Federation citizenship?"

Picard turned to Koli. "Lieutenant?"

"There would certainly be numerous complications arising from such a case . . ."

"More complications." Picard gave a curt nod. "These, at least, are purely hypothetical. We have already traded significant goodwill simply by informing the Romulans that we know about the revised blast radius. Relocating refugees across the Neutral Zone into Federation space is a step too far. We will work with your other scenarios, Lieutenant Koli, and hope that we soon hear good news from the Daystrom Institute." He checked the time and rose from his chair. "You must excuse me. Governor Menima has asked for a meeting in advance of our arrival on Arnath. I gather she has some questions about the facilities there. I know nothing beyond what her own government is telling her, but I would prefer to keep her happy before we face the task of disembarking."

After he was gone, Raffi turned to Koli. "I'd like to see a more fully worked-through version of that last scenario. If we did decide to cross the Neutral Zone."

"But you heard what the admiral said. That can't happen—"

"Sure," said Raffi, "that's what he says today. But if there's one thing I've learned about Admiral Picard, he would do anything if it meant saving lives."

Koli was puzzled. "But he's so by the book . . . everything so carefully done."

"He gave up the *Enterprise* for this mission," said Raffi. "Who knows what else he would do?" She smiled at the other woman. "You're probably right—it might not happen. They'll get the breakthrough at the Daystrom Institute, and we'll have more ships than we know what to do with. This will be a conversation that we will forget we ever had. But I like to be prepared. So let's do the research, and have the information tucked away somewhere. And if and when the admiral finds himself having to choose between a treaty and saving lives, we'll be able to say, 'Here's what you need to do, JL.'"

"All right, Commander," Koli said. "Does he mind," she went on as they left the room, "that you call him JL?"

Raffi pondered that. "He's never said. Anyway, it gets his attention."

5

Admiral's Log: After the weeks of our journey, our arrival at Arnath was marked by the uncloaking of eight birds-of-prey: hardly the most welcoming sight after our long voyage. The vessels in our fleet are primarily people carriers, and while we carry sufficient firepower to defend ourselves, I am not eager to find myself in the middle of battle. However, our conversations with the officer in command here on Arnath, Tholoth, have been if not cordial, then at least efficient. The first group of our guests—the governor, her entourage, and two dozen other officials—have all been transported to the surface, and the mass evacuation will be underway within the next few hours. Across all our ships, our relocation specialists are making their way down the decks—answering questions, alleviating fears, offering help.

While this voyage has not been without its trials (we have learned a great deal about how to manage the expectations and concerns of our guests, and the news of the revised figures for the blast range necessitated a thorough reappraisal of our resources), I am cautiously satisfied with how the mission has progressed so far. We have brought nearly ten thousand souls to safety, away from the imminent destruction of their world, to a place where they can begin a new life, in peace.

The sight of these refugees will remain with me for a very long time. We cannot, in truth, compensate for the loss of one's home—the exile from a beloved place to which it is impossible to return—and while we cannot make these partings anything other than bittersweet, we can try to make the transition to a new way of life as painless as we possibly can.

VERITY

The evacuation process had been underway for twenty-one hours when Picard received a message from Subpraetor Suvim requesting an urgent meeting. Suvim had continued to be a thorn in his side throughout the voyage, but Picard had found that treating him with courtesy had gone a considerable way to mollifying him. Raffi had remarked on his forbearance on numerous occasions.

"I try to remember, Raffi," he said, "how I would feel—torn from my home, cast adrift. Suvim was a man of authority—a man who commanded considerable respect. At the end of his life, when he should be resting on his laurels, his world has shrunk to the size of a small cabin, granted to him by the charity of his enemies."

"Huh," said Raffi. "Quite a *large* cabin. But I get your point."

Besides, whenever Picard reached his limits, he was able to send Koli Jocan to Suvim, to listen to tales of his glory days. He brought Koli with him this time. "Who knows," said Picard as they stood in the turbolift. "Perhaps Suvim wants to thank us for his comfortable journey, and the excellent conversation you have provided." He glanced at the young woman. "You have been a great help, Jocan. I am grateful."

"You won't believe this, Admiral, but he has been very interesting to talk to. He lost his wife some years back. I think he's lonely."

"I'm grateful, nonetheless. He is a changed man."

Arriving at Suvim's quarters, however, they could see that all was not well. Suvim, glancing up and down the corridor, hurried them inside. What was he concerned about? Could he not still believe that he was not safe, here on a Starfleet vessel, after all these weeks? As soon as they were inside his cabin, Suvim hastened them over to the computer. "I have something to show you," he said. "This is footage from the surface of Arnath. Please, Admiral, look closely."

Picard leaned in. The images were fuzzy, disjointed, and angled from low down, as if someone was recording using a concealed device held close to their side. Nevertheless, it was quickly clear what was going on. High fences, tents, dust. Picard frowned. Still . . .

"I am not unaware of the irony," said Suvim, "that I am complaining about accommodation yet again. And I know that these images are not clear. But I have had other messages, from the ground, from people begging me to help them. They tell me that they are being held prisoners, that they are living in the dirt, that they are not sure there is enough food or water." His voice was becoming desperate. This was a war veteran, Picard thought, someone who had been courageous and bold. To be pleading with his enemies for help . . .

Suvim, glimpsing the pity in Picard's eyes, began to change his tone. "It is unacceptable! We were promised homes, schools, hospitals! I will not have it—!"

"Subpraetor," Picard said calmly, "let me speak to the authorities on the ground. They might permit a brief visit from Starfleet."

It was a little easier said than done, Picard thought as he stared at the comm screen in his ready room, but the trick was not to be the one to blink first.

"Commander Tholoth," said Picard to the stern-faced young Romulan who was flatly denying his request to take a small team down to Arnath, "I understand that this is a Romulan world, and that these are Romulan citizens. Nevertheless, they have been our guests for some time, and we should like to see them settled comfortably."

"Why should they not be comfortable—?"

"I would ask you to consider whether you would like to facilitate this visit, or whether I should speak directly to your ambassador to the Federation. But may I suggest to you, Commander, that it is never good for an officer's career if their name first comes to the attention of their superiors as a participant in a diplomatic incident."

The screen went dead. Picard waited. Raffi, sitting across from him, lifted an eyebrow. The comm chimed. A message from the ground, granting permission for two Starfleet visitors to come to the planet's surface. Picard smiled. The gambit had paid off.

Raffi whistled. "I didn't think you were going to pull that one off, JL."

"He was a young man," said Picard. "All I had to do was pull rank."

Resettlement Facility 124
Arnath

Raffi fussed a little about allowing him down on the surface, but he insisted, taking Koli with him. And found, to his dismay, that Suvim was not exaggerating. The outlook on Arnath was bleak. Within seconds of their arrival, both he and Koli were coughing from the red dust, screwing up their eyes, which were quickly running from the grit in the air. The overwhelming impression was of barrenness: a dry world, lacking life, lacking the conditions that would permit life to flourish. Picard, surveying the dismal scene, murmured, "What has happened here?"

He was looking at a fence—a high fence—and beyond that all he could see were rows upon rows of tents. In the narrow gaps between them, soldiers—armored, helmeted, visored—were patrolling in pairs, kicking up red dust as they passed. More pairs stood at the intersections between the tents, disruptors at the ready. As for the people . . . they were barely visible. He saw a face here and there, peering out from under a tent flap, disappearing rapidly back inside as a patrol went past.

Koli, too, was looking around in horror. "This isn't what I expected . . ."

"No," said Picard sternly. "Not in the slightest."

Picard pondered, briefly, what his expectations *had* been. The impression they had been given from the Romulans was that work had been underway for some time on Arnath to receive settlers. He had not expected a fully built town—that would take a while, and require local resources—but he had at the very least expected structures. Houses, not pens. On Cardassia, he recalled, after the Jem'Hadar destroyed the infrastructure, the relief mission had used industrial replicators and large-scale archi-printers to rapidly produce modular buildings. Homes, of various sizes according to need; medical centers; schools; recreation facilities—even the headquarters of the relief effort had used them as its building blocks. They had not been beautiful, but there had been a spare functionality and orderliness about them that inspired calm, or a sense that everything was under control.

There was none of this here. There was order, yes, but it was the order brought by the threat of force. There was the order commanded by fear. Tapping his combadge, he said, "Raffi, get me images of the area around here."

He heard footsteps crunching behind him, and turned to see a Romulan officer, followed by two armed guards. "Admiral Picard," said the officer. "My name is Telak. I'm the commander of this facility—"

"Facility?" said Picard. "We were expecting a town."

Telak, cut short, gave him a cold look. "Whatever we call it is our business. Can I ask why you're here? Tholoth insisted I allow this visit, but I could not see any reason why—"

"I'm here to ensure that our guests have arrived safely—"

"Once they leave your ships, they're no longer your responsibility."

And while that might be technically correct, thought Picard, in the narrowest legalistic sense, it was certainly not, in any way, morally correct. "I disagree—"

Beside him, he was aware of Koli, shifting uneasily.

"We're grateful for your help, Picard," said Telak, "but these are Romulans. We'll take care of them. Go now."

Picard looked beyond the fence, and then back at the implacable officer in front of him. This was not, he sensed, somebody who could be manipulated into standing down. He tapped his combadge. "*Verity*," he said. "Two to beam up."

The dust and misery of Arnath disappeared, and he and Koli were back on their sleek, safe ship. "Raffi," said Picard. "Have you got me those images yet?"

DAYSTROM INSTITUTE
OKINAWA, EARTH

A couple of months into Estella Mackenzie's assignment to the Daystrom Institute, Maddox was grudgingly admitting that the gruff engineer knew her stuff. Still, bio-neural circuitry . . . it was hardly the work he had dreamed of doing. More than ever, he was glad that Agnes Jurati was around; someone he could talk to, who knew what this work was costing him. Someone who understood his frustrations and regrets. They had taken to meeting away from the campus. They wanted privacy. They would choose a city in turn, where they were unknown, anonymous, faces in the crowd. He had made her go hiking in New Zealand, where she had been woefully underprepared and got blisters within half an hour. She had gotten her revenge by dragging him to the carnival in Venice, making him dress up and dance. She chose a mask for him with a long beak while she wore something encrusted with red beads and crowned in feathers. He had doubled down with Machu Picchu ("More damn hills!") and she had responded with a show in Las Vegas.

But now they were sitting in the campus coffee house. He was drawing a picture on a napkin, explaining, after she had asked, about the latest upgrade in the circuitry, and the problems they were having making it interface with the casings that they had designed to house the circuitry. The bodies, he supposed he should think of them.

"So damn frustrating," he said. "The circuitry is solid, I'm sure—complex enough for the task at hand. But if we can't get it to work within the casing, then it's no better than a brain in a jar. I feel like I'm missing something obvious."

He realized that she had stopped responding some time ago. When he looked up from his notes, he saw an image of dejection. She was sitting, shoulders slumped, looking down at her uneaten cake.

"Aggie, what's the matter?"

She shrugged.

"Tired?"

"No. Yes. It's . . . difficult."

"Okay . . ."

He started folding the napkin. They sat for a while in silence.

"My time's up the end of next week," she said, after a while.

"Oh," he said.

"It's been nice, hasn't it?"

"Very nice." He started twisting the napkin around his fingers, like a ring.

"It's been great watching you work," she said. "I know you're not keen on the project, but it's been a thrill to see the new facility set up . . ."

"Yeah, the space is amazing, isn't it?" He gave a slightly bitter laugh. "A dream come true. Astonishing the resources that Starfleet can find when they have to."

"It's good work," she said, her voice high and false.

"I guess." He began to shred the napkin. She put her hand on his, to stop him. They looked straight at each other. "Aggie," he said urgently, "I know you were only here to take a few classes. But why don't you stay?"

She stared back. "What do you mean?"

"I mean—there's nobody here who understands what it's like . . . what it means, to move my focus away from my own research and have to work instead on this . . ."

"Do you want me to work with you on the nonsynthetics?"

"You should be doing doctoral work, Agnes," he said.

"I'm already a doctor," she said brightly. "MD."

"You know what I mean. You're smart, so very smart. Come and work on this. Get the doctorate in robotics—you'll race through it. I've read your dissertation—you know it's going to get one of the highest grades we've given out for a master's—"

"Are you supposed to be telling me that?"

"With that behind you, you can work on whatever you like. Work alongside someone else . . ."

"Work with you, you mean?"

"Well," he laughed, "I've got this whole new facility."

"Making toys," she said.

"There is that . . ." He chewed his lip. He knew, somehow, that if she was here, then at least some of the dream would remain alive. He knew, somehow, that she was a necessary part of his dream, that without her he would not be able to continue. What he did not know was how to tell her all this. "But if you'd rather go back and practice medicine, I'd understand."

He looked back at her, almost afraid to see what was there. But her eyes were shining. "Bruce," she said. "It's what I wanted. Of course I'll stay."

VERITY

Picard, Raffi, and Koli gathered in his ready room to study the images from the surface of Arnath. The facility was easy to see—it stretched out, for miles, row after row of tents, set in the middle of nowhere. They could see little in the way of infrastructure. They could see a great deal in the way of fences, guards, and towers.

"Facility," said Picard, and shook his head. "It's a prison. Tents in a desert. There's nothing there."

"What do you think happened?" said Raffi. "Did they run out of time? Is this temporary?"

"Resources stretched too thin," said Koli. "They made promises to get these people to leave their homes, and then they weren't able to deliver."

"Suvim, Menima... these are pretty high-ranking people," said Raffi. "If the Romulan government isn't able to supply homes and facilities for them, what's it going to be like for the people without their influence?"

"They're not *that* influential," said Koli. "Not in the great scheme of things. They're provincial officials. Perhaps they were causing too much noise so they were sent on their way so quickly. Send them off; shut them up."

"But if they couldn't build what they'd promised," said Picard, "why didn't they simply ask for help? We have industrial replicators, large-scale printers, all ready for use."

"Secrecy," said Raffi. "It's the Romulan way."

"Let's make the offer to Commander Telak, at least," said Picard. "Although how it will be received..."

"Nothing ventured." Raffi asked Marshall to open a channel to Commander Telak.

"What's your advice, Jocan?" Picard said. "How do we help?"

She sighed. "The problem is—I don't think we can..."

"But you saw that camp," said Picard. "I cannot, in good conscience, allow the people we have brought here to be left in conditions such as that—"

"What do you propose to do, Admiral?"

"Summon Telak here and ask him to explain himself—"

"Why would Telak come?"

"Because—" Picard stopped. There was, of course, no reason for Telak to come, and no way to compel him.

"You see the difficulty?" said Koli. "This is an internal Romulan affair. We have brought them here, at the request of the Romulan Senate, but it's exactly as Telak said—once they have left our ships, they are no longer our responsibility—"

Raffi's combadge chirped, and she tapped it and jumped right in. "Commander Telak, Admiral Picard would like to discuss the possibility of supplying you with industrial replicators."

"Commander Musiker, this is a Romulan matter. We will handle this. You will continue transporting all Romulan citizens down to Arnath."

The channel snapped shut. Before Picard could reopen it, his combadge sounded. *"Picard!"*

Lieutenant Marshall cut in. *"It's Subpraetor Suvim, sir. He's refusing to leave the ship. There's two hundred of them who say they won't go."*

"Well," said Raffi, *"now* it's getting interesting."

"This is not what we were promised," said Suvim. "This is not why we left our homes—"

"I understand," said Picard. "Although I am at a loss to know what I can do to help, Subpraetor. I have very limited authority here—"

"Take us away," said Suvim. "Take us somewhere else."

Picard rubbed his cheek. He had suggested this to Telak (he had made many suggestions to Telak over the last few hours), but the only response had been the commander's expectation that the transportation of Romulan citizens under his care would continue, and on completion of this task, the Starfleet vessels would leave local space. After a while, even this response had stopped. What solution was there?

"I'm unsure such a location exists, Suvim," said Picard. "Commander Telak is very clear that this is where you should disembark. He says that these are temporary accommodations—"

Suvim snorted. No, he didn't believe that either, although Picard was surprised that he was prepared to voice the opinion so openly. Picard opened his mouth to offer further assurances, and then he took another look at the old veteran. This wasn't good enough, he thought. This was not a just reward for this man's life and service.

"Subpraetor Suvim," he said. "You are perfectly correct that this is not an acceptable solution. Let me speak to my superiors. I shall do everything in my power to help."

INSTITUTE OF ASTRONOMY
CAMBRIDGE, EARTH

On the day of the symposium, the two Romulans arrived precisely three minutes before the first session, bypassed the conversation in the hall, and went straight into the seminar room. Safadi, following Haig, stood at the door and watched as they chose where to sit. The seating was arranged in a horseshoe shape, three banked levels, with the speaker standing between the points of the horseshoe. The exit (there was only one) was to the right of the speaker, near one end of the rows of seats.

"Let's see what they make of this," said Haig, mildly amused. "They'll want to be able to study the speakers and their presentations closely, but they'll also want to be close to the exit."

"They could split up," said Safadi.

"Oh no," Haig said. "If one of them is a real scientist, the other is their Tal Shiar handler, and will want to stay at the scientist's side. If they're both Tal Shiar, they'll want to work as a unit."

"And if they're both real scientists?"

"That was never going to happen," Haig said. Cheerfully, he added, "Of course, knowing the Romulans, it's possible they don't even know what the other one is. Tal Shiar watching Tal Shiar."

"That's madness," said Safadi.

"It's certainly not an efficient use of resources," said Haig. "And yet they are the most effective secret police in two quadrants. Only the Obsidian Order compared—and they don't exist any longer. It's almost as if extreme paranoia isn't a viable survival strategy." He eyed her. "What do you think?"

"Don't ask me," she said. "I'm an astronomer, not a sociologist."

Eventually, their Romulan guests chose seats at the end of the back row, near the door. If they hoped to be unobtrusive, it didn't pay off. Everyone who came in had to walk past them to take a seat, taking a good long look as they went past.

"I hope they *are* Tal Shiar," said Haig with barely suppressed glee. "They must be hating this."

"Now, now," chided Safadi. "That isn't in the spirit of scientific collaboration."

Haig took his seat at the other side of the room, in the back row, directly facing the two Romulans. Once he was sitting, he gave them a cheery salute, professional spy to professional spy. Safadi took her place at the front of the room, checked that the mic, the visual tagging for sign users, and the universal translators were all working fine. She opened the symposium.

The morning went quickly, fascinatingly, informatively. Safadi, sitting at the end of the front row so that she was on hand to help any speaker struggling with the equipment, also had a good view of the two Romulans. One was entirely focused on the presentations. The other took more interest in the room. Safadi watched as, one by one, he studied each attendee. Every so often, his lips moved silently; she guessed he was subvocalizing, somehow recording his impressions. Had Haig done a sweep for that kind of technology? Or had he simply decided that he would let them get away with it? They were all at universities and research institutes, Safadi thought, you could look up their resumes. She turned back to the proceedings. This mindset, she thought; you could lose yourself in a vast maze: pathways and alleyways turning back on themselves, dead ends, false entrances and exits. It was nonsense.

At the break for lunch, and at Haig's request, Safadi made her way straight to the two Romulans, who stood uneasily on one side of the room, holding plates and staring straight ahead.

"Hi," she said. "Welcome to Cambridge. We're glad to have you here."

Up close, they were younger than she had expected and certainly young enough to convince as graduate students. They made eye contact, briefly, and looked back down at their food.

"I was wondering whether you'd had a chance to discuss the program with Doctor Vritet. Whether he had any thoughts. I was hoping to send him my paper beforehand, get a response from him, but . . ."

One of them, the slightly older one, said, "Doctor Vritet sends apologies for his absence."

And that was as far as she got with either of them. After a few more minutes of vague and opaque exchanges, she had to return to the hall to get ready for her own presentation. Haig, passing her by on his way to his seat, said, "Anything?"

"Nothing," she said. "I'm not even sure that they know who Vritet is."

And then it was time for her to speak, to put her figures out there and live with the consequences. Throughout her presentation, she was conscious of both Romulans, taking assiduous notes as she explained her figures. As she came to the end of the explanation of her calculations, and began to summarize some of the ramifications, she knew that the room was completely silent, everyone's eye on her. She saw one or two people watching her but writing at the same time on padds, uploading her presentation in real time for two quadrants to read. The message was getting out there: the progress of the supernova was moving faster, and its effects would hit harder, than anyone had predicted. She heard blips and chimes on people's various devices as responses started coming back. She tried to put this all aside and focus on delivering the research.

When she was done, she stopped, and looked back at the formulae on the display screen behind her. *Well*, she thought. *It's all out there now.* "That's the math," she said. "I guess . . . it's over to Starfleet."

There was a brief silence, and the room exploded into applause. Hands were shooting up around the room. She looked around, and saw the two Romulans stand up and leave. She never saw them again.

She took the questions, and then the room pored over her figures, examined them, asked questions about them, concluded en masse that she was accurate. After that, and a few closing remarks, people began to make their way back to the transporters for their journeys home. Haig, on his way out, said, "Good work, Doctor Safadi. I'll be in touch."

The day was over. Safadi chatted for a while to a couple of the postdocs, and then took one last look around the lecture room. Cups and plates and remains of people's lunch were still strewn about, giving the room a forlorn feeling. She had that sense of deflation that always came after a presentation; the sense that something special and important had happened, but was now finished, and would never return.

I'm tired, she thought. *Time to go home.*

She went back first to her office to leave her notes on her desk: she wouldn't work on them again today. But before she left, she opened her computer, and wrote a message.

> *Dear Doctor Vritet,*
>
> *A short note to let you know that the symposium today went well, although your presence and expertise were greatly missed. May I compliment you, however, on your students, who asked such penetrating questions. They are a credit to you.*
>
> *I am sending you my paper. I hope it is of interest. I would welcome any thoughts that you might have.*
>
> *These are difficult days for you and your people, and while I am sad that you could not join us, I hope you know that you have an open invitation to visit us here at the Institute at any time. Above all, we are scientists, and that work—while it might not transcend other ties—nonetheless connects us all in a very special and particular way.*
>
> *I remain your colleague, and hope one day to be your friend—*
> *Doctor Amal Safadi*
> *Institute of Astronomy, the University of Cambridge, Earth*

She read the message over, and then sent it. If she had taken advice from Haig, from anyone with any expertise on Romulan affairs, she might have thought twice. She might have thought what this letter looked like, read through the ever-watchful eyes of the Tal Shiar. She might have thought twice before holding out the hand of friendship.

DAYSTROM INSTITUTE
OKINAWA, EARTH

Agnes Jurati's paperwork had come through, and she was now officially a doctoral student at the Daystrom Institute, under the supervision of the Chair of Robotics, Professor Bruce Maddox. They went to Istanbul to celebrate. Staring at the mosaics in Hagia Sophia, he started burbling suddenly, about when he came here as a kid with his mother, who was mad about Byzantine art, only he wasn't. Kids are never interested in what their parents do, and that was one reason he had never wanted kids, but then she had shoved a poem by Yeats in front of him, and he had read about enameling and hammered gold and clockwork birds and bodily forms and natural things, and he realized, then, what it was he wanted to do. Make life. Make something so beautiful it would keep an emperor awake. Aggie stood and listened to every word, her mouth open, her eyes bright.

That night, he went back to the lab. All was quiet. He wandered around the new big room, kitted out with everything Starfleet could throw at him. The lights were down. At the far end was the tall chamber containing the parts of the prototype that he and Mackenzie had been laboring over. The creature stood motionless, in shadow. He stared with faint loathing at its immobile features. The skin was golden; they had not bettered the materials used on Data. But what lay within was a pale shadow.

"Are you ever going to wake up?" Maddox said. "Are you ever going to set me free?"

He pulled out a padd and a stylus. He started to doodle, his head still full of the mosaics. And then he saw it—the solution; the way to bridge the gap between Mackenzie's circuitry and the casings he had so grudgingly designed. He turned to the nearest computer and began to program. Ideas were flooding through his mind, each one opening out onto a new one, like the fractals of a Mandelbrot set. He keyed in some words; deleted them, laughed, and keyed in some more. Behind him, something stirred. And then came a small voice, as rusty as a tin man caught in the rain.

"*Daisy . . . Daisy . . . Give me your answer do . . .*"

Maddox turned to look at his creation. "Hello," he said. "I guess you're my redheaded stepchild."

VERITY
IN ORBIT OVER ARNATH

Picard spoke directly to both Bordson and Clancy. The C-in-C, despite his obvious sympathy, was implacable. *"I'm sorry, Jean-Luc, but Commander Telak is correct. These are Romulan citizens. They're under his jurisdiction—"*

"They are still on board the *Verity*."

"Then they must be persuaded to leave."

This was all very well for the C-in-C to say, thought Picard, but he had not met Suvim. "The reality is that I have several hundred terrified refugees who have nothing to lose." He thought again about what he had seen on Arnath. "Victor, if you could see the conditions down there. It is *desperate*. People were promised homes—a place to resettle and start their lives once again. Facilities such as these . . . I cannot even call them facilities! This is a *camp*! We cannot be a part of that. We should speak out in the strongest terms, not allow this to go ahead—"

"The president has spoken directly to the Romulan praetor," said Bordson. *"We've expressed our disquiet. We've made offer after offer. And we've been told—these are their citizens, and they will care for them—"*

Clancy added, *"The timing's unfortunate. Safadi's research hit the public comms yesterday. The Romulans are furious, calling it bad faith. They're muttering about cutting back our involvement entirely. Perhaps before that, we might have been able to persuade Telak's superiors to allow us to help set up new facilities, at least. But we've been shut down. They've been embarrassed, publicly. They want to resolve this on their own terms—"*

"Victor," said Picard. "These people are refusing to leave my ship and I sympathize entirely with their plight."

"They have to leave," said Bordson. *"It's as simple as that."*

"I assume," said Picard, rather coldly, "that you are not authorizing the use of force?"

There was silence, and he wondered, for a moment, whether he had overstepped the mark.

"I am by no means authorizing the use of force to transport refugees into the camps," said Bordson. *"I understand that you're under a great deal of pressure, but when you're ready, I'll accept your apology for that."*

"Sir, I apologize unreservedly."

"Good." Bordson looked at him sympathetically. *"We're all struggling with the ramifications of this mission. We support you entirely."*

"It seems to me," said Clancy, *"that we have two options."*

Picard noted, and appreciated, the "we."

"We transport these people directly to the surface, or we permit the Romulans to transport them."

"One of those options seems like cowardice, Captain," Picard said. "Can we at least continue to press our offer of material aid?"

"We can press," said Clancy. *"I am pressing. But they're not buying what we're offering."*

"I'm sorry, Jean-Luc," said Bordson. *"But if this is what it takes for us to continue the mission, then this is what we need to do."*

"Understood. Picard out." He cut the comm and looked over at Raffi, who had been sitting and listening.

"One bite at a time, eh, Raffi?"

"You know what, JL? Turns out some things are hard to swallow."

Picard spoke to Suvim privately, and face-to-face. He thought the man might rage, complain, refuse, but as he spoke—as he explained the situation in full, the impossibility of it all, the limits on his ability to act—he watched the subpraetor crumble. The Romulan seemed to age. It was terrible to behold. Picard thought: *This is the death of hope.* He never wanted to see this again: a man brought so low.

In the end, Suvim, and the others, went quietly to the transporter rooms. They stood clutching their possessions, and their dignity. Picard stood quietly by as a witness. Before the transporter took him, Suvim looked at Picard and said, "*Zheven'tar*, Jean-Luc Picard. I curse you—you, this ship, this fleet, this mission. May you taste ash. May the fruits of your labors wither on the vine. I curse you, Starfleet, and the Federation, who offer the hand of friendship, only to snatch it away."

And then he was gone. Picard felt Raffi's hand upon his shoulder, the briefest of touches. He was glad—very glad—that she was there.

"Well, Raffi," he said, without turning to look at her, "have we heard back from Telak as to whether we might place independent observers on Arnath?"

"Oh yes, we've heard, JL," she said.

"I assume he said no."

"He said no."

Picard cleared his throat, tugged at his uniform jacket. Koli, at his other side, said, "I know this is hard, Admiral. It is never easy. But we have done the right thing. We have no legal jurisdiction to intervene in Romulan domestic affairs."

Ah yes, he thought. *We retain our moral purity.*

"Yet you know, don't you," said Raffi, "that there'll be abuses of power down there. The first sign of trouble, those soldiers will shoot."

Picard's combadge chimed. He tapped it, and Marshall spoke. *"All of our guests are down on Arnath, sir. The facility has now been cloaked."*

"Thank you, Lieutenant," said Picard. He looked at Raffi and Koli. "We're finished here. We should move on."

Raffi fell into step alongside him as they walked down the corridor. He felt the subtle shift of the ship's impulse engines. "Ten thousand down," Raffi muttered. "That's nearly a billion, huh?"

VERITY

After Arnath, the admiral's black mood hovered over the whole ship, and threatened to engulf the entire fleet. Raffi was caught out by this aspect of the man: he seemed to move through life on a higher plane, she thought; calm, measured, sometimes driven to exasperation, but always seeming to be in possession of some deeper, wider sight that gave him perspective. To find him brought low—it surprised her. Ever practical, she knew this was something that had to be managed, and that this was her task. She made a point in her daily updates to highlight successes: the addition of another three refitted ships, the successful transfer of five thousand people to a newly built garden city on a small conservation world and the grateful messages sent by their children. The distraction was good for her too, keeping her from brooding over her increasingly chilly conversations with Jae. She had begun, in recent weeks, to notice that Gabe was adopting more and more of his mannerisms, his ways of speaking. She remembered her son when he was tiny, when he had still seemed an extension of her. She dreamed, sometimes, of putting him in a little boat, watching the boat drift away.

She was here, and she had her duty. She conferred with Koli, whom she had begun to confide in more and more. Koli advised patience. Later that week she issued an invitation for the admiral and Raffi to join her in her quarters. When Koli let them in, they found that her cabin was lit only by candles.

"*Peldor joi*," she said to them. Picard smiled, for the first time in weeks.

"*Peldor joi*, Koli Jocan." He turned to Raffi. "The Bajoran festival of gratitude. Come, Jocan, let us say farewell to our troubles."

Koli explained the ritual to Raffi: write your worries on renewal scrolls; burn them in the fire. Picard wrote at once. Raffi thought for a while, then wrote: *Losing my boy*.

They consigned their troubles to the flames. "*Peldor joi*," they said to one another.

"Thank you, Jocan," said Picard, after they had eaten together, "for sharing this with us."

The ritual had the desired cleansing effect, lifting the admiral's mood, although he did remain subdued. Without more ships, without news from the Daystrom Institute or from Mars, they were still limited in what they could do. Eat a herd of damn elephants, with fifty more arriving each day.

A few weeks later, Raffi joined Picard in his ready room as he was speaking to the captain of one of the other ships. Seeing Raffi, he indicated that she should come in and sit down. He twisted the screen so that she could see Captain Xotis, on board the *U.S.S. Dignity*.

"The *Dignity* is at Sithu," he said. "Almost the whole population is now on board."

Raffi nodded. The original intention had been to take the inhabitants of Sithu to Lukol II. That now fell within the revised blast range and would need its own evacuation plan.

"I'm glad to report we have a solution," said Xotis. *"Of sorts."*

"We've had an offer from a small colony world," explained Picard. "They're able to accept a limited Romulan population."

"What's the catch?" said Raffi.

"It's a human colony, on Torrassa," said Xotis. *"That's just outside the Neutral Zone. In Federation space."*

"Ah," said Raffi. "So not a solution."

"Oh, I rather think it is," said Picard. Raffi, shooting him a quick look, saw that his mood had lifted. He was poised, eager, ready once more to act. "Captain Xotis, when your guests are all on board, you should proceed with all speed to Torrassa."

"Are you sure, Admiral?"

"Those are my orders, Captain Xotis. I'm quite sure. Picard out."

He stood up and moved from behind his desk. At the door, he halted and looked back at her. "What is it, Raffi?"

"I didn't say anything."

"You don't approve?"

Raffi folded her arms. "I wholly approve of saving as many lives as possible."

His mouth quirked into a smile. "Good." He walked out onto the bridge to take his chair. Raffi, on her way to her own seat, passed Koli. "Jocan," she said as she walked past, "remember that thing I said would never happen? It's happening."

Raffi took her seat beside the admiral. He was already issuing his instructions.

"Lieutenant Miller," he said, "set in a course for the Neutral Zone."

A murmur, quickly suppressed, passed over the bridge, although Miller, to his credit, did not even blink. Raffi leaned over to Picard. "JL," she said softly, "quick question."

"Yes, Raffi?"

"Are you *quite* sure you don't need to ask for permission to dismantle the Neutral Zone?"

The admiral shrugged. He had never seemed so French. "Better to ask forgiveness than permission, Raffi."

"I'll look forward to using that on you one day," she said.

"I'd be disappointed if you didn't." He leaned forward in his chair. "Engage."

Daystrom Institute
Okinawa, Earth

It was the last day of the old year. Bruce Maddox, watching his audience of two, said, in the manner of a showman about to perform an illusion, "Prepare to be amazed."

Mackenzie leaned forward, excited. La Forge folded his arms and looked as if he had come a long way not to be impressed. Maddox opened the door beside him, and said, "Come on out."

There was movement behind the door. Then a figure walked through, slowly, but steadily, and smoothly. Mackenzie gasped. La Forge said, "Well I'll be damned."

"Allow me to introduce the Daystrom A500," said Maddox.

He looked at the face of his creation and felt repulsed. Gold pseudo-flesh, too reminiscent of Data, but the most reliable thermoplastic they had found for the casing. It would endure. Golden eyes that blinked, too regularly, too carefully. But these creatures were not aiming for verisimilitude. They did not need to pass for human. They simply needed to function.

"Damn, Bruce," said Mackenzie. There were tears in her eyes. "You've done it!"

Yes, he thought. *I have made a toy. A machine. But not life.*

Both Mackenzie and La Forge hastened over to examine the thing. Put it through its paces. Held a conversation. Asked it to perform simple functions. Then complex functions. Then more complex functions. *Oh yes*, thought Maddox, *I have done everything you have asked.*

"How many of these do you have?" said La Forge.

"At the moment—this one," said Maddox. "We have four more almost complete. We can start a production line. By the end of the month."

"Amazing," said Mackenzie. "Oh, this is going to make all the difference!"

La Forge was standing and shaking his head. "At last," he said, "some good news!" He grinned. "The admiral is going to be delighted!"

"As if that would make it all worthwhile," Maddox said bitterly to Jurati. They were walking around the campus lake. It was late, dark, and cold.

Winter. Maddox kicked viciously at the dead leaves on the ground. Suddenly, he stopped, and put his hands to his head. "Oh God!" he said. "These damn things! This is what I'll be remembered for, isn't it? These hybrids, these half measures, these goddamn *jokes*!"

There was a crunch of leaves beside him. He felt her hand rest upon his arm. "Bruce..."

"I know, I know! 'It needs to be done, Bruce! Think of all the lives you're saving, Bruce! A greater good, Bruce!' Well, you know what, Aggie? *Fuck* the greater good."

She withdrew her hand. "What I was going to say," she said, "was that I have complete confidence in you. Yes, this is not what you want to be doing but it's a... it's a stepping stone, isn't it, on the way to success? The dream of fully sentient life."

"This isn't a stepping stone, Aggie. It's a dead end!"

Again, she placed her hand upon his arm. She made a small, soft, wounded sound. He looked up at her. She was crying, very gently. "I believe in you," she said. "You'll do it. But you have to keep on going, Bruce. Don't give up. Don't ever give up. You're brilliant."

In the distance, the fireworks began. The year was turning.

"I think," she said, "that you might be the most brilliant man alive."

Part 2

THE BEST

2383-2384

6

Admiral's Log: As ordered, Captain Xotis has taken the *Dignity* across the Neutral Zone and entered Federation space. He and his guests are due to arrive on Torrassa within three weeks. I have already received a communication from a group of Torrassan Elders who represent the population. They ask me to extend the hand of friendship to the Romulans traveling to their world, and make sure that they know that they will be welcome. More importantly, these sentiments are being backed up by detailed plans. The Torrassans have asked for as much specialist help as the Federation can offer. Resettlement experts from the UFPHCR have already arrived, and Commander Gbowee and my team back at Starfleet Command were able to divert four industrial replicators to Torrassa. I remain in awe of the skills and dedication of my procurement team, who are enabling a very rapid and positive response to this change in our mission. The reports I am receiving from Torrassa show that building is well underway, and that homes are already prepared for nearly a third of those that Xotis is taking with him. Images from Torrassa arrive daily, showing the progress of this work. It's all very encouraging after our experiences on Arnath.

Despite what my XO might say, I am not unaware of the complications arising from taking Romulans citizens across the border into Federation space. The Neutral Zone has been the keystone of our relationship with the Romulans for generations, ensuring peace (more or less) and providing a boundary beyond which neither party was to cross without good reason. I have not made this decision lightly. These lives were at risk. There was nowhere within the Romulan Star Empire to take them—and, after Arnath, I would not be able to trust that any world suggested would in fact be fit for habitation. A Federation world has offered these people succor. What other choice was there? Treaties can be reconstructed, renegotiated, remade. Lives, once lost, are gone for good.

Nevertheless, I am glad to hear of the progress on Torrassa, not least because this means I have concrete and positive news to bring to my somewhat urgently arranged and imminent conversation with Starfleet Command.

VERITY

Picard, sitting in his ready room, watched Koli as she examined the model ship on the far side of the room. The *Enterprise*-E: his home, still, in many ways. He had been on board this ship now for the best part of two years and felt as if he had barely begun to unpack. Some of his more beloved effects remained in a storage facility on Earth. He should make an effort to have them sent to *Verity*, to give his accommodations a less improvised and impermanent impression. After all, he intended to be here for the long haul.

"Do you miss the *Enterprise*, sir?"

A thorny question; one he was not entirely able answer to his own satisfaction. He deflected. "Why do you ask?"

"You were there a long time."

He was saved from having to come up with a response when Lieutenant Marshall signaled an incoming communication from Starfleet Command. Koli came quickly around the desk to take a seat beside him. The screen showed a split image: Bordson in his office, Clancy in a small conference room that, from the décor, Picard recognized was the Federation Council building in Paris. He felt a brief twinge of guilt—very brief—grip him. Clancy had presumably been meeting various members of the Council to discuss the ramifications of his orders to the *Dignity*. She looked harried, and not happy. He did not envy her this task. Admiral Bordson was less easy to read, but Picard was prepared to assume this particular expression did not signify joy.

"Can you tell me, Jean-Luc," Bordson said, *"what in your orders conveyed to you the impression that you had the authority to unilaterally cast aside two centuries of foreign policy?"*

That, thought Picard, was the closest he had ever heard to outright anger from Victor Bordson.

"Not to mention our treaty obligations," said Clancy.

So they were presenting a united front. Very well, he thought. He might be outnumbered two to one, but he had right on his side. He would stand firm.

"You do understand what you have done?" said Clancy.

"I understand perfectly, Captain," he said calmly. "I know both the history and the politics extremely well, often at firsthand—"

"Then why would you think—"

"The simple answer is that we are on a mission to save lives," he said. "We have limited time available. Given what we now know about the blast radius, a vastly increased number of people to move, and a suddenly decreased number of options as to where we can take them."

"All of which is true," said Clancy, *"and all of which needed to be discussed with the Council, the president, the Romulan ambassador, and, oh, perhaps the commander-in-chief of Starfleet, Admiral Bordson."*

"I was given this mission," said Picard, "an unprecedented one, we agreed. The heart of the mission was to save as many lives as possible." He leaned forward, keeping his voice low, but emphatic. "The greatest risk to the success is that we lose sight of our goal. That is the priority, the moral imperative. Therefore, if we concern ourselves with the niceties of diplomacy, or the fine print of agreements made by our respective governments in very different times, well . . ." He shrugged. "So be it."

"The niceties of diplomacy . . . ?" Clancy was staring at him. *"Jean-Luc, do you understand what you have done?"*

"Yes. I ordered a Federation starship to cross the Neutral Zone from Romulan to Federation space, carrying Romulan refugees to a human colony world that welcomes them with open arms."

Koli, who had been sitting quietly throughout this battle of titans, leaned forward. "If I might offer some thoughts here?"

Clancy, exasperated, turned to the Bajoran lieutenant. *"Perhaps we'll hear some sense."*

Koli folded her hands before her on the table. Picard could not help but respect this woman, who took such care over her work, even as she was likely to be handing his superiors the means to remonstrate with him further. All he hoped was that he would not be instructed to order Captain Xotis to return to Romulan space without depositing his guests at their new home. He would not give that order.

"These are always difficult situations," said Koli. "Always fraught. This is the most complex refugee crisis I have ever encountered. On Bajor—we needed help. We needed assistance to get back on our feet, and we were prepared to accept what the Federation had to give. Across Cardassia, too, after the Dominion War, what was needed was help—physical assistance."

"More in the case of Cardassia," said Bordson, who had been there. *"We helped rebuild organizations from the ground up."*

"But *at* the request of the Cardassians," Koli said. "And in each case, the home remained. The *homeworld* remained. There was some center that could be rebuilt, even if lives and more had been lost. But in this case . . ." She held her hands out. "They cannot return home. Home will be destroyed. And there is certainly no desire to change culture, way of life, values. If anything, it makes it more precious."

"What are you saying?" said Clancy impatiently. *"That Romulans should stay in Romulan space? This makes sense to me. In fact, it's what I've been saying—"*

"It's not that easy, Captain Clancy," said Koli. "It's never that easy. And what we have to keep at the forefront of our mind is self-determination. That has to be the key principle behind any relocation. And in this case,

I believe all parties were willing. The Romulans on Sithu have made no complaint about being taken from their world."

"That has certainly not been the case for other missions," pointed out Picard.

"And no complaint," continued Koli, "at being taken into Federation space."

"Sithu, as I understand it," said Clancy, *"is an agricultural colony so impoverished that the infant mortality rate was among the highest across the Star Empire—"*

"They were glad to leave," said Picard.

"But not without the permission of their government!" Clancy said.

"Have they sent ships to stop us?" said Picard.

Bordson said, *"You know they have not. We have, however, had a formal complaint from the Romulan ambassador, whom I will meet later today. Sulde is not a happy woman—"*

"A complaint, yes," said Picard, "but no action has been taken to stop the *Dignity*. Might we then go so far as to assume that this mission is going ahead if not with enthusiasm on the part of the Romulan government, then at least with their tacit consent?"

"They're probably glad to see the back of them," said Koli. "Like you said, Captain Clancy, the people on Sithu are poor. The Empire sees little value in them but can hardly leave them to die. They are a problem that can be passed on to the Federation. If we want them—we're welcome to them." A slight flush rose on her cheek. "Like so much rubbish."

"What do the residents of Torrassa make of the plan to bring them a colony of desperate Romulans?" said Clancy.

"They've invited them," said Koli. "They've offered their help. I'm not saying that the process won't be difficult, but the will is there."

"All signs from Torrassa are positive," said Picard. "I suspect the Romulan government will try to make political capital out of this, nonetheless."

"From the summary dismantling of the Neutral Zone?" said Clancy. She

gave a dry laugh. *"You bet they will. And all for the sake of a few hundred thousand hayseeds!"*

"If we are not prepared to throw away our diplomatic advantage for the sake of the poorest," said Picard, "then it is no advantage at all."

Koli was nodding. "Captain Clancy, Admiral Bordson—we are doing the right thing."

"Well," said Bordson, *"who are we to argue with the experts, Kirsten? All right, Jean-Luc, I will defend your outrageous decision to the Federation Council with every breath in my body."*

"I am deeply appreciative, Admiral," Picard said. And he meant it. "Thank you."

"But don't expect them to be enthusiastic. Not least because once this colony of 'hayseeds' is established, there will be a significant Romulan presence in Federation space!" Bordson continued, not looking pleased. *"Issues of citizens' rights and jurisdiction alone are enough to make me break into a cold sweat. Has anyone prepared a briefing on how that might work?"*

Koli nodded. "I have."

All three of her senior officers eyed her thoughtfully. *"Preparing for a rainy day, Lieutenant Koli?"* said Clancy. *"Or have you had something like this in mind for a while, Jean-Luc?"*

"The admiral did not request this and knew nothing about my report. This was my own initiative," said Koli. "But it might be helpful?"

"It will," said Bordson. *"Thank you, Koli."*

The call ended on friendlier terms than Picard had expected. When the screens returned to the Starfleet symbol, Picard turned to Koli. "Thank you for your support, Jocan."

"We are doing the right thing, sir."

"Thank you also for your foresight in preparing a briefing on matters of jurisdiction."

Koli rose from her seat. "For that, sir," she said, "you should thank Commander Musiker."

As so often, Picard thought. *As so often.*

STARFLEET COMMAND
SAN FRANCISCO, EARTH

Ambassador Sulde was petite, elegant, and very angry. She swept into Bordson's office and refused the offer of a seat. "Admiral Bordson, this is—"

"An outrage, indeed," said Bordson. "And under ideal circumstances we would maintain the treaty and territorial agreements that have kept the peace between us for so many years. But the circumstances are far from ideal, aren't they? Your whole civilization is under threat."

Sulde looked at him in shock. Bordson, who had in recent months spent increasing amounts of time with Romulan officials, had discovered that complete frankness was by far the best way to handle them. They were simply not equipped to deal with it.

Sulde rallied. "That is an overstatement, as you well know! We are well able—"

"I'm sure you know your domestic business much better than I, but perhaps our officers on the ground among the threatened worlds have better information than either of us? Admiral Picard—"

Sulde glowered at the name.

"Whatever your private opinion of him, Jean-Luc Picard is no fool. If this was what was needed to save those Romulan lives, then this is what had to be done."

"He has ordered a Federation vessel to kidnap over a hundred thousand Romulans!" exclaimed Sulde.

Bordson sat back comfortably in his chair. "Now you are the one indulging in overstatements."

"Taken hostage! No doubt demands will follow—"

"Ambassador, you and I both know that your military leaders are *delighted* to have a Romulan presence on our side of the Neutral Zone."

"Hardly a presence! A motley bunch of farmers and their families. All at the mercy of Starfleet. I must insist that we are allowed to send a ship of our own to act as protection to them—"

Bordson smiled. "Allowing Romulan citizens and their Tal Shiar minders to take up residence within Federation space is one kind of folly. Allowing a warship to station itself permanently on our side of the border is another."

"I must insist that these people are protected in some way!"

"There is no threat to them—"

"There is to their way of life!"

Bordson had no doubt that as soon as these refugees could, they would become Federation citizens. "Very well. I shall make this suggestion. It would be customary for these people to receive Federation citizenship automatically within five years of residence. We are content to waive that—"

"Quite right."

"Instead, they will be welcome to *apply* to become Federation citizens after the five years are up."

He watched Sulde weigh the pros and cons of all this. Her demeanor became slightly less combative. "Very well," Sulde said at last. "But I have one last request."

"Yes?" said Bordson carefully.

"It seems to me," said Sulde, "that many of our problems arise from miscommunication. A lack of understanding about cultural norms."

"Perhaps," said Bordson cautiously.

"Then let us open more direct and immediate channels of communication."

VERITY

"'Cultural liaison officer'?" Raffi was not impressed. "That's a euphemism for spy if ever there was." They were on their way to the transporter room, to welcome the latest addition to the crew.

"Lieutenant Tajuth has been assigned to us, and we shall make him welcome," said Picard.

"Typical micromanagement from Clancy," she muttered. "You know he'll be Tal Shiar?"

"I would expect nothing less, Raffi." He considered letting the comment about Clancy slide, knowing how much time Raffi spent handling queries from her office, but he could not in good conscience. "I believe this was a request from the Romulan ambassador."

"Koli wasn't."

"Koli is a fine crewmember. You have said as much to me on many occasions."

"First thing he'll do is try to hack our systems," Raffi grumbled. "The hours I'll waste, trying to fend all that off . . ."

"It is my hope," said Picard, "that we can establish an open relationship with him."

Raffi stopped dead in her tracks. "A *what*?"

"Raffi, have you ever considered that too much time spent trying to think as a Romulan may have given you an overly suspicious cast of mind?"

"It's not paranoia," said Raffi, "when they really are out to get you."

"We have a chance here," said Picard. "A Romulan officer, sent to serve alongside us. I believe firmly—and all my experience bears me out on this—that hosting officers from different worlds leads to trust and increased understanding. Look at Captain Worf. I remember when he was assigned to the *Enterprise*. Nobody believed that a Klingon could serve Starfleet faithfully. Everyone believed that his loyalties would be fatally divided. Now he commands our flagship."

"Yes, but—"

"Or consider Data. What we learned from him, serving alongside him, about ourselves, our humanity. Such interactions are at the heart of Starfleet's remit to seek out new life and learn from them."

"Seriously, have you ever considered that insufficient time spent trying to think as a Romulan may have given you an overly credulous cast of mind?"

He put his hand to his head. "I must *hope*, Raffi! I must hope that we may find a way through our differences."

"Seriously, JL?" She looked at him with frank disbelief. "You're living in hope that a Tal Shiar officer sent to spy on us will learn the error of his ways from our example? There's hope and there's blind faith in the face of all the evidence. What are you gonna do to make him love us? Sign him up to a string quartet?"

They entered the transporter room. Picard gave a bark of laughter. "Who knows. An encounter with Beethoven might be the making of the man."

"It might do something to him. Jeez, though, this might backfire. He might make us listen to Romulan indeterminate polyphony."

"Raffi," he said, with some amusement, "you never cease to amaze me. What on *earth* is Romulan indeterminate polyphony?"

"You really want to know?"

"Of *course* I want to know!"

"It's singing, yes? Voices, unaccompanied."

"That part," he said, "I understood. How about the indeterminacy?"

"They don't know what the other people are singing."

There was a pause. Picard glanced at Lieutenant Shriv th'Kaothreq, on duty by the transporter controls. The Andorian shook his head. *Don't look at me.*

"You're not telling me the truth, are you, Commander?"

"JL, I swear on my mother's life that every word of this is true. They are given a starting note, a musical key, and a tempo. The performers are in separate rooms. The audience sits in a gallery above and looks down on them. They're given the cue to start, and off they go."

Picard contemplated this. He had not considered how the Romulan principle of secrecy might play out in their art. "What a fascinating idea . . . How does it sound?"

"How do you think it sounds? It sounds fucking awful."

Behind them, th'Kaothreq stifled a laugh.

"Then let us by all means prevent any move toward establishing a Romulan glee club," said Picard gravely. "In lieu of which, I shall endeavor to kill him with kindness." He gave the nod to th'Kaothreq.

"There are quicker ways," said Raffi, "to kill a Tal Shiar agent."

By luck rather than design, she finished speaking exactly as Tajuth materialized. He was tall and spare with distinct cranial ridges. "A northerner," murmured Raffi.

"Is that significant?" asked Picard.

"They can be chippy," said Raffi.

Picard stepped forward. "*Jolan tru*," he said. "We're very glad to welcome you on board, Lieutenant Tajuth. We look forward to working with you." He turned to introduce Raffi. "This is my first officer, Lieutenant Commander Raffi Musiker."

"Hi," said Raffi, with a touch of acid.

Tajuth looked at them both down his long nose. Then he looked around the transporter bay. He sighed, as if he didn't want him to be there either. "It has been a long journey," he said. "If I could see my quarters, and then we'll discuss the next mission?"

"Of course," said Picard, and gestured to Tajuth to follow him. Raffi, following behind, muttered, "Sounds fucking awful."

FEDERATION COUNCIL
PARIS, EARTH

Kirsten Clancy knew that many of her colleagues resented the round of functions and drinks parties that seemed to clutter one's diary once you were promoted past a certain point. She did not mind. Not because she particularly enjoyed small talk, although she did not find it difficult, and she threw herself into the task with the same dedication that she brought to every aspect of her work. She knew how much crucial information could be learned during the course of these events. Drinks flowed, and tongues loosened, and people were trying to impress everyone, hinting at sources of information to which others did not have access, anxious to make themselves seem close to power. Clancy, moving around these spaces in her dress uniform, was someone looking to be cultivated. She listened to everything and drank synthetic sparkling wine. She was an expert in making people believe they'd had a full and frank exchange of views, when mostly she had learned a great deal and they had been told very little in return.

This function, an annual reception for newly elected members of the Federation Council, was a regular fixture in Clancy's diary. This year's new councilors were next year's committee chairs or policy leaders, or, one day, even president. Clancy wanted to know who (or what) was heading her way. She had observed, over the years, that they generally fell into one of two categories: those who were stunned into silence, and those intent on making a great deal of noise. The latter Clancy looked out for; they generally caused her some small trouble at some point along the line. This year, she was on the lookout for someone very specific.

She had heard of Olivia Quest, the new junior council member for Estelen, before even entering the room. Estelen was a small world close to the Neutral Zone, and Quest was a descendent of one of the original settler families. She had been the chief executive officer of that family's large-scale agricultural operations on Estelen and its moons. An engineer by training, with a specialty in terraforming, she was reputed to be extremely smart, not to mention frustrated by the lack of influence that such small worlds had on Federation policy. She had run on a platform of setting up a committee to scrutinize the Romulan relief mission, to which Quest had argued during her campaign, too many resources were being allocated.

Jean-Luc Picard's remarkable decision to take Romulan settlers into Federation space had proven a godsend for Quest. Her face had hardly been off the newscasts. *"Is this policy now? Will all the worlds along the border be asked to take Romulan settlers? Will the point come where we will be required to take them? Our hearts go out to these people in need, but surely there are questions to be asked about whether this is the best solution. The border is destabilized. Floods of refugees. Do we have the ability to help them properly? Do we have the right? Maybe we should be considering whether Romulan space is better for Romulans."*

You could hear the dog-whistle a klick off, Clancy thought sourly. Nevertheless, these interviews, which gathered pace in the last ten days of her campaign, had propelled Quest into office. In her victory speech, she had promised to come to the Council to ask serious questions about the mission. *"We owe it to ourselves, and to the Romulans too."* Several councilors from other worlds along the border had already signaled their interest in serving on a scrutiny commission beside Quest. "We need new blood like this," one said. "Shake us up; stop us doing business as usual. Ask the right sorts of questions."

The function room was packed. Bright lights glinted off decorations from countless worlds. The babble and chatter of dozens of conversations filled the space. Still, there was a noticeable ripple when Quest arrived. Clancy, talking to an aide from Trill, had positioned herself carefully to be able to watch the entrance, and saw Quest enter the room. She stood for a moment, the doorway forming an arch around her, surveying the gathering. Everyone turned to look. She was tall, rather masculine in feature, her jaw slightly square. Her white-blond hair, very straight and fine, came down to her ears; her eyes, deep set, were a bright and piercing blue. She was wearing a silver dress, which looked stunning; she knew exactly how much impact she was having. She let everyone look at her, and then she swept into the room, where a senior councilor from Coridan and a high-ranking official from the Federation Science Bureau gathered her up and started introducing her to key players.

The captain, courteously disentangling herself from the young Trill, started to circulate around the room. As she moved, she caught snatches of conversation: *"Real questions about what this means for worlds on the border. My wife's cousin left his post at Utopia Planitia, you know, couldn't get the resources he needed for his work. Got to wonder about the impact on the defensive capabilities of new ships if all we're doing now is making damn ferries. I don't want this to sound bad, but maybe Romulan space really is best for Romulans."*

Clancy, hearing all this, taking the temperature of the room, thought, *Next time you come up with a smart idea, Jean-Luc Picard, you might want to run it past Command first.*

A waiter offered her some canapés. She said, "No, thanks, I'm good." At the sound of her voice, Quest turned and looked at her. Her eyes were bright, intelligent, amused, and calculating. She nodded at Clancy—she plainly knew exactly who she was—and then turned back to her conversation. They spoke only once, in passing, much later in the evening, when Quest was on her way out, in the company of several other more senior councilors, all from worlds close to the Neutral Zone. Nodding in greeting as she passed, Quest said, "Captain Clancy, I'm sorry we didn't get a chance to talk. I look forward to making your acquaintance another time."

This one, thought Clancy, watching her leave in a shimmer of silver, *is trouble.*

VERITY

"How is your new cultural liaison officer settling in?"

"Fine," said Picard. "He and Raffi have only come to blows once." Seeing Bordson's face, he said, "I'm joking, Victor. But Raffi has good reason not to trust the Tal Shiar—as do we all."

"We have no evidence that Tajuth is Tal Shiar."

"If we had evidence," said Picard, "he would not be a particularly effective member of the organization. But we shall win him over. I shall play good cop; Raffi can be bad cop."

"*Where on earth did you find that extraordinary expression?*"

"A detective novel from twentieth-century Earth. As yet, Tajuth's presence has caused no difficulties."

"*Well, as long as it keeps the Romulans happy. But we have another set of people who are asking questions, Jean-Luc, and whose concerns must be assuaged—*"

"There are always people like that. Must we bother with them?"

"*Since they are elected members of the Federation Council, I'm afraid we must.*"

"What was it that Churchill said about democracy?" said Picard dryly.

"*Your knowledge is wider than mine, Jean-Luc.*"

"He said it was the worst form of government except for all those other forms that have been tried. Who on the Council is asking questions?"

"*Councilor Olivia Quest.*"

Picard searched his considerable personal knowledge, and said, "I've never heard of her."

"*She represents Estelen, a planet very close to the Neutral Zone. She is naturally concerned about the ramifications of your recent decision and how it could affect her world.*"

"That seems reasonable enough."

"*And as a junior councilor, she will be seeking reelection in four years.*"

"Ah," said Picard. "Now we get to the heart of it."

"*She's a young woman in a hurry, and she's keeping herself very busy. She's persuaded the Council to set up an oversight committee for the relief mission. She's heading it, of course.*"

"Who else is involved?" Picard asked. Bordson immediately sent over the list, which Picard read through with a sinking heart. "Is everyone here suspicious of Romulans in some way?"

"*There are good historical reasons for that, Jean-Luc.*"

"We are not living in the past. We are living in an unprecedented present—"

"*Nevertheless, these are elected officials. Their opinion carries weight—*

and public scrutiny of how our resources are being used is only appropriate." Bordson sighed. *"I wish you were more sensitive to the political ramifications of your decisions, Jean-Luc. This mission will fail without political will behind it."*

Picard frowned. The careers and jockeying of some minor functionaries were as nothing compared to the number of lives they were trying to save. He said, "What can I do to help, Victor?"

"A few high-profile successes wouldn't do any harm."

"We are successful all the time. The situation on Arnath, and again on Sithu—these might attract attention, but the real work of this mission goes on quietly. Is Quest aware how many people we have already successfully relocated? Has she taken the time to visit some of the towns we have helped to build, or to speak to some of the people whom we have saved? Has she taken the time to visit the mission headquarters there on Earth? Spoken to Crystal Gbowee about the logistical work in which she and her team are engaged? Or T'Kautunn on Starbase 32 about coordinating the fleet? Or visited Mars, or the Daystrom Institute, and asked questions about the technological innovation being undertaken—?"

"Sending her to Mars might not be a bad idea," said Bordson. *"Technological innovation in ship design is something she should be able to understand— a concrete ancillary benefit from all this—"*

"We are not undertaking this mission to push forward ship design," said Picard.

"You're not," said Bordson, *"and I'm not. But other people are not as selfless as you and I."*

Picard shook his head. "Saving lives should be enough."

"Romulan lives," said Bordson.

"I seem to hear that a great deal these days. It makes no difference to me."

"Unfortunately, to some people it does."

"I'm glad you're the one having to speak to them, Victor. I'm not sure I would be able to restrain myself."

"Kirsten Clancy will handle Quest and her committee, Jean-Luc. But they exist, and their demands and their concerns are real, and could well have an impact on this mission. Give me a big win that I can take back to them. Politicians are simple folk. Let us give them a story that they can easily understand."

Bordson closed the channel. *Easy to understand*, thought Picard. But the fact was that some tasks—some missions—were complicated; they required complex solutions. There was no conjuring trick he could perform to solve this crisis, no spell that he could cast that would spirit their problems away. The true magic of this mission lay in its daily grind: moving supplies and people around, attention to detail, forward planning, and careful logistical work. Such things were not suited to easy stories and headlines. That did not make them any less heroic in Picard's eyes. Quite the opposite. The combined action of many people, the steady, patient, and dedicated work—that, he thought, was the real heroism. Later, when he was bringing Raffi up to speed on the conversation, he said, "Bordson wants a big win."

"Jeez," Raffi replied. "Don't we all."

ROMULAN ASTROPHYSICAL ACADEMY
ROMULUS

Even for a Romulan, Nokim Vritet was a solitary man. Brought up in a family that, while well connected, was nevertheless riven by the feuds and quarrels of multiple factions, he had decided at a very young age that the best way to rise above it all was to look up and up, at the night sky. At the age of six he petitioned so fiercely for a telescope that his parents, used to a silent and somewhat biddable child, immediately supplied one. He proceeded to teach himself about the stars, and, having learned that this combination of extended periods of silence punctuated by sudden and clear demands was an effective tactic to get what he wanted, he would occasionally surface to make clear and specific requests: for extra tuition, for further equipment, for introductions to relevant people. His family, who were amused if baffled, indulged these demands. At sixteen, Vritet presented his first paper. At twenty-one he completed doctoral studies and took up a research post at the Astrophysical Academy. His entire goal was to be left alone to look at his beloved stars, those silent comrades who made no demands, who moved at their own pace, who spoke of a larger pattern behind the random noise that seemed to be the stock-in-trade of the people around him.

Nokim Vritet was therefore entirely unprepared for his area of study to become the most hotly contested field in galactic politics. He worked quietly and unobtrusively. He was entirely ignorant, for example, that for over a year now all of his incoming and outgoing communications had been monitored, intercepted, censored, and some deleted. He had no idea that the two new colleagues in the office next door were Tal Shiar, sent specifically to observe him. He was unaware that he had been invited to a symposium on Earth, and that Doctor Amal Safadi (whose work he admired) had sent him messages. He certainly did not know about her paper, and its contents. But numbers do not lie, and nature cannot be fooled, and it was therefore only a matter of time before a man as meticulous as Vritet replicated Safadi's results.

He was sitting at his desk in his office, which was situated in a rather poky corner of the academy and had been his private sanctum for nearly two decades. He had made the most of the space available. Visitors to Vritet's office had to negotiate two sliding doors that shifted about in a complex fashion such that one had to be open a very precise amount before the other was unlocked. This, as well as the abstruse nature of his research, meant that he rarely had visitors. This was what he preferred. His long-suffering doctoral student, seven years into her project with no end in sight, had given up trying to see Vritet face-to-face. In fact, she was in the process of shifting herself and her work over to the Astronomical Unit on Utux. (She would then complete her thesis in seven months and, not incidentally, save her own life by getting away from the Romulan homeworld so early. It would be almost a year before Vritet would even notice she was gone.) But this morning, even Nokim Vritet realized that the wider world was soon going to be knocking on his door.

He had noticed the irregular readings from the Romulan sun toward the end of the previous year, and, comparing these with data published by other researchers, had concluded that they were looking at sunspot activity that, while at the upper end of the range, was nevertheless within normal parameters. Still, the phenomenon interested him, and he began compiling his own dataset, acquired from several probes upon which he had, as a teenager (and thanks to a wealthy and influential uncle with business interests in this area who had a fondness for the family eccentric), quietly installed a number of sensors. These had, over the years, privately supplied him with all manner of interesting information. The source of his data was, therefore, not controlled by the government, and, unknown to him, much closer to the readings that Doctor Safadi had taken. He had been compiling the data for a week or two now, modeling the effects of the supernova. This morning, he was confronted with the results. The supernova, that global disaster that everyone was vaguely worrying about, was coming much sooner than anyone had thought. All of it. The changes in climate, and the ultimate end.

Even a man as isolated as Vritet (one who had not yet connected the rising cost of fresh food on Romulus with the strain on infrastructure that the relocation effort was causing) immediately understood the ramifications of his results. His first reaction, as he watched the rings fan out quicker than ever before, taking in more and more worlds, was a cold sense of shock that almost sent him into panic. His second reaction (for someone so solitary, he remained at heart a scientist) was to want some independent verification of his figures. His third reaction was to realize, with dismay, that he would have to go and speak to someone else.

He rose from his chair, picked up his handheld device, and went in search of his direct superior, Academician Nurius, the director of the academy. Nurius was a big, bluff man whom Vritet sometimes suspected of being more politician than scientist. In the past he had deplored this. It might come in useful now.

"Well," said Nurius, "a most startling analysis, Nokim!"

"I'm extremely worried about it," said Vritet. "Has the Federation done any work on this? There are a few people on Earth who I know have an interest in this field. There's Amal Safadi . . ." He went on to list a handful of people, which Nurius noted down to pass on to the Tal Shiar to add to any communications blacklist.

"Federation research is hard to come by, of course," said Nurius. "They are not exactly friendly."

Vritet, who found it easier to believe propaganda rather than waste valuable time deciding for himself, nodded. "Yes, yes, very sad . . . Still, I do think that these figures are sufficiently alarming. We should try to get some independent verification."

"Let me send this on," said Nurius. "I'll pass on your request for anything that the Federation might deign to make available to us." He stood up, and so Vritet did the same. "In the meantime, I'd say get back to work and don't worry." Nurius laughed and maneuvered the other man out of the door.

"But if the star is going nova this quickly, the evacuation of Romulus should already be well underway—"

"And I'm sure that if that was the case, the authorities would already know. As you say, there would be a plan underway for our evacuation, wouldn't there? But don't worry, Nokim. I'll pass this upward. Our superiors will have everything in hand. Our leaders wouldn't cut and run and leave us all to die, now, would they?"

Vritet left and went back to his office. He tried to turn his attention to his current project, but he couldn't get those concentric rings out of his mind. Midafternoon, he received a message from Nurius sending him a report plastered in Federation and Starfleet logos, and Amal Safadi's name, which, on reading, told him that Federation figures agreed not with his new data, but with the previously accepted model that put the blast range at 9.7 light-years, and the pace of the nova at the original rate. He was puzzled, but he respected Safadi, and the people at Cambridge, and so he decided that he had made a mistake. It was hard, sometimes, working alone, like wandering through a maze where you frequently went down the wrong path and then had to go right back to the beginning. He had wandered many such mazes on the various family estates over the years. Sometimes he still had nightmares about them. He considered whether his research student might be able to help, and then thought that bringing her up to speed would be too much distraction. Instead, he decided to get a new set of readings, and run the model again, from a fresh dataset. In the meantime, he would try to do what Nurius had suggested, and put the whole thing out of his mind.

But whenever he closed his eyes, he saw Romulus consumed, and he saw all the people left behind.

After Vritet left his office, Nurius was extremely busy. He went to speak to the two Tal Shiar agents who had been installed on Vritet's corridor some months back. They examined Vritet's model with interest and sent Nurius a report that they told him was written by Doctor Safadi, at the Cambridge Institute of Astronomy on Earth, which had, coincidentally, arrived earlier that morning, and which showed that Vritet was certainly mistaken. Nurius had no reason to ignore their request to pass the report on to Vritet. And once he had done that, he put in a request for a transfer to a research institute on a remote world halfway across the quadrant, where his daughter had settled some years ago. Nurius, at least, did not doubt Vritet's genius, and made haste to be gone from Romulus by the end of the year. (He survived long enough to retire in some comfort, until a bite from a hunting hound went septic. Problems with maintaining supply lines to his new home meant that the necessary drugs were not available, and he died within days, a secondary victim of the times in which he lived. But at least he escaped Romulus.)

7

Admiral's Log: It is a scant six weeks since I first heard the name Olivia Quest, and now it seems to be everywhere. I believe this is not simply a matter of perception. The councilor has wasted no time since her election, and—remarkably, some would say, for a politician—has gotten to work immediately in keeping her chief campaign promise, to set up a committee to scrutinize the relief mission. A number of other councilors—not all of whom represent worlds close to the Neutral Zone—have put their support behind her, and, as a result, the committee, which comprises half a dozen councilors, is now well established. My office at Starfleet Command has been approached for full access to files and staff. This is a not inconsiderable burden for my already very busy teams, who now increasingly find themselves facing sudden requests for information, or to attend interviews with the committee. I do resent these incursions on their time, when we are overstretched, and on what seems, from this distance, to be meddling on Quest's part. We have a clear and difficult task to perform, one of an unprecedented nature, and naturally mistakes are likely to be made. Mistakes are, after all, how we learn. The mission is not served—and the staff not rewarded for their herculean efforts—by a sense that a group of politicians are watching over their shoulders, eager to interpret any misstep as evidence that the mission is out of hand.

Curious about Quest, I asked Raffi to assemble her election speeches into a compilation for me to see. I confess I found these concerning viewing. The phrase "Romulan space is better for Romulans" appeared with depressing regularity, and I understand from Raffi that it has gained some considerable currency since, not only within political circles—from people who should know better—but among the general population. I find sentiments such as these narrow and even reprehensible. The best place for any person is a place where they can live in peace. I am not personally inclined to indulge Councilor Quest but, nevertheless, at the request of Victor Bordson, I have been reflecting upon where this mission has hitherto been most successful, so that representatives from the Federation Council might see that the work we do is achieving measurable results. As ever, I am able to rely on Commander La Forge to be able to demonstrate excellence and achievement, and I have therefore advised that Councilor Quest and her colleagues begin by visiting the shipyards at Utopia Planitia, to see the scale of the operation there, and the success that Commanders La Forge and Mackenzie have had in implementing their plans for upscaling production. My sense is that technological breakthroughs such as these are a concrete and straightforward way in which people can see that the Federation is gaining benefits from this mission.

Admiral Bordson advises me that while technological achievements are certain to impress Quest, others on the committee will be looking at the relief effort to see how the mission fares. We have many achievements to report: tens of thousands of Romulans ferried from one world within the Empire to another, but naturally Bordson is keen to demonstrate that my gamble of settling Romulans in Federation space can work. After close consultation with Raffi and Koli—and, I must admit, our resident Romulan, Lieutenant Tajuth— I am taking our core of ten ships, including the *Verity*, to Inxtis, a world close to the Neutral Zone, whose inhabitants are to be relocated to Federation space. The people on the Federation world of Vashti, in the Qiris Sector, have offered to welcome these refugees, and have been preparing facilities for them. My hope is that this mission will provide us with the "success story" we need to address the concerns being raised by the committee, and, not incidentally, continue to justify the policy of moving Romulans into Federation territory. I do not underestimate the challenges of introducing a Romulan population into Federation colonies, but I believe that with dedication and intelligence, and the appropriate support, these situations can be managed in such a way as to allow the settlers to flourish on their new worlds.

Hostility between Federation citizens and Romulans is understandable. Centuries of mistrust lie between us, and the Romulan habit of secrecy is so deeply ingrained that one might almost call it an instinct. But I remain optimistic that somewhere within Romulan space there are people who believe that this mission can succeed in its wider goal of bringing about friendship and understanding between our two great civilizations.

Utopia Planitia shipyards
Mars

Olivia Quest knew that she was ruffling feathers, and, frankly, she didn't give a damn. She was intelligent and ambitious, but she was also the product of a small and easily overlooked world. Her ambition had, early on, outstripped what she could do with her family's agricultural holdings. A brief period studying on Earth for a doctorate in xenoagronomy had opened her eyes to the wider Federation of which Estelen was a member. As the years passed, she became increasingly and deeply frustrated with the structural imbalances she saw in the Federation. For a society that prided itself on its inclusiveness and equality, there was, she knew, an unstated hierarchy at work. The founding worlds—Vulcan, Earth, Andor, Tellar—all held considerable sway. Quest understood that they had the weight of history behind them—not to mention size of population—but these facts, surely, should not be allowed to give them such influence over the destiny of other worlds? Yet what could these smaller worlds do? The Big Four had the informal means by which they brought members into the Federation, making the new blood beholden to them. How could a small world, like hers, combat this?

Quest had not been surprised, during her first months as a Federation councilor, to learn how many others from small worlds shared her opinion. During private conversations in quiet corners at social functions, or in confidences exchanged at dinner parties, person after person from world after world told her of their frustrations at how the Big Four pushed through policy; how lip service was paid to them, but that their concerns were often passed over and forgotten when one of the founding worlds had a more important concern.

Take this Romulan relief mission. That told you everything you wanted to know. Many of the small worlds along the Neutral Zone were concerned by the sudden influx of Romulans. Some were frankly terrified that they would find themselves pressured into accepting considerable numbers of refugees among communities who could never love a Romulan. What would this mean for the stability of their worlds? Where had the promised infrastructure projects gone? Why were the replicators and archi-printers busy producing homes for Romulans? The spaceport on Nytis was in desperate need of renovation, and the promised transporter links between the two hemispheres of B'rq were going unbuilt. Hadn't there been a plan to terraform another three of t'Lottei's fifteen moons? What had happened there? Sometimes it seemed to these small worlds that the big powers felt they had more in common with Romulus than with the people of their own Federation. This was not right, many were saying this, more and more openly. This was unjust. Quest was here to do something about it, and she found that among the many tiny worlds that comprised the Federation, she had allies. She was here not simply to ask questions—she was here to get answers.

The committee that she had promised to establish had taken off even more rapidly than she could have hoped. She had expected stonewalling, but the head honchos at Starfleet Command had proven surprisingly willing to give her access. She had spent a week on Earth, following Commander Gbowee, and her helpful shadow, Lieutenant Kaul. Other senior players in the Romulan mission had also been very useful: T'Kautunn sent her such detailed and meticulous overviews of the fleet's schedules that she almost suspected him of trying to overload her with data. But above all, Quest longed to bring the public face of the whole mission—Admiral Picard—in front of her committee. (Imagine the vids! The 'casts would be delighted with her!) But she knew that this would have to wait until she had significantly more political capital. Picard was much admired, much respected. She would look like she was overreaching; she might look as if she had become overly self-satisfied. Who was she, after all? A junior councilor from a small farming world on the border. It could wait. In the meantime, her inquiries were taking her to Mars.

Quest had multiple degrees in engineering and was experienced in the kind of targeted terraforming projects that made her world viable. She was therefore confident when interviewing engineers and scientists; she would not be fazed. Sometimes they tried to blind politicians with technical language, but this wasn't going to work with her. And, in all honesty, she was excited to see the shipyards at Utopia Planitia. She was, she knew, a product of her civilization: she was Federation trained; she believed in the transforming potential of science and technology; she believed that groups of diverse people could band together to achieve great things. But she was sick of not having her chance to be on the inside, making policy, deciding what projects were pushed through. Now was her chance. She believed it was her duty too. She was here to serve her world, and those worlds that shared her sense of grievance and dispossession, and therefore give them back their voice.

Arriving on Mars, she was greeted by the project leads, Commander Geordi La Forge and Commander Estella Mackenzie. They began the tour of the groundside facilities. Quest was, quite simply, stunned by the scale of what she saw. She was not pleased.

"So far, most of our work has been refitting existing ships," said La Forge as he walked her through one of the vast hangars where pieces of hulls were being tested, "but ultimately the intent is to produce a fleet of purpose-built ships."

"What sort of numbers are we talking about?" said Quest.

"Between fifteen hundred and two thousand ships over the next year. Eventually ten thousand ships will be built."

Quest stopped dead in her tracks. Her mouth fell open. Her homeworld had fifteen decent-sized but increasingly elderly vessels at its disposal. *All this,* she thought, *for Romulans. Where are* our *new ships? What are we getting from this?*

La Forge, mistaking the nature of her surprise, grinned and said, "Pretty impressive, huh?"

"I am amazed," Quest said, "at how quickly you have been able to get this operation up and running. Any trouble getting the resources?"

"Well, it's been a major task, obviously," said La Forge, "but Starfleet has always come through."

"Has it?" Quest said dryly. How good it was, to have friends in high places.

"The biggest worry," said Mackenzie, "has been the workforce. Making sure we have enough labor to get the work done."

"So we had to get creative," La Forge offered.

"Oh yes," said Quest, "I've been hearing a lot about this. Advances in robotics, I understand?"

La Forge and Mackenzie shared a look of great pride and contentment. "More than that," said Mackenzie. "Come over here, Councilor."

Quest followed the engineers to a gallery that overlooked a long production line. She watched a dozen people moving around. She had seen many production lines—watched sorting lines on her family's large farms, looking for efficiencies in time and motion—and she grasped immediately that something was different here. After a moment, she realized exactly what it was: it was the figures. Not the speed of their movement, although that was impressive enough, but their *uniformity.* "Are these . . ."

"The Daystrom A500," said La Forge proudly. "The most advanced synthetic yet created. Well," he said, "they're not Data."

Quest stared down at the machines that she had taken for living beings. "These are remarkable . . ."

"Aren't they?"

"They're not . . ." She hesitated over the word. "*Sentient?*"

"What?" La Forge quickly disabused her of that idea. "Oh no. No! Data was unique in that respect. You should go and see Bruce Maddox at the Daystrom Institute. See the synth production facilities there."

"I will. I shall." Quest pulled her gaze away, remembered why she was there. "I have to ask again, though—this is the point of my inquiry, after all—isn't this all a huge drain on resources? From other projects, I mean. Haven't various projects here on Mars been put on hold? Some even canceled?"

La Forge said, "We all knew when we signed up for this mission that a lot of things would have to be put on hold. But it's the right choice—"

"It must be hard, though, to have your research put on the back burner while everything shifts over to this. How did people here respond to this change in priorities?"

She did not miss them exchanging a look. "Engineers are practical people," said Mackenzie. "There's no point coming up with innovative materials for deep-space exploration vessels if deep-space exploration is a secondary concern right now. We all like to see our work in use—"

"Well, you raise an important point there, Commander," Quest said. "Plenty of people have been asking how much of Starfleet's core mission has to stop in order to support this work. And whether it's right for such a large proportion of Federation resources to be poured into . . ." She let the end of her sentence hang in the air.

"Helping Romulans?" said La Forge. He was frowning.

"We've been enemies a long time," said Quest. "Is it wise, to throw away an advantage?"

"I guess compassion often looks foolish," said La Forge. "I know I for one don't mind looking foolish, now and then." He gave a disarming laugh. "I guess I'm old-fashioned in that way."

"I'm not talking about leaving them to *die*, Commander!" Quest said. "I hope you don't think I meant that! But we have to keep on asking whether this is the best use of our resources. It's not as if the Romulans have welcomed our efforts with open arms, now, is it?"

"You'd need to talk to Admiral Picard about that," said La Forge. "I've not been out there. My job is to work on ways to build as many ships as possible, as quickly as possible. The quicker we get those people to safety, the quicker we can get back to what we were doing before."

Quest looked down again at the production line, and marveled. "I think we all know that nothing will be how it was before."

VERITY

As the months passed, Picard had found that arriving at each new threatened world brought a particular kind of intellectual and emotional struggle. This came from the fact that you had to keep your distance from the fear and despair with which you were confronted, while still resolutely maintaining the hope and the focus to alleviate the distress. He, Koli, and Raffi had talked about this balance often, and he sometimes received missives from Deanna Troi on the subject. For himself, work was the answer: being solidly and actively involved in this mission, at every level. Hope alone was insufficient. If it did not translate into concrete, planned, and targeted action, then it was nothing more than fine words, and those meant nothing to these poor exiles. Above all, he knew, despair was not an option. The Starfleet uniform provided a significant shield that permitted one some aloofness, especially to Romulans, but that also signaled that help was here.

Still, arriving at yet another world to be greeted by the sight of thousands upon thousands of frightened, dispossessed people was not easily borne. If Picard had been a different kind of man, he might have begun to relish the role of savior. But each face he saw—each child too dulled to be able to play, each old person with one hand pressed against a cheek as if that might offer some protection from the chaos all around—each of these humbled him. Sometimes, in the quiet of night, he would be reading through reports from all across this vast mission—Gbowee, T'Kautunn, La Forge, Clancy—and he would find himself deeply and acutely daunted.

The simple impossibility of the task that they had set for themselves—that he had set for himself—would be suddenly overwhelming. He felt beset by the requests from juniors, the questions of superiors, the demands of politicians and officials. The task was so great—was he sufficient?

In his heart, Picard had no answer to this, and suspected that only history would be able to judge what was being done during these days. He could only do what he believed was required. And he would put his doubts aside, and find some equilibrium, remind himself that there was a world beyond those lost sad souls. He would put down the reports and listen to some music; Brahms, perhaps, *Ein Deutsches Requiem*. He would find consolation in the reminder that all flesh was as grass, that in the end all our striving came to nothing, but that in that brief aching and vivid time that we call life, one must do all that was possible to protect, conserve, and nurture this phenomenon of life. Do all in one's power to help it flourish. Whether he was sufficient would be decided in time. For now—he would continue to bring relief to those in need.

He brought the *Verity* to Inxtis with hope, as he arrived at all worlds that it had been his privilege to visit. The *Starship Nightingale* had already been at Inxtis for a fortnight, and its captain, Jex Pechey, had been sending daily reports. All signs, Pechey reported, were positive. The population of Inxtis seemed less restive than other places they had visited, calmer, somehow, as if trusting that the rescue would come through in time. The reports from Vashti, the Federation world in the Qiris Sector that these people would soon be calling home, were, quite frankly, a joy to read. Clear plans had been laid out, they would have ample housing and facilities. And, apparently there was genuine excitement among the locals at welcoming the Romulans. Picard felt a sense of pride at these reports, sensing that the days of their apprenticeship were coming to an end, and that as they became more experienced, the mission would progress ever more smoothly. At Raffi's suggestion, and with Koli's blessing, Picard had suggested Bordson send a few news organizations to Vashti to report on the work being done. Still, none of this removed the fact that he would soon have yet another close encounter with the realities of frightened, poverty-stricken people.

"*Admiral,*" said Raffi's voice on the comm. "*We're now in orbit over Inxtis. We've received a communication from one of the settlements—Sordsol Township. We are invited to meet someone named Zani.*"

He went down to the transporter room, where Raffi and Tajuth were waiting. "Zani?" he said to Raffi. "Any idea who this might be?"

Raffi shook her head, nodded toward Tajuth, and put a finger to her lips.

"Yeah, I have a hunch about that," she said. "But let's keep it close for the moment."

Sordsol Township
Inxtis

Inxtis surprised Picard immediately. Beaming down with Raffi and Tajuth, he found himself standing in a long and pleasant valley. A wide slow river ran through; the fields on the gentle slopes were heavy with the harvest. The world's sun shone lovingly down. It was the very end of summer, in a temperate region, and the greens all around were on the cusp. Picard caught the first hints of red and yellow and brown in the leaves of the trees. In a few weeks, he thought, he might return here to see that most glorious sight: a full and rich autumn. The poignancy of this was almost unbearable. This harvest that he could see would not be taken in; this autumn would be the last for Inxtis. This world was damned, and not through any crime or sin, but through an event on a cosmic, stellar scale. This time, he thought, the fault *was* in the stars.

Raffi, ever alert to the immediacy of her surroundings, checked her tricorder and said, "Numerous life signs. We must be on the edge of the township."

Picard followed her, Tajuth behind, wondering where the buildings were. They saw a huge tree ahead, multitrunked, like a banyan tree, but with the individual trunks much wider, and much farther apart. Here he saw the first signs of civilization: wooden decks, interlocked, lay around the trunks, and hanging from the branches and between the trunks were wide sheer nets. Beyond other trunks, he saw other wooden decks, and behind the sheer nets, he saw the dark shapes of figures moving swiftly. He heard voices from amidst the trees, singing, speaking, and the sound of children playing. He understood, *these* were the homes.

Picard took a moment to orient himself. He had, over the past couple of years, become used to the claustrophobic nature of Romulan homes; the back doors and hidden passages that concealed even members of the same family from each other, as if the ties that would naturally bind each Romulan to the other must be disrupted, and a veil of secrecy thrown between each and every one of them. Doors, and partitions, and sound barriers, anything to prevent someone in one room knowing whether anyone was in the room next door. But this, here—this was the complete opposite. A house that lay open to all comers: that advertised its inhabitants, that let their voices carry on the air. How had this happened? What made them feel so secure, to live in this way, when so many other Romulans lived with such a sense of palpable fear?

As they came closer, they saw a very old Romulan woman sitting on a barrel, her back against the trunk of a tree almost as gnarled as she was. She saw them, sat up, placing her hands firmly upon her knees, and called out, "Zani! The humans are here! And they've been stupid enough to bring a damned *tok'tzat* with them!"

A voice from behind the nets called out, "I'm coming, Shai! Keep an eye on the *tok'tzat*!"

Picard heard Tajuth mutter something that from the plosives was surely a curse. Picard's grasp of Romulan profanity had improved markedly in recent months, but some dialects were still a mystery to him, and Tajuth's voice, Picard noticed, had gone oddly nasal, as if he had fallen back on some childhood accent. Raffi, hearing, smiled, as if something had been confirmed to her.

"Well, Raffi?" Picard said.

"Qowat Milat," she murmured. "Well, I never thought I'd see this . . ."

"Say that again, please, Commander."

She repeated the words, and he tried them on his tongue. *Qowat Milat.* "Not bad!"

"Who are they exactly, Raffi?"

"They're nuns, JL. Warrior nuns." Putting her hand on his arm, she moved him away from Tajuth. "Guardians of truth. Traditional enemies of the Tal Shiar. Look at Tajuth. Red alert. A secret policeman's lot is not a happy one."

And, indeed, Tajuth—usually so unreadable—was manifestly on guard, his hand resting upon his weapon.

"Told you he was Tal Shiar," said Raffi smugly. "They *hate* the Qowat Milat, and the feeling is mutual."

The old woman, on her barrel, was watching Tajuth with her lip curled. She looked so fierce that Picard was not entirely sure that he would bet against her if it came to blows.

"What makes them such enemies, Raffi?"

"Well, these things are always complicated, but, as I understand it, there's a fundamental difference in ideology. The Qowat Milat follow what they call the way of absolute candor . . ."

"What does that mean?"

One of the nets slung between the trees was pushed back, and a nun, younger than the one sitting on watch, came out, wiping floured hands upon her skirts. Raffi said, "I guess we're about to find out."

Picard glanced back at Tajuth. No, not a happy man. "Absolute candor. That doesn't sound very Romulan."

"And yet here they are," said Raffi. "It's a funny old universe, isn't it?"

"Warrior nuns. Romulan warrior nuns. You know, Raffi, I am grateful."

"Grateful?"

"That the universe can still delight me."

The nun moved, with speed and grace, to greet her visitors. Standing in front of Picard, she held her hands together, palm to palm, and then opened them, slowly and with great care, as if they were a book, or as if she was offering something; her heart, perhaps. "Admiral Picard."

"Zani?" he said, uncertainly.

She smiled. "Yes, I am Zani. Our house and our hearts are open to you, Picard."

Picard was suddenly, and deeply, moved. He had not realized, until this moment, how often, on arrival at these worlds, he had been greeted with anger, demands, resentment, hostility. It was not that he expected gratitude—he had not taken on this mission for rewards or thanks—but he had hoped for moments of amity. Now it was being offered. Here, on this quiet and lovely world, a Romulan had offered the hand of friendship. Carefully, he copied her gesture: pressed his hands together; opened them to her. He tried to think of some suitable words. "*Jolan tru*," he said. "We come in friendship, and with open hands."

She looked delighted. She and Raffi exchanged the gesture, and Raffi said, "Qowat Milat. I am . . . Well. Wow."

Zani laughed, a full laugh straight from the depths of her belly. Then her eye fell on Tajuth. "You are welcome, Starfleet—despite the company you keep."

They did not get a chance to discuss this further. Something tiny but very fast-moving came rushing out of the house, pushing itself in the middle of their group. Picard, looking down, saw a boy; about four or five years of age, had he been human—small, serious, and extremely grubby.

"Are these the humans?" said the child. He looked steadily at Picard. "They're ugly."

"Thank you," said Picard gravely.

"Absolute candor," Raffi reminded him.

"I believe we were both included in that assessment, Raffi." Awkwardly, Picard bent down on one knee. "Well, young man," he said. "I am Admiral Jean-Luc Picard. And who are you?"

"Elnor," said the boy. "I wanted a present."

Raffi laughed. Picard panicked. "Um. Do you like books?"

"Wow, JL," said Raffi, "you're a natural . . ." She glanced at Zani. "That was a lie. Sorry."

Zani nodded to show she understood the curious human tendency toward sarcasm. The boy stared at Picard. "Yes," he said. "I like books." He shoved his filthy little hand into Picard's and began to pull him toward the house. "You can come and read to me."

Picard glanced over his shoulder to Zani, who said, "Yes, follow Elnor. He knows the way." She looked back at Tajuth. "Your Tal Shiar friend can come too, if he's feeling brave."

They were welcomed into the house beneath the trees. There were women everywhere; old and young, and girls too, some wearing the same robes as the older women, but in a paler shade of blue. Postulants, Picard thought, or novices, if the Qowat Milat had such gradations. They did not strike him as the kind of people that would trouble themselves with such hierarchies. The convent—for such, he saw now, was the nature of the place—was a hive of activity, and while nobody seemed to be issuing orders, everyone seemed clear on the tasks that needed to be done. The new arrivals sparked considerable curiosity, and the presence of Tajuth attracted considerable amusement.

"Is he really here for supper?"

"Don't tell him, Sister, but he *is* supper."

Picard suppressed a smile; Raffi was less diplomatic. The expression on her face mirrored what Picard was feeling: delight that this place existed; amazement that it was so ineffably, so completely *Romulan*. After so many months of navigating the choppy waters of Romulan sensibilities and secrecies, the place was like a glass of cool, clear water.

Zani took them through into a common area. The space was clearly being made ready for people to eat together. At one end, a group of five women were putting away their weaving; others were pulling back net curtains to open the area up farther. As Picard watched, younger girls began to carry through low round tables, and set them around the room. Eight tables all together, set around to form another circle. Circles upon circles. Other women dashed around, setting the tables with plates and dishes and cutlery, and small pots filled with tiny bright sweet-scented flowers. From beyond the far end of the area, Picard caught the tantalizing smell of cooking. The kitchen, he guessed. He heard voices, busy and chattering, "Do the humans eat this kind of thing?" The laughter of women.

Picard followed Zani as she led them around the tables. The boy's hand was still shoved stickily into his. He realized now that he had seen no other men. Only himself, and Tajuth—who was still attracting attention and the odd hoot of derision—and the child, Elnor. Were there no men at all here? How had the boy ended up among them? Was it permitted in some way?

They came to the table closest to the kitchen space. There were no chairs. Picard glanced at Raffi, who shrugged. "Don't ask me," she murmured. "I thought they were a legend until about half an hour ago."

"I'd hate to offend," he murmured back.

"I kind of get the feeling they'd tell you straight out if you did that."

The boy had started tugging Zani's hand. "Can I stay up?" he said.

"It's getting late," said Zani. "Look!" She pointed through the curtains, now tinted with a red glow. "The sun is setting."

"I want to look at the humans," said Elnor firmly. There was no whining or pleading. He simply stated this as a fact. "I want to eat supper with you."

"But you are very small," said Zani. "And that means that you need more sleep. Also, you are happier in the mornings if you go to bed early. You are not pleasant company when you stay up late."

The boy frowned. This assessment clearly had the unmistakable ring of truth.

"If I stay up late tonight," he said, "I promise to go to bed earlier tomorrow."

Zani reached over to tuck a strand of the boy's long, dark hair behind his ear. "Promises are prisons, Elnor," she chided him. "Do not take the risk of walking blindly into a lie."

"But I want to stay up," he said again. He looked at Picard. "I think you should tell her I can stay up."

Picard was aware of Raffi behind him, enjoying this—damn her. She was a mother; she had probably suffered through this battle numerous times and was enjoying being a bystander for once. "I think," he said to the boy, "that you should obey Zani."

"Oh no," said Zani quickly. "I would never require obedience from anyone."

"Then . . ." He looked at Zani for guidance, not wishing to interfere with her way of bringing up the child, but she was not forthcoming. He thought for a moment. Compromise, he thought. That was what he would want to teach a child. How to negotiate; how to compromise. "I think that you should stay for a little while, and then go."

"But I want to stay until everyone else goes to bed."

"And yet Zani wants you to go earlier. So let us find a way that will make both you and Zani happy. You said that you liked books."

"Yes . . ." said Elnor, with some suspicion.

"If you go to bed when Zani asks, I will read something to you. A human story."

"Story?"

"A fiction. A tale. Something made up."

"A lie?" The boy looked puzzled.

"No," said Picard gently. "A human way of telling certain truths."

Elnor thought for a while. "Very well," he said. "We will eat together, and when Zani says so, I will go to bed. And you will read something to me."

Elnor sat down on the floor. He reached up to tug at Picard's sleeve until Picard sat down next to him. Zani took her place at Picard's other side. Raffi next to her. Zani indicated to Tajuth to take his place opposite her. "Sit there," she said, "where I can see you."

Tajuth, stiffly, did as he was asked. He did not look happy. He looked even less happy when the old woman who had been keeping watch for their arrival came and sat down next to him. "There you are, *tok'tzat*. Now, behave yourself. I don't want my supper spoiled."

Others were beginning to take their places. Soon the hall was full of women. And then the food came: a thick and spicy stew that reminded Picard of the kind of lamb dish one might eat somewhere in the Mediterranean, accompanied by another made from pulses that he thought was very like a dahl. There were huge round flatbreads, cut into triangles; *prezhan*, Zani called them. Many of the women did not bother with spoons or forks, and simply dug in with the bread, spooning up the food. Raffi did the same, eating with obvious pleasure. Tajuth picked at pieces of bread and drank only water. Picard was offered, and took, a pale yellow wine that he was sure his family would have been proud to produce. Raffi accepted cup after cup. Zani asked perceptive questions about the mission, and Picard found himself answering frankly and openly. He talked in some detail about the multiple frustrations of juggling both the expectations of his superiors, and of trying to navigate the conflicting messages that came from Romulan officials.

"A little more frankness all around would do no harm," she said, and he agreed.

The plates were gathered up and taken out, and then dessert came.

"Ah," said Zani, a gleam in her eye. "Have you tried *hanifak* before, Admiral?"

"I'm not sure I know what it is," he said.

A plate was set down in the middle of the table, piled high with candies. Each was formed into a small square, and there were many different colors. The effect was bright and cheerful.

Picard reached to take one, pressing it gently between thumb and forefinger. It felt slightly soft, like marzipan. Zani took one, popped it into her mouth. "So sweet," she said. "I shall miss this."

Picard had found, over the long months of this mission, that there were simple moments that pierced him suddenly, as if he had been stabbed. A woman eating a favorite treat, not knowing whether she would be able to find them again in the place where she was going. Such losses, he thought, which seemed so small, the comforts and pleasures of life—these would be the hardest to replicate. They might never be replaced. He put the *hanifak* into his mouth. She was right; it was so very sweet.

Picard made sure Elnor got to bed, as he promised, and recited to him some of *The Little Prince* that he remembered. The tale of a lost and lonely little boy, who saw things differently from those around him, finding a home in the stars. Picard had loved it as a child, and asked his mother to read it to him many times. He watched as Elnor's eyes grew heavy, the small fist on the pillow slackening and releasing, sleep taking him. He stopped and, very carefully, touched the child's brow, as if to bestow a blessing. Then he went back to the common room. Tajuth had gone back to the ship. Raffi was sitting with Shai and a few of her cronies, playing a card game that looked both complicated and merciless. He watched for a while, and then went in search of Zani.

He found her sitting on a bench outside close to the tree trunk, looking out across their lands. It was long past sunset. The sky was inky, and a breeze was lifting, sending the nets all around drifting. Lamps were lit, great round lamps that showed pathways through the valley. The trees, too, were gleaming. From somewhere farther, he heard the gentle tinkle of wind chimes. Seeing Zani, he went to join her.

"The boy's asleep," he said, sitting down next to her.

"Good," she said.

"He liked the story I told, although I fear he may have thought it was all true."

They sat companionably for a while, looking out across the gardens.

Under the lamps, a small group of women had gathered together to perform a set of exercises, rather like *tai chi*, Picard thought. He breathed, deeply; night flowers were blooming and releasing their scent. The whole place had a blissful feel to it.

"This has been a good home," she said. "But times have changed, and to try to remain here would be self-deception. I regret, though, that we shall not have a chance to bring in the harvest. It is a great waste."

A sadness washed over Picard at the thought of all the harvests that would not be gathered as this tragedy unfolded; fruits and crops left to rot on abandoned worlds, the people who had cared for them dragged far, far away. And, at last, the great fire that would consume them all . . .

He collected himself. "It has not escaped my notice," he said, "that you're all women."

"Yes, indeed." A smile quirked across her face. "No surprise to me that Elnor took to you. He rarely sees men."

"There was Tajuth . . ."

She gave him a look that said: *Unlikely.*

"How did Elnor come to be with you?"

Her face saddened. "He was left with us, abandoned. If there is a mother or father still alive, we don't know. The intention was to find him a home, as quickly as we could—our houses don't permit males, not even boys. But when a home is not to be found, what is to be done? He was safe with us, and so I decided he should remain."

"You broke the rules of your order?"

"Yes, I broke the rules, and I shall continue breaking them as long as Elnor remains safe. Are you shocked, Admiral?" She gave him an amused glance. "I don't know a great deal about Starfleet, but you do seem fond of rules and regulations."

"I believe," he said, "that my superiors might wish I was more of a stickler for them."

"Oh," she said, in surprise, "do you have superiors?"

"One or two."

"I imagined you were the leader."

He was both touched by the compliment and diverted at the thought. And surprised, to some extent, at her unworldliness in this respect. She had otherwise struck him as very practical, very grounded. Perhaps it was simply that Starfleet had, until recently, meant nothing to her.

"Did you suffer consequences for your decision to protect the boy, Zani?"

"Consequences? None that mattered to me. Some disapproval from some of the sisters, but I am more than used to hearing their opinions voiced, and I am perfectly capable of not listening. Refusing to help Elnor would have been worse. What is the purpose of rules," she said, "if they do nothing to protect the vulnerable—no, more, *succor* the vulnerable. Protection is not enough. Nurture is also necessary. Elnor is nurtured. Any rule that prevented that is not worth obeying."

Listening to her words, Picard felt a deep sense of hope and love—call it fraternity, or sorority, or simply fellow feeling—envelop him. These were words, he realized, that he had been longing to hear said. From his superiors he heard, be diplomatic, consider the political ramifications; from the Romulans he met he received demands, anger, hostility. And yet it all seemed so simple to him: it was incumbent on them to use all their talents, skills, and resources to bring relief. To help the helpless. At last, here on a hillside looking down at a Romulan world, someone had spoken straight to his heart.

"Yes," he said. "Yes. That is how it is."

She smiled at him. "Certainly not what I expected to hear from a Starfleet officer."

"There is no purpose to Starfleet if it cannot fulfill this function," he said firmly. "I will give everything to this mission. There is no more important task."

From down in the valley, there came soft singing. Zani said, "I will help you however I can."

He had grasped, already, that Qowat Milat did not make promises. This he understood to be a statement of fact, of clear intent. Once again, he was moved. He had come this far, and at last he found someone who shared his values. He had hoped that there would be a kindred spirit among the Romulans—and he had been proved right. He must not forget this, he thought; he must not fail to hope.

8

Admiral's Log: We have begun the evacuation of Inxtis, and Zani has been as good as her word in offering us all the assistance that we require. The Qowat Milat have been everywhere: soothing tempers, calming fears, persuading even the most intransigent to board our ships. My heart grieves to see this beautiful planet abandoned, to think of the homes that have been left behind, and the communities that have been transplanted. If I were a resident here, I might not have left willingly. But it seems that the Qowat Milat inspire trust. I imagine this has been years in the making: open houses to which people can come when they are lost, or friendless, or—I should guess—in trouble with the Tal Shiar. The rivalry between them is a sight to behold. Tajuth did not want them on board and approached his ambassador to request it. I will forgive him for going behind my back: they are rather daunting en masse. Having watched a little more of the practices of these women, I understand now that they are true warriors. Old Sister Shai's wooden staff is not simply to help her walk but conceals a rather sharp and deadly blade. I see many of the sisters carrying these staffs, *tan galankhs*, they call them. Regulations state they should be surrendered before coming on board ship. I have no intention of asking, and neither does Raffi. A regulation that we are quietly ignoring.

Summer is rapidly coming to an end on Inxtis, and we hope to have the entire population on route to Vashti within the next two weeks. This task, often so grim, has seemed less heartbreaking this time, and for this we can only thank the Qowat Milat, for their patience and their courage. I can see how a mother in need might choose to leave her child with these women, and trust that the right thing would be done by him. Elnor is something of a permanent presence these days. He has pronounced *The Little Prince* "odd" but has nevertheless invited me to read more to him. I say "invited"; it was rather more in the nature of an instruction. I shall have to wrack my brains to recall what I liked to read as a boy. I was something of an eccentric child—but then, I suppose, so is Elnor.

Sordsol Township
Inxtis

Picard walked through the empty house in search of Zani. Lieutenant th'Kaothreq, in the transporter room, had told him that she had gone back down to the surface of Inxtis a few hours earlier, saying that she had forgotten something important.

"Zani!" he called as he walked between the trunks of the big old tree. The nets were gone, folded and packed, as was everything else that had helped make this place the busy house that he had first seen. Leaves were now drifting through forlorn, bare rooms. Picard walked through and out again into the garden, where he had sat with Zani on that first night, under the starlight and the lamplight. Some of the lanterns were still hanging, chains creaking in the breeze, never to be lit again. He walked on, down the path, until he reached the river. There, her skirts tied above her knees, stood Zani, up to her ankles in river water. She was skimming stones. They bounced—one, two, three, four.

"Zani!" he called out, waving when she turned to look at him.

She waved to him to join her. He stood on the bank and watched the stones, each one sending out ripples and shockwaves, ring upon ring that spread across the silver stream. After a moment or two, she came to join him on the bank.

"My favorite spot," she said. "I would often come here to think." She shivered and wrapped her shawl around her. "But it's cold in there today."

He put his hand upon her arm. "Let me take you home," he said. "Or a place that you can make home."

She turned back to the river and stretched up her arms, as if to touch the sky. "Thank you," she said, to the world she had lost. "You have been a good home. I will remember you as long as I am able." Then she said, "Time to go."

"Th'Kaothreq," he said. "Two to beam on board."

Within seconds, they were gone. The river ran on. The leaves drifted. And, in the valley, the wind chimes sang a song that would never be heard again.

DAYSTROM INSTITUTE
OKINAWA, EARTH

Olivia Quest left nothing to chance. The Daystrom Institute was likely to be interesting, yes, but she sent Danny, one of her aides, there first and waited to receive the account of his visit. He was a slick young man who never usually deigned to rise above an air of jaded cynicism. Quest often found this pose tiresome, but he was a master of press releases, and she also owed his family several favors after the help they had given her to get elected. When his report from the synth production facility arrived, it was unexpectedly gushing, and therefore of considerable interest to her.

Liv, you have got to get yourself over here ASAP. It's AMAZING. Bring the networks. Bring as many holo-cameras as you possibly can. PS happy to report that the sushi even in the cafeteria is AMAZING. Think you should move your office here TBH.

Ciao for now. Danny

Quest—who had developed a warm and friendly relationship with the press during her campaign for election and was always happy to provide them with curated content—quickly arranged passes and permits for the usual members of the fourth estate. They arrived in Okinawa with considerable fanfare: forty altogether, coming through in groups of four to the faint alarm of the director of the Institute, Sisra Koas, a pleasant if rather absent-minded and elderly Trill who allowed herself to be positioned exactly where Quest wanted her. Smiling, Quest didn't fail to notice that there were UFPHCR logos all over the place. Those guys didn't miss a trick . . .

Inside the main building, Quest's mask of enthusiasm was replaced by something much more genuine. Steering Director Koas gently but firmly, she hurried them past the usual sights, to get to the synths as quickly as possible. This involved a short monorail ride out to the far end of the campus, to a long, low building that she knew was the brand-new synthetics production facility. More UFPHCR logos. Starfleet logos. Where was the Council in all of this? Most strikingly, the whole place gleamed. It was spacious, it was staffed, and it was all brand-new. This, she thought bitterly, was where Estelen's new transporter links between the planet and its moons had gone. Earth got whatever it wanted. Quest entered the facility prepared to be angry. But she was too much of an engineer not to be blown away.

She had learned from her own researches that the facility could produce up to five synths at any given time. Koas led her past the bio-neural replication bays, the casing displays, and, at last, toward the five chambers where the final assembly of each synth happened. The place where they came to life—or to not-life, as the case may be. She had to remember that they were nonsentient. They were not alive; they were machines. A member of staff, standing by, ran them through the final initiation process, and they all stood and watched as one of the synths was switched on. It lay there in its chamber, inert. Then the eyes flickered, and opened, and gleamed gold. Quest almost gasped out loud. It was like watching a spell being cast. But then she looked more closely at the eyes and saw that they were flat, blank, without any spark. They saw; they even processed—but they did not *live*. They could act, could even decide—but they could not judge. There was no free will here, no freedom. This realization was almost a relief.

Lurking nearby was a tall man with a beleaguered expression. After watching the A500 perform a series of functions, like a wind-up toy, she crossed over to speak to him. "Doctor Maddox," she said, "I'm delighted to meet you. Your work here is very impressive—"

He jerked his head, as if to reject what she had said. "Credit where credit is due." He struck her as rather prissy. "The project owes a great deal to Commander Estella Mackenzie of Starfleet. She was the one who came up with the idea of combining her research into bio-neural circuitry with what we can do here at the Daystrom—"

"Of course . . ." Quest waved these niceties away, thereby unwittingly earning Maddox's contempt at her airiness toward the science and his irritation that his name was the one attached to this whole damn thing. "But the real breakthrough is here, isn't it?" she said. "These incredible creations of yours . . ." She gestured at the chambers all around. Another synth was being assembled, its arms being carefully attached to its trunk. "I have to say that machines like this would have a tremendous impact on my own homeworld of Estelen." She glanced across at the holo-cameras and smiled for anyone watching. "It's a farming colony—"

"Is it."

Suddenly, Quest grasped that this conversation was not unfolding as successfully as she might like. "I'm sure you can see how nonsentient synthetics would be useful on worlds like that."

"Yes, well, somebody has to do the dirty jobs."

Cameras whirred; Quest, with some effort, did not frown. "But seeing them now—seeing how complex they are, how sophisticated—well, why stop at manufacture or at farming? Surely you can see how revolutionary machines like this could be?"

"You'll have to enlighten me, Councilor. I merely spend my time building them."

She gave a bright smile. "They're being used for industrial applications, but why not domestic applications too? All kinds of work. A synth in every home! Your Daystrom A500s could be as ubiquitous as . . . well, as a replicator!"

A more unfortunate simile Quest could not have found. Maddox went very still. Quest, unaware of the bear trap opening in front of her, carried on blithely.

"You know, the more people who can see something in this project that will benefit not only, well"—she balked at saying *Romulans* so openly—"*others*, but will benefit people across the Federation, the more goodwill you earn. Not only from people like me, but from the public at large." She laughed. "Though of course it doesn't do any harm to keep people like me on your side—and looking at all this, I am. I am *very much* on your side."

Maddox stared at her with open dislike. "That's not the point of all this, though, is it?"

The cameras were watching. Quest blinked. "What do you mean?"

"Councilor Quest, I'm sorry to speak bluntly—"

Christ, she thought, *don't do that. There are journalists here . . .*

"—but I didn't get into research to please politicians. Nobody involved in research of any kind should be thinking about whether or not it pleases politicians. The work comes first. The work must always come first."

Quest gave a smile intended to smooth these unexpectedly ruffled feathers. "But political support is what gets you resources, Doctor Maddox—"

"Something that I find pretty repellent, to be honest."

"Repellent? What do you mean?"

He threw his hands up, exasperated. "I mean, the politicization of research like this! The politicization of *all* damn research! Don't you get what we're trying to do here?"

"You're trying to help the relief mission—"

He cut her off with an impatient wave of his hand. She would never forgive it. "We're trying to create *life* here!" he said. There were red blotches of color on his cheeks. "Not curry favor! Politicians like you come and go, you know. Research like this takes decades!"

Quest was, frankly, furious. The sheer damn nerve. Who the hell was this man anyway? Who the hell did he think he was? Sure, a respected scientist, and brilliant, by all accounts—but had anyone elected *him*? There was an arrogance in some circles of Starfleet, Quest thought; you got the sense that they considered themselves unaccountable to anyone. But they *were* accountable, and they had to remain accountable. Maddox's manner could not go unpunished, that was for sure, but Quest was far too canny an operator not to be mindful of the journalists all around, eager for a story. She considered carefully what to say.

"Well, I still think this is very fine work you're doing here," she said. "What an achievement, after decades of work, Doctor Maddox! What a legacy!" She turned to him. "A synth in every home!"

That hit, and hard. She heard good-natured laughter from all around and knew that would be the headline. She smiled and waved at the holo-cameras.

Maddox felt as false as the machines he had created. All through Quest's visit he had tried to keep cheerful; tried to keep up the pretense that he was enthusiastic about the work he was doing, but finally he had cracked. *A synth in every home.* He knew that her parting shot had been intended to wound, and she had certainly done the job. He stood in the darkened production room, staring at the synth currently under construction. The smooth face, too perfect, lacking any blemish to give it personality or uniqueness; the golden empty eyes, without any spark . . . A travesty of life. A joke. That was his work now: a joke. He was a punchline.

Hearing footsteps, he turned to see Agnes.

"Hey," she said. "How did it go?"

"Oh, she loved it all," he said. "She loved everything she saw."

Agnes came closer. Uncertainly, she said, "That's good, isn't it?"

"Yes, great, if what I wanted to do with my life is put a synth in every home. That's what she said, you know. That can be your legacy, Doctor Maddox. A synth in every home. *Shit!*" He banged his hand against the side of the table. The synth nearby did not react. There was nothing there, and there never would be. They were inert, a mockery of life; a mockery of his life's work. He closed his eyes.

He heard Agnes moving. "Bruce," she said, in a muffled voice. "I'm not the enemy."

Guilt spasmed through him. He turned to face her. She was chewing at her lip, looking at him apprehensively. She was so young, he thought, still so full of optimism, of hope. But hope for what? This was their work now. This was all that there would be for them. There would be nothing else. No new life. No offspring. Nothing. A dead end, for both of them.

He realized that she was crying. Very softly; she was trying hard to hide it from him. She was so smart he forgot, sometimes, that she was the student and he was the professor. He reached out to touch her wrist.

"Agnes . . ." he said. "Aggie. I'm sorry. I'm so sorry. This isn't your fault—"

"It's not that I think you're blaming me," she said. "I understand that you're angry. It's that you lose faith in yourself. I hate to see you like this."

He felt ashamed. She was so loyal; he didn't deserve this. He didn't deserve her . . . "Aggie, I . . ."

"This is an *opportunity*," she said fiercely. "You say she loved what she saw? Then use that! Use *her*! She's powerful, influential. She can put resources our way—"

"That's what she said," Maddox said bitterly. "But to do what? She wants miners, domestic servants, field hands. Labor, not life!" *Not Data*, he thought, aching for that perfect lost creation. Quest wouldn't understand these emotions; she wouldn't understand his glorious dream—to create synthetic life so beautiful, so perfectly imperfect, that it could not be distinguished from the real thing . . .

"Then give her that! Give her what she wants! You've built a bio-neuronic synthetic—everything else will be trivial, a question of specialization—"

"Aggie! This line of research won't go there!"

"You don't *know* that! Maybe it's a step on the way! Every synth we build is something new learned! Every synth we build is one more step toward the real goal . . . Don't you see? This *is* your work! Your real work! Everything we do, everything we have to hand over or is given to us—we can use that!" She reached out, took one of his hands in hers. "I believe in you," she said. "I believe that you can do this."

They were close now; he had never stood so close to her before or looked at her so clearly. She was lovely, wasn't she? She was so present, so *alive* . . . She leaned forward; kissed him. He accepted; reciprocated. For a few moments, it was blissful, uncomplicated, the most human thing imaginable. And then he sprang back. "Shit, Aggie, I'm sorry, I shouldn't have— *Shit*, what was I *thinking*!"

Her hand had been on his shoulder. She yanked it away, and pulled back, as if she had been slapped. Her face crumpled. She put her arms around herself, like armor. "I'm sorry to hear I'm so repellent—"

"God, Aggie, no; that's not what I meant!"

"I'm not some kind of *toy*! I have feelings, you know, I *feel* things. I'm not one of your damn plastic people!"

They're not mine, he thought, but said: "You're my *student*, for Christ's sake!"

"Bruce," she said. "*I* kissed *you*."

She moved toward him once again, laid one hand upon his chest, and the other upon his cheek, as if claiming possession. "I am not a child!"

No, he thought as they kissed again. She was not a child, not at all. She was . . . a partner, a confidante, a friend. Someone to trust; someone to believe in him; someone who understood. The kiss became hungry; deepened.

She came back to his apartment and stayed the night. In the morning, when he woke, he watched her, pressed against the pillow, snoring very softly. He tucked a falling strand of hair behind her ear. When she woke, they made pancakes. She danced around the kitchen, wearing his shirt, singing "Cloudbusting," and he thought: *You are the only person who has ever understood me. I can do this . . . with your help. I can do anything if you are beside me.*

VERITY

The Qowat Milat not only aided the evacuation of Inxtis, they eased the passage of the fleet to Vashti. Picard and his crew found that the usual round of complaints and quarrels were quickly dealt with and defused. They had, with the permission of the nuns, dispersed them in small groups so that there were a handful on each deck, ready to dispense advice, rulings, and anything else that the Romulan guests needed, but for some reason did not want to ask from Starfleet. The remaining women took a group of adjacent quarters on deck twelve, where, with Zani's quarters in the center, a temporary convent was formed. Here the women came to train, sing, and work. The whole deck was quickly thrown open: the doors to each cabin set not to close, nets thrown up at need, and one room had the furniture removed so that they could sit on the floor together and eat. Picard heard from other captains in the fleet that the same had happened on other ships. They set up schools, too, and day care. He was content to let them get on with things. It all seemed to work very well. He asked Koli to go around the ship, speaking to people, asking them to record short messages about their experiences so far. The resulting short vids were seized on with delight by Clancy at Starfleet Command, who tasked a small group of cadets to compile them into a documentary, showcasing the success of the mission.

They were seven weeks into their journey to Vashti before the first—and only serious—incident of the flight took place. He was receiving an update from Captain Pechey on the *Nightingale* when an urgent message came in from Raffi.

"Deck twelve, JL. As soon as you can."

He gave his apologies to Pechey and made his way down. Raffi came to meet him.

"What's the problem, Raffi?"

"One word. Tajuth."

She led him down the corridor toward the "abbey," explaining as they went. "It turns out that one of the people who came on board on Inxtis is wanted by the Tal Shiar," Raffi said. "The Qowat Milat gave him sanctuary eighteen months ago. Tajuth has somehow gotten wind of this, and decided to arrest this guy—"

"Any idea what he did?"

"Zani tells me that he was a cartoonist. Stupid pictures of politicians, that kind of thing. Only they touched a nerve. He got away from Romulus—Zani won't tell me how, but I get the impression of an underground railroad of some kind—and hid on Inxtis. The Tal Shiar don't go there much, as you might imagine. And now he's here on the *Verity* and Tajuth wants him."

"And the Qowat Milat are not helping with his inquiries, presumably?" said Picard.

"You could say that," said Raffi, and pointed ahead.

Picard saw six Qowat Milat, three rows of two, blocking the corridor, *tan galankhs* in hand. Standing in front of them, black clad and with his back to Picard, was the stiff figure of Tajuth. Peering over the block of nuns, Picard caught a glimpse of Zani, in her blue robes, standing tall and resolute outside the door to her quarters. "Oh, Tal Shiar," she said. "Please choose to live."

"Wow," murmured Raffi appreciatively. "They really *are* warriors."

Picard stepped forward. "Lieutenant Tajuth," he said calmly. "Can you explain what's happening here?"

Tajuth swung around. He was plainly angry. Picard had not seen him lose this much control before. "They're concealing a wanted criminal! These damn women—!"

"Thank you, that's enough." Picard peered past the implacable rows of nuns. "What are you hoping to achieve here, exactly?"

"I want him in custody."

"I don't think that's going to happen," said Picard.

"It shall! It *must*—"

"Lieutenant Tajuth," said Picard, "there are two ways past these women. I doubt you will be able to persuade them. And I will not permit the use of force."

"I demand that your security officers help me gain access! They are committing a crime against the Romulan government—"

"Let me be clear: You want me to shoot these women?" Picard shook his head. "You know as well as I do that that will not happen. This is, to all intents and purposes, a Qowat Milat province, and this is an internal Romulan matter. You're welcome to take the risk trying to enter—but you'll do it without Starfleet's assistance."

Tajuth wavered. Picard moved closer. "Let us talk about this in private," he said. "There is nothing to be achieved here, and a great deal of face to be lost."

Tajuth turned, and marched back down the corridor. Picard followed. From behind the armed nuns, he heard Elnor's voice, high and clear. "That *tok'tzat* is an idiot."

Picard could not fault the boy's assessment. In his ready room, he turned on Tajuth, eyes flashing. "This was wholly unnecessary. If you had concerns about anyone who had boarded this ship, you could—and should—have come first to me." He saw Tajuth's mouth open to protest and cut straight through. "Don't say that this was an internal matter. You were ready to ask for my help to shoot these women. And with the boy present!"

Tajuth tried to get himself back under control. "They are harboring a criminal."

"They are harboring someone who has irritated someone in your government—"

"His work lowers morale—"

"I imagine there is more lowering morale than a few drawings, however barbed. Your mistake, by the way," Picard went on, "was choosing to fight this battle over a political prisoner. If you'd come to me claiming they were protecting a murderer, you might have found me more sympathetic. But the Qowat Milat wouldn't do that, I imagine."

"You're very sympathetic to them, Admiral."

"They have been very helpful, Lieutenant," Picard said. "You're dismissed. I don't want to hear another word about this. If you want this man arrested, you can go through the appropriate channels when we reach Vashti. But don't try your luck again with the Qowat Milat." He sat down at his desk, and heard, rather than saw, Tajuth leave.

Later, Raffi groaned when he reported the conversation to her.

"So how's that killing with kindness going?" she said, with slight malice, he thought.

"I'm prepared to be patient," he replied.

"Uh-huh?" Raffi did not look convinced. "Well, I'm prepared to bet on the death of the universe happening first."

But there was no more trouble on that voyage.

ROMULAN ASTROPHYSICAL ACADEMY
ROMULUS

Nokim Vritet did not like having his routines disrupted, so he had been very unhappy when the small café where he ate his breakfast every morning had suddenly closed. Nobody cooked *votlik* eggs the way that old Chimiu cooked them; nobody got the consistency right (neither too runny nor too thick) or used the right amount of gray pepper. It was most annoying. But there it was. Vritet had come out from his apartment one morning, only to find that the little eatery was locked and dark, and no matter how much he hammered on the door, Chimiu did not appear, grousing and grumbling as he always did. Eventually the woman in the flat upstairs leaned out of her window, told him to stop that bloody racket or she'd knock something out of him, and, no, she didn't know where he was gone, but if he had any sense he wouldn't be coming back.

So much for his breakfasts, Vritet thought as he wandered sadly down the street to the tram. Over the following weeks, it proved surprisingly difficult to find a satisfactory replacement, not least because he couldn't seem to find *votlik* eggs in the shops, and when he did find them, they seemed terribly expensive. Vritet, morosely, took to eating in the campus cafeteria, hardly his preferred option, since it was always so noisy, and he couldn't regularly get his preferred booth at the back near the courtyard, and there was always the terrible risk that colleagues or students might see him and want to strike up a conversation.

This morning, after placing his order, he slipped to the back and took the empty table in the booth, blessedly surrounded on three sides by screens. He did not want to be disturbed. He had a great deal to think about. His plate of eggs arrived. (Too watery! But at least the bread was decent for once.) He laid out his notes in front of him. He was reading his report through for one last time before sending it upstairs to his superiors. Vritet's new dataset had given him precisely the same results as before, and the model he had built had told him exactly the same thing: the supernova's range was much wider than believed, and the speed much faster. And this meant that the evacuation of Romulus should by now be well underway. He was sure of his work—of his own brilliance and eye for detail—but still, for the first time in his life, Nokim Vritet wished for a colleague to whom he could show his calculations and with whom he could discuss his findings. It would be good to have someone who could confirm what he knew. He had gathered, dimly, that other species ran scientific research in this way. Not Romulans. Somebody might be stealing your ideas or reporting you to the Tal Shiar for straying too far from permitted areas of research.

Vritet glanced across the cafeteria. It was busy now and people were looking for free space. A big man came and sat in the booth with him. Vritet quickly gathered up his notes, hiding them from view. He concentrated instead on his disappointing eggs and tried to decide what to do next. Nurius had retired, gone offworld, and had not yet been replaced. Vritet was not entirely sure now whom he should report to—and whether he should. But the figures said the same thing. If only he had someone to confide in . . . someone to tell him what the right thing to do was. So many lives depended on this . . .

The big man opposite finished his breakfast, belched mightily, stood, and went on his way. Vritet watched him go, glad to see the back of him. Then he realized the man had left something behind—a little handheld device. He stood up, to call after him, but the man was already through the door. Vritet reached for the device, intending to look for a name or some other identifying feature. As he touched it, the screen sprang to life. Odd, he thought; why would it recognize *his* bio-signature? He glanced down at the screen and saw the name *Safadi*. He began to read what was scrolling past—and his world fell apart.

Vritet took the handheld back to the quiet of his office to study the contents more carefully. He knew Doctor Safadi's name, of course; she was one of the most respected figures in their field. He had sometimes wished that he could meet her or, at least, communicate with her. But permits for communication with Federation citizens were very hard to come by, not to mention expensive, and he knew his family, who could afford the fees, would never allow it. Why would anyone want to communicate with someone from the Federation? They were scum. They were smug and overbearing, and held Romulans—even the best, good-blooded Romulans such as him!—in contempt. But now, somehow, he had come into possession of this paper. Well, not somehow. Vritet might be monastic in his habits, but he was not a complete fool. Whoever the man in the cafeteria had been, he had certainly intended Vritet to see this report. And for good reason. Safadi's data, and her model, exactly replicated Vritet's own work.

For the rest of the morning, Vritet sat alone behind his desk and worried. He knew now, without doubt, that his calculations were correct: the blast radius of the supernova was well beyond official measures, and many more worlds were at risk. But what could he do? Whom should he tell?

And how? And why, *why*, was nobody doing anything about it? Surely there should be information about the evacuation of the planet by now? Surely people should have left by now; many, many people should have left by now. They wouldn't simply leave everyone . . . would they?

No, that was not possible. That was unthinkable! They were keeping the news quiet, of course, but they were organizing everything behind the scenes, so that there was no mass panic. Surely that was the case? Then another idea struck him. Perhaps they *didn't* know . . . Perhaps Nurius, hurrying to leave, had forgotten to pass the information on. Perhaps Vritet was sitting here, the only person within the Empire who understood the threat.

There was a tap at the door. Hastily, he concealed the handheld in his pocket.

"Come in!"

It was one of the new members of staff—newish, he should say; the two of them had been here several months now—who had offices next to him. They had smiled once or twice, nodded greetings, but they had never talked to each other before. Vritet didn't make friends easily and didn't particularly want to. He wanted to work.

She said, "I thought I'd drop by and say hello." She gave him a close look. "Is anything the matter? You look rather fraught."

Vritet considered for a moment what to say. He could not reveal the device: there were identifying features on it that would lead back to his informer, and the man did not deserve that. But he could still talk about his dataset.

"I'm glad you came in," he said. "I'm very worried. Do you think you could take a look through these numbers?"

Vritet went to bed feeling more cheerful than he had in some time. His colleague, Chokitha, had listened as he talked her through his figures, and explained their ramifications. She had nodded when he told her his worry that the message had not got through from Nurius to the people that mattered. He was worried, very worried, that the necessary preparations were not being made. She had listened patiently, and, when he was done, said, "I understand your fears. You should send your report up again—send it to the director of the academy."

It went against his nature to draw attention to himself, but with Chokitha's help, he wrote a short message, and sent the report on. When this was done, she said, "Can I ask—what has made you so anxious about this today? From what you've told me, you've had these figures for some months."

He didn't miss a beat before responding. Evasion was the first trick that all Romulans learned. "I thought I must have made a mistake and so I took some new readings. I finished analyzing them today." No need to mention handhelds, and strange belching men in cafeterias, and Doctor Amal Safadi.

"I see." She nodded. "Well, I hope I've helped."

There was something else preying on his mind, but he wasn't quite sure how to explain it. Chokitha, seeing his face, said, "Is there something else, Nokim?"

"There is something." He glanced around and lowered his voice. "I'm struggling to make sense of these readings. How they can occur. They don't fall within anything I would expect from this type of star . . . It's almost as if . . ."

"Go on," said Chokitha.

"As if . . . there's something unnatural about it."

She blinked at him. "What do you mean, Nokim?"

"I mean, I can't find a natural explanation for this. But I don't know what it would mean for this to be . . . well. Manufactured. Done deliberately."

"You're tired," she said. "And you've been very worried. I'm sure, when you look through your figures again, you'll see what you've missed. Go home, Nokim. Get some sleep. You don't need to worry anymore."

She left. He tidied up his desk and turned off the light. How fortunate, he thought as he walked home, that she had come past when she did, exactly when he needed some help. She was right. He would sleep well tonight, knowing that someone was going to act . . .

He woke, suddenly. There was a bright light in the room. He thought for a moment that he was dreaming, but then the light shone even brighter. His eyes began to water. A dark figure moved behind the light.

"Who are you?" he said. "Who's there?"

"You know who we are," said a voice. It was coming through an electronic filter. It sounded like a talking machine. Vritet shuddered. Things like that were the stuff of nightmares. "Your work is done now, Nokim," said the voice. "We have your report. It's been passed on, and you should move on. Do you understand?"

"I . . . But has it reached the right people . . . ? Do they see what it all means—?"

"Do you understand?"

"But the figures! The numbers! I must be sure that someone has them! Does the relief mission have them? Do they know how desperate the situation is? The evacuation! It should be well underway by now—"

"This is out of your hands now. It is no longer your concern. Your superiors have all the information that they need. They will act on it. Do you understand?"

"I . . . I understand."

"Go back to sleep."

The light went out. He closed his eyes and lay there for a while, until exhaustion caught up with him. When he went to his office the next day, Chokitha's desk had been cleared, and his own had been searched. He touched the handheld in his pocket. Later that day, he destroyed it completely.

NORTH STATION
VASHTI

The Federation News Network was out in force on Vashti. Picard, with Raffi and Koli beside him as ever, walked over to join Commander

Gbowee, who had made the journey from Earth for this occasion. Lieutenant Kaul was at her right hand. Picard, remembering the young ensign who had taken such good care of him during his first hours commanding this mission, greeted her warmly. She was clearly delighted that he remembered her.

Then Picard moved along to speak to Kirsten Clancy. "I'm grateful that you've made this journey, Captain. We're a long way out."

She looked smart, neat, and unperturbed; the very model of a Starfleet functionary. "Well, you said that this one was going to be the big success. So we thought we'd throw our support behind you."

"And what do you think?"

Clancy looked around. He watched her clever, calculating gaze take in the square in which they were standing. Vashti was no Risa, far from it; the sun gave the world a dry and dusty air. But the locals had done their best to give North Station a festival feel, to welcome the new arrivals due shortly to set foot on their world for the first time. There were ribbons and streamers, and banners that said: *WELCOME TO YOUR NEW HOME!* in both Standard and Romulan. The whole town, it seemed, had come out. There was a carousel and a Ferris wheel, and a band playing in one corner. There was to be dancing later, and the promise of fireworks. Raffi had said the whole thing reminded her of a school fair, but that made it no less heartfelt. Picard watched Clancy's face crack into a smile.

"I think everyone on the Council is going to love this," she said.

He tapped his combadge. "Lieutenant th'Kaothreq," he said. "Is Zani ready?"

"Whenever you are, Admiral."

Gesturing to Clancy to join him, Picard walked over to where the governor of Vashti and representatives from the local town were waiting, looking rather nervous in their finery. "Shall we begin?" he said.

The governor nodded. Picard tapped his combadge and said, "Lieutenant th'Kaothreq. Proceed with the first group of guests, please."

There was a hush—even the band stopped—and then the first twenty Romulans—all Qowat Milat—arrived on Vashti. Zani was at the front, Elnor beside her. The governor stepped forward, and with an anxious air, pressed his hands together, as if holding a book, then opened them again. "*Jolan tru.* Welcome to Vashti. Our homes and hearts are open to you."

Picard, catching Zani's eyes, smiled. The governor had jumbled up the order of words slightly—and his Romulan accent was dreadful—but the sentiment was unmistakable. With infinite grace, Zani mirrored the gesture. "We thank you. We open our hearts to you, and the homes that are to come."

There was a big cheer. When that died down, and the band was about to strike up, Elnor stepped forward. His eyes were wide. He was staring at the Ferris wheel and, more particularly, at a unicorn waiting for a rider. "What," he demanded imperiously, "is *that*?"

A human child—a girl of about seven—slipped out from the crowd. She shoved her hand into Elnor's and dragged him off. "I'll show ya," she said, and helped him climb onto the beast's back. She jumped up behind him and wrapped her arms around his waist—and then they were off. The girl shrieked her delight; Elnor gave a grave smile.

It could not have been better. The holo-cameras caught everything and sent the images straight back home. Clancy looked pleased. Picard, breathing a deep sigh of relief, whisked her off to inspect the new houses that were being built, and left his teams to get on with bringing the settlers down to Vashti. Later that evening, escaping the party to come back on board the *Verity*, Picard summoned his staff to join him on one of the starship's emptied decks, where partitions had been removed to open up a reception room. Champagne was poured, and he toasted them all, and the success of their mission.

"Well done, all of you," he said. "My deepest, most heartfelt thanks to you all for this great success."

"To the admiral!" someone called out; and they all took up the cry: *To the admiral! To Admiral Picard!*

Watching them, smiling and laughing, their tired faces shining with the knowledge of a difficult job well done, he believed that this was the happiest moment of his entire life. All the hard work, the trials and tribulations, the doubts, the struggles—everything was coming together. They had come together, and they were succeeding.

To the admiral!

9

Admiral's Log: After four months, we leave Vashti confident that the refugees whom we have brought here are settling in their new homes. The welcome they received from the local population is surely the most encouraging and even moving sight I have seen in my many years as a Starfleet officer. It epitomized all that I think is best of the Federation: open-minded, open-hearted, generous, and curious. I have great faith that the Romulan settlement on Vashti will in future years be a byword for the success of this mission, proof that this great gamble of ours has paid off. As well as the welcome, we saw clear signs that the practical realities of settling so many people on the world were not being underestimated. The people of Vashti—both Romulan and human—will go to sleep for many years from now listening to the *pop-pop* of archi-printers constructing their new homes and facilities. My understanding is that many small worlds along the border with the Neutral Zone resent diverting resources to the Romulans, fearing they would lose out. Vashti shows how an entire world may benefit.

Captain Clancy was on Vashti for five days before returning to Earth. I have been keeping her informed. The messages I have received from her recently indicate that the images sent from Vashti have gone a long way to shoring up support. The sight of Elnor and the young girl making friends has proven particularly popular. I am both touched and charmed to think that this unusual boy now symbolizes this mission in the hearts and minds of many. Vashti, the Qowat Milat, Zani, and Elnor all hold a special place in my heart. I believe that during this mission in particular we have demonstrated how ambitious our work is, and how successfully it can be implemented. I am not so hubristic as to believe that our mission will be plain sailing from here on, but I do believe that as our experience grows, so does our ability to cope with whatever situations we may face. We become, daily, more fit for the task. If I did not take time to be proud of how far we have come, and how much we have done, I would not be human.

It would be remiss of me not to note how a large part of our success is due to Zani and her sisters in the Qowat Milat, and continued success on Vashti will depend in large part on them. A personal note: it has been a privilege for me to have met her, and to have established our friendship. From the start of this mission, and despite the numerous setbacks we have faced, not least the lack of openness from the Romulan government, I have always had faith that somewhere within Romulan space I would find a kindred spirit—someone whose values were congruent with mine, someone who understood that when life is at risk, all must be risked to save it. When I left Vashti, Zani said to me that the gifts we had brought were beyond measure. I would say that the gifts she has given me are at least as great: counsel, comradeship, and courage. If I should ever doubt this mission again—and I have no doubt I shall in the coming days—I will think of Zani, and of Elnor, for whom she risked all.

But now we must leave Vashti in her capable hands and turn the *Verity* and the rest of the fleet toward our next mission. I hope we shall have at least some of the success of this last one, but preliminary reports indicate that we face a considerably more difficult situation than that we found on Inxtis. The border world of Nimbus III, despite the hopes invested in it at its foundation, has historically been a lawless place, a haven for black marketeers and other malcontents. My understanding is that in recent years, the inhabitants have worked hard to bring law and order to their world, and that this has only been achieved recently, and at considerable cost. I will not be surprised to meet resistance here: a home so hard won will not be easily surrendered. This is one of the many small tragedies of this catastrophe. Rich or poor, young or old, no one can escape the effects of this disaster. It is our task to protect those who cannot protect themselves. Nevertheless, as we proceed toward Nimbus, I find myself turning as ever to Lieutenant Koli, and relying on her advice to tackle those who do not wish to leave their homes . . .

CAMBRIDGE, EARTH

Spring had come to Cambridge, a sweet season in a temperate region of a planet that had learned from the calamities of the past and had organized in order to do what was needed to save all its species and the world itself. Doctor Amal Safadi, waking to see that it had rained during the night, foresaw a lazy Sunday morning ahead: catching up on her reading, biking into town for brunch with friends, a swim later at Jesus Green. As she passed by her desk on her way to the kitchen to put on the coffee, however, she saw a little red light flashing on the screen, indicating she had received a communication from someone she had flagged as *crucial*. She hesitated, thinking of her plans for the day, but she knew that she would not relax, thinking about that flashing light. She sat down and opened the message.

The message was from Haig at Romulan Affairs at Starfleet. A brief text note, saying, "This just in. Important. Get back to me as soon as possible."

She knew Haig didn't waste words. Important meant . . . what? Game changing? She opened the file he had sent over, her trepidation rising as she saw the author of the report.

Nokim Vritet.

Surely this is good news, she thought. A communication from Vritet? Perhaps it signified movement on the part of the Romulan authorities, an indication that they were willing to start sharing the information that they had about the supernova. Safadi respected Vritet, and she also knew how good her own work was. Vritet was surely writing to confirm that his figures bore out hers.

She was rapidly disappointed, indeed, shocked at what she read. Vritet's report stated in the strongest terms that his latest set of figures did not replicate hers, that her revised estimate of the blast radius was vastly overstated. He confirmed that he had received Safadi's figures via his students at the Cambridge symposium, that he had analyzed them numerous times, and that he had compared them to datasets that he had acquired from several sources back on Romulus (Safadi noted that these were not included).

She could not believe what she was reading. The worst part of the whole message was the note that had been attached by the Romulan intelligence officer who had sent the report to Haig, his opposite number.

"We are at a loss here to understand what Doctor Safadi intended when she produced her malicious report, or, indeed, what the whole team at Cambridge was hoping to achieve when they gave institutional backing to her efforts. We are trying to assume it was in good faith, given Starfleet's continued insistence that they are acting in the same fashion. Nevertheless, these are difficult times for us, and it is hard not to believe that some mischievous or unfavorable intent was behind Safadi's work. Why else would Federation scientists—who we all know are directed in their work by Starfleet—make these outrageous and inflammatory suggestions? We are well aware that these claims, if they became public, could create chaos across the Empire. This is a very serious matter, and should any evidence come to light that such was the intent, we would consider it a prelude to war. Let us remind you that the Romulan Star Empire will not take attempts at destabilization during this trying time lightly. If such was the purpose of this report, we must insist that your government more carefully scrutinize work being conducted in this field and ensure that its scientists are held to the highest standards. At the moment, we are not convinced that this is the case."

Safadi sat back in her chair, shocked. Had Vritet honestly dismissed her work out of hand? For a moment, she doubted herself. Had there been a mistake, a slip? It was so easy to get too close to your work. But that was what the team was for; that was why you had people around you. Check the work. Check the thinking. That had been the point of the symposium: to take the group's findings and bring them before the wider scientific community and get them to make sure that there were no errors. That was how the whole thing worked. Besides, Safadi was able to judge her own work, and she was sure, completely sure, that there was no mistake. What the hell was going on?

Her comm chimed. Durnyam Bekri, looking worried, appeared on the screen. *"Amal,"* she said, *"I got Haig's message. Have you read Vritet's report?"*

Safadi nodded miserably.

"What is happening?"

"I don't know," Safadi said. "I can't . . . This can't be right. Something must have happened at Vritet's end—I can't believe he would falsify results."

"Do you think he doesn't have access to the data?"

"I honestly can't say. All I know is—my model is right. You know that too; so do the others, so does everyone we showed the study to."

"I know, I know . . ."

Safadi looked anxiously at her friend's face. "Durnyam, some of the things they were saying . . ." *Malicious*, she thought, and shuddered. "Is this going to be okay?"

"I'm not sure . . . Listen, there's more. I got a message from Councilor Olivia Quest—have you heard of her?"

"Yes." If you took an interest in the 'casts at all—and Safadi liked to be well informed—then it was hard to miss Councilor Quest these days. Not that Safadi could remember the world that the councilor came from. She was slightly embarrassed by that. Maybe these small worlds had a point about how easily they were forgotten. "Isn't she the one heading the relief mission oversight committee?"

"Yes, and she's very keen to speak to us in the light of all this. She's sent a message asking us—you and me—to come and speak to the committee. I say 'ask,' but it's more a summons. You won't believe this bit, Amal. She reminded me that she has the right to compel us to attend."

"She doesn't need to compel me to attend a committee hearing. It's my duty and my pleasure. But what is she expecting us to say? That we're very sorry, and we made a mistake adding up, and that they should cancel the mission?"

"I don't think you'll need to go that far. But we'll need to be prepared to explain the figures in the simplest terms possible. Quest is an engineer—but she's not our only audience. The ordinary person is."

Safadi cut the comm. She stared out of the window, where the bright sun was refracting through the water drops on the glass. Outside, on the garden fence, a blackbird hopping along stopped dead and turned one inquisitive eye toward her, before flying away in search of breakfast. Safadi opened her files. So much for a lazy Sunday.

Verity

Admiral Jean-Luc Picard, receiving his weekly update from Mars, sat and listened as La Forge ran through his figures. In truth, Picard had few concerns. The Daystrom A500s were proving a boon to the mission, and they were on schedule for rolling the first batch of specifically designed *Wallenberg*-class ships off the production line by the start of next year. As long as there were no more surprises. But then there was only so much for which one could prepare. Life did not run like clockwork. Other people, light-years away, made decisions that you knew about, and others that you would never know anything about. Eventually, the consequences were felt, and had to be dealt with. He cleared his throat.

"*Admiral, you've stopped listening, so why don't I stop talking, send you this file, and you can tell me what's the matter.*"

Some people simply knew you far too well . . . "My apologies, Geordi. But you're right. I've seen that people from the Institute of Astronomy in Cambridge have been asked to appear before Councilor Quest's committee, and that there is some query over their calculations."

"*Yeah, I've read that report too. There's some very unhappy people in Romulan Affairs right now, I bet.*"

"Do you think there's any truth in it?"

"*Do I think Doctor Safadi made a mistake?*"

Picard nodded.

"*You know, Admiral, those people are smart. I mean—super smart. Not only at what they do, but in the way they go about doing it. There are checks* and balances. She published, dammit! People have been poring over her figures for months! The most high-profile piece of research in decades! There'll be someone out there dying to make their name by proving her wrong. But, if it is wrong—I bet Safadi and her people would want to be shown how and why. And if they've made a mistake . . ." La Forge held up his hands. "Well, that's good news all around, isn't it? I have half a dozen people here who would be happy to get back to their old projects."

"Do you think Safadi's report is solid?"

La Forge rapped his knuckles against his desk. *"Solid as Mars rock. Whether she can persuade that committee, though—well, that's another question entirely."* He sighed. *"I should go. I have a genius at the Daystrom Institute to harass. La Forge out."*

Picard smiled. He turned his mind back to Nimbus III. Doctor Amal Safadi could surely take care of herself.

FEDERATION COUNCIL
PARIS, EARTH

Safadi, sitting outside the committee room, watched Durnyam being interviewed. She thought about how she used to joke that her mother didn't have a clue what she did, but loved to see her on the news. *Well, Mama—be careful what you wish for.* Durnyam was acquitting herself well, answering the questions clearly and carefully, explaining the composition of her team, their qualifications, and their methods.

"What is your assessment in particular of Doctor Safadi's abilities, then, Doctor Bekri?"

The camera shifted to Durnyam. She looked as if the question made no sense. *"Doctor Safadi is one of the best scientists I have worked with. She's meticulous, scrupulous, and very well informed."* Safadi, listening, smiled quietly to herself. It was good to know that people had her back.

At last, Durnyam was released, and Safadi was called. They passed each other as Safadi was brought in, and Durnyam gave her a quick hug. "Be brilliant, Amal," she said, "like you always are."

Still, Safadi thought as she took her seat in front of the committee, it was hard not to feel anxious, and hard not to feel faintly as if she were on trial. The committee—seven of them in total—sat in a semicircle in front of her. Safadi sat alone, at a desk, facing them. She placed her padd down—it was good to have notes to refer to, in case of nerves or surprises, although she was confident that she could speak without them.

A fair-haired woman, about Safadi's age, was sitting in the middle of the semicircle. Safadi recognized her immediately. "Doctor Safadi, I'm Olivia Quest, junior councilor for Estelen, and chair of this committee. Do you give permission for this interview to be recorded?"

"Of course, Councilor."

"Thank you, Doctor Safadi. If we could begin with you giving an overview of the study you carried out that revised your understanding of the impact of the Romulan supernova?"

Safadi tried to relax. She knew this material well, and she had presented versions of it to all kinds of audiences: to experts and peers, to newscasts, to local science groups that had invited her to speak. She knew that Quest had a scientific background, as did one or two of the other committee members, but not all of them did. So she pitched it relatively low. If they wanted details of the math, they could open their computers and look at the equations. It was not like she was keeping them hidden.

Her presentation went smoothly enough. There were one or two queries, which she answered clearly and crisply. When she was done, she waited for the next salvo. Quest, she noticed, had been sitting with her head down throughout, taking copious notes. At last, the councilor looked up, pinning Safadi with her bright blue gaze.

"I have one question. Doctor Safadi, the math behind this is very complicated. Do you think it is possible that you could have made a mistake?"

"Councilor Quest, everything is possible. Could I have made a mistake? Yes. Do I think it likely that I made a mistake? No."

"So if you think you made a mistake—"

"You're misrepresenting what I said."

"If you think a mistake is possible—"

"Unlikely."

"But *possible*, yes? Those are your own words?"

"My words are—possible, but unlike—"

Quest stopped her, "If you think your model is possibly flawed, why are you pushing it?"

"Because given the evidence it's the most likely scenario."

"But that's precisely what Academician Vritet says is not the case, isn't it? Doctor Safadi, isn't science about consensus?"

"The consensus among me and other colleagues is that the threat from the supernova is considerably greater than the official Romulan figures."

"Don't you think that's rather extreme?" said Quest. "Almost *apocalyptic*? Why push this particular reading of the data? Why not something more balanced?"

Safadi took a deep breath. "Councilor Quest, I am not writing science fiction. I am interpreting data. If that data signals an apocalypse, it's my duty to report that accurately. It's up to people like you to decide what action to take to mitigate the effects."

"But don't you think this is all very Cassandra-like?"

"Cassandra," said Safadi, "was telling the truth. The problem was that nobody listened."

There was a small ripple of laughter. Quest covered her displeasure. "But Doctor Vritet says something different—"

"I want to be absolutely clear about one thing," said Safadi. "I greatly respect Nokim Vritet and his work. But this report cannot be true. Whether he is working from incomplete data, or whether scientists on Romulus are being censored, I know for a fact that the figures presented in the report sent to me under his name are not and cannot be true."

There was a short silence. "Those are some pretty strong accusations, Doctor Safadi," said Quest. "Are you saying the Romulans are lying to us?"

"I have no idea," Safadi said. "None whatsoever—"

"There are political ramifications to a statement like that—"

"Councilor Quest, I leave politics to the politicians. But we must be very clear—math is math. Let me remind you what a great scientist once said, when asked to make mathematics bend to the wishes of politicians. 'Nature cannot be fooled.'"

Around her there was a great stir. Quest looked uncomfortable.

"My job," said Safadi, "is to tell you as clearly as possible what my observations of nature are telling me. I've told you that, Councilor Quest. Now you must decide what you want to do with that information."

One of the other committee members leaned in to whisper something to Quest, who then said, "Thank you, Doctor Safadi. You've been very helpful."

Hey, Mama, thought Safadi as she made her way out into the corridor, *I hope you were watching.*

Haig was waiting, arms folded, back against the wall. "Well done," he said.

"Thank you."

"You said everything that needed to be said—and no more."

She considered this. "You know," she said, "there's something that still worries me."

"Oh yes?" He pushed himself up from the wall and began to walk toward the exit.

She followed him. "What's happening to the Romulan star—I don't have an explanation for it. Correction: I don't have a *natural* explanation for it."

"No?"

"I think it was . . . made. Created. Not naturally occurring."

"Do you."

"What does Starfleet think?" she said.

They reached the exit. He grasped for the handle but did not open it. "I think that you don't have any evidence, Doctor Safadi. It's just a feeling, and you should put it out of your mind." He gave her a wan smile. "Stick to science. Leave the politics to us."

He opened the door. Durnyam was standing outside. She took Safadi by the arm and hurried her past the waiting journalists. "Come quickly and quietly," she muttered in Safadi's ear.

"Where are you taking me?" said Safadi.

"For cocktails. You've earned them, Amal."

Safadi let herself be led away. But back at her quiet home that night, watching the blackbird on the fence, she pondered what Haig had said, and tried to persuade herself that he was right. *If I could visit Romulus*, she thought, *get close to their sun . . . Make sure . . .* But that was never going to happen and, besides, she had other worries. Shivering, she remembered the cold gleam of anger she had seen in Quest's eyes, and she wondered if she had made a mistake—or even an enemy.

Nimbus III

"We shall not go."

Raffi, tired, her eyes full of dust, looked at the woman opposite and tried to sympathize.

Delike Hurer was a small, thin, tough Romulan who had a long white scar running down her forearm. Raffi suspected that Hurer was not as old as she looked; not surprising, given the life she must have led on this benighted world. Nimbus was a desert, and until ten or twelve years ago, despite being nominally ceded to Romulan control, had been without any effective government. It had also been plagued by the worst kind of mercenaries. *Imagine trying to scratch a living out of this dump*, Raffi thought. Imagine trying to build something, always living in terror that it would be taken by force, that someone would kill you, simply because they could. Some people harbored their survivalist fantasies. They snuck off into the wild to have the excuse to live out some vision of themselves as all-powerful, inviolable. The people of Nimbus III had seen them off, they triumphed in the end. Now they didn't want to leave their world behind.

"I understand the reasons for your resistance—" Picard began.

Hurer cut him off. "No," she said. "You do not. You cannot. We have built a home here. We will not have it taken away."

Raffi glanced at JL. He was nodding at Hurer as she spoke, and listening too, listening closely, as if he believed that if he was attentive enough, he would somehow find the key to unlock her, the means by which she would be persuaded to think his way. But he wouldn't. There was no key to unlock this woman; there was no argument that would make her see the light. Hurer's attachment to this place was emotional, not rational. Staying here was not rational. Therefore, she could not be reasoned out of this.

"Do you understand," Picard said, "that this world is at risk? You will surely feel an impact from the supernova—as the situation worsens on Romulus, whatever support you get will disappear competely. It will become harder and harder to survive here—"

Hurer laughed, a rasp that ended up in a coughing fit. A young woman, sitting next to her, put her hand upon Hurer's arm, and passed her some water. Hurer drank sparingly, enough to help with the cough but not more, and set the cup down again with reverence. Water. There mustn't be much of it here. They had certainly not been offered any.

"Hard to survive?" Hurer said. "You're describing Nimbus as it is right now! Hard to *survive*!" She looked at him in scorn. "If you want to help—give us some replicators. Then go away and leave us alone."

"Madame," said Picard, addressing her as if she were an ambassador from a huge and wealthy alien power. (*To give JL credit*, Raffi thought, *he always speaks this way; he does not discriminate between the great and good and the small and not so good.*) "Eventually you will run out of resources. If you remain here, you are going to die."

"Never thought I'd make it in the first place," said Hurer. "I've seen famine, plague, watched crops burn for no better reason than to amuse some warlord or other . . . yet here I am. We got through before. We'll get through this."

"Madame—"

"The simple fact is," said Hurer, "that I don't believe you, Mister Starfleet. Why should I? The people who settled here, all those years ago— Starfleet was meant to protect them. Promised to protect them. But at the first sign of trouble, they were gone. The planet of galactic peace. My ancestors were left to die. But they didn't die. They *didn't* die. They got through. And they told us—never trust Starfleet. Because they're liars." She looked at him as if he were dirt on her shoe. "Why should I believe you, Mister Starfleet?"

For a moment, Raffi thought JL was going to make the mistake of trying to explain to this woman why Starfleet had pulled out of the Nimbus project. It would only make matters worse. A Starfleet admiral, lecturing this woman about her own history. But JL, fortunately, had good sense. He glanced at Koli, inviting her to speak.

Raffi had been surprised when Koli had announced that she would not be wearing her uniform for this mission. She could see the wisdom in it now. Instead of speaking for Starfleet, Koli was speaking as a Bajoran. It brought credibility to her words. Bajorans too had been caught between great powers; they had had their world taken from them, and they had struggled to rebuild. And they had accepted Starfleet's help. Raffi hoped this would be enough.

"Madame Hurer," said Koli, "there is no reason for you to trust us. There is every reason to suspect that we have come to take this world from you by deception—"

Raffi saw Hurer flinch. Yes, clever Koli, that was what was going on, wasn't it? The locals suspected some trick, some ploy, to get them off planet. They must think that the world had in some way acquired sudden value. New mineral deposits under the ground; a strategic advantage in the changing galactic order following the breaching of the Neutral Zone. Whatever it was, the people of Nimbus wanted their share.

"All that I can say to you," Koli went on, "is that is not the case. What we showed you is true. Your way of life is under threat from the blast range of a supernova that will destroy the Romulan homeworld. There is no fairness to this, no justice. If there was, you would live out your days in peace on the land that you have fought so hard for. But that cannot happen. Madame Hurer, it's not fair. The Romulan sun is going supernova, and you will be left to fend for yourselves. We are here to offer you safe passage. Please—"

Choose to live, thought Raffi suddenly.

Koli held out her hands. "Please let us help."

Hurer had been looking at Koli carefully throughout this speech. When the Bajoran finished, the older woman took another sip of water, licked her lips, and looked around at her three visitors. Her eyes narrowed as she saw the Starfleet uniforms. Then she clenched her teeth.

How this conversation might have ended, Raffi would never know. At the time, only a few weeks after Vashti, she had believed that Hurer was about to concede, allow them to help. She would call for water to be given to them and shared around. They would eat together—they always ended up eating together, on these worlds, once the agreement had been made, the universal gesture of friendship—and they would begin their plans to evacuate the world. That was what Raffi imagined at the time. Later, she was not so sure. Had that last sip been one of resolution? The prelude to a refusal, a rejection? A response based on suspicion and mistrust? Later on, Raffi would find it hard not to think that was what it had been.

Either way, she was not to be allowed to find out. Suddenly, the door swung open and a young man ran in. He was clutching a rifle. Raffi, jumping to her feet, put herself between him and Picard. Later (Raffi had a lot of time on her hands, later; a lot of time to go through all her steps and missteps), she wondered whether that might in itself have finished off any chance of trust between them and the people of Nimbus: the assumption on her part that any interruption presaged some attempt on their lives. But the young man was not looking at them.

Breathlessly, he said to Hurer, "Tal Shiar. They're here!"

Hurer stared at him, and then at Picard. "Did you bring them here?"

And Raffi, watching JL's jaw harden, thought: *Not us. Tajuth.*

The chief settlement on Nimbus III was a collection of low buildings huddled around a red dirt square. Raffi, ducking her head to pass under the low door, looked out to see a crowd of around two dozen people gathered outside. Some had their hands held high or placed on top of their heads. Looking beyond these, she saw a dozen black-clad figures, armed with disruptors. Tal Shiar.

"Shit," she said, and gestured to Picard to stay inside. From behind her, she heard his combadge chime, and Lieutenant Marshall's voice come through.

"Admiral Picard, I have Admiral Bordson on a priority channel here. He wants to speak to you immediately."

Raffi came back inside. Picard had turned to Hurer. "Madame, that is the commander-in-chief of Starfleet. May I take the message in your office? I am sure he is advising how we may help."

Hurer pointed at the desk over on one side of the room. An office was overstating it, Raffi thought. *Typical JL, bestowing dignity where there was none.*

Picard took a seat behind the desk and turned on the beaten-up old comm. Hurer, despite the protestations of the young woman with her, went outside. Koli followed them. Raffi, at the door, said, "JL, shall I go?"

"Stay here but out of sight," he said. "And close the door."

A chill went down Raffi's spine. She realized, suddenly, looking at his grim expression—he wasn't expecting help. He was expecting to be told to stand aside.

"Victor."

"Jean-Luc—"

"Who called them in?"

"I don't know. But the Romulan ambassador informed us about an hour ago that they were sending their own people to Nimbus, and that they would oversee the relocation effort from now on."

"Why? Why here? There's nothing here—"

"Who knows, Jean-Luc. Maybe they're angry about Doctor Safadi's appearance before the committee. Maybe they want to punish the locals for disobedience. Maybe there are secret bases on Nimbus that none of us know anything about, and they don't want Starfleet there."

Or maybe, thought Raffi, Tajuth was paying them back for Inxtis.

From outside, there came a shout, and then a burst of disruptor fire, short and quickly over. "Mother f'ers!" muttered Raffi. She pulled out her phaser, opened the door a crack, and peered out into the square beyond. Everything was deadly quiet. From behind her she heard the voices of the two admirals.

"Victor, they are firing weapons—"

"Admiral Picard, you have your orders. You must not intervene. Return to your ship at once. Starfleet Command out."

Raffi looked out. Koli was kneeling over someone, trying to save their life. Hurer was standing beside her, weeping openly. Raffi, looking at the body on the ground, recognized him as the young man who had come to tell them the Tal Shiar were here. Who was he? Hurer's son? Grandson? Someone significant.

"Raffi," Picard called out, "what is going on out there?"

"Bad things, JL. But nobody's shooting right now."

"Put the phaser away. We'll go out. Try to talk to them."

"JL, I don't think that's a bright idea—"

"You heard Bordson. We have no jurisdiction here. Let's not make this worse, Raffi."

Bitterly, she put away the phaser. Picard stood up, straightened his uniform, and gathered himself. She followed him out into the square. She counted five Romulan weapons immediately turned their way. Picard lifted his hands: a gesture of peace, but by no means surrender. "There is no need for this," he said.

One of the Tal Shiar holstered his weapon and came toward them. "Are you Picard?"

"I am Admiral Picard, yes."

"You and your people can leave now."

Koli was still trying to breathe life into the young man. Picard looked toward her. "Not yet," he said. They watched, in agonized silence, for what could surely have been no more than a minute. At last it became plain to everyone there that the young man was dead. Raffi wanted to go over to her colleague, help her, put her hand upon her shoulder. No chance. "Jocan," she said. "It's over. You've done all you can—"

Koli sat up. She reached over and closed the young man's eyes. She sat back on her heels. Her eyes were wide and sightless. There was blood on her hands. Beside her, Hurer began to wail. The Tal Shiar officer said, "You can leave."

"Get Tajuth here immediately."

Raffi, one arm still around Koli, nodded to Lieutenant th'Kaothreq. "Come here and look after her." Th'Kaothreq hurried around and Raffi hit her combadge. "Tajuth. Transporter room two. Now."

He was with them almost at once. He stood with his hands tucked behind his back, looking calmly back at them.

"Lieutenant," said Picard, "did you request that the Tal Shiar be sent to Nimbus?"

Tajuth blinked. "Admiral, I keep my superiors informed as to the progress of our mission. If, on reading my reports, they choose to intervene, that is their right as a sovereign—"

Koli sank down on the transporter step and began to weep.

"I swear," said Raffi, "I am going to punch you out."

"That would be a hostile act, Commander Musiker," said Tajuth.

"And yet one feels some sympathy with it," said Picard. "Why here? Why now?"

"You would have to ask my superiors—"

"Very well. I shall. Meanwhile, in your capacity as liaison officer to those superiors, please give me your best assessment of the situation down on Nimbus."

Tajuth swallowed. A request for assistance, thought Raffi, was not what he had anticipated. "I am not sure," Tajuth said. "Nimbus III has for the most part been left to its own devices for many years. Perhaps the relocation was taking too long, somebody decided that they could be made an example of—"

Koli, sitting nearby, said, "I want to go back down."

Tajuth said, "I don't think that will be permitted—"

"You'd better ask," said Picard softly.

"Admiral, my superiors have been very clear. This particular relocation effort is now the direct responsibility of the Romulan government. And my understanding is that *your* superiors have been very clear to you too."

There was a short silence. "JL," said Raffi, "there's going to be a massacre—"

"Admiral, please," said Koli. Tears were running down her face. "Let me go back down there!"

Picard looked at Tajuth. Slowly, he shook his head. "We have direct orders from the C-in-C," he said. He knelt down before her. "Jocan, I'm sorry. Our hands are tied. There's nothing we can do."

Raffi helped Koli back to her quarters. She suggested a sedative, but Koli refused. She watched as the Bajoran woman lit candles all around the room.

"What are you doing, Jocan?" She was reminded of the gratitude ritual they had shared here with the admiral, all those long months ago, but she didn't think this was the same thing. Koli had a bright, almost feverish look to her eye, and she was whispering under her breath. "Jocan? Are you okay?"

"I'm fine. I'm praying. This is what we always did, after there was murder. When the Cardassians arrived, and people were taken away. Light a candle. Say a prayer. Wait for the Prophets to remember us, and dispense justice . . ." She looked at Raffi. "I told you and the admiral what was going to happen. I won't forget this."

Raffi left her to it and went to join Picard in his ready room. "Are you sure there's nothing we can do, JL? Jocan is sure that there's going to be blood spilled—"

"We don't know that, Raffi. But Bordson insists. An intervention here would be a serious risk to the wider mission. Councilor Quest was embarrassed by Doctor Safadi at the committee. Tempers are running high—"

"You're kidding, right?" Raffi couldn't believe what she was hearing. "Some damn councilor from some stupid little border world didn't get her own way, and to make her feel better, we have to sit on our hands while the Tal Shiar murder helpless people—"

"We don't know," Picard insisted, "that that is going to happen. We *do* know that we have explicit orders from our C-in-C not to get involved."

"I've seen you play pretty fast and loose with explicit orders in the past, JL!"

"I don't think you have, Raffi," he said mildly. "I think you've seen me play fast and loose with the discretion and authority granted me as an admiral."

There was a pause. "Sorry, sir."

"I'm sorry too, Raffi. Nobody wants this. Nobody in their right mind, at least."

"Except Tajuth."

Picard looked thoughtful. "I'm not even sure he wanted this either."

The *Verity* remained in orbit over Nimbus for the next ten days, ostensibly to assist at any point in removing the population. No request came from the Romulan government for aid. Eight Romulan vessels were now in orbit over Nimbus, and exchanges between the two fleets had been terse and tense. On the tenth day, a communication arrived from the Romulans that the population was now settled on their ships, and that they would shortly be on their way. They were asked to leave the system.

Raffi stood on the bridge and watched as the Romulan ships departed. She saw Tajuth standing by and went over to him.

"Satisfied?" she said softly.

He turned to look at her. "Lives have been saved. Romulan sovereignty has been maintained. Yes, I'm satisfied. It is telling that you are not."

"Tell me one thing. *Did* you call in the Tal Shiar?"

He did not deign to reply. She looked back at the empty world. "Damn," she said. "What a damned mess."

"And yet the relocation has been successful, Commander Musiker."

"Some definition of success."

He moved away. Her combadge chimed.

"Raffi," said Picard, *"could you join me?"*

She turned from Tajuth and headed toward the ready room. Koli was in there, sitting in front of his desk, her hands twisting together in her lap.

"Everything okay, JL?"

"I'm afraid not, Raffi. Jocan has handed in her resignation."

Raffi stared at the other woman in disbelief. "What? Why?"

"Her concerns over our handling of events on Nimbus III."

"Jocan, you were there—it was an impossible situation . . ."

"There was more we could have done—"

"We had direct orders," said Raffi.

"Which have been ignored before. These people—they were vulnerable, desperate—"

"We did everything we could, Jocan."

"I don't believe we did, Raffi." Her face was tear stained. "We backed away at the first sign of trouble."

"If we had intervened after that boy was shot, there would have been more deaths down there."

"You think there weren't more deaths?"

"That blood isn't on our hands—"

"We did nothing. The Tal Shiar arrived, murdered someone in cold blood, and we *retreated*!"

There was a short silence. Picard said, "I find it hard to disagree with what you say, Jocan. You have taught me—that these missions are complicated. That there is never a right answer. We did what we could in a difficult situation—an explosive situation. Raffi is right—if we had intervened then, more people would have died."

"How many people do you think died after we left?"

He shook his head. "We don't know that happened, Jocan. We can't berate ourselves over hypotheticals—"

"These are not hypotheticals!" She reached into her pocket and threw a tricorder onto the table. "Look! Watch what's on there!"

Raffi picked it up. She ran it around in her hands, turned it on, and set it to play. A small flickering image, recognizable as the ramshackle square of the main settlement on Nimbus, appeared. She could make out figures—nearly fifty people, hands on their heads. Then the shooting started. It didn't stop until everyone was lying on the ground, dead.

"*Mon dieu*," whispered Picard.

"How did you get this, Koli?" asked Raffi.

"They knew down on Nimbus what was going to happen," she said. "But they knew I was a friend. They found a way to send it to me. I told you this was going to happen!"

"Jocan," said Picard, his hands held open, his face aghast.

"You have chosen on many occasions to step beyond your authority, Admiral. What I cannot understand is why this was not one of those occasions."

He knew why: because the loss of life would have been greater. But he knew that she did not want to hear this. He knew that in her eyes he was lessened by his decision—and that this disillusionment was no small part of her distress.

"I *told* you this was going to happen!" she said. "This is why you have my resignation, Admiral."

10

Admiral's Log: Koli Jocan has left the *Verity* and is now, as I understand it, on her way back to Earth, where she has agreed to meet Captain Clancy and report on Nimbus III.

I understand the depth of Koli's feeling about what happened on Nimbus. The situation must have been a terrible reminder of what she witnessed during the Bajoran occupation. I have gone through the events on Nimbus numerous times, considering whether there was a point where we might have intervened, but I struggle to see what could have been done differently. Once the Tal Shiar were present and had assumed authority over the relocation effort on Nimbus, I believe that any direct intervention on our part might well have led to a loss of Starfleet personnel and ships. I know that this is little comfort to those who witnessed the massacre, those who lost people. It cannot bring back those who were murdered. But all my experience tells me that the death toll would have been greater had we chosen to escalate the situation. The people on Nimbus III clearly counted as nothing to the Tal Shiar, and I believe that they would have been prepared to obliterate the settlements there rather than countenance further disobedience.

I remain at a loss as to why the Romulans chose this particular world at this particular time for this horrific show of strength. Raffi's reports from the people at Romulan Affairs can shed no light. If there were secret military bases or other facilities on Nimbus, then why were we permitted to proceed there in the first place? Raffi suggests that the branch of the Tal Shiar that gave us permission might not have been aware of these installations, and when those in the know were alerted to our presence, they came as quickly as they could. I find these Romulan rabbit holes deeply frustrating—indeed, they make me increasingly angry. Time and resources—and, most importantly, lives are being lost playing these spy games. It is unforgivable.

It is not yet proven either who called for the Tal Shiar's assistance. Raffi and I believe that it was Tajuth, but we have no evidence. I should note, however, that Tajuth has recently received promotion to commander. One would like to think that this is a mere coincidence; one can hardly avoid thinking that it is not. When I reflect upon what happened on Nimbus, it is hard to see who has gained. Not Koli, resigning her commission. Not me, or this mission, losing a dedicated member of staff. Not the Romulans, I must assume, who now face difficult questions from us, their allies in this crisis. And most certainly not the people of Nimbus, some of whom have been murdered.

I wonder, in the cold light of day, whether Tajuth truly considers the promotion worth the price. And I wonder too—what kind of man is he, if he believes it is? Perhaps Raffi was right about him all along.

Starfleet Command
San Francisco, Earth

Kirsten Clancy watched with compassion as Koli Jocan took the seat opposite her. The Bajoran woman's hands were shaking as she picked up her glass of water.

"Jocan," she said. "I'm so sorry that this has happened."

Koli nodded. "To some extent I was expecting it," Koli said. "But to be there . . . to see it happen. And for nobody to *intervene*." There were tears in her eyes. "Admiral Picard, of all people!"

Clancy sat and listened. If Koli could talk for a while, then she might begin to put some of the shock of this behind her. She might even be persuaded not to give up her commission. Clancy understood the woman's revulsion. But from various reports, Clancy was struggling to see what else Picard could have done in the circumstances. Any intervention on his part might well have led to considerably more loss of life. For once, she thought, Picard had obeyed the orders of the C-in-C and understood that his decision would have consequences for the entire mission. Picard had acted for the good of the many. He had done, in fact, exactly what Clancy would have done.

"I know how difficult it is to understand this from Earth," Koli was saying. "I understand that. But this case was clear cut. I said that there would be a massacre. And there was."

"Are you sure, Koli?" Clancy asked softly.

Koli looked at her in surprise. "What do you mean? You've seen the footage, haven't you?"

"Yes."

"Then why would you . . . ?" Suddenly, Koli sat back in her chair. Realization was dawning on her face. "Oh, I see. I see what's going on now."

"There's nothing going on, Jocan."

"No, there'll be nothing at all. I see that now. No inquiry, no questions, no scrutiny. Those people have been massacred, and nothing will be done. Nobody held accountable—"

"I've read the reports," Clancy said firmly. "Nobody did anything wrong. Correction—nobody within *Starfleet* did anything wrong. And it's not within my remit to bring Romulan officers before a court-martial."

"So that's it," said Koli. "Finished, as far as Starfleet is concerned."

"By no means," said Clancy. "I'll be talking to the Romulan ambassador later today—"

"I'm sure angry words will be exchanged on all sides."

"Jocan," said Clancy, "you are the one who has always argued that we need not to overstep our authority. That we must uphold Romulan self-determination—"

"As far as is reasonable! As far as is moral! They *murdered* people, Captain!"

They looked at each across the desk, across the gulf. "I can't do anything about that," Clancy said.

"No," said Koli. "I see that now." She stood up. "I'm wasting my time here."

After she left, Clancy sat for a while, rubbing her eyes. Then she went back to work. She tried to put Koli out of her mind. A half hour after Koli had left her office, Clancy's comm chimed. It was her aide-de-camp.

"Captain, you need to switch on the FNN 'cast right now."

Clancy complied.

And put her head in her hands. There, on the screen, for the whole Federation to see, was the footage from Nimbus: grainy, frightening, and utterly savage. Her comm chimed again.

"I have Councilor Quest on the line, Captain."

"I bet you do," muttered Clancy.

STARFLEET COMMAND
SAN FRANCISCO, EARTH

Whatever the Romulan government was paying Sulde, Clancy thought, it probably wasn't enough. Perhaps the promise not to summon her back to the homeworld was sufficient to ensure her loyalty. Whatever it was, the Romulan ambassador didn't blink when they played her the footage from Nimbus. Clancy had to avert her eyes at several points.

"Ambassador," said Admiral Bordson, "can you give us any explanation for this?"

"For the existence of faked footage attempting to discredit Romulan officers struggling to do their duty in difficult circumstances? I would suggest you approach your own intelligence agencies, Admiral. This lie would be in their interests, surely?"

Clancy and Bordson exchanged a look. So this was how they had decided to play it.

"You realize the difficulties this is causing us?" said Clancy. "I'm dealing with Federation Council members who want to know why Starfleet officers are being put into situations like these." Personally, Clancy thought

Quest had a damn nerve using that line, but she was not beyond using it herself. "Worse than that, it's hardening public opinion against the mission. There are polls showing that a substantial proportion of Federation citizens are now asking whether the mission should continue in its current form." And damn Quest for that too, she thought, putting out a poll with a question like that in it.

"Yes, I've seen those polls," said Sulde. Her mouth pursed, as if the idea of forming policy based on the opinions of ordinary people was highly distasteful. "You neglect to mention something about them, Captain. That a growing number of people believe that Romulans are 'ungrateful.' Ungrateful! It's an insult—"

"That is not official Federation policy," said Bordson. "But it is what people are saying." He corrected himself. "Some people."

"We have our own footage," said Sulde, pushing a small holo-player across the desk. "Here are some images from Dondut, where the people of Nimbus are being taken. See—here is the town that is being prepared for them. The homes. The medical center. You may keep this," she said, "scrutinize it. Hand it over to your people in Romulan Affairs. They'll struggle to find problems with it."

"I imagine they will," said Bordson dryly.

"And when you are content with it," said Sulde, "you can broadcast this to your people, correcting the lies that have been propagated. I believe this is what is called 'responsible journalism.'"

With that, the ambassador rose from her seat. She gave a small bow that somehow managed to convey both courtesy and contempt—and swept out of the room.

Clancy turned to Bordson, almost admiringly. "The damn nerve. As if we'd ask the FNN to broadcast Romulan state propaganda. The absolute damn . . . *nerve!*"

Bordson picked up the holo-player. "Nevertheless, they will surely make this publicly available, and their denial that anything happened on Nimbus will be a matter of public record too."

"Tell a lie often enough, someone will believe it."

"It's worse than that, Kirsten. Tell a lie often enough, and it stands a good chance of becoming the truth."

FEDERATION COUNCIL
PARIS, EARTH

Quest did not waste time ensuring that political capital was made from the events on Nimbus. She was due to speak to the Council, ostensibly to report on the work of her committee, but she knew this was the ideal time to get her voice heard by a wider audience. Taking her place at the lectern, she addressed the Council, and the electors.

"I was elected to serve the people of my homeworld, Estelen, and I am proud, privileged, and honored to be their representative. My priority is to act as their voice within the wider community of our great and diverse United Federation of Planets.

"We're a small world. We're not famous. We're not on a tourist stop. That's a shame, because the hiking and the cooking are outstanding. We're a good people. We're friendly, we're hospitable, we're community minded. But we don't have a high public profile. We worry that we're not being heard.

"When I speak to folks back home, they ask me questions about the Council's priorities. How much do they think about small worlds like us? Do they only agree to projects that have a higher public profile?

"Take the Romulan relief effort. Somehow, this has become Starfleet's core mission. Somehow, a whole generation of Starfleet officers will come of age without the chance to explore space, discover new worlds and new life, broaden our horizons as a Federation. Instead, their careers will be devoted to just this mission.

"I am not saying that we should not help! Nobody could look at the footage from places like Vashti and not see that we are doing fine work, important and compassionate work. Other places . . ." She drew the line at mentioning Nimbus III specifically, but everyone would understand. "Well, I wouldn't like to be the one having to make those decisions.

"I'm not saying that there aren't benefits for us from this mission. In particular, let me praise the work of our scientists, who for the past few years have been pushing boundaries. And then there's the technical ingenuity of our engineers on Mars, working to produce new starship designs. Most of all, let's not forget those geniuses at the Daystrom Institute. I've been to their labs there and let me tell you that what they are doing is going to benefit every single person in the Federation. A synth in every home! It's amazing.

"We cannot think that we can do everything. There have to be limits to what we do, because we have many priorities. We need to be clear that when we offered aid to our Romulan neighbors, we did not intend that aid to come with any strings attached. We have to tread carefully.

"And so I come back to my work on the oversight committee promising a fuller and closer scrutiny of all our rescue and resettlement programs. We must ensure that they are aligned with Federation interests. We must ensure that our people on the ground do not overstep their authority or interfere with domestic Romulan affairs.

"And most of all, we must ensure that our neighbors know that we have not come to take advantage of them in their hour of need."

She opened her hands, an open-book gesture.

"We are not conquerors."

VERITY

Picard muted the sound.

"Hey," said Raffi, "I was listening to that!"

"I was barely able to hear the councilor over your commentary, Raffi."

"Well, it's the same old bullshit, isn't it? Since Nimbus III, she thinks she's got a mandate."

"She's an elected member of the Federation Council," Picard said mildly. "She *does* have a mandate." He looked at his XO's frustrated face. "All we can do is keep going," he continued. "Keep demonstrating through our actions that we are making a difference."

They both sat in silence, staring at the screen as Quest continued her speech. Her actions were getting increasingly urgent.

"I wish Koli hadn't quit," said Raffi.

"I wish for many things," said Picard softly. Most of all, he wished he had understood the full extent of the threat that had been posed to the people of Nimbus III.

"You know, JL," Raffi said, after a moment, "you should go on the offensive. Take this game right back to the politicians."

"In what way, Raffi?"

"Get out there, talk about what we're doing. You're the public face of this mission. Everyone knows who you are. Respects you."

Picard was shaking his head. "I can't, and I won't."

"People would listen to you, that's all I'm saying. You've got gravitas—"

"I'm gratified by that, Raffi, but flattery will not work in this circumstance. It is not my job to stand up and make speeches—"

"A short interview would do a world of good . . ."

The thought filled him with mild revulsion. His job was here, on the ship, at the head of this fleet. He was here to *show* the purpose of this mission, not to *tell* it. "It's not appropriate. Starfleet answers to the Federation Council. A response from me to Quest would be to dishonor my oath."

"But if you won't make the case, Admiral, who will?"

"That's Bordson's job. The C-in-C is the place where the politics and Starfleet meet."

Raffi did not look entirely satisfied.

"He will do the right thing," said Picard. "We're lucky to have him, Raffi. Other C-in-Cs would have buckled under the pressure much sooner. We've been given largely a free hand."

Raffi stood. "As long as he understands how difficult these people are making this for you, JL. As long as he stays on our side."

VERITY

The events on Nimbus III and whether Tajuth played a part in it preyed on Picard's mind. He was acutely aware that he knew no more about Tajuth than from the day he had arrived on board eighteen months ago. Cool and self-contained, Tajuth did not socialize with other members of the crew. Picard was aware that he had occasionally met Koli when they were both off duty. Not for the first time, Picard regretted Koli's departure; regretted the loss of the small acts of courage and honesty that had done so much for the mission. Now there was no real point of contact between the Starfleet officers on the *Verity* and the Romulan assigned to liaise with them. He would have to begin building trust all over again.

I must remember, Picard thought, *that such trust is possible.* When the footage of the massacre had been revealed, he had got in touch with Zani. Her counsel, as ever, had brought him back to himself. *"You are not responsible for the choices made by others,"* she had said. *"To attribute to oneself that power is to assume that you have the right to compel others. And that is to deceive yourself. Do not lie to yourself that you could have done more than you did."*

Still, Koli held him responsible for what had happened on Nimbus, and it was difficult not to believe he was culpable in some way. He had been the senior Starfleet officer present, and people had died. No matter how often Raffi said—how often he told himself—that their withdrawal had prevented a widespread massacre. His actions had prevented the mission from coming under further threat. But he could not free himself of a sense of blame.

Did I save lives that day? Did I lose lives? When did this become a matter of addition, subtraction, profit and loss?

The door to his ready room chimed. "Enter," he called, and watched as Tajuth came in, as cool and impenetrable as ever. Picard indicated that he should sit, and they studied each other carefully. Secrets and evasions. The Tal Shiar way.

Let me try absolute candor.

"The methods used by the Tal Shiar on Nimbus III were unacceptable," said Picard, and lifted his hand when Tajuth began what he assumed would be a denial that the people there had been Tal Shiar. "Unacceptable and unproductive. You can't kill the patient as part of the cure."

There was a pause. Tajuth said, "Did you want me to respond to that?"

"I would prefer open dialogue with you, Commander," said Picard.

"Open dialogue," murmured Tajuth. "With Starfleet . . ."

"May I suggest," said Picard, "that our old habits and instincts will not serve us in this situation. Only trust."

"Trust . . ." Tajuth seemed to ponder the idea. "Lives were saved on Nimbus, Admiral. The only people who died were attempting to prevent the relocation from happening."

"We would have persuaded them."

"I do not believe that would have happened."

"We were hardly given the chance!"

"You'd been there some time, Admiral," Tajuth said. "There are other and worthier worlds than one inhabited by a bunch of criminals and bandits."

"No life is worthier than any other. No one is worthier than anyone else. Everyone is worthy of respect—"

Tajuth smiled. "Fine words. But, as ever, Starfleet says one thing and does another. We asked you to stand aside and allow us to handle the situation on Nimbus the way we saw fit. And, once again, we found that you do not believe that our requests are worthy of respect. Our authority should be undermined, when it suits the Federation. You do not mean what you say, at all."

"People were *murdered*—"

"More lives were saved than lost. Time and resources that were being wasted on a small colony that are now available to save others—"

Picard said, "That does not excuse what happened—"

"Admiral, this is the Romulan way. You cannot expect thousands of years of Romulan culture to bend to your will because one Starfleet admiral wants it to."

"Not one admiral," Picard said. "Many of us, including Lieutenant Koli." He caught a flicker in Tajuth's eyes then. Yes, his instincts had been correct; Koli had made a connection there. "The methods that were used on Nimbus were not acceptable. They are not something Starfleet can be associated with."

"Saving face?" said Tajuth.

"No," said Picard. "Acting according to our values."

"Let me try again," Tajuth said. "Let me try to explain. To many Romulans, it seems as if Starfleet's intervention is conditional. That the aim is not simply to give aid when requested, but to undermine Romulan politics—"

"The Empire faces an unprecedented crisis that would undermine any political system," Picard pointed out.

"And that process does not need outside help. This is what our people are coming to believe. That the aid the Federation gives depends upon changing our way of life. Changing our culture. Do you understand, Admiral?"

"I understand that Romulan culture is not as monolithic as your leaders would have us believe."

Tajuth frowned. "In what way?"

"I've seen many different aspects of your culture now, Commander. If anything belies the notion that you are all alike, it is the Qowat Milat."

Tajuth froze. *Damn*, thought Picard. *That was a mistake.* "Please," he said. "Let us put all this aside. Let us deal with the immediate issues—the need to help. Are you still willing to help me, Tajuth?"

Tajuth looked back at him—almost sorrowfully, Picard thought. "I have always helped," he said. "But this does not necessarily mean that I will act in a way that you want, Admiral. Romulus is not the Federation. You need to remember this. You need to *respect* this."

"As Koli did?"

Tajuth did not reply immediately. "We will all miss Lieutenant Koli," he said, and Picard sensed genuine regret in his voice. He stood up. "She gave you good advice, Picard. Respect us. Respect our values. I wish she was still here to advise you."

Daystrom Institute
Okinawa, Earth

Later in life, when time and change and entropy had taken away from him much that he held dear, Bruce Maddox would remember the early mornings with Agnes Jurati as among the happiest moments of his life. What made these memories most precious to him, he recollected, was that they were theirs, and theirs alone. At his request, they were keeping their affair private. There were no longer questions of his role as her teacher; she had received her doctorate in robotics earlier in the year. But he did not want people to know that they were together. The time he spent with her was an escape from the world; they inhabited their own bubble, where he felt completely at ease. He sometimes thought of them as living inside a snow globe, protected from everything beyond the dome, safe inside their own fine and private place.

Once, just once, she said to him, "Are you ashamed of me, Bruce?"

"What? What do you mean?"

She was sitting in the chair by the window, wearing his robe. She looked young, and vulnerable, and sad. His heart went out to her. He thought she was lovely.

"I guess . . . maybe . . . because you won't be seen with me?"

He came and knelt down before her. He took her hands within his. "Aggie," he said, "you are my inspiration. My courage. I . . . I guess I don't want to share you."

It seemed to convince her, or to satisfy her, at least, and they went back to how it was. Her arriving under cover of darkness; leaving the apartment early, and without him. In between, she was everything to him. He spent his days working on a project so far from everything that mattered to him that he felt disassociated from it. He went through the motions—a mechanical man, no less—answering questions, directing research, thinking through problems, keeping the synths rolling off the line—but a part of him remained aloof. Some small, critical part had . . . not malfunctioned, not that, but had detached itself from the world around him. Only Aggie kept him from sailing away for good.

Late one night, they lay together in bed. The lamplight formed patterns on her pale skin. Gently, he mapped these with his fingertips. She shivered with pleasure.

"I've been thinking," he said slowly.

She froze beneath his touch. "Oh god," she said, "that's usually the prelude to 'goodbye.'"

"What?" He saw the fright in her eyes. She looked like a small creature, cornered by the hunter. "Aggie, of course not! I mean, I've been thinking about work. I have some ideas . . ."

"Shit," she said, putting her head in her hands. "I thought you were finishing with me!"

"Whatever would make you think—"

"No, it's me," she said. "Stupid me. Stupid Aggie. Go on," she said. "I'm listening. Take me through it."

"It was something you said, of course—well, it's always something you say, isn't it? But this was something specific. The first time we met."

She flushed. "Oh god. I was starstruck. I was hoping you'd forgotten that—"

He ran his hand along her arm. "I'll never forget meeting you."

"Charmer," she said. "Anyway, what did I say that was so inspirational? Amongst all the inspirational things that I must say, all the time?"

"You asked me if I'd thought about the capabilities of a single positronic neuron."

"Did I? Yes, I did! And did you, ever?"

"Yes, I have."

Beneath the covers, she dug into his leg with her toes. "Clever boy."

"Ow," he said. "Well, some part of me has been thinking . . ." He drifted off, into his thoughts. She poked her toes into him again.

"Go on!"

"Soong's work, it's in B4," he said. "We have the building blocks. I thought, what if I go back down, right to the very beginning, right to the building blocks. What do I have there? A few dozen neurons."

Her face puckered into a frown. She was adorable. "Is that all?"

"Uh-huh. So, I thought, what can I do with that?"

"Not much, I'd guess?"

"You'd think so, wouldn't you? But I thought, no, I won't let them win. I won't let Quest and La Forge and everyone else get away with this."

"Good for you, Bruce! This is what I've been saying to you all along!"

"I can't do much with one. I need more. So how about I clone them?"

"What?"

He sat up, wrapped his arms around his legs. He could hear his ideas coming together, as he described them. "Fractal neuronic cloning, Aggie. It builds on what we've done with Mackenzie. But it builds on Soong's work too. Do you see?"

He reached for a padd, began to sketch his ideas out for her. One neuron. That's all they needed. And from that came . . . everything else. As he ran her through it, he watched her face. He watched her lips move, silently, as she worked through his ideas for herself. He saw the moment when understanding dawned; when his ideas came to life in her eyes. He saw that she grasped what he meant. She was, she would always be, his most gifted student. "Bruce, this is it! This is really it!"

"Well, I think it could be . . ."

"You are a genius!"

Could anyone ever tire of hearing that said? "There's a way to go yet, Aggie! A lot of work to be done—"

She pulled him into an embrace. "You'll do it."

"And there's synths to build still, all the work for Mars—"

"Who cares about Mars?" She held him as if he were the most precious thing in the world. "This is creating *life*!"

ROMULAN ASTROPHYSICAL ACADEMY
ROMULUS

Some days, Nokim Vritet could persuade himself that everything was the same as ever. Some days he was able to buy food and catch the tram that went straight to the academy. Some days he would even be able to work at his desk all day without suffering a power cut, and not have to retreat home, sitting huddled over his books with a solar lamp, until fear of that running down would make him turn it off, and leave him sitting staring into darkness. Some mornings he would not need to put on his face mask, and he could step outside and think: *The pollution is better today*. Some evenings, walking slowly home, he would look up and think: *What beautiful colors! What a fine sunset!* He would look at the sky and tell himself that he did not feel afraid.

But the truth was that he felt afraid almost all of the time, and bewildered. He seemed to be caught between two worlds, one in which everything was continuing as it had throughout his whole life, and another in which a horror was hurtling toward him, a horror so vast, so unimaginable, that the simplest thing to do was ignore it, and carry on as best you could, pretending that everything was fine. He was used to this. Romulans were used to lying to each other, and to themselves. But even so—he could not completely ignore what was going on around him. The food shortages. The blackouts. The hotter days. The odd skies. The whispers all around him. The imminent and rapidly approaching end.

Some truths are simply too big to ignore. As a child, Vritet read voraciously, preferring a sensational kind of literature in which far-flung alien worlds were beset by terrible apocalypses: great wars, overwhelming floods, cruel invasions, devastating fires that could not be extinguished. His parents, used to their son's oddities, had humored him until he had started to have nightmares, and then the books were deleted, and he was instructed to focus on his studies. The cold stars, and their steady rhythms, had been a balm. But even the stars, it seemed to Vritet, had betrayed him. Everything he had expected was coming true: the accelerated changes in climate and temperature, the sense that the structures upon which his world depended were breaking down. His calculations, he knew, had been completely true.

And yet nothing was happening. Or, at least, not that he could see. Some people had gone, that was true, a few senior administrators at the Academy, a few politician friends of his family. But, as far as Vritet could tell, the life of the capital city was continuing as it had always done—or was trying to, at least. Why was nothing happening? Why was nothing being done? He knew better than to ask—he did not want to hear from the Tal Shiar again. He assumed that next time they would not simply pay him a visit. They would want him to spend some time with them—and nobody wanted to spend time with the Tal Shiar. Their reach, their power—he did not think that even his family connections would protect him. But each night, as he lay in bed, and tried to sleep, his mind would soon wander to thinking about the horrors of what Romulus would soon face . . . Somebody, somewhere, had to be doing *something*. But who? What? Where?

At length, he couldn't bear the uncertainty any longer. He had to have news—but whom could he ask? He did not trust the propaganda that his government was putting out, which assured the people of Romulus that everything was fine, that evacuation plans were well underway, and they should wait to hear from local officials about their designated departure dates. He did not believe the footage that he saw of happy Romulans settling into bright new homes on bright new worlds. He did not trust colleagues either, or those that remained; he assumed half of them were Tal Shiar, and the rest were either paid off or intimidated. He knew that he needed external confirmation of his work, someone objective who could tell him that his predictions were right.

The name came to him one night when he had gone to bed early, there being no light, no power, and no food, and he lay hungry and restless, listening to disruptor fire on the far side of the city.

Safadi.

She would know what was happening. She was an expert.

As soon as he thought this, he tried to put the idea out of his mind. It was madness, he thought; there was no way that he could contact her. But who else was there? Who else could tell him that his work was accurate? Who else could he ask?

He spent a great deal of his personal fortune on getting the communication arranged. An uncle who had always had a soft spot for him, who had indulged the boy's eccentricities for many years, and who happened to own a fleet of ships that operated along the border, agreed to send the message for him via his Federation contacts—for a fair price. So Vritet sent his message, written in both desperation and hope, to Amal Safadi on Earth:

Please confirm you have seen my work and agree. Please confirm help is on its way.

And then—back home to wait. Hope that somehow the message would get through; hope that it got through undetected. Hope that whoever she was working with in her own intelligence services had the ability to see that this was not a fake and had the skill to use the information encrypted in his message to send the response back safely. He waited, and he waited.

At last, there came a knock at the door.

About ten minutes later, Vritet sat in the back of a vehicle speeding through the city, wedged between two Tal Shiar agents. They had hit him, very hard, and then put a hood over his head. They had dragged him down the stairs, his legs crumpled beneath him. They pushed him into the back of this vehicle and made him sit with his head down between his knees and his hands clasped behind his neck. All through this, particularly after they had hit him, his mind had floated away. He thought: *Did I think it would end this way?* And he knew that half of him had, and half of him had not. That dual world all Romulans inhabited: one of reality, one of self-deception. At last, after time had lost meaning to Vritet and he had passed into limbo, the vehicle stopped. He was bundled out, and dragged inside, and then marched—where? For a long time, down echoing corridors, up flights of stairs, down more flights of stairs . . . He tried to tell himself that all of this was simply an attempt to disorient him, to frighten him . . .

The problem was—it worked. It worked very well.

And it ended where it was always going to end: Vritet strapped in a chair, with lights shining in his eyes, and two shadowy figures behind the lights, talking to him. *Take us through your calculations. We believe there are errors . . . We would like you to outline these for us . . .*

Through parched lips and a broken nose, he said, "There are no errors."

Try again, Nokim. There are certainly errors here.

"There are no errors!"

Look harder. You will find them, if you look closely enough.

Look harder, Nokim. If you try very hard, you will see your mistake.

DAYSTROM INSTITUTE
OKINAWA, EARTH

After his conversation with Jurati, Maddox went to ground. She left him message after message, and he would think: *This isn't fair, I must get back to her.* But then he would open up his files, and turn back to his work, and he would become lost. He would become lost to everything except the pursuit of his beautiful, elusive dream.

Dimly, he perceived that this change in his habits was not going unnoticed. Even Sisra Koas, the rather shambolic director of the Institute, had left him a handful of cordial and circumlocutory messages that he knew were asking: *Where the hell are you, Bruce?* Estella Mackenzie, keen to get started on the next generation of synths, was plaguing him almost hourly, it seemed. And then the messages started to arrive from Geordi La Forge. *What's going on, Bruce? Where are you?*

But he could not put his work aside. This idea—this brilliant idea, of fractal neuronic cloning—he knew that there was something there, and the thought of this consumed him. He felt like a boy again, poring over the books and datafiles utterly absorbed, forgetting the time and everything around him. He began to remember how it felt, to be caught up in ideas, to be pursuing a breakthrough. The need to be wholly immersed, to be without distractions, to absent oneself so thoroughly from the world around you. He took long walks, out into the countryside around the Institute. He turned off his handheld, his comm at home, and then his comm at work. Somewhere, in the peace and quiet, lay the answers he had been looking for all his life.

He was utterly unprepared for Geordi La Forge's arrival. A summer morning, very hot. Maddox getting to his office late and distracted. La Forge standing outside his locked door, arms folded.

"Hey Bruce. What's going on?"

The whole day lost to this. He remembered the story of Coleridge, waking from a fever dream with the whole of *Kubla Khan* inside his head, sitting at his desk and getting down only a few lines before there was a knock at the door, and a person from Porlock kept him talking until the poem was well and truly dead . . .

La Forge put him through his paces. He wanted a full tour. He wanted detailed reports. He wanted the team heads in. He wanted to hear everything they had to say. He wanted to know how the next generation was coming along. He wanted fifty more synths as quickly as possible. Maddox hardly heard a word of it.

"Bruce," said La Forge, partway through the afternoon, "are you even *listening*?"

Maddox looked up. The whole team was staring at him. La Forge looked . . . pissed off.

I have to get a grip. Just for today.

"Of course I am, Geordi," he said, and he pulled his mind back to whatever the man wanted. That night the team took their visitor out for dinner; fourteen of them, plus Maddox and La Forge, a very cheerful and lively occasion. Agnes sat at the far end of the table, looking sad, and he smiled at her until she began to glow, ever so slightly. *Get through this evening*, Maddox was thinking, *and you can get back to work*. On the way out of the restaurant, Agnes brushed past him, smiling brightly, and said, in a quiet voice that only he could hear, "Are you okay? Have I done something wrong?"

He touched her arm. "Everything's okay, Aggie. Work."

And he left it at that, because he did not want a long conversation. He did not want distractions. As soon as he was sure that La Forge was content, he hurried off, back to his apartment. He listened to yet another message from Agnes (*"Hey, I know you said everything was okay, and, so, I don't mean to hassle you, wondered if a coffee might be on the agenda soon."*) He promised himself he would reply to her in the morning. He was afraid, terribly afraid, that if he lost the thread he would never find it again.

Maddox lay down. The night was hot, and the temperature regulators were struggling. Through the open window, he heard the endless chirrup of the evening cicadas. He closed his eyes. But he did not see darkness. Instead, he saw fractals. He saw them vividly, lit up, golden rays and spirals that began to spin, that drew him in, ever deeper and deeper. He knew he might lose himself inside this maze. And he knew that this was what he wanted—because the deeper he went, the better he would understand. And somewhere in this maze, he knew, he would find the key. In the dark, eyes closed, he pressed the thumb and forefinger of each hand together, forming circles. Then he pushed the circles together so that they interlocked. *The key*, he thought; *the key to unlocking life.*

Part 3

THE LAST

2385

11

Admiral's Log: Reports have been reaching us that the situation on the Romulan homeworld is deteriorating rapidly. Significant changes in climate, and the concomitant strains, are leading to an infrastructure breakdown. I cannot imagine what conditions must be like on Romulus as a result of this. Highly complex civilizations, reliant as they are on long supply chains, can be extremely vulnerable to even mild disruptions, and they are long past that point now. What are the effects of such disruption? Urban centers—which rely on the rapid transportation and delivery of goods—cannot feed their populations. Are these supply chains still functioning? Is the power still on in the major cities? Is clean water still readily available? If this fails, then there is a serious risk of the outbreak of communicable disease. Famine, thirst, plague—truly this would be the end of days.

Our knowledge of conditions on Romulus is limited. Receiving good intelligence was always difficult even in the best of circumstances. My understanding is that we still have some agents on Romulus, but it becomes harder to justify their continued presence there, given the imminent risk. Interestingly, Raffi is of the opinion that our intelligence has become slightly better in recent months, but that this is one further sign that Romulus is in deep and serious trouble. She suspects that as the strains on the Romulan government and the flow of refugees outward become ever greater, information has become harder for the authorities to control. As a result, we are able to learn much more than we ever did in the past, and much more than the Romulan government would like. They are no longer able to contain the leaks. Nevertheless, despite all evidence to the contrary, the Romulan government insists that their ongoing evacuation effort of the homeworld is proceeding steadily, and within necessary time frames.

Admiral Bordson has told me of several tense conversations with Ambassador Sulde in which she flatly denies that any help is needed on Romulus.

I am sympathetic to the desire to save face, but I simply do not believe Sulde. Whether they are lying to us or deluding themselves, it is clear to me that Romulus is now on the brink, and only a concerted evacuation effort can save what remains of the population still there. But the call has not come. At all times, I try to remember the Romulan predisposition toward secrecy, and that there are still many gaps in our intelligence as to the operations of the Romulan military and the Tal Shiar. It is my fervent hope that one or both of these groups is coordinating evacuation operations that we know nothing about. But my heart tells me that they are no longer able to marshal the resources to do this. At some point, Starfleet will be asked to help. I cannot imagine the devastation, the loss of life, if the Romulan authorities would prefer to save face rather than save their fellow citizens. I cannot believe that the plan has never been to evacuate their people, but to leave them to their eventual and inevitable fate.

Raffi, I should note, does not find this difficult to believe. I have noticed, particularly since the tragic events of Nimbus III, a hardening of the commander's attitude toward the people whom we are trying to help. Let me correct this. I have noted no change in Raffi's desire to help ordinary Romulan people. But it is plain that her opinion of the Romulan authorities—government, military, and Tal Shiar—has lowered considerably during the past year. Thinking about how matters must be on Romulus, and how we stand ready to help, but remain unasked, it is hard not to agree with Raffi. But I must continue to hope that we will persuade the Romulan authorities that we are their friends—or, at least, that we are not their enemies . . .

FEDERATION COUNCIL
PARIS, EARTH

The popularity of politicians will rise and fall. Olivia Quest, three years into her time as a Federation councilor, was discovering that one cannot remain the people's darling indefinitely. To her credit, she was not caught unawares. Since her visit to the Daystrom Institute, she had spoken on numerous occasions, and with great enthusiasm, about the synthetics program. Upon reflection, she could see that to an outsider, it signaled a significant shift in her position, even allying her with the factions within Starfleet that insisted that the Romulan relief mission should continue at the same pace. She tasked her aides to conduct some quiet polling, and the results were a wake-up call. A worrying number of people on Estelen, whom she depended on to keep her job, were starting to say that she had "gone native." Her time on Earth had turned her into yet another Federation lackey, out of touch with her homeworld.

Quest did not intend to lose the forthcoming election, and if that meant listening to her constituents, and not to her colleagues, then she was prepared to do just that. Taking advantage of the yearly Council recess, she traveled back home, and spent the break touring the major conurbations on Estelen and its moons. She held town hall meetings, took the reprimands from her constituents. She heard what people were saying and told them she would return to Earth with their interests foremost in her heart. She was too canny an operator not to also further her own goals. After some considerable wrangling, she was able to take home a Daystrom A500; she presented it at separate meetings of farm managers and terraformers and asked them to think about what these machines could do for them. And when she saw their amazement at these creations, and the gleam of understanding about how their productivity might be transformed, she secretly thanked Bruce Maddox for his work on her behalf.

She returned to Earth for the new Council session determined to balance these competing demands and find a way through that would satisfy her constituents' disgruntlement with the relief mission while discovering ways to expand the synthetics program for them. Could there be a way to sever the synthetics program from the relief mission? She found that during her time at home, momentum against the mission had certainly grown. When she arrived back at her office in Paris, her aide sat her down.

"Liv," he said, "things have gone crazy while you were away. The representative for Dorrax wants to see you."

Dorrax was a small Federation world like Estelen: far from Sol, close to the Neutral Zone, its population alarmed about the continued diversion of resources toward the Romulans. "Let's get him in here as quickly as we can."

The Dorraxian councilor, Thebi, was in her office the following morning—and he was not alone. He had brought three others with him: two other representatives from outlying worlds and a vividly beautiful androgyne from a species that Quest did not recognize. Thebi introduced this person as Vhokti, an ambassador from the unaligned Neutral Zone border world Intassa, which was not a member of the Federation. All were deeply concerned about the Federation's increasing involvement in the Romulan crisis. But why, thought Quest, was Vhokti here?

"You said it yourself, Olivia," Thebi said. He was a thin, rather worried-looking man, whose hands moved nervously throughout the conversation. "This mission is a strain on resources. Transport ships to Dorrax have been halved in the last two years. The ships have all been pulled away to the Romulan effort!"

"We're not saying," said one of the other councilors, a felinoid named Inkyne, "that they don't need relocating. Of course they do! We're not monsters! We don't want them to die! But at what cost? It won't be the Big Four that pay, will it? It will be worlds like ours."

"You know that I understand," said Quest. "I understand completely."

"You seem to have been distracted recently by those damn synths," Thebi said.

"Only because I think we can use them," Quest said quickly. "I am absolutely committed to ensuring our voice is heard at the top levels."

The other councilors exchanged a look. "The fact is, we're not sure whether we want a voice any longer," Thebi said. He glanced at Vhokti. "We've been exploring the possibility of secession."

Quest didn't blink. *Secession?* "That's a . . . drastic solution to our troubles."

"But it's one that we should think about," said Thebi. "Consider our worlds, Olivia. All on the border. I know Estelen was settled by humans, and I appreciate that the cultural ties to Earth are strong, but some of us joined the Federation because we thought we were becoming equal partners in a great collaboration. But as far as we can see, it's the Big Four running the show, and they've got more in common with the Romulans than with us."

"But *secession*," said Quest. Even saying it sounded faintly treasonable. Why should the idea be unthinkable? What power prevented her from even wanting to think about this as a possibility? "Ambassador Vhokti," she said. "Forgive me if this sounds mistrustful but—what exactly is in this for you?"

Vhokti looked at her with silver unblinking eyes. Hard to read. Quest wasn't sure what to make of it. "I want to assure you," said Vhokti, "that I am not here to cause strife. My world has a great deal in common with yours. We are small, we are agricultural, we trade widely both within the Federation and beyond. We were approached nearly a century ago about the possibility of admission to the Federation, and we debated the idea thoroughly. In the end, we chose to remain outside of the Federation because we were afraid of cultural contamination. We were afraid of Romulan invasion, yes, but that is no longer a threat. They are no longer a power. The Neutral Zone is breached. In five years, the border will be transformed. It's wise for the worlds who will be most affected to look to each other, rather than to another power, to ensure mutual aid and protection."

Quest folded her hands in front of her. It was a bold vision, she thought. What would be best for Estelen? "I have to think about this," she said. At the very least, it might be possible to use the idea of secession as leverage. Persuade the powers that be—whether in the Council or Starfleet—that something had to change.

"By all means think about it," said Thebi. "But you must bear in mind—we are not the only people thinking this way. Momentum is growing. Councilors from a half dozen planets have approached me to discuss secession. And think about your own world, Councilor. Things are changing. Starfleet has overreached. The Federation has overreached. Perhaps the days of the Federation are done. We should look to our own worlds, take care of ourselves, and find allies closer to home."

"Read the mood carefully, Olivia," said Inkyne, green eyes glowing. "Starfleet, the Federation—with each decision they make, each ship they divert to this mission, each project they start that aims to aid the Romulans, they are telling us that we are of less importance to them than a long-standing enemy. Perhaps it's time to break, truly. Stand up for ourselves. Stand with each other."

"Like you say all the time, Romulan space is best for Romulans," said Thebi. "And perhaps our worlds are best for us."

"And I am here to assure you that you have friends outside of the Federation," said Vhokti. "If you choose to leave, we will be there."

When the group left, Quest sat with her mind reeling. *Secession.* She had not seen that coming. It was almost unthinkable. Could it be done? Would it be best? She thought carefully. Thebi had said something, about Estelen being a human colony, and the cultural ties to the Federation being strong. That gave her pause. In her heart, Quest was not sure that she would countenance the idea of leaving the Federation. Many of them made trips back to Earth at some point. They looked up their family trees. They visited the cities and countries that their ancestors had left. Yes, those ties were strong, and her instincts told her that she could not sell this, at least, not without careful preparation. In the meantime, Estelen's continued involvement in the Federation was worthwhile. And that, in turn, meant that she needed to show some concrete benefits, and soon. A diversion of resources away from the mission, and back to the borders.

Starfleet brass had controlled the narrative on this for far too long. It was time to think the unthinkable; say the unsayable. It was time to debate this mission, debate the fundamentals and let the Council speak.

Quickly, she wrote out the motion, and sent it for consideration. By the end of the day, the debate was timetabled.

The Romulan crisis is a domestic matter. Starfleet's involvement has exceeded its mandate and should be immediately scaled back.

This might be the thing that stopped these secessions from happening. The thing that could stop the breakup of the Federation.

STARFLEET COMMAND
SAN FRANCISCO, EARTH

Captain Kirsten Clancy, sitting in her office, following the debate, heard Councilor Inkyne say the word *secession*. She thought at first that the universal translator had failed. Then she began to believe that she had just seen the opening move that would lead to the Federation's demise. For a moment, she glimpsed that future: hundreds of worlds, rudderless, each out for their own gain; pressing their own advantage and treating each other as competitors rather than partners. Hostility. Suspicion. Chaos. War. Clancy—practical and unemotional, dedicated and intelligent— damped down the sentiment immediately. She was damned if that was going happen on her watch.

One eye still on the screen, one ear still following the speeches, she began scribbling a list of people whom she needed to see and stat. Borderworld representatives, Inkyne, Thebi. She made a note to ask Starfleet Intelligence how the unaligned border worlds were reporting all this. Then Inkyne said, *"Romulan space for the Romulans—"*

"Christ!" Clancy said, and threw down her padd. That damn phrase was everywhere these days. She loathed it; loathed the subtle undercurrent of racism; loathed how it was invariably followed up by the statement *Oh, it's not that I want them to die—I simply think it's their own business.* Dammit, hadn't people got it yet? If Starfleet wasn't there, then all those people *would* die.

Her comm chimed. It was the C-in-C.

"Kirsten, are you watching this?"

"Damn right I am!"

"I've asked Picard to speak to us later today."

"I'm clearing my damn schedule!"

"This is all extremely concerning—"

"It's a damn fucking mess!"

Bordson blinked. *"Kirsten, I have never heard you swear this much."*

"Take it as a mark of how fucking deep my concern runs, sir."

Clancy spent the rest of the day chasing meetings and taking soundings. By the time she went to join Bordson for their conference with Picard, she was by no means in the best of moods. She listened to the careful and measured discussions of the two men with increasing annoyance.

"All of this is irrelevant compared to the true purpose of this mission," said Picard, *"the rescue of people in need."*

Clancy couldn't believe what she was hearing. She imagined the dinosaurs looking up at the asteroid, thinking: *Perhaps we can be friends.* She leaned forward to speak, but Bordson was already talking.

"I'm afraid that things are changing rapidly here, Jean-Luc."

That was phrased considerably more politely than she could have managed, but it was the basic point they needed to get through to him.

"They are changing rapidly in Romulan space too—and not for the better."

Nope, it hadn't gotten through.

"And while I continue to be sympathetic to their plight, I am saddened to say that for many people in the Federation, this is less and less true. I understand. Smaller worlds, on the border, finding that promised resources have not materialized. Some of these worlds have suffered at Romulan hands in the past—"

Picard was shaking his head. *"Then they must put aside their grievances, listen to the better angels of their nature, and make a sacrifice that is necessary for others to survive."*

"Nobody," said Clancy, "wins elections telling people to make sacrifices."

Picard was looking at her as if she were speaking a language that his universal translator could not parse. *"I fail to see the relevance—"*

She shifted impatiently in her seat. "There are worlds now threatening to secede. The idea is gaining momentum. 'If the Federation won't look after us, we'll look after each other.'"

"Secede? That would be an entirely irrational decision. They are manifestly better inside the Federation than out."

"These decisions aren't made rationally, *sir*," she said. "They're coming from anger and resentment. They come from a growing sense of tribalism. You hear anti-Romulan sentiment even on Earth in places you wouldn't believe."

"We cannot base our response to this mission on such sentiments—"

"No," said Bordson, calmly intervening, his hand placed upon Clancy's arm, "but others will. We gain nothing by ignoring such sentiments or allowing them to fester and gain ground."

"Would you pander to xenophobia?"

"I would not," said Bordson, sharply for him. "But the mission needs a big win, Jean-Luc."

"Vashti," he said immediately.

"Old news," said Clancy. "We need more. Happy Romulan children. Smiling Starfleet officers. Federation citizens, welcoming them with open arms—"

Picard's look, she saw, was pure distaste. She felt a flash of anger.

"Rather coarsely put, Kirsten," said Bordson, "but the sentiment is correct. We need another Vashti."

"Surely it wasn't unique?" Clancy said.

"I understand. Verity *out."*

Bordson eyed her thoughtfully. "You think we need more, don't you?"

"It's not that I think we need more, Victor, but that I think this mission is going to become increasingly difficult to sell. The concerns that these people have—they're reasonable. I said this at the start—we were getting ourselves involved in a project that had no clear end date and might expand in ways we couldn't foresee. And it has! The whole of the Martian shipbuilding facilities pulled into the service of this mission. A generation of Starfleet officers and civil servants all working on this. We've invented a new form of synthetic life! We're five years into this, and the mission is still growing."

He was listening. "Your advice?"

"I advise that we start putting some resources back into Federation projects."

"Picard isn't going to like that—"

"Picard," said Clancy, "is going to have to lump it."

Bordson sat for a while, deep in thought. "Secession," he said at last. "Do they mean it? Or is it a bluff?"

"I think we should meet with these people. Talk to them. In the meantime, I'm going to see what we can pull back. People, ships, replicators, printers. Not the whole mission, but something. Enough to make them understand that we're listening." She looked at him. "Do you want to take the meeting with Quest, or shall I?"

"I think," he said, "you should handle her."

VERITY

Picard received with some anger the news that a dozen ships, three hundred staff, and five industrial replicators were to be pulled. They were going to support infrastructure projects on remote worlds. The decision had plainly been taken without consideration to his objections. Therefore, all he could do was mitigate its effects. He suggested that the use of these resources might be contingent on the recipient worlds aiding Romulan refugees. Whereby when a new transport came online, the worlds would agree to take a few thousand settlers. Clancy quashed this idea at once. Indeed, he thought she quashed it with unusual vigor.

"Are you kidding me?" she said. "I put that to the councilors for Dorrax and they'll secede on the spot!"

Picard was at a loss to understand why this idea met with such resistance. It had struck him as a rather elegant solution. Privately, he believed that these mutterings about secession were no more than empty threats. Who would dare leave the Federation? Who would willingly exile themselves from this great diverse community of worlds, each seeking to benefit the other both materially and culturally? These worlds would be forced to rely on only their own resources during a deeply uncertain time. Nevertheless, he knew that Clancy was closer to the politicians, and reluctantly accepted what he was sure would be a short period of retrenchment. He also held numerous conversations with La Forge about how the shortfall in the ships might be made up.

"That depends on Maddox," said La Forge, *"and how soon he can get this new batch of A500s to me."*

"Is there a problem, Geordi?"

"No . . . but the work has slowed down. You know Maddox. He gets distracted."

"Then he must undistract himself," said Picard acerbically.

"I'll send him that message," said La Forge, *"and I'll say it comes straight from you."*

Clancy's parting shot in their previous conversation was preoccupying Picard. Was Vashti unique, then? Once again, the grind of the mission began to wear at him. The slow procession of lost souls, clutching all they could carry. Would the children ever recover? Was the damage, the trauma, too great? He found himself researching everything that was known about the psychology of Romulan trauma. Ignoring Clancy's pleas not to add personnel, he requested that Gbowee recruit psychologists to begin longitudinal studies of the Romulan settlers in Federation space. He fretted over the cabin layouts. Did they do enough to mitigate stress? Raffi indulged him at first, but he knew she was starting to become impatient.

He turned to Zani, hoping she could provide answers he could not see.

"I fear we have done unwitting damage," he confessed to her. "I fear Starfleet may have created wounds that will never heal."

"What would you have done differently?" Zani said.

He pondered this. He might wish that events on Nimbus III had not ended in the way that they had, but he could not see what he could have done. "Nothing," he said.

"Then what can I say other than—act honestly. And listen honestly."

Was that a rebuke? Did he sometimes not listen honestly? He believed that he was a thoughtful man, a compassionate man, one who tried to take all opinions into account. Nevertheless, he was grateful for her counsel and for her friendship. He did not—he *could* not—believe that such a friendship was unique, that among their peoples, they were the only two who understood each other. There had to be others, who could put everything aside, and do the right—the *necessary*—thing.

Picard received a request for another conference with Admiral Bordson with some trepidation, fearing that there would be more bad news, further demand for retrenchment to placate the isolationist elements that seemed to be emerging across the Federation.

"Admiral Picard," said Bordson. *"I'm patched in with Ambassador Sulde in Paris."*

The Romulan ambassador to the Federation, Picard thought. *What could this mean?*

Sulde's face appeared on screen. Picard had not dealt with her—that had been Victor Bordson's duty. His impression of her in the vids that he had seen was of a controlled, canny, and extremely suave woman. This was not how she appeared today. There was an air of exhaustion—and, yes, grief—about her that she could not hide.

"Ambassador Sulde," he said, "how may I help?"

"Help," she said, and a bitter smile passed across her lips. *"Admiral, I have been authorized by my government to request Starfleet's assistance in the evacuation of Romulus. We . . ."* She halted, as if the words stuck in her

throat, and lifted her hand to press it against her mouth. Picard watched with compassion as she gathered the tatters of her dignity. *"We are no longer able to keep pace with the need."*

Picard nodded. He hated this. He hated to see these proud people brought low. He remembered what Koli used to say: "We must not let the Romulans become the beggars of two quadrants." He had no desire for that, no taste for it. All he wanted was to bring Sulde's people to safety, to allow them to live. And, perhaps, to prove to the Romulans beyond doubt that the Federation were their friends.

"*Jolan tru*, Ambassador," he said. "We honor your people. We honor the sanctity and the privacy of your homes. We understand how hard this request must be. I promise you our help, and our discretion." He glanced at Bordson. "Do you wish our fleet to proceed to Romulus itself?"

Sulde looked away, her eyes down. *"That . . . is not possible."*

No, thought Picard, he had suspected not. "Then where, Ambassador? Our fleet is at your service."

"*Vejuro,*" she said.

Picard knew the world: it was in the next system along from the Romulan star, one of the most populated settled worlds beyond the home system. "How advanced is the evacuation?"

She did not look at him. *"It has not yet begun."*

He thought he heard Bordson murmur something. "I see, Ambassador. We shall do all we can."

She did not speak but touched her mouth and her heart. Then she was gone.

Bordson remained on the channel. *"I've never seen her like that before. I was . . . Well. I hope never to see her like that again. The situation must be desperate, Jean-Luc. What the hell is happening there?"*

Picard thought of the many worlds that he had seen so far. He thought of the conditions on some of the worlds where his fleet had been. They had faced floods and fires. They had brought medical aid to places where plagues and diseases had taken advantage of squalor and crowding and lack of clean water. They had helped bury the dead. How much bigger this disaster would be. The sheer numbers involved . . .

"We will try to meet the need, Victor. Will you help us?"

"However I can."

"There can be no half measures," Picard warned. "We need every resource. Most of all, we need the ships."

His commander-in-chief nodded. *"I am doing everything I can. In the meantime, godspeed and good luck."*

Picard sat alone for a while and contemplated the gravity of this new mission. He was about to send a message to Zani when the door to his ready room chimed.

"Enter."

It was Tajuth. "You've heard?"

"Yes."

Tajuth circled the room, eyeing Picard warily, and refusing the offer of a seat. At last, he said, "Will your people make political capital from this?"

Picard leaned back in his chair. He held his hands out. "My people?"

"You know what I mean. Your politicians."

"I cannot control what the politicians do," said Picard. "But my superiors want to help. As do I. You know that already."

He watched Tajuth struggle to maintain his composure. "A big win," he said. "Isn't that what your superiors want?"

The Tal Shiar's sources of information were still solid, Picard thought. Or Tajuth simply knew his enemy. "Yes," he said. "That's what they say to me. I'm never entirely sure what they mean. Each life saved counts as a victory, as far as I am concerned."

"Let me guess, then," said Tajuth. "Holo-cameras. Romulans falling gratefully into Federation arms. Thanking their saviors." He was angry. "And for those images to come from so close to Romulus itself—even better!"

"None of that will happen with my permission," said Picard. "You have my word."

Tajuth gave a bitter laugh. "That I should believe the promise of a Starfleet officer," he said. "How far we have fallen indeed!"

Picard studied him thoughtfully, and with compassion. "Why do you loathe us so much?" he said. "After all this? Is there anything more that we could have done? I wish only for there to be friendship between our peoples."

"That is not a possibility," Tajuth said. "There's too much history. Too much mistrust." He made for the door. "But beggars cannot be choosers."

FEDERATION COUNCIL
PARIS, EARTH

Kirsten Clancy took the meeting with Olivia Quest. She even went so far as to go to Quest's territory—her office in the Federation Council chambers. She wished for a better day. When Clancy stepped out of the transporter across the square from the great building, Paris was wet. The sky was cloudy and gray. The city of lights, dimmed.

Quest welcomed her into her private office with some reservation. Clancy accepted the offer of coffee. She apologized for the weather. "You should stay a day or two," she said. "Tomorrow might be very different."

Clancy shook her head. "I'd like to, but there's too much happening."

Quest gave a closed smile. "I wondered why you were here."

"The Council will be informed within the hour, but it seemed courteous to come and speak to you first. Given your, ah . . ." Clancy looked out at the blurred sky. "Your particular interest in the Romulan relief mission."

"You're canceling the whole thing," Quest deadpanned.

"I'm afraid not," said Clancy. "We've been asked for further assistance in the evacuation. Vejuro. The most populated world in the next system along from Romulus."

Quest stood up and walked across to the window. "By whom?"

"Ambassador Sulde."

"Ah," said Quest, "a genuine request, then."

"And one made in desperation. Starfleet is helping."

"Of course you are," said Quest.

Clancy put down her cup. Truth was, she'd had enough coffee today already. "I've no idea how you intend to play this," she said. "Because try as I might, I'm never quite able to grasp what motivates you."

"Serving Estelen motivates me."

"Sure, yes, absolutely," said Clancy. "But what else floats your boat, Councilor? I don't quite see. You like to be at the center of things, I know that. Fair enough. I think you're right when you say the Federation has taken some of these small worlds for granted."

"That's heartening to hear."

"But you like to gamble, don't you? Or keep your options open. I don't think you have any intention of pushing for Estelen to secede. Swapping a large stage for a very small one? Not in its interest. Not in your interests. But those other worlds—you won't stop them if they want to go, will you?"

"They are free to make their own decisions."

"I'm here to try to alleviate your fears about the mission—but the problem with that is, I'm not sure what they are. I don't think you're afraid of much."

Quest turned to look at her. Very cool. Very untroubled. "No," she said. "Not much."

"Let me speak freely. We're going to help the Romulans. We're working flat out on Mars to make sure we have more ships. Same at the Daystrom Institute, trying to get enough synths out. We're pulling everything back into this, not only because the idea of the Star Empire collapsing entirely and the chaos that would follow keeps me awake at night, but also because it's the right thing to do."

Quest lifted a hand. "You're pulling *everything* back in?"

"For the next few months, at least. Is that going to be a problem?"

"From me? No."

The captain, who had expected resistance, was momentarily stunned. Then she got it. "I see," she said.

"I gain nothing," said Quest, "by being seen to block this. What kind of monster would do that?"

"No," agreed Clancy. "That would make for some bad optics."

"The fact is," said Quest, "that this mission cannot go on indefinitely. At some point, the Romulan star will go supernova, but that's not the end of it. It's what comes after that concerns me."

Damn, thought Clancy, *she's cold*. "What's your expectation?"

In other words, Councilor, what's your price?

"I'll think of something," Quest said. She reached out her hand, which Clancy, after a moment, shook. "Thank you for coming to see me today, Captain Clancy. I'm sure this is a very busy time. I'll be in touch."

Clancy, chilled, made for the door. Quest called after her.

"I can give you my word that I won't speak against the expansion of the mission. But you must understand that I do not control the councilors for other worlds. They might think differently. And remember, Captain—at some point, this all has to come to an end."

Clancy walked back through the rain to the transporter. *Did I just give everything away?* The trouble was that she couldn't be sure.

VERITY
APPROACHING VEJURO

As the first of thirty Starfleet ships entered the Vejuran system, a small vessel asked permission to pass through local space on the way back to the Federation. Picard had a suspicion who this was, and, if his guess was correct, any remaining hope he held out for the situation on Romulus was now completely dashed. The passenger on that little ship would not have left before the end.

Lieutenant Marshall, on comms, took an incoming message. "Admiral," she said. "There's a message for you. Sir, it's—"

But he knew already who it was. "I'll take it in my ready room."

Picard opened the channel as soon as he was alone. "Ambassador Spock," he said as the Vulcan's face appeared on screen. "How are things on Romulus? As bad as we fear?"

"That and more, Admiral."

"I was afraid you were going to say that."

"I have stayed as long as I dared, but I have my own people to consider. They must be taken to safety."

"You'll have no trouble entering Federation space, Ambassador. We'll make sure of that."

"Thank you. And I have a request to make, Admiral."

"Whatever I can do."

"You will find that the elites will demand to leave first. I have brought on this vessel a small number of vulnerable people. But there are many more on Romulus. They have already been betrayed by their leaders, and my fear is that they are facing further betrayals. Do all you can to assist them."

"You have my word, Ambassador."

"Then live long, Admiral," Spock said. *"And prosper."*

VERITY

Raffi Musiker, more than a little drunk, stumbled back toward her quarters. "I'm not coming home for a while," she'd said to Jae, earlier that evening. "We're going to Vejuro."

Jae had said, *"I don't think you should come back."*

And she'd said, like a fool, "From Vejuro? It's going to burn to a crisp, Jae!"

"I mean home, Raffi."

She didn't know how to respond. She tried, "Excuse me?"

"We've moved on, Raffi. Gabe and I. We're . . . we're done waiting. We can't wait forever."

"Jeez, Jae, this has come from nowhere!"

"No, it has not. And the problem is that you don't see that, do you? Raffi, this has been years *in the making."*

What followed had not been very dignified. Neither of them had covered themselves in glory. Eventually Jae had cut the comm. She had yelled, *Fuck you!* She guessed that meant the marriage was in difficulty, huh? Anyway, there was no point brooding, so she got out of her quarters and headed down to the officers' mess and found something close to Scotch, and she'd drank most of that pretty quickly.

And now she was staggering back to her quarters. *Hell, this corridor seems so long all of a sudden . . .*

She stumbled. She started crashing down. Something stopped her hitting the deck. Bleary eyed, she found herself staring up into the face of the enemy.

"Might I suggest," said Tajuth, "that you get yourself back to quarters, Commander. You should not be seen by anyone."

"Fuck you," muttered Raffi. It came out garbled. That was when she began to realize exactly how drunk she was. Incredibly drunk. She glared at Tajuth. He had one hand pressed against the wall. She sniffed and caught the scent of something vinous. "Hey," she said. "I'm not the only one, am I?"

"No," said Tajuth. He gripped her arm and started walking her down the corridor. She wasn't quite sure who was propping up whom. After a brief shuffle, they reached the door to her quarters. As she thumped in the key code, he leaned against the wall. "My world is about to end. What's your excuse, Commander Musiker?"

He didn't wait for an answer. He pulled himself up straight and stumbled off. *My excuse? Same as yours.* She fell into her quarters and onto the bed. *This damn mission. It'll eat us all up and spit us out.*

12

Admiral's Log: Throughout this mission we have struggled with the Romulan need for secrecy and privacy, and with their understandable desire to save face. I have tried to respect their autonomy, within the goal of this mission—to protect and preserve life. I have made decisions that have overthrown treaties, redrawn the boundaries, and brought hundreds of thousands of Romulans into Federation space. I have learned that my decisions have threatened the very essence of the Federation, bringing some worlds to the brink of secession. I have gone as far as I dared, and perhaps, on occasion, beyond what is justified. But now, confronted with the situation on the Romulan homeworld, I know that I should have gone further, sooner, and with less doubt in my heart.

We trusted that the Romulans were helping their own. As soon as we arrived on Vejuro, I could see the extent to which they have not. Whether through denial, incompetence, or an inability to meet the vast requirements, or simply because they did not care, the Romulan government's plans to evacuate this world have been entirely insufficient. I am aware that details of the ultimate impact of the supernova have been kept from ordinary Romulans, and I sympathize with the desire to prevent panic. But there must have come a point—long past—when it was clear that something on Romulus was going horribly wrong. Yet many people—even among the elites, most of whom have been privy to the information—seem not to have believed the evidence of their own eyes. They seem to have wantonly refused to connect the dots between the increasing heat, the storms, the floods, and the freak weather pattern. I struggle to understand why. Perhaps some truths are simply too much to face. Perhaps the Romulan habit of secrecy and compartmentalization is so deeply ingrained that Romulans are psychologically able to believe that there is more than one truth. Perhaps people have been too afraid to confront the reality—not only because speaking out might carry sanctions, but because the truth is too terrible to admit. As a result, many of the elites have preferred to continue as usual. "If the situation were so bad," they seem to have told each other, "then our government would be doing something."

Their government has not. Their government has failed.

Moreover, most members of the government are not to be found. The messages we receive from high-ranking officials come from systems away, well beyond the blast radius. The very highest echelons seem to have persuaded the rest of the population that they are not at risk, ostensibly to prevent rioting and keep order, while simultaneously ensuring their own escape. I do not know whether this counts as a crime under Romulan law. But I believe wholeheartedly that these decisions and actions are immoral: an abnegation of duty and responsibility that may yet lead to the deaths of many hundreds of thousands of people, if not more.

I am grateful that someone within the Romulan government has seen sense and turned to us for assistance. I can only guess at what has happened behind the scenes, what deals have been struck, what offers made, what promises given. Let those involved trouble themselves with this. My own concern now is that our arrival has come desperately late. We are running out of time. Romulus is doomed, and many more places besides; whoever remains on these sad, lost worlds is also doomed.

How does one help in an apocalypse? What does one do?

One does one's best.

OJUL CITY, VEJURO

Raffi Musiker woke each morning to look out across a city of the damned.

She had worried sometimes throughout this mission that she was becoming inured to the sight of the pain of others. She worried that she was becoming blasé, that nothing could shock her anymore. She had raised this once—and once only—with JL. He suggested counseling. As if that was ever going to happen. No way. But Raffi could sense within herself a kind of strange distance growing. Sometimes, when she was in the thick of things, she would feel herself detach from proceedings, as if she were floating above. She listened to words coming out of her mouth—orders, reflections, suggestions—and marveled at how good she had become at this job. Like a machine. She found that she spent more of her off-duty hours alone in her quarters, scrolling through intelligence reports, drinking. Not that she was drinking that much. Maybe. Never mind. She was doing fine, wasn't she? Yes, she was doing fine.

The main part of the fleet had arrived at Vejuro three weeks ago. Two weeks had been spent wrangling with the local authorities to get permission to set up a base of operations. Eight days ago, JL decided enough was enough, and instructed that the damn structure should be put up without any damn permission, and if they didn't like it, they could damn well live with it. JL resorting to even the mildest curse was a call to arms. Twenty hours later (a record for the mission, but then, they'd had a lot of practice), United Federation of Planets High Commission on Refugees HQ Ojul City was standing: eight prefabricated plasticrete rooms, transported from the *Verity*, put together rapidly, and filled with the workstations, comms units, and myriad specialist staff needed to start processing people offworld and onto the fleet of ships in orbit overhead. At last, they were able to get to work.

Two days later, a squad of eight armed police arrived to take the building down. Raffi, looking below at them from the roof of HQ, thought they were a pretty sorry bunch. Most of them looked like kids, not much older than Gabe was now. They seemed unhappy, as if they wanted to be somewhere else. Something everyone had in common around here. Their leader, however, was different. Raffi knew his type: a thug, motivating his unwilling troops chiefly through threats of violence. Still, it was an effective technique, in the short term, and it had the potential to make things nasty. Raffi, coming down from the roof, went in search of Tajuth.

"We're going to need your help here, Commander."

Tajuth said, "Let's wait a minute or two."

They stood together and looked out from an open second-story window. From the moment that the base had started construction, people had begun to arrive. The news that Starfleet was here had clearly gone around the city. By word of mouth, Raffi assumed, since the local 'casts were rubbish. Sentimental holodramas and advertisements for holidays on the coast. Did anyone believe any of this? It infuriated her. They should be advising on where to go for help. Telling them what they needed to pack for the journey. Directing them to the nearest relief center. It wasn't as if this anodyne crap was keeping people calm any longer. They got reports of riots every day. People were on the move, whatever the government was saying.

Even before the HQ was finished, there were hundreds camped outside, each wanting to be first in line. By the time the police squad arrived, there must have been nearly two thousand there. *Damn*, Raffi thought, *they are a pitiful sight.* Family groups, possessions strapped on their back, leaving hands free to keep hold of their kids. Raffi's heart clenched at the sight. Some of those little ones, you lost hold of one of them in this chaos, you'd never find them again. Raffi thought of Gabe at that age, his small hand within hers. She thought of him slipping away.

The most striking thing about the encampment was how subdued it was. People weren't fighting, or jostling for position, or making demands or getting into fights. They were simply . . . waiting. And then the squad arrived. They shoved their way to the front, where a fence separated the HQ building from the camp, letting them siphon the flood of refugees into a steady trickle that went through a gate, past the desk, and to transporters beyond.

The squad leader rattled the gate. He began to shout, *"Open up!"*

And then the damn idiot started to explain why he was there. *"This is an illegal installation! You must open up and remove this facility!"*

Raffi watched as word passed around the camp. Turning to Tajuth, she said, "Holy shit, this is going to be a bloodbath—"

"I don't think so," said Tajuth. "Watch."

Within the crowd, people were rippling forward. Five, ten, fifteen huge Romulans. Blue-collar, Raffi saw: worn clothes, hard faces. People who had worked like hell their whole lives, who had been left behind to burn in it. They pressed forward to the gate, and, without any words, formed a barrier between the squad and the crowd. One of them shifted forward, their ringleader, and began to speak to the officer. He lifted his disruptor and pointed it straight at the ringleader.

"Shit," said Raffi. "Tajuth, we need to do something—"

"*Wait.*"

Everything paused for a moment. The ringleader turned his head away from the squad leader and looked at the kids that had come with him, one by one.

Something got through. One of the young men, hands trembling, lowered his disruptor. He gripped it by its snub nose, and held it out, offering it to the ringleader. The others (they were so young, these boys, this could be Gabe) stared at him open-mouthed.

One by one, the others followed suit. Soon, only their officer was armed, and he was looking down the barrel of seven disruptors. The ringleader gestured to him to hand over his weapon. Raffi thought for a moment that he wasn't going to do it—but then, those guys were very big. He did what he was told and slunk away. The crowd shifted, opening up a path for him to leave, staring at him as he hurried through. The boys from the squad stared blinking and terrified at the ringleader and his men. Then one of them pulled off his gear and melted into the crowd. Soon they were all gone. The ringleader and the others exchanged a few quiet words, and then they too slipped away, hidden and protected.

Raffi relaxed. She glanced at Tajuth, who stood motionless, arms folded. "That was a gamble," she said. "At least you haven't had to pull Tal Shiar from elsewhere."

"No," he agreed. "I doubt I could have found anyone in time."

He turned and walked away. Raffi, watching him, processed the ramifications of what he'd said; the glimpse into the power vacuum that she had been dropped into.

It was all one great almighty clusterfuck. And it was only ever going to get worse.

Verity
In orbit over Vejuro

Picard wearily took his seat behind his desk, activated his comm, and drank a mouthful of tea. The Starfleet logo dissolved, and Admiral Victor Bordson appeared on screen.

"Jean-Luc. You look tired."

"A long day, Victor."

"Any good news?"

Picard pondered this request. What constituted good news these days? A riot prevented. An outbreak of a waterborne fever detected, and the carriers quarantined just in time. A lost child reunited with relatives on board the ship. An official's anger over some imagined slight deflected. "I was about to ask you the same question."

"Let me see. I have found another two ships, which will be with you within the week—"

Two. A drop in the ocean. "Thank you."

"Kirsten has somehow persuaded Olivia Quest not to block these emergency requisitions."

"Has she? I wouldn't like to think what that has cost."

"I imagine we shall learn in time."

Picard rubbed his eyes.

"I received your reports, Jean-Luc. Tell me, exactly, how bad is it?"

How bad? They had no idea.

"Whatever you are imagining, you should increase it a thousandfold."

"I was on Cardassia Prime after the war . . ."

"That must have been hell. This . . . this is worse, Victor. So much of what we face could have been prevented if we had been asked sooner. But, no. The self-respect of the Romulan elites had to be upheld at all costs. But they are not the ones paying for it. Most of them are gone. The ones suffering are the ones without power, and they are now beginning to understand the nature and the depth of that treachery."

Bordson had been listening with compassion. *"Tell me,"* he said, *"in all honesty and in complete confidentiality—do you believe that you will be able to remove everyone in time?"*

Picard folded his hands together and rested his chin upon them. *No*, he thought, and then pushed the thought back down into whatever part of his subconscious had offered it up. That answer was unacceptable. It was not to be countenanced. "I believe that we must try."

"I see," said his commander-in-chief. *"Let me leave you in peace, then. I'll wait for good news."*

As shall I, thought Picard as Bordson closed the channel. He reached for his tea, which had gone cold. He drank it anyway. He read reports from across this poor damned world, and he dug deep, deeper than ever, and found within himself what he had hoped he would find: yet another vein of courage and determination. As he drank his cold tea he read about the death of fifty people when a bridge collapsed on the Buhina river. *"Heart be the keener, mind must be the greater, while our strength lessens."* He waited patiently for good news.

Vulmab District
Vejuro

From a shuttle, a less experienced man might look down and persuade himself that all was fine. But Picard was now too well versed in the visual grammar of collapse, and he could read the signs quite fluently. The charred and blackened remains of trees in the wake of a forest fire. Abandoned groundcars blocking a major highway. A group of nearly two hundred people, walking across a hillside. The inevitable group of stragglers, falling steadily behind. Left alone, there would, in a week or two, be fresh graves. After that, there would be unburied bodies. He tapped his combadge and sent a message back to HQ, alerting them of a group of refugees in the Tihe hills, sending precise coordinates, and their direction of travel. Someone would come, and he hoped it would be in time for everyone.

Picard did not want to leave the city. The sheer amount of work that needed to be done . . . but a message had come from Bordson, who had been contacted by Ambassador Sulde, alerting them to a problem in the Vulmab District. It was a rather remote region several hundred kilometers from Ojul City. The senator who represented the region, Kurrem, was an aristocrat, rich and powerful enough to keep his district in a state of near feudalism. It was, Picard thought, remarkable that such situations still arose in what was, or had until recently, been an interstellar power. Picard, who knew intimately the history of his own native land, understood thoroughly the authority that such men could wield, keeping their retainers and dependents in a state of vassalage. He imagined that as the threat from collapse had become more acute, many tenants had been forced to go cap in hand to their overlords. Some of these—not many, but some—had acted responsibly, organizing evacuations, and in some cases transportation offworld for their people. Perhaps it had been a sense of duty, or they had hoped that by doing this it would be a source of power in their new homes.

Whatever the motivation, Picard could only wish more had acted this way. It would have alleviated the burden on the authorities—and Starfleet—considerably. Many, he knew, had departed as soon as the danger had become clear, but had left their people behind. Now Starfleet had to pick up the pieces. Raffi had reported back on some of these: shocked loyal retainers, who had served for generations and could not believe that they had been thrown to the wolves. Some had not wanted to leave without express permission, and certainly not on the advice of a Starfleet officer. Tajuth had been indispensable in these circumstances. Nothing focused the mind like a Tal Shiar officer.

But in this already complex web of betrayals, Senator Kurrem was something else entirely.

"*I gather he's always been something of an eccentric,*" Bordson had explained. "*At least, that's what Sulde has been hinting. But now he's excelling at it. He's refusing point-blank to leave.*"

"The senator is of course more than welcome to fend for himself when the blast comes. But we'll be long gone."

"*I'd be tempted to advise you to say that to him, Jean-Luc, and I'd ask you to make a recording of his response available to me. Unfortunately, the situation is more complicated.*"

"In what way?"

"*He's not allowing anyone in his district to leave either.*"

Picard frowned. "Can he do that?"

"*He's the senator, as well as the major landowner and employer in the district. He can do whatever he likes. He can revoke travel permits, for example. I believe he may have the power to revoke citizenship, or, at the very least, the influence to be able to get that done.*"

Picard, quickly searching the databanks for information on Vulmab, read the basic information with some dismay. "*Merde*, Victor, there's nearly half a million people out there!"

"*None of whom have permission to leave.*"

"Yes, I see the problem. I am happy to speak to the senator in person, but how likely do you think it is that he will see me?"

"*Ambassador Sulde has received permission for you to visit. But the senator forbids the use of transporter technology to enter or exit the area. One of his eccentricities.*"

It was also, Picard noted, a very good way to keep the local population bound to the district. Nevertheless, this was why he was using a much-needed shuttle, heading out toward Vulmab, in the hope that he might negotiate the release of nearly half a million people from a bondage that seemed to be verging on serfdom. Raffi had offered to come, but he needed her back in the city overseeing the operation there. Everyone knew that when Raffi spoke, she had the admiral's authority behind her. There was no one else that he trusted as much on this mission. No one else who had so consistently come through for him, supported him, kept the burdens from overwhelming him. He did not know what he would do without Raffi Musiker.

He still missed Koli Jocan. There was so much she could have done here. Instead, he asked Tajuth to come with him. Raffi, to his surprise, had not argued against it. "He knows his business," she said. "I guess he might come in useful."

That was a change, Picard thought, and quite a significant one. What lay behind that? From his seat, he eyed Tajuth covertly. The man was piloting, sitting calmly as ever, looking out across the land below. What must it be like to look down upon the ruin of one's home? What must it be like to know that soon all this would be gone, and gone for good, and that there would never be a return? The boy that he had been, once upon a time, unhappy and restless on Earth, had looked at the stars and promised himself that one day he would live among them. Picard knew that he was fortunate not to be bound to a single world. His home was the space between the stars, which was vast, and would always be there for him.

The shuttle's engine tone shifted, and they began their descent. Tajuth, turning, saw Picard looking at him. "Have you seen one of our great houses before, Admiral?"

"I regret that my visit to Romulus did not allow me to indulge my cultural curiosity."

Tajuth gave a sly smile. "Your education is about to begin."

Tajuth, who had been given precise coordinates for landing, had brought the shuttle down in an empty field. Behind them lay open countryside, rather bleak even for the very end of winter. In front of them was a high green hedge. There was nobody there. No welcoming committee; more positively, no armed guards.

"Are we in the right place?" said Picard. "We were given permission to land—"

"Oh yes, we're in the right place," said Tajuth. "The house is behind this hedge."

"I assume there is a gate somewhere . . ."

"Probably. I wouldn't try going that way, though." Tajuth started walking along the hedge, his left hand brushing along the foliage, clearly feeling for something.

Of course, thought Picard, the hidden doors and entrances that were there even on the smallest Romulan building. A wealthy man like this was sure to have something considerably more, well, *byzantine*. Twenty minutes later, still on the outside of the hedge, Picard realized he had vastly underestimated exactly how byzantine this could be.

"Is this one of Kurrem's eccentricities?" he asked Tajuth. "Or are all your stately homes this difficult to enter?"

"I'd say this was fairly standard," said Tajuth. He knelt to rummage in the foliage at the bottom of the hedge. Standing, he held out a stone, covered in small marks.

"Is this significant?" asked Picard. He could make no sense of the markings.

"Well, it tells us we've found the entrance."

"To the house?"

Tajuth looked at him with pity. "To the *maze*, Admiral." He reached to pull the greenery apart, opening up a gap in the hedge. Picard looked through, and saw a narrow green passage formed of leaves ahead.

"A maze?" he said faintly.

About an hour later, they came to a halt. They had wandered along more green and twisty passages than Picard thought possible. There had been small clearings too—one with a bench and a fountain, where they sat for a while, drinking the water, which Picard had found uncharacteristically generous. Tajuth would also stop every so often, bend down, and find more stones. Some, he said, gave clues to the maze, some were misdirection. And no, he added, there was no particular rhyme or reason that he could discern. Picard, growing impatient, had suggested returning to the shuttle to use the sensors, but Tajuth would not. "There'll be jammers," he said. "No, we have to make our own way through."

It was not hard to guess the cultural significance of such a feature, Picard thought as they trudged on. Defensive, yes; only the most dedicated of visitors would not give up and leave. But it was also manifestly a display of wealth. To grow and maintain something like this was a not insubstantial use of resources. And, of course, it put anyone who did get through at a significant psychological disadvantage. Already they had to admit the power that the master of the house held over them. He murmured, "Are we there yet?"

Tajuth nodded. "I think so."

Yet they walked on for another five or ten minutes. At last, Tajuth stopped and reached out again to pull apart the foliage. Two minutes later, they were out of the hedge and standing in front of the house. "How did you know that the exit was there?" said Picard, looking back, and genuinely impressed.

"That was a fairly old-fashioned layout," he said. "Many of the houses of this period have something similar. You visit enough, you get to know the design."

So Tajuth is a regular visitor to stately homes, Picard thought. Another piece of data about this solitary man. He looked up at the house. Four stories high, it loomed over them. It was built from yellow stone, and the façade was intricately decorated. Picard saw several figures from legends and tales that he had begun to recognize from his travels in the Empire. There was Tuthus of the Two Faces, the trickster that presided over Year Turn. Vanauka and her many masks. Laleen and her eight white wolves. Surri, who kept the tally and devoured suns. Kalle, the deceiver, most honored of the demigods, with his guard of eight thousand snakes. Lotro, who had built an image of herself out of silver, and for that crime had been sentenced to burn for eternity and never die. A remarkably gruesome bunch, even by the standards of the average pantheon. The Greek gods of Olympus seemed tepid by comparison; the lords of Valhalla rather tame. Picard also noted that there were no real doors or windows as far as he could see. Everything that looked like it might be a means of entry was painted. A feint. A misdirection. A lie. All praise Kalle, the deceiver!

Picard sighed. "How do we get in?"

"There'll be a trapdoor somewhere," said Tajuth. "It might be on this side of the house. There's occasionally a double bluff—you assume that it will be round the back, and they usually put it at the front. Let me think."

After a moment or two, he led Picard around the side of house, through a flower garden. The *meritak* was beginning to bud. The garden would be bright in the summer, should summer come. At the far end, a wall jutted out, covered in brambles. Tajuth began to shift these away. After a few minutes, a doorway was revealed. Tajuth pressed his hands against it. He hunted through the brambles again and found a keypad, a surprising piece of contemporary technology in the midst of all this fairy-tale baroque. Tajuth tapped in a series of numbers. There was a grinding noise, and the door opened.

"How did you know the code?" said Picard.

"The stones in the maze, Admiral. The marks on them. Were you not paying attention?"

"Apparently not."

They walked through the door. They were in a little anteroom, with two more doors up ahead. "In early centuries," said Tajuth conversationally, "we would of course have faced numerous booby traps from here on. Poisons, spears, trapdoors, and so on."

"Let us hope Kurrem is not too much of a traditionalist," Picard said, and followed Tajuth to the right-hand door. Again, Tajuth found a keypad and entered a code.

The door opened. They passed through into a huge hall, dimly lit. Picard, looking up into the darkness, guessed that the hall was the height of the whole building. Staircases ran up both sides, and he glimpsed dark galleries at each level, hinting at warrens of rooms behind. Standing in the hallway, rubbing his hands together, was a tall, well-built, and very expensively dressed Romulan. Kurrem, surely.

"Admiral Picard!" He walked toward them, looking delighted. "How well you have done! But I think you might have had some help?"

"Senator Kurrem, I assume. May I introduce Commander Tajuth, my guide."

"Commander, eh? You deserve a promotion for that, boy. One of the best times I've seen—certainly the best by a northerner."

Tajuth gave a cold, tight smile. Then his attention was suddenly grabbed by something—a movement, in the shadows. A figure emerged, dark clad, armed. Tal Shiar? Picard could not say. Tajuth most certainly did not look pleased to see this person—but then the Tal Shiar, like all instruments of the Romulan state, was so faction-riven that they might wear the same uniform and serve entirely different masters.

"My guard," said Kurrem off-handedly. "Molula. Forgive me if she stays nearby. She's rather suspicious of Starfleet." He clapped his hands together. "But we're all friends here, are we not?"

That, thought Picard, *remains to be seen*.

"And I'm forgetting my manners. You've walked some way this afternoon, haven't you? Let's have a drink!"

So began one of the more surreal episodes of Picard's time on this mission. Kurrem led them up the staircase to the third story, then along a series of passages until they reached a small wooden door beneath a stone archway deeply etched with indecipherable markings. Picard was reminded uneasily of the tallies kept by prisoners in dungeons and cursed his own familiarity with Dumas. Kurrem unlocked the door with a huge iron key, and led them down, down, down a winding and uncarpeted stone staircase until Picard could no longer guess which floor of the mansion they were on. Another series of corridors followed, these lined with small recesses filled with statues, carvings, glassware, various other *objets d'art*. Under other circumstances, Picard would have been delighted to see so many and varied pieces of art, but instead he found himself starting to feel rather impatient. The attempt to overawe was so blatant. The art was not loved for its own sake, for its beauty and the pleasure that it brought. It was loved only for the power it gave the owner over others.

At last they came into a big hall. A long table, made of heavy dark wood, took up a large part of the room. There were three chairs on one side, and three on the other, with one at each end, bringing the total of available seats to eight. The table was set with three places, with Kurrem at the head and his guests on either side of him. His guard, Molula, who had been following all this time, pulled out chairs for Picard and Tajuth. Picard, sitting, looked around the dimly lit room. There were doors leading off from all four walls. Hangings here and there that could be concealing more exits as far as he knew. Yet another gallery overhead. But the most striking feature was on the wall behind Kurrem's chair.

Here hung a huge brass disk, about three feet in diameter, with deep grooves and markings set all around. Picard counted these: five groups of five. Twenty-five hours, the length of the Romulan day. A brass pendulum swung slowly at the bottom. A clock. Within the disk were other circles, each similarly grooved and marked: seconds and minutes, presumably. The whole piece would be already impressive, but the most alarming element was the feature that lay on top of the disk. A huge black metal sculpture of an insect, like a grasshopper, which, with each beat of the clock, opened and closed its mandibles.

Kurrem, seeing that Picard was gazing at the contraption, said, "Do you know what this is, Admiral?"

"No," said Picard. Even if he had known, this was surely the answer that Kurrem wanted.

"It's called a chronophage," said Kurrem.

"A time eater," said Picard.

"Well done, Admiral!" said Kurrem.

Picard looked away from the thing and back at the table. "Most impressive," he murmured. He thought the whole display was hideous.

The food was immaculately and intricately prepared. Part of the point, as far as Picard could make out, was to decipher which utensils were the appropriate ones for the dish presented. One of the forks turned out to contain a concealed fish knife. Another spoon had serrated edges that were sharp enough to draw blood from the unwary. All very tiresome. Nevertheless, they dined well, and listened as Kurrem boasted about his possessions. At last, Picard pushed his plate aside and said, "I must explain the purpose of this visit, Senator."

A rather petulant look passed across Kurrem's face. His mouth puckered. "Must you? We were having such a pleasant time."

"You do understand why I am here?"

"Of course I do! I know quite well why Starfleet is here."

"I'm glad to hear that—"

"You and your colleagues are here to take advantage of the current political crisis. And how well it's working! I imagine you have a Starfleet officer on almost every street corner throughout the Empire by now. Well, not Vulmab!" He wagged his finger at Picard, some of his bonhomie returning. "Never Vulmab! Not as long as I have breath in my body!"

Picard was taken aback. He glanced over at Tajuth, who was looking blandly past him at one of the tapestries on the wall behind, as if he was not listening.

"I'm afraid I don't quite understand, Senator—"

"No? A typical Starfleet ploy. I'm amazed you've had so much success, but then, the civil service doesn't recruit from the better kind these days." His eyes flicked over at Tajuth. "All sorts getting into senior ranks. People with no family to speak of. Credulous. And here we are—everyone running around like it's the end of the world, and Starfleet crawling all over the Empire like a particularly unpleasant infestation of vermin."

Suddenly Picard understood. This was no ploy of Kurrem's to wrong-foot him. He was not trying to discompose Picard; he was not trying to gain some advantage over him in their negotiations. He ... simply did not believe. A chill went down his spine.

"Senator," he said, "let me assure you that there is no such ploy—"

Kurrem snorted.

"The Empire is in very real danger. Already there is significant climate change on Romulus itself. The end cannot be far away—"

Kurrem yawned. "So they say. Nothing wrong here. Weather's fine. Snow came a little later than usual. Nothing too drastic. Harvest should be fine. The people will get by. They always do."

There was unlikely to be any harvest. Picard tried again. "I can show you footage from Ojul. The situation there is quite desperate—"

Kurrem waved his hand in dismissal. "Federation propaganda. Do you think I'd be taken in by a Starfleet holodrama?"

For a moment, Picard was at a loss as to what to say. How could he counter this? This was beyond denial. This was delusion impervious to evidence or reason. Helplessly, he turned to Tajuth, who this time did meet his eye, but simply shrugged.

"Senator," Picard said in a low, urgent voice. "Let me assure you that this is no lie. You and your people are in very grave danger. You must allow the evacuation of this province. It is a matter of urgency—"

Again, that sulky, peevish look. "Why would I do that?"

"People will die. Half a million people in this district alone!"

"My district. My people."

"With all due respect, they are not your property."

Kurrem said, "That's an interesting legal position! Feel free to try it out in court. The peonage laws were never quite struck down."

"Senator—"

"Admiral, I'm aware of your activities throughout the Star Empire. Your high-handedness. On Arnath, among other places, transporting unwilling refugees. And for some reason those idiots in the government have let you strut around as if you owned the place. Let me warn you now—I won't allow that here."

"You might not," said Picard with some asperity, "be able to prevent it."

"Yes, I can," said Kurrem. He looked very pleased with himself.

"How so?"

"I'll have the entire district shielded." He laughed. "I will, you know. Not one person is going to leave Vulmab, from the very top to the very bottom. This district is mine, Admiral. It's been in my family's possession for over six hundred years. No Starfleet officer is going to steal it from me." He rose from his chair. He looked bored with the conversation. "I'm going to bed. You're welcome to stay the night—Molula has had rooms prepared for you, I think."

Molula, in the shadows, nodded.

"But I want you gone in the morning. And I don't want you back."

Pushing aside one of the tapestries to reveal a hidden door, Kurrem left the hall.

Shielded. Nobody would get out. The whole half-million of them, stuck behind the shield. They would die most horribly . . .

"Tajuth," Picard murmured. "What is happening here?"

Tajuth put down his glass. "Well," he said, "you were warned he was eccentric."

"*Eccentric?*" said Picard. "It goes rather beyond that!"

Tajuth tilted his head. "Let me rephrase that. He is quite insane."

13

Admiral's Log: We have accepted Senator Kurrem's offer of a bed for the night. Accordingly, I found myself led by two silent and surly armed guards, presumably Tal Shiar, through a vast and impenetrable country house. I hesitate to call this typical Romulan hospitality. But I might go so far as to say that I am enduring a quintessentially Romulan experience. From the maze, to the entry codes, to the layout of the house, to that brass monstrosity devouring time, Kurrem's home seems to represent all that is most Romulan. The room to which I have been brought is itself another puzzle box: a chest of drawers that turns out to have only false frontages, an enormous wardrobe that conceals a bed. I am not sure what the vast four-poster bed that dominates the center of the room might conceal—I find myself loath to take my chances and am considering whether an arrangement of cushions on the floor might be the safest option. Of course, this might be what they want me to think.

I am trying to find some levity in this bizarre situation, but it can only be gallows humor. We face a very serious challenge here. I am unable to put my conversation with the senator out of my mind. Kurrem does not believe that his homeworld's sun will soon be a supernova, and that the effects will be calamitous. I am aware that Vulmab is a relatively distant province, and it is clear that the senator has placed himself behind numerous defenses (that extraordinary hedge maze not least), but to be so completely impervious to the facts? To deny the reality that is all around him in such a way? The more I reflect upon this, the more horrified I am. A mindset so rigidly formed that it cannot be changed is a terrible thing, the product of a culture of secrecy and lies that will lead to disaster. For this to be the mind of a man who wields so much power over the lives of others is more appalling.

I spent some time considering how I might go about opening the senator's eyes; how I might persuade him of the truth of the catastrophe that his people face. But I have come to the conclusion that this is simply not possible. Whatever I show Kurrem, he will not believe. I could show him footage from the homeworld itself, and he would claim that it was false, or edited to show that the situation is worse. I suspect that even if he could be persuaded to visit Ojul City in person, even were I to walk him around the streets, show him at firsthand the desperate huddled crowds, the riots, the lack of power and water, he would no doubt claim that I had staged these sights. He is firm in his belief that Starfleet, for some extraordinary reason, has somehow persuaded the Romulan government that a disaster is imminent, and is pouring resources into giving this scam complete verisimilitude. I can think of quicker and less costly ways of invading a world. But the senator is trapped in a maze of his own making, a labyrinth of lies from which I do not think it is possible for him to escape.

Were Kurrem the only one at risk from his delusions, I would be happy to leave him here in Vulmab to face the consequences. We have limited time, and a great deal to do elsewhere on the planet. But the fact is that nearly half a million people are at risk from his intransigence, his (yes, I shall describe it thus)—his insanity. In these dreadful times, Vulmab has reverted back to feudalism, to absolutism. Would Kurrem truly carry out his threat of shielding the entire district, thereby preventing even those who want to leave from leaving? I am sad to say that I believe he would. Reason has taken flight. One cannot argue with a man lying to everyone around him, and above all to himself. One must neutralize his effects as quickly and as painlessly as possible. How might this be done?

VULMAB DISTRICT
VEJURO

"Jeez, JL, he sounds like a nutcase."

Picard smiled. Always he could rely on Raffi to cut through the nonsense. He might wish occasionally that her language would be more sensitive, but he could never deny her precision.

"It was certainly not the most rational conversation I have ever had." He shuddered once more. "Quite the contrary."

"You should be careful. You might find the room where all his wives are kept in cupboards."

"I have seen no wife or children."

"Of course not, he's keeping them in cupboards. What are you going to do, JL?"

"I believe we must take seriously his threat to shield the district. Could you investigate what we might do to stop that? The authorities in Ojul might be able to assist—"

"Authorities? What authorities would they be?"

"Is there nobody there?"

"It's getting worse here by the hour. I haven't been able to raise even a junior official for the last three hours. I think they're all getting out. The senior staff are gone already, on Romulan ships."

Leaving far too many behind. Picard wished he could be shocked, but in truth nothing would surprise him. More and more, he was coming to think that people such as Zani were a vanishingly small proportion of sentient life. That selflessness was so rare as to be almost nonexistent; that only a thin façade lay between civilization and savagery. Nevertheless, he knew upon which side of the line he wished to stand. He would not surrender himself to this, and he would not surrender the mission to this. Silently, he vowed to himself that Starfleet ships would be here until the end, and they would save every single life that it was possible for them to save.

"*Is there anyone else there you can apply pressure to? Anyone around him?*"

"Kurrem has a guard . . ." Picard said doubtfully. "Very loyal, as far as I can see."

"*Some kind of personal Praetorian Guard?*"

"I'm not entirely sure, Raffi. I think she might be Tal Shiar, although she doesn't seem particularly keen on Tajuth."

"*Well, he's an acquired taste.*"

"One would hope for some fellow feeling between secret policemen."

"*This band of bastard brothers, eh? There are lots of different factions within the Tal Shiar.*"

"One might also hope that such petty concerns might be put aside in the face of a crisis of this magnitude."

"*Yeah, well, people can be assholes.*"

"Indeed they can, Raffi."

"*Get some sleep, JL. We'll work on trying to find out whether those shields are a genuine threat, and what we can do to get past it. As if we didn't have anything else to do.*"

"Thank you, Raffi," he said. "How are things proceeding there?"

"*They're proceeding. Four more ships arriving tomorrow, earlier than expected. The other eleven are on target. I've spoken to Zani, and she confirms that the authorities on Vashti have agreed to take another three thousand, if the Qowat Milat are able to receive them.*"

He breathed silent thanks to the woman who had done the most to make him keep heart.

"At last," he said, "some good news."

"*When shall we expect you back?*"

"We've been instructed to leave in the morning, so tomorrow afternoon."

"*You're missed, JL. We'll sort it out. We always do. More or less. Raffi out.*"

He sat, pondering his situation, straddling the very thin line he often trod between contemplation and brooding. After a little while, he sighed, and stood. He looked at the vast bed in the center of the room, and the one concealed within the wardrobe. Which was more likely to be weaponized? The hidden one might tip up again. The four-poster, by its very grandeur and obvious comfort, was the more enticing, and surely that way lay danger? He shook himself. He was starting to think too much like a Romulan. Eventually, he took the path of least resistance, reached for several pillows, and spread them out on the floor. That would have to be sufficient for tonight, and he would hope—among all his great hopes—that it would be enough to allow him to see the morning.

He was about to lie down when he heard a tap at the door.

"Who's there?" he said.

"Please open the door," said a quiet voice. "I mean you no harm."

For once, he thanked Romulan paranoia that the door was equipped with a peephole. Molula, Kurrem's guard, was standing in the corridor outside, peering at him, slightly misshapen as was the way with the glass in these devices. He could not see any weapons, but they would surely be concealed, and they would surely be legion.

"Please," she said again, softly. "I only want to talk."

Raffi would not like it, he thought. In fact, she would be furious with him when he told her. But somebody had to break the deadlock here.

He opened the door.

Molula looked at him. "I have some questions, Admiral," she said. "May I come in?"

He admitted her. He still hoped—beyond hope—that even this late in the day he might find another Zani, another person driven to help. If they could find enough of them, he thought, if there could be a critical mass of them, they might save everyone.

Molula was not, he had to confess, particularly promising. She stood stiffly next to the closed door, clearly wanting to have an exit route available to her. He held out his hands, unconsciously mimicking the open-book gesture of the Qowat Milat, and then decided that was not the best strategy if she was in fact a Tal Shiar officer. Clasping his hands together, he said, "I know that as a rule Romulan culture values secrecy, and that the open-handed and open-hearted are considered fools at best and dangers at worst. But we have passed that point, and we passed it a long time ago. Your world—your entire civilization—is at risk."

She folded her arms in front of her. "We receive limited information out here," she said. "The senator controls which news services are able to broadcast in the district, and in the past few months we've been able to watch only one."

Picard guessed which one. State propaganda gone out of hand. He doubted a single truth had been broadcast on that service in the last year. Gbowee, whose staff monitored the transmissions, had once told him that they had an ongoing sweepstakes on the longest gap between established facts. Last he checked, it had been ninety-four days and counting. Bordson had raised the issue with Ambassador Sulde many times, suggesting that slowly introducing the population to the idea of the evacuations would ultimately make the process easier. The suggestions had always been rebuffed, Sulde insisting it would cause panic. And yet panic was happening anyway.

"My understanding is that there have been some severe weather conditions that have caused some problems with infrastructure," Molula went on. "But . . . I am starting to believe that it has gone past that."

"Yes," said Picard gently. "Very much so."

"My superiors have not been in regular contact for some months," Molula went on.

Picard imagined they were long gone. "You must be feeling increasingly isolated."

She bristled slightly at this hint of compassion. "My feelings are immaterial," she said. "What I want is information. Proper information."

"We can tell you everything you want to know—"

"You'll forgive me, Admiral, when I tell you that I don't trust the word of a Starfleet officer."

"Yes," he said. "I'll forgive you."

"I want to see for myself."

"Of course." Picard tapped his combadge. "Commander Tajuth, apologies if I've woken you. But could you join me in my room?"

Tajuth was there within minutes. He was still dressed and did not look as if he had been asleep, but Picard was prepared to believe he slept in his uniform. Tajuth and Molula eyed each other carefully while Picard explained Molula's request.

"That's easy enough," said Tajuth. "I'll fly you to the capital. We can leave now. Kurrem won't know you're gone until morning."

"No," said Molula quickly.

"Why not?" said Picard.

Tajuth turned to Picard. "I would imagine that she doesn't want to get into a flyer with me."

Picard, beyond impatient now with nuances of rivalries that he could not hope to understand, said, "I'll fly the damn thing!"

The two Romulans looked at him in surprise. "Well," said Tajuth, "a glimmer of passion from Starfleet's finest. You hearten me, Admiral."

Picard, who had been faintly embarrassed by the outburst, realized that for some reason it had done the trick. As he and Tajuth followed Molula back through the house, he puzzled over this. Why had a sudden flash of temper been so persuasive? Should he have appealed to emotions much sooner? He would never, he thought, entirely understand Romulans. Each encounter revealed hidden depths and hinted at more layers concealed. Was there any core? Or did the secrets carry on down into infinity, like fractals? One could die before coming to the end.

They came via a narrow and unadorned servants' staircase to the basement. From here they entered a long, straight passageway. Picard said, "Where does this go?"

Tajuth, behind him, said, "Beneath the house and under the hedge, I imagine. You might want to delay access to the house while still being able to exit quickly."

Molula did nothing to confirm or deny this hypothesis, but simply walked on. At length they came to a third staircase, steep and narrow, leading up. A wooden door at the top opened to a bitterly cold night. Flakes of snow were falling. Picard thought of the buds in the flower garden; they would not survive this. The dark shape of the shuttle huddled ahead, and they hurried over and got inside. Picard, taking the controls, rapidly lifted off. He sent a message to Raffi, explaining what was happening, and then laid in a course due south, back to the capital.

Dawn rose on their left as they traveled, revealing to them a falling world. Molula sat with her face pressed against the shuttle's ports. Every so often she would point out some notable feature below: a town aflame, the slow winding lines that evidenced migration. A people, a world—a whole civilization—in flight. Could they possibly believe that this was all a sham? Were they as deluded—as *programmed*—as Kurrem? At length, they began to fly over the outskirts of the city. Here, the evidence of ruin was surely not to be denied. Picard, deliberately, circled the shuttle several times above the refugee transit center alongside mission HQ. The huge press of desperate, terrified people, hoping that they would get the chance to reach the transporter to safety. The thin veneer of organization that was the Federation compound. He landed the shuttle behind the fence. Raffi was there to meet them.

He brought his guest over. They stood inside the compound and looked out beyond the fence at the people huddled there.

"This is no ploy," Picard said to Molula. "No scheme, no trap, no falsehood. Your world is on the brink, and we are here to do all that we can to save as many lives as possible. Senator Kurrem," he went on, "is putting many people at risk. There is still time to save them, but this will not be the case forever."

"We can have two ferries above the district capital by tomorrow," said Raffi, "if we can guarantee that they will be filled. If not—I need them elsewhere."

"Can you help?" said Picard, looking at Molula carefully. "Can you persuade Kurrem to cooperate?"

Her face was pained, grieved. She said, "I have a better idea."

• • •

This idea involved cutting out Kurrem completely. With the help of Raffi, Molula began to marshal the resources to set up operations back in Kindiba, the Vulmab District capital. The crew of the *Verity* were old hands at this exercise now: they knew where to build their temporary bases; they knew how to get hold of census information; they knew how to spread the word around that they were there without causing panic, persuading people to come to the transition camps in orderly fashion. They also knew how to make it clear that rank would not help people to the front of any queue, and that the young and old and sick, and their families or careers, would be taken first, regardless of name or wealth or status. This last inevitably caused some quarrels—and across the years various people had attempted to argue that this was Federation cultural imperialism, imposing an antihierarchical ideology onto Romulan society. It was surely no coincidence, Picard thought, that the people who said such things were invariably in the process of pulling rank.

The operation felt strangely like a breath of fresh air in the streets of Kindiba. At first, the locals were puzzled by the sudden arrival of Starfleet in their midst. Quickly they began to understand why they were there. They were met with relief, as if a long-kept secret had suddenly been brought out into the open. Kurrem's news blackout had clearly only had limited success, and the population of Vulmab had a good grasp of what was happening to their world. Perhaps they did not know exactly how bad the situation was—the district had been mercifully free of the freak weather conditions hitting other parts of the planet, and there had been no shortages of food. This helped make the relief mission easier. They were ready to leave; they were not, as yet, terrified beyond reason. In this case, thought Picard, they might maintain the illusion a little longer. There was no need for these people to know how close they had come to a brutal death until they were safely on their way.

By the third day, the mission was well established. The local police and militias, and some who were plainly Tal Shiar, were coordinating in a most helpful fashion. Already over a thousand people had been transported to the ships that had moved into orbit directly above the area. Picard was beginning to think that he might apprise Bordson and Clancy of their work; they would surely want to make political capital from this success.

And then the huge black ship arrived.

Kurrem burst into local mission HQ like a hurricane, the force of centuries of privilege propelling him forward. "Where is she?" he yelled. "Where's the traitor?"

Picard, who been expecting this, and had therefore been delaying his return to the capital, came to greet him. "Senator," he said. "Welcome."

"*Welcome?*" Kurrem looked ready to reach for his throat. "You scheming, conniving, *puk*, Picard! *Qezhtin! Koga—!*"

Picard had heard worse on a thousand other worlds. "Senator," he said calmly, "there are children present. Outbursts such as these frighten them unduly in what is already a most destabilizing situation—"

"*Zheven'tar!* They're mine anyway! My people, my district! You're not wanted here, Starfleet! Pack up your filthy goods and get out of here or I swear by Surri herself that I'll destroy you!"

"We shall not," said Picard. "And you will not. Your ambassador to the Federation, on behalf of your government, has sanctioned my presence here. The evacuation will continue, under our aegis. You are welcome to board one of our ships, Senator, but if you continue to disrupt proceedings here, I will be obliged to have you removed."

"Fuck *you*, Starfleet!" Kurrem looked around. "Where is she? Molula! Show your damn face!"

Molula stepped out from a nearby office.

"Molula," said Kurrem, "after all I did for you! Helped you, promoted you, protected you—"

"Helped me?" she said. "You'd have let us all burn."

The senator changed tack. "I know they've got to you, dear girl," he said, his voice down almost to a croon. "Starfleet—they lie with every breath. All this"—he looked around—"they're playing a game with us—and it's working! They're bringing Romulus to its knees—scattering us to the four winds! Don't listen to them, Molula. Listen to me. I've been a father to you; better than a father—"

She wasn't persuaded for a second, Picard saw. Kurrem saw it too. "You stinking street rat!" he yelled. "You'd still be whoring on the docks of Volisa if I hadn't saved you—"

Picard saw Tajuth move suddenly beside him, but too late. Kurrem already had his disruptor out. He aimed, and fired, and Molula, screaming, fell to the ground. Tajuth, his own disruptor now out, fired at Kurrem—but a split second before the shot reached him, the senator was gone, pulled away by the beam of a personal transporter.

"Raffi," said Picard, "where the hell has he gone?"

Tricorder out, she had an answer in seconds. "Back to his house," she said.

"Can we get him back?"

"Uh-uh. Whole place is shielded."

Picard shook his head. Much as he would like to see the senator facing a murder charge, he had to admit that his removal was one less thing to worry about. He turned to look at Tajuth, who was kneeling down beside the body of Molula. Picard watched as Tajuth closed her eyes and laid his hand upon her chest.

"*Jelit ma*," Tajuth murmured. "Sister. Comrade. Rest now, in the privacy of death." He stood, his hands closed together, and then left the room. Picard heard Raffi stir beside him. "Killed with kindness, eh, JL? Looked pretty fucking brutal to me."

They received no further word from Kurrem, and no further intervention. The evacuation of Vulmab, once started, was one of the smoothest, most rapidly executed projects of the entire mission. It was a resolution, but the whole affair left a sour taste. Once the *Verity* had its full passenger manifest, Picard set course for Vashti, where they were to be resettled, and where, not incidentally, he would be able to see Zani. Vashti remained his touchstone—a place where refugees had been welcomed, without condition, and had not been treated as interlopers or burdens, but had been integrated, the spaces shared, in the hope that each group would learn from the other. As long as Vashti continued to be a success, he would not lose faith in their work.

In his ready room, he finished updating his log. The door chimed, and Raffi came in. She sat down opposite and stretched. "I am not sorry," she said, "to leave this place behind."

"No," he agreed. He found a bottle of wine and poured out two glasses. They sat quietly for a while and drank.

"It's that time again," she said.

"What time?"

"When we head toward Vashti."

"And the significance of that . . . ?"

"That generally means you need some cheering up."

Was he so transparent? "Raffi, appointing you was the single best decision I have made on this mission."

"Oh, I think you've made a couple of other decent ones, JL. That one where you ripped up the treaty and smashed up the Neutral Zone? That was a particularly good one."

"We got away with it," he said.

"More or less."

They drank a little more. "I don't deny that visiting Vashti gives me hope."

"As it should. Hard to think of anywhere else that works so well."

"Given my way, I would have a group of Qowat Milat on every world to which we take refugees."

"Me too, if I'm being honest."

He eyed her over the rim of his glass. "You don't regret accepting this duty, do you?"

"What? Where the hell has that come from?"

"It's kept you away from home for a long time."

He was startled, briefly, by the alteration in her face. Suddenly she looked ten, fifteen years older; there were lines and cares etched onto her that he had never seen before. He caught a glimpse of how she would look as an old woman. Then she lifted her glass and knocked back the contents. When he could see her face again, she was the same as ever: his XO, Lieutenant Commander Raffi Musiker, one of the very few people on this mission who had come through for him completely.

"Nah," she said. "It's fine. Besides, where else should I be?"

All manner of places, he suspected.

"Where else could I dine every day on elephant?"

The journey to Vashti was comparatively smooth by the standards they had set for these voyages. Some fistfights to break up; a handful of suicide attempts, two tragically successful. Rival gangs briefly brought anarchy to deck nineteen; a combination of Raffi, their mothers, and a night in the brig had them swiftly under control. There were some poignant moments too: a small group held a festival of mourning. One of their passengers turned out to be a composer, and a makeshift orchestra performed her new choral symphony. The Starfleet officers on board learned about the whole thing when they realized that the Romulans had taken down many of the internal walls on one deck in order to have a performance space. Picard let them proceed, on condition that he and his officers could attend. The piece was called *Laments for Homes and Hopes*. It turned out that composer had been raiding the *Verity*'s databanks, where she had found an old human prayer and included lines from it, "We cry, we sigh; we mourn and weep in this vale of tears . . . After this our exile, let us find mercy; let us find peace."

In the darkness of the performance hall, Picard brushed away tears.

"After this our exile . . ." What would come after, for many of them? He hoped it would be mercy. He hoped it would be peace.

"Not exactly a glee club," said Raffi. "But I'm glad I heard it nonetheless."

This, thought Picard, would be the pattern of his life for some years: slow and patient work of carrying lost souls away from their home and toward worlds that they could hope would welcome them. And when they were all saved, what then? Then, he knew, the mission would move into its next stage: the continued construction and maintenance of these new communities. They had never talked about this. Picard had never raised the subject, but he would. As Raffi was wont to say, "One impossible thing at a time, JL. One impossible thing at a time."

At last they reached the Qiris Sector. They stopped first at Diamanta, where a quarter of their guests disembarked. Then on to Vashti. He felt the weight of the world lifting steadily from his shoulders thinking of the quiet convent, its ordered and grounded way of life, the wise and centered friendship of Zani. He packed a bag and put *The Three Musketeers* inside for the boy. He transported to the surface. He walked through North Station, saw the work being done. Romulan children playing with human children; Romulan builders working with human builders. The steady *pop-pop-pop* of archi-printers filling the town with new buildings. Then, a small boy heading toward him like a bullet. *Sanctuary*, he thought when he saw Zani, in her blue robes, following.

The next morning, he play-fought with Elnor, and was entirely unprepared when the message arrived from Raffi.

"What do you mean," he said uncomprehendingly, "'synths attacked Mars'?"

He let a careless promise slip through. "I'll come back."

On the bridge of the *Verity*, there was a profound hush when the admiral arrived. Picard, who was only beginning to comprehend the scale of the tragedy that was overtaking them, had one question uppermost in his mind.

"Can anyone tell me yet," he said, "whether they have heard from Commander La Forge?"

Romulus

Six weeks after the Tal Shiar dumped him unceremoniously on the doorstep of his apartment block, Nokim Vritet ventured outside again for the first time. Hunger had driven him out, and pain; the bones that had been broken had not been set correctly, and his whole body ached. Something cruel gnawed at his belly. He had eked out his supplies as long as he could, but he had run out four days ago. The replicator was not working, and this morning the water had stopped running from the faucet. He thought that if he could simply make his way to his office, he might see a friendly face, someone who could help him buy some food, and even be persuaded to bring him home.

He could make little sense of the streets around him. Familiar landmarks seemed to have gone up in smoke. He heard disruptor fire in the distance. He made his way along, tripping over his feet, or loosened stones. He found a fountain on the street that was still working, and drank thirstily, before wandering on his way. He listened for the familiar rattle of a tram to take him to the interchange and then on to the academy, but nothing came past. It was all very odd. He rubbed his eyes. He didn't see as well as he used to.

By midafternoon, through persistence and denial, Vritet had managed to drag himself to the academy. He wandered through an empty building. There were no lights on anywhere. Was it a holiday? That would explain the absence of the trams. Was it Year Turn already? The Festival of Masks? He had always liked the Festival of Masks. As a child, he would sit on the stairs, watch his parents' guests arrive, their faces hidden behind bright, macabre, and glorious creations. He would watch them carry candles to set around the huge and gaudy multifaceted statue of Vanauka. Was that the day? There should be fireworks. Or was it something else? He couldn't quite sort out the dates in his head. He wandered through the abandoned building, until he reached his office.

Here everything was calm and orderly. He tried the lights several times, but nothing happened. Never mind. He didn't care for lights these days. He would be happier in the darkness. He found that his computer wouldn't turn on. There'd been a few power cuts recently, hadn't there? What was going on there? Power brownouts. Well, that kind of thing happened in every big city, didn't it, across every civilized world. No matter, the authorities would have everything in hand; they'd soon fix everything. Vritet opened a drawer in his desk and found some crackers stashed there. They were rather stale, but he gobbled them down. Then he located actual paper, and a pen, and began to work on some equations. The task was peaceful and soothing. Math was always so peaceful and soothing: the complexities of living in the world, which Vritet had never quite mastered, all disappeared.

He woke at dawn. He had fallen asleep at his desk with his head upon his folded arms. He considered going home, but the thought of the walk filled him with a sudden, terrible weariness. He put his head down, and was on the verge of sleep once more, when he felt someone shaking him awake.

He looked up into the face of a colleague. What was her name again? "*Tzakh*, Nokim, what are you playing at?"

"What? I'm working! I know it's a holiday, but—"

"One of your neighbors got in touch, said they'd seen you come out of your apartment! Everyone thought you were dead! Nokim, it's time to go! It'll soon be too late!"

He couldn't make sense of this. He looked down at his papers. What was her name again? He had always found her very annoying. "Go away! I'm busy! I'm thinking!"

"Nokim, we have to leave! You know why—your figures! Your model!"

He began to shake. He put his hands over his ears. "You're disturbing me! Why does everyone have to always be disturbing me! Go away!"

"There's a place for you, please, Nokim, come with me now! I'll walk with you—"

"Go away!"

He heard a shuffle of footsteps, and then her voice came, from by the door. "I can't stay any longer . . . I have to go . . ."

"Good! Go away!"

Soon he was left in peace again. He picked up his pen. Lies, lies, lies. Starfleet lies. His figures had not been right. They wouldn't lie.

14

Admiral's Log: The shipyards on Mars are burning. This we know. Our best intelligence indicates that the Daystrom A500 synths went rogue, attacking the people around them and then activating explosive devices. This is all data from long-range sensors. There are, as far as we can tell, no survivors.

I am in no position to judge the veracity of these accounts, and I am in no position to judge whether such behavior lies within the spectrum of possibilities of the Daystrom A500s. I will wait to hear what our experts tell us, when they have had a chance to examine all available data. In circumstances such as these, I would approach my own expert, but there is, as yet, no word from Commander La Forge, and my deepest fear is that he must be numbered among the dead on Mars.

Mars shuttle
En route to Earth

Geordi La Forge opened his eyes to a new day and a new world that, while he was sleeping, had become less brave and more fearful.

"Lights!"

He began his morning ritual, the same wherever he was. He opened the foldout running machine and did his morning 5K. Showered. Pottered around, listening to jazz, whipping up a pretty good breakfast from the replicator. Scrambled eggs. Brown bread toast with a dab of butter. Black coffee. Brushed his teeth. Whistled as he put on his uniform. Whole thing took a little over an hour, and he didn't interface with the outside world until he was all done, and the working day could officially start. Taking his chair at the little desk, he opened up the cabin's computer, and the messages began to flood in. He read the first three.

"What the—?"

He hunted down the FNN channel. At first he thought he must have accidentally gotten the wrong feed, that he had found one of those weird multi-user immersive experiences where you acted out a disaster scenario. Someone back on Mars was yanking his chain. They had signed him up as some kind of joke. Well, La Forge would get to the bottom of who the culprit was when he got back. He didn't think this prank was in particularly good taste. He started flipping through the stored messages, wondering why they hadn't gotten through, then he saw one from Admiral Picard: *"Where are you?"* He tried answering but could only send a delayed message. "Somewhere between Mars and Earth." He went back to the FNN. Something wasn't right.

Hearing voices outside his cabin door, he went out and was confronted by the sight of one of the other passengers in tears. A woman, one of the civilian crew, was trying to comfort him.

"No, no," the passenger was saying. "I can't believe this. My wife is back there. She was going to come with me . . . She changed her mind at the last minute!"

That was when La Forge realized that something very bad was happening on Mars.

He got the crew woman's attention. "Hey," he said, "what's going on?"

She gave him a distraught look. "There's been some kind of attack on Mars . . ."

The passenger started going into hysterics. The crew woman was trying her best, but she was obviously in considerable distress herself. Most likely she was from Mars. She probably had family back there, too, and was desperate for news but trying to do her duty.

La Forge, putting his hand on her arm, said, "Take him to see the medic. It might be a good idea for him to have a sedative. And make sure you take some time for yourself."

The woman gave grateful thanks and began to maneuver her charge along the corridor. La Forge, mind racing, headed off to get fresh news.

La Forge did not tend toward catastrophic thinking. By predisposition and by training, he was optimistic and solution oriented. He didn't waste time imagining catastrophes. He waited until they landed in his lap, and then he got on with fixing them.

He soon reached the small mess area. Almost all the passengers were gathered there, in silence, watching the FNN 'cast. La Forge stood at the back and stared at the appalling images coming from Mars orbit. There would be ships in orbit, trying to bring help. But as he watched, everything went from bad to worse. Some kind of chain reaction had been set off. More and more explosions; more and more of the shipyards caught up in the conflagration. Not many, he figured, had the dubious honor of seeing their last five years of effort burn. He got to see, in real time, friends and colleagues die. He watched as the secondary assembly line in plant fifty-two exploded. If he stopped to think about it, he could probably say exactly who was on duty. Who exactly had died.

La Forge fumbled his way to the nearest chair and sat down.

"All of it?" someone said. "The *whole* shipyard?"

He couldn't quite take it in. La Forge had been there himself, twenty hours ago . . . He looked around. He could see the same emotion on the faces of the others there: how close they had been to all this, how lucky they were not to be among the dead. The logical engineer part of his brain provided the term: survivor guilt. He'd be dealing with this for years to come.

The news broadcast went on relentlessly. La Forge tried to piece together the situation. An attack on the shipyards? But whom by? How? *Why?*

"The synths," someone on the 'cast said. It started going around the room. The synths, the fucking synths. Those fucking things! Dimly, he perceived the extent of the anger, which soon would be raging like wildfire.

Suddenly, the enormity of what was happening hit him.

"Holy shit," he murmured. Someone unobtrusively pushed a cup of water into his hands. He took a sip. He felt cold, clammy. *Shock*, murmured a calmer part of his mind.

Because it wasn't only the construction yards, was it? It wasn't only the ships. It was everything. It was *everyone*. Everyone he had worked with over the past few years. Everyone who had grumbled and groused and complained, and eventually had decided that, yes, all right, they'd throw themselves behind this insanely complex project. They had come around, and seen the impact that they were having, the material good that they were doing, and had turned slowly but steadily into cheerleaders; defending their work to all comers, providing information at the drop of a hat for people like Olivia Quest and her committee. Every last damn one of them was dead, from the newest junior tech to all the division heads. Estella Mackenzie, that tough, no-nonsense, dedicated woman who had been his first and stoutest supporter, the first person to knock on his door with a solution, and not a problem, who had been behind their best breakthrough. She was *dead*.

The synths, he thought. *What happened? Did we miss something? Did we make a mistake?* The cruelty of this was almost too much to contemplate. Estella Mackenzie had not deserved this. *Maddox*, he thought wildly. *You haven't had your eye on the ball for a while now. What the hell has been going on down there in your damn lab?*

Then the Martian stratosphere ignited.

"No, no, no," somebody said. People began to cry, openly. Someone started to pray. La Forge detached himself entirely from any emotional reaction and shifted gear into a cool and purely intellectual response: *That's going to burn for years.*

VERITY

The *Verity* hung silently in orbit over Vashti. Picard raised his head from his hands when Raffi entered his ready room. "I've had a message from Geordi La Forge," he said, "but I'm not sure when he sent it."

"I've raised him. He's on a shuttle back to Earth," said Raffi. "JL, are you okay?"

Picard, briefly, put his hand back to his brow, covering his face. He heard Raffi shift uneasily in her chair. "JL?"

"I'm fine. I'm very relieved to hear about Geordi, that's all."

"The other news isn't so good..."

He didn't move his hand. "Tell me."

"Everyone at the production facility is dead. They're trying to evacuate other parts of Mars. The stratosphere's on fire." He listened as she steadied her voice and tried to report properly to her superior officer, tried to hold herself together. *Mon dieu*, he thought, *we are all going to need to find a deep well of courage.* He thought, fleetingly, of those Saxon warriors, facing imminent annihilation, somewhere finding it within themselves to lift their spears and their shields for one last, fruitless defense. He thought he knew, now, how that must have felt.

"The ships, JL..." Raffi said. "All the ships... They're *gone*..."

"*Thought must be the harder,*" he murmured, "*heart be the keener, mind must be the greater, while our strength lessens...*"

"What?"

He looked up at her. Her cheeks were wet with tears.

"Simply gathering my strength for the battle ahead."

"The battle..." She understood. Of course Raffi understood. "What's this going to mean for the mission, JL? It's *all* the ships..."

"This will *not* stop us. It cannot. But we need solutions."

"Ships," she said. "We need ships."

"Then let us look at what we have, and let us look at what can be found—"

The comm chimed. They both started at the noise, as if caught in some indiscretion, and glanced at each other. *"Admiral, Starfleet Command."*

"Jean-Luc," said Bordson. *"I want you back on Earth, immediately."*

"Victor, I—"

"That's not a request, Admiral."

Paris, Earth

Maddox contacted Agnes Jurati, and they arranged to meet, immediately, but not at work, not at their café, not even on the campus. Not a place where they might be seen or known. He wasn't sure why he thought they needed privacy and secrecy. They hadn't done anything wrong, after all, had they? No, they hadn't done *anything* wrong.

After some negotiation, they agreed on Paris. One of the cafés beneath the trees in the Jardin des Tuileries. It wasn't hard to find her: she was one of the few people there. What kind of person went out socializing on a day like this? This was the kind of day where you stayed at home with your loved ones, holding them to you. The kind of day that in years to come you would suddenly remember, and a cold chill would envelop you, and you would turn to the person with you and say, "Where were you when you heard about Mars?"

She was wearing a headscarf and black sunglasses: Audrey Hepburn–style. Hot chocolate and croissant. *Jeez*, he thought, *what is up with her?* How could she have any appetite? There was a book on the table beside her, the cover showing. *Frankenstein*. Was that supposed to be funny? He nearly grabbed the damn thing and tore it to shreds.

He sat down opposite her. She took off her glasses. She looked haggard. Her eyes were red from weeping. "Oh Bruce," she whispered. "What have we done?"

"Nothing," he said. "We've done nothing—"

"Are you sure? Can you know for sure?"

"Aggie! Shut up for a minute! Let me think!"

A waiter came to take his order.

"No, no, nothing!" he said.

"You have to get something," said the waiter. "These seats are very popular. If you don't want them, someone else would like them."

Maddox looked around the empty garden. "There's nobody here!"

"You are, sir."

"Who the hell is out drinking coffee today?"

"I have something," said Agnes, pointing at her cup and untouched croissant. "Isn't that okay?"

"I'm sorry, *mademoiselle*, but the gentleman needs to order as well."

"Damn, man!" Maddox exploded. "Don't you know what's going on?"

"I know what's going on," said the waiter in a quiet voice. "Even less reason to be rude. And you still need to order—"

"All right, I'll fucking order! I'll have a fucking Americano!"

There was a pause. "With hot milk?"

"Yes."

"That's not an Americano, sir. That's a café au lait. Unless you want the milk steamed, then that's a latte—"

"Just get me a fucking coffee!"

"I'm just trying to get your order right."

"For fuck's sake, I didn't want anything anyway!"

"Bruce, *please*!"

Maddox stopped. To his shame, he realized that the waiter was crying. "I'm sorry. Black coffee is fine. I'm sorry."

"Yeah, well, fuck you," said the waiter. He went off to get the order. They sat in silence, burning with embarrassment. Jurati started to tear the croissant between her fingers. The coffee arrived: black with a little jug of hot milk. Maddox turned his face away. Even looking at it made him feel nauseous. The waiter finally left them in peace.

"Bruce," Agnes said, "did we do this?"

Maddox calmed himself. He leaned in to speak in a low voice. He felt exposed out here, naked. Unprotected in some way, as if there were a target painted on his back. As if someone were coming for him. Maybe they should have met at the lab. But the truth was, he hadn't been able to face going there yet. He hadn't even begun to think what he could say to the team.

What have I done?

"It can't be the synths," he said firmly. "It's not in their programming—"

"But you weren't only working on the A500s, were you?" she whispered. "Were you?"

He didn't answer. He started to pour the milk into the coffee. Swirls and spirals, spinning around, like fractals. The nausea hit him once again.

"*Were* you, Bruce?"

"Dammit, you know I wasn't!"

"What *happened*, Bruce? What did we *do*?"

He put his head in his hands. If he could, he would have put his head down on this café table—here, in the middle of the most beautiful city on Earth, the city of light, the city of *Enlightenment*—and wept like a child. He knew, whatever the truth of what had happened on Mars, that he was finished. His work was finished. His career—finished. He had overreached. He had tried to do too much, to work on what was wanted by others, and at the same time to do the work that was necessary for himself, the work he had to do to keep himself *alive*. He had been proud, and vain, and too sure of himself, and now Nemesis was hammering at the door.

A couple sat down at the next table.

"Bruce," she whispered again, "is this our fault?"

He ran his hand across his face. He was sweating. Was he catching a cold? Or was this shock? The truth was that even though he could close his eyes and picture every last piece of circuitry inside every one of those damn toys, and even though he couldn't see anywhere—*anywhere*—that could have led to this, it had still happened, hadn't it? And he could not, hand upon his heart, with the scrupulous truth required by science, say that he had not made a mistake.

Agnes was looking at him, lips parted, eyes trusting. He said, "I don't know."

Her face went slack. "No," she said. He could see panic setting in. "Oh no, oh no, oh no, what have we done—"

"Aggie, stop it—"

The couple next to them were staring at them.

"Oh god, oh Jesus Christ—!"

"Aggie," he hissed, "shut the fuck up!"

She pulled back, as if he had slapped her. But he hadn't slapped her. He hadn't done that.

"Okay," she said, subdued. "I see. Okay."

"I'm sorry, please . . . Please, Aggie, I'm upset . . ."

"Okay. Yes. I get that. Of course. I'm sorry. It's okay. I'm okay now." She put her palms down flat on the table and took deep, steadying breaths. "Yes, okay, calming down now." She gave him a weak smile. "What do we do now?"

"I don't know. There'll be an inquiry."

"Okay."

He looked at her carefully. She hadn't grasped yet what was going to happen, had she? She thought they had a chance. But they didn't. The people who were in charge, who had been behind the whole thing—they were going to turn everything off. They couldn't be associated with a disaster as huge as this. The robotics program at the Daystrom Institute was dead and buried. They might as well not bother going back to campus. No, he thought, seeing her smile at him. She hadn't seen that yet. But she would, very soon.

His handheld chimed softly. He pulled it out of his pocket and looked at the incoming message. He was nearly sick again.

"Who is it?" she said.

"Geordi La Forge," he said. "He's on his way to the Daystrom Institute. He wants to see me. *Shit!*" He jumped up out of his seat. The jug of milk went flying, spilling its contents all over her book.

She picked the book up. "Oh," she said. She was crying openly now. "I loved this book . . . I loved this cover . . ."

"I'm sorry," he said. "Aggie, I'm sorry."

He looked down at her for a moment, and then he ran away. He left her there, sitting crying over her ruined book, and he dashed back to the public transporter, and fled all the way to Okinawa.

Daystrom Institute
Okinawa, Earth

Commander Geordi La Forge transported direct from the spaceport to the Daystrom Institute transporter pad. The director of the Institute, Sisra Koas, was there to meet him.

"Commander La Forge, I am so sorry. I can't even begin to imagine—"

He knew that he would have versions of this conversation dozens upon dozens of times over the next few weeks, months. Hell, it was going to be *years*, wasn't it? Because he was still alive when everyone else on Mars was dead—and he knew he was going to need a strategy to cut people off straightaway. Because he couldn't go through the rest of his life having versions of this conversation. He couldn't go through life being known as the one who got away. He wouldn't.

"Thank you, Sisra." He glanced around. This wasn't quite the welcoming committee he'd been expecting. "Is Bruce Maddox here?"

"I've been trying to raise him . . ." Koas looked embarrassed, as she might, given the absence of her most prominent member of staff, who was the man of the moment. "It's most odd." She laughed nervously. "You know Bruce. Like herding cats . . ."

Gone to ground, hey? La Forge tried to clamp that down. He had no evidence—none whatsoever—that Bruce Maddox was in any way responsible for this catastrophe. La Forge knew that grief did strange things to you, and one of the things that it did was make you thrash around trying to pin the blame on someone. And sometimes, there simply wasn't anyone to blame. There was only sheer damn bad luck. He had to keep that in mind . . . Besides, that wasn't why he was here. He was here to start asking the right kinds of questions that would get answers. But for all his training, for all it was in his nature as a decent human being not to prejudge anyone, La Forge was finding it hard not to damn Bruce Maddox. He could at least have had the common decency to be here.

"Well, whenever he's ready. How about we go over to the production facility?"

La Forge didn't say the word *synth*. Everyone else was doing the same right now. Had the word acquired a cursed aura, as if simply saying it could draw disaster to you? La Forge was certainly not superstitious, not in any way, but the word still stuck in his throat. *Give yourself time*, he told himself firmly. *You're going to need time.*

Koas led him over to the monorail that ran out to the far side of the campus, the brand-new facility where the synths had been created. She tried a few conversational gambits, and then thought better of it, leaving him to sit in silence. The whole campus was deserted. Whether this was out of fear, or out of respect, La Forge could not guess. Speaking for himself, he never wanted to go near one of the damn things ever again. He sympathized with anyone who was keeping away from the place where they'd been made.

At the production facility itself, however, he saw many people, none of them working. Bunched together in twos and threes, watching the 'casts. Whispering. Some of them crying; some consoling. Everyone distressed. He walked through, thinking about the time he had been here with Mackenzie. Their delight and excitement; the incredible feeling that they'd cracked the problem, that they had at last found the key to unlock the mission, to build all the ships that were needed to save a people.

And now he was here, and Estella Mackenzie wasn't, and what he couldn't stand, most of all, was that she'd offered to stay here, keep an eye on things, because you knew Bruce Maddox, the man needed someone standing behind him with a *poker*. And La Forge had said, "Come back to Mars, Estella." Because she was his pal, and his fiercest supporter, and he wanted her around. If only he had let her stay . . . maybe she would have seen something. Maybe she would have stopped whatever had gone wrong. And even if she hadn't, she wouldn't have been on Mars when those damn things had gone on the rampage.

Estella, he thought, *one day I might forgive myself.*

They came at last to Maddox's office. Sitting behind his desk, alone, but watching the 'casts like the rest of them, was the man himself. Koas brought La Forge to the door. Maddox rose from his seat. She looked at the two men and said, "I'll leave you to it."

"Bruce," said La Forge. "What the hell happened?"

Maddox opened out his hands. The gesture made him look extremely vulnerable. "I don't know, Geordi. I wish I did, but I don't. I can't understand it, their programming didn't allow for it—"

La Forge looked back over his shoulder. The wall was transparent, and he could see that there were many people in the office beyond looking in at them, pretending not to, but looking, nonetheless. He didn't blame them. He'd be doing the same thing. He drew in a steady breath. It was very important, he thought, that he did not lose his temper now. There was too much pain going around at the moment to cause more. He needed to be constructive; he needed to ask questions and find answers, and with that done, he would be able to let the dead rest in peace.

But first—the questions.

"Bruce," he said, "tell me straight. Did you take your eye off the ball?"

La Forge watched the man pale.

"*What?*" Maddox whispered, and La Forge knew he'd been right.

"Bruce—did you cut corners?"

"I . . . I . . ."

"Bruce, you have to trust me. You have to tell me the truth. Were you working on something else?"

"I . . . Maybe I was thinking about other things as well . . ."

A whole chasm of grief and horror opened between them. "Oh, Bruce, man! What were you *thinking*? What the hell were you thinking?"

"Geordi, you have to understand . . . My life's work . . . !"

"You kept on, didn't you? Like I told you not to. You kept on, working on sentient synthetics—"

"It's my dream, Geordi!"

It was that present tense that bugged him. Even now, even after all this, Maddox couldn't admit that he was done. La Forge gripped his head between his hands. *People are looking*, some calmer part of his mind said. *Well, let them look.*

"Everyone on Mars was pulled onto this, Bruce! Most of *Starfleet* was pulled onto this! Everyone sacrificed their projects, their goals! Sure, they hated it—man, they hated it! Those people on Mars? All those dead people? Do you think they liked being asked to stop working on their projects? But they got on with it because they knew it had to be done. Oh, but not Doctor Bruce Maddox! The only genius among us? Is that what you told yourself? Your work—so special, so important!"

"Yes," Maddox said, fiercely, dumbly, "yes, it *is*—"

"Bruce . . ." La Forge tried to calm himself down. "I understand your passion—I do, I really do. Look around you! Look where it's *led* you!"

He watched as Maddox put his head in his hands. He did understand; he understood the loss too. Softly, Geordi said, "Data was unique, Bruce. You can't ever re-create him. Never going to happen. *It's never going to happen.* And look where it's ended. You think there's going to be work like this done ever again? It's over, all over. It's cost thousands upon thousands of lives. This is the *end*, Bruce."

VERITY
EN ROUTE TO EARTH

Raffi Musiker lay in the darkness listening to the soft steady rhythms of the ship. After thirty hours on her feet, gathering information about what was happening back on Mars, JL had ordered her to go and get some rest. She'd returned to her cabin, eaten, and showered. She had thought about trying to speak to Jae and Gabe, but found that she couldn't face the conversation. Couldn't face the strain, the awkwardness, the unvoiced but ever-present reproach that had seeped into all their interactions . . . She could cope with the death throes of her family or the death throes of the mission to which she had sacrificed that family, but she couldn't cope with both.

She lay in bed, eyes tired and burning, thoughts whirling restlessly, like leaves stirred by sudden squalls. This attack, she thought. It could *not* be random. Nothing in the universe was random. There was a pattern to everything, if you looked hard enough. There had to be. Otherwise . . .

Otherwise the universe was meaningless. And Raffi couldn't bear that. She'd go insane, if that was the case. Raffi clenched her fists together beside her in the darkness. She was not going to give up this mission, not without a fight. She had given *everything* . . .

She got up and dressed. She looked at the half-empty bottle on the table. She was tempted for a moment, but she didn't want to risk having the smell on her breath. She left her cabin and went in search of her captain.

As she'd predicted, he wasn't sleeping either. He was sitting alone in his cabin. Contemplating. Pondering. *No*, thought Raffi, *this is full-on brooding*.

"Can we talk, JL?"

"Of course, Raffi."

She sat down on the couch opposite. She gave him a wan smile. "Hey," she said. "I thought we'd ordered each other to get some rest."

"I thought I might try asking your forgiveness later this morning."

"You know what a soft touch I am."

"Was there something in particular you wanted to talk to me about, Raffi?"

She leaned forward in her seat, planted her hands firmly on her knees. "Yes, JL. Yes, there is . . ."

"Go on."

"It's kind of wild."

"I'm open to any ideas right now that might help me make sense of this catastrophe."

"Okay," she said. "Then try this. The more I think about this whole thing, JL, the more I think it can't be an accident. I mean, Maddox is insisting, isn't he, that it can't be a flaw in the programming."

"These are complex machines, Raffi—"

"But Maddox knows them."

"That's true," he conceded.

"So if it's not a flaw in the programming, then it has to be deliberate—" She saw his expression. "Listen, JL. Hear me out. These synths—Maddox says it couldn't happen this way. They're androids, toys, nothing more. It would be like . . ." She hunted around for a comparison. "Dammit, like your *tricorder* attacking you. It's not possible!"

"What else could it be, Raffi? Maddox has admitted to La Forge that he was preoccupied with other projects. That he was still working toward creating sentient life—"

"No, not that, not the synths . . . I know this is going to sound crazy, JL, but I think there's something else going on."

"Something else?"

"Something premeditated. Something *planned*—"

"Raffi . . . You have to understand—when you're dealing with artificial life in any form, you never know what to expect."

He's going to mention Data, she thought.

"Data . . . at every turn, Data exceeded his programming. He became more and more alive." A small glow suffused his face.

Data, she thought. What was the special magic that that lost creation had contained, which inspired such love, such devotion? What had been the power this machine had held, to so enchant all those around him?

"In many ways," said Picard, "he was the most alive being I have ever encountered."

"But these synths weren't Data, JL," she said.

"No," he said. His face became sad. "No, they were not. But everything I have seen—and, Raffi, I have seen *so much*. So many marvelous, awe-inspiring—and, yes, *terrible*—things. After so many sights, I can well believe in the possibility that these synths came to consciousness."

Whether it was the lack of sleep, or the drink, or the sheer toll of the past two days, she was not making herself understood. "JL, all I am saying is—"

He reached out to her. He lifted one of her hands and pressed both of his around it. She knew he was trying to console, but she had never felt so distanced from him. He was the wisest man she had ever known, and he had not understood what she was trying to tell him. The most important thing she had ever had to say, and he had not understood.

"Raffi," he said. "It's natural to look for someone to blame. Many, many people are dead. But the fault is . . . Who knows? Maybe Maddox overreached, didn't take enough care, made a mistake. Or maybe, just maybe, something sparked within these creations . . . Something emergent, something we could not have calculated for. Maybe they woke, and looked around, and decided that they did not want to be our slaves."

"JL, please, listen—"

"We made them, Raffi. Perhaps we made them better than we intended. And when they woke—to consciousness, to sentience—they saw that their creators had made them only to make use of them, and they took the only action they could."

She stopped trying to explain. She was too tired, too heartsick. But she knew—she *knew*—that she was not wrong. She might not have the proof yet, but damn it all, she would find that proof. She could not be wrong about this. Because that way lay only chaos.

He released her hand. She felt a powerful surge of love for him, but for the very first time it was tinged with disappointment.

"Go to bed, Raffi," he said. "We are heading for Earth. We need to sleep, and we need to be sharp, because there are many lives depending on us. Many people who as yet have not been brought to safety. Let us not lose sight of this. The next few days will be critical, and we need to be ready to do whatever we can to save this mission."

She left and went back to her cabin. But she did not go to bed, and she did not sleep for a long while. Instead, she poured some whiskey, and she started watching the 'casts, and those led her to the dark virtual chambers where people trade in conspiracy and supposition, and she began what was to be a very rapid slide down—down, down, down to somewhere a very long way from Wonderland.

15

Admiral's Log: We are now within six hours of Earth, and my meeting with Starfleet Command. The journey time here has been spent pulling apart our mission goals and trying to determine what will be needed in order for us to be able to continue our work. In this, as in so many things, Commander Musiker has been invaluable, developing duty rosters, ship manifests, and all the necessary information for us to redeploy our resources. What is clear is that there is an interim, short-term period where the mission will inevitably have to be reduced in scope, not only while we move ships from other tasks, but retool them for the purposes of ferrying our Romulan refugees to their new homes. While this is, obviously, a significant logistical task, I believe it is important for us to remember that all the preparation work to receive the refugees is comparatively unaffected by this Mars tragedy. A large proportion of the worlds to which we were carrying refugees have nearly completed the necessary infrastructure projects. Some will have to scale back (we are no longer so easily able to transport extra building material and other supplies to them, and refugees must take precedence), but these are activities that can be recommenced at a future date. The most important task is to ensure that the transportation of Romulans from the blast zone to safety continues uninterrupted. If we must resort for a while to small ships—Dunkirk comes to mind. We will still be able to save lives that would otherwise be lost.

The alternative is unthinkable, and I cannot believe that anyone within Starfleet would countenance it. These people are blameless. They are guilty of no crime.

The morning after the news broke, Tajuth came to see me, and, for the first time, I glimpsed some warmth within the man. Perhaps it made a difference to him to be the one able to offer, rather than to be the object of, sympathy. At the same time, I could see that he was anxious to know what this would mean for the relief mission but was not indelicate enough to ask outright. I have tried to assure him to the best of my ability that as far as I am concerned, this alters nothing: there is no evidence or even suggestion of Romulan culpability in the Mars tragedy, and therefore no reason why our mission should be diminished. It is of great importance, I believe, to keep our clarity about the relief mission. There are many desperate people in dire need of our help. I intend to suggest to Admiral Bordson that we now approach ambassadors from other powers to ask what further aid they might offer. Enmities between the Romulans and the Cardassian Union and the Klingon Empire go back many years, but each might well be reminded how the Federation came to them in their hour of need, and thus be persuaded to offer assistance.

Raffi and I have not spoken again about our conversation the night after the attack, but I sense that our exchange then has put something at odds between us. I believe she has not set aside her suspicion that there is some deeper scheme—some hidden intent—behind this catastrophe. I am aware that beyond the immediate tasks I have set her, she has been asking her former colleagues within Romulan Affairs for a report on Tal Shiar activity as comprehensive as they can possibly muster. I imagine that this is temporary on Raffi's part. We all must process shock and grief in our own ways.

For myself, I try, when I can, to speak to Zani. To know that something is still right is very important right now. Vashti remains my lodestone, the north on my compass. While Vashti flourishes, this mission has not failed. And this mission must not—cannot—will not—fail.

STARFLEET COMMAND
SAN FRANCISCO, EARTH

Picard was sweating. For some reason, he had been expecting a cold day. In fact, it was bright, sunny. He pondered this miscalculation. Somewhere along the line he had lost track of the seasons; he had fallen out of synch with Earth.

The benches outside Starfleet HQ were hardly the best place for a briefing—or a pep talk, for that matter—but Raffi had insisted on coming down with him, and, given the opportunity, would probably have walked him to the door of Bordson's office, handing him newly updated duty rosters all the way there. "Raffi," he had said at last, "everything will be fine."

"I want to be sure. Let's go through it one last time."

So, because he owed her so much, he went through everything, one last time.

"They'll start with the ships," he said. "But I can point them to the inventories from Beta Antares and Eridani A. So, then they'll try staffing. But we have the duty rosters from personnel . . ."

She nodded throughout, even mouthed along with him at a few points, and, when he came to the end, she grunted and looked satisfied. "Good," she said. "Yeah, that's good." She gave him an appraising look, and then reached out to fiddle with the admiral's insignia on his collar, like a mother fussing over her son's uniform on the first day of school.

"You'll do. I guess."

"Thank you, Lieutenant Commander Musiker." He watched her put her hands flat along her sides, trying to command her own nerves.

"Okay," she said. "This is a minor setback, isn't it?"

"Raffi. Relax. We'll be back at work before we know it."

"Okay, well, we have a plan—and not just any old plan, it's a *great* plan—"

He put his hand upon her shoulder. "You've done good work, Raffi, under difficult and trying circumstances. I promise you that I will not let this mission be curtailed. We have to do what is right, even when we have been so grievously injured. *Particularly* when we have been so grievously injured."

She gave him a wry look, tempered with affection. "Make a speech like that, and we can't go wrong. I'm glad you're the one fighting this battle, JL. Nobody's further up on the moral high ground than you."

"I think that was a compliment, Raffi."

"I meant it that way."

"Then I'll take it that way."

He checked the time. Ten minutes until his meeting. It took him seven and a half minutes, he knew, to get from this spot to the door of Bordson's office. There was no harm, however, in being timely.

"Right," he said. "Let's get this done. Let's get back to work."

"Good luck, JL."

He walked toward the entrance. Before he went inside, he glanced back over his shoulder, and saw her sit down again on a bench. She already had a padd out, diving into some research or other. He smiled, fondly, and went inside.

Inside, the mood within the building was taut as wire. People dashing about, no chatter. Action; any kind of action. He had seen this before, after stressful events. The need to keep busy, to do something. An ensign, waiting for him, hurried over, and moved him briskly toward the elevator, but did not meet his eye. He went into the commander-in-chief's office confident: sure of himself and his purpose. Sure of his plans, and of their overwhelming rightness.

Bordson was there. Clancy. Two other admirals' holos were projected over the long table. Murim, from Trill, and a Vulcan, named Charu. Picard knew them but he had not been expecting them. Their presence made no difference. He was sure of what he had to say.

"Admiral Picard," said Bordson. "Thank you for coming. Please, sit down."

Picard took the seat that Bordson offered. Clancy was sitting opposite. She looked exhausted. His heart went out to her. They had been sheltered on the *Verity* from having to deal with the immediate ramifications of the Mars tragedy. "Kirsten," he said warmly.

She nodded, rather brusquely. "Jean-Luc." Even her voice sounded ragged.

"Before we start, Jean-Luc," said Bordson, "I would like you to be clear that we have received all your reports and we have studied them in considerable detail."

Picard looked at him with a little surprise. "I am sure that you have, Victor."

"Good. So that you understand that we are not making any decisions lightly—"

"Of course not." Picard frowned. What decisions could be made, until he had shown them the revised evacuation plans? "We should look at those reports in more detail. I have some further amendments to them that, as you will see, make the plan even more sustainable—"

"The problem," said Admiral Murim, *"lies in the fact that we have in one fell swoop lost our shipbuilding capabilities. The ships that do remain will have to perform double, triple duties—"*

"Yes, naturally I understand this concern," said Picard. "Let me draw your attention to these most recent inventories from Beta Antares and Eridani A. There are a number of retired ships that, with some work, can be retooled—"

"Who will do this work, exactly?" Charu asked. *"There is also a question of labor—"*

"Duty reserve officers," said Picard promptly. This was going exactly how Raffi had predicted. "We have been speaking—"

"The mission," said Murim, *"depended on synthetic labor."*

There was a pause. Picard, noting that past tense, began to perceive that something was not right.

"I understand that there are significant concerns about synthetic labor—"

He heard Clancy, opposite, breathe out. *Exasperation?*

"Let us turn," said Bordson, "to the matter of the synths. You need to know, Jean-Luc, that there is, with immediate effect, a ban on the production of synthetics within the Federation. Furthermore, there is a ban on research that might lead in any way to the creation of any form of synthetic life."

"That is a very stringent ruling, Victor—"

"In the face of thousands dead," noted Charu.

"It's also a direct order from the Council," said Bordson. "The synth production facility at the Daystrom Institute is, as we speak, being shut down, and once the forensic inquiry is finished it will be completely decommissioned. There is no question of further use of synths within the Federation."

"Of course," Picard said cautiously. He and Raffi had discussed something along these lines—not so draconian as a complete ban on research—but certainly cutting back on synths for the immediate future. "Naturally this leaves us with some questions about how we can meet our objectives in terms of ship construction, but I am sure that—"

"Admiral Picard," said Clancy. "The shipyards on Mars have been obliterated. The Martian stratosphere is on fire. There *is* no ship construction."

The switch to his title set the alarm bells thoroughly ringing. Quietly, but persistently. "I understand, Captain, but there are other options—"

"None of which can meet the scale that this operation requires—"

"And we will have to," Picard said gently, but firmly. "The Romulans manifestly do not have the capacity to remove the people remaining within blast range. I will not be surprised if we are called on soon to assist in evacuating the homeworld itself—"

Bordson raised an admonitory hand. "Please," he said. "Jean-Luc, I am afraid that you have not been privy to the kinds of conversations that Command has been conducting over the past few weeks. The appetite for this mission was already waning—"

"That's an understatement," muttered Clancy.

"The will has gone," Bordson stated.

Now the alarm bells were something more of a red alert. "Victor, you can't—"

"I appreciate the time that you and Lieutenant Commander Musiker have put into these plans, Jean-Luc. But they are unfeasible. The relief mission is over."

For a split second, Picard thought that he had misheard. But no: Bordson was looking back at him, calmly and compassionately; Clancy was looking at him implacably. The others . . . they were not meeting his eyes. Suddenly, he sensed the fear in the room, even from the Vulcan admiral. But this fear; this was not how a decision of this magnitude should be made . . .

"I'm afraid," said Picard, "that is not acceptable."

Clancy pushed back in her chair. "The alternative, sir," she said, "is the breakup of the Federation. You've been gone a long time. I've spent every day—day after day—trying to keep the Council on our side . . . We've come close to having worlds *secede* over this! The entire Federation is starting to ask again what exactly this mission has brought us. And they look at Mars and see—nothing but grief."

"That is not the fault of anyone in Romulan space, Captain," said Picard. "You know that as well as I do! It is imperative that we distinguish between the tragedy that has happened on Mars, and what continues to be happening, on a daily basis, within Romulan space—"

"Sure, yes, I know the difference. And yet still I have fourteen member worlds telling me that they will start the process of seceding from the Federation if this mission continues," Clancy shot back. "We needed a win. And instead we got . . ." She threw her hands up. "We got *hell*."

Picard turned to Bordson. "Sir," he said, softly, urgently, sensing that the other man was not entirely sympathetic to this course of action. "This is a grotesque decision. This is a renunciation of the Federation's core values in the most unforgiveable way. There are still many, many people in desperate need." He looked bitterly at Clancy. "You say that I don't understand, Kirsten. I've seen the refugee camps. The desperation, the sheer *need*—"

Bordson cut in. "I'm sorry, Jean-Luc," he said. "This is the decision of the Council, agreed by the president. The mission is over. I have spoken already to Ambassador Sulde. We have agreed a number of replicators and archi-printers will remain for a period of time on the worlds to which they have already been assigned. But the ships must come home."

Dead silence.

"Jean-Luc?"

"I will not do that," said Picard.

"That is an order," said Bordson. "You must instruct the fleet home. A number of them will be tasked with the Mars cleanup."

"No," said Picard. "Starfleet may accept my revised evacuation plan, or it accepts my resignation."

"For god's sake, Admiral, it's a direct *order*!" burst out Clancy. "The mission is over!"

"Admiral Picard," said Bordson again, mildly. "If you can't accept these orders, then . . . then I will accept your resignation."

(Later, sitting in splendid isolation in his manor, M. Picard would often wonder whether what he did had been meant as a threat or a gamble, or whether he had known when he said it that the game was over. Whatever the case, it was his last throw of the dice, his last chance to salvage something from this terrible situation. His last, best chance to save lives.)

"Then I resign from Starfleet with immediate effect."

If he had been expecting some protest, it did not come. He rose to his feet. "It seems we are finished here."

"It seems we are," said Bordson. "Jean-Luc, for what it's worth, I am very sorry—"

"Don't," said Picard. "I don't want to hear it."

He turned, walked away from them, and left the room. He left the fleet, and the mission, and—yes, he left Starfleet—behind him. He was striding across the atrium before the enormity of this decision hit home. It hit him physically, a tremendous and sudden shock that left him trembling. He had no idea how the events of the last half hour had happened. He had no grasp of the paths, the decisions, the steps that had brought him to this pass. Picard had not, for many years now, experienced so profoundly, so devastatingly, what it was to fail, and to fail so completely.

Where do I go now? What shall I do?

He walked out into the square. Raffi was still sitting where he had left her.

What do I say to her?

His hand went up to his face, reached to touch his deepest and most abiding scar.

What good am I? What am I for?

Who am I, now?

DAYSTROM INSTITUTE
OKINAWA, EARTH

Bruce Maddox stood outside the meeting room, and for a moment thought he could not do what he'd come here to do. *All I wanted*, he thought, *was to be left to do work . . .* That was the bitterest pill to swallow, in the end. They had come to *him*—demanded that he turn his mind toward this project—and now here he was, the man who had created the monster. *Not my fault!* a part of him screamed, while another part taunted: *Are you sure of that, Bruce?*

But one thing was true: it was certainly not the fault of the people waiting for him beyond these doors. They had done everything that had been asked of them, and more, and he had a duty to them, to tell them why their world was coming to an end. He swallowed, took a deep breath, and pushed open the door and went inside. His team looked up at him: some fearful, some hopeful, and some . . . well, they knew where the cards were falling. Over in the far corner sat Agnes Jurati. She met his eye, briefly, and gave the saddest of smiles, and stuck both thumbs up. *Oh Aggie*, he thought. *Why are you so good to me?*

He stood at the front and folded his arms.

"Thanks for coming," he said. "I know this isn't easy. The first thing I want to say is—I couldn't have asked for a better team. All of you. You're outstanding. You won't struggle to find posts after this—I promise you. Koas has given me her word." He gave a faint laugh. "You know, not everyone gets to have their name attached to a catastrophe like this. But it's my name that's attached. Not yours. I want you to know that. Your scientific careers won't suffer because of . . ." *Me*, he thought. "This," he said.

"Bruce—" said someone from the back. He carried on quickly.

"The program's over, immediately," he said. He heard a soft cry go up from someone; not all. "I'm sorry. This is the only outcome. The synths are banned—"

"But everything we did . . . we didn't do anything *wrong*—!" someone said.

"I know. I know that. None of you did anything wrong. But we can't appeal to reason right now. We can't appeal to science. People are *scared*. They look at the A500s, and they see killing machines. They see mass murderers—"

"They weren't *like* that!"

Already their work was in the past tense, even from those protesting.

"I know," he said. "But that's the way it is. Everything is being turned off. Everything is being dismantled. Everything is being destroyed. You're welcome to stay here at the Robotics Division, but if you do, you have to understand that your lines of research are about to become severely limited. You'll be able to work on abstract design—but you will never be able to build another synthetic—"

"Bruce, that's absurd—they can't shut down a complete line of scientific inquiry! That's dark ages stuff, man!"

"They can," he said. "And they have. You try building something now and you're going to find yourself in jail. My advice—leave the Institute. At the very least, particularly for those of you still working on doctorates, find another line of research as quickly as you can. I know this might mean throwing away two or three years of work, and it's damn unfair, but that's the way it is. You are not to blame for this, and you will not be held accountable. But you need to put your time here behind you and move on as quickly as you can."

He opened the floor to questions and answered them as calmly and as rationally as he could. As he expected, most of the people in the room were now anxious about what they should do next. He did his best to suggest people to speak to, topics to pursue, anything to get them going on another path of research and put this whole house of horrors behind them. At last, they were mostly satisfied, and started to filter out of the room. Eventually, there was only one other person left.

Agnes Jurati closed the door behind her colleagues. "Bruce," she said. She looked pale, shocked. "This can't be over. This can't be the end."

"It is, Aggie. It's finished."

"What are we going to *do*?"

"You heard my advice. Get out. Find some other work. I know you're further on than others, Aggie, I know it will be harder—"

"I'm not leaving here! I'm not leaving you!"

He could not quite meet her eye.

"Bruce? What's going on?"

"I won't be here, Aggie. I'm finished here. I'm quitting, right now. I'm gone."

She looked at him in dismay. "Bruce, you can't go . . ."

"I have to. I can't stay here. If I can't work . . ." He reached out one hand, although he didn't quite dare touch her. "You could come with me, Aggie."

"Where would we go?"

"I don't know . . . Somewhere. A place where we can carry on this work . . . Our beautiful, important work." Suddenly, he saw how it could be: the two of them, together, side by side. The necessary pair that would make this breakthrough . . .

"Bruce," she said. "I can't go . . . I'm too . . ."

Castles in the air, collapsing all around him. No, of course she wouldn't go with him. Why would she? "All right. I understand."

"Bruce, I'm sorry—"

"It's all right. Forget I ever asked. Goodbye, Aggie."

He turned his back on her and left. He could hear her calling his name, but he didn't answer. *I'm gone*, he thought, and while he did not know where he was going, he did not think: *Who am I, now?* or *What shall I do?* Bruce Maddox had never really doubted himself, or his great elusive dream. He never did.

Some say that history is the deeds of great men; others say that history is women, following behind with a bucket. After the great men weary of performing great deeds, after they lay down their tools and retire from their quests—what happens next?

Life goes on—at least, until it ends.

Some people were barely affected. Doctor Amal Safadi, for example, who had done good work—done her best, no less—and showed courage in the face of adversity, and had not backed down, and had given people the information they needed to save millions of lives—she was largely unaffected. She was shocked, of course, as anyone else within the Federation would be, first by the news of the attack on Mars, and then, again, at the abrupt ending of the Romulan relief mission. She, like many others at Cambridge, was deeply concerned by this. She, unlike many others in her circle, went to the trouble of contacting her representatives, and registering her disappointment and distress that the Romulan people were being abandoned. She never received a wholly satisfactory answer, and she began to realize that her view was in the minority. Even some of her more enlightened acquaintances were heard to say: "Perhaps we'd done enough. Perhaps we need to look after our own people." What upset her the most, she realized as the months went past, was that she could find no trace of Nokim Vritet. She still did not believe he had written the condemnation of her report that had led to her being called before a Federation committee. She knew he was too meticulous, too good a scientist. She worried about what had happened to him, in those last terrifying days. For many years after, Safadi held out hope that she might find him, tucked away in a refugee camp somewhere. She would bring him back to Cambridge, find him a quiet office, and they would work together. For many years, she held out this hope, long beyond anything rational. Long after he had died.

Olivia Quest had played her cards carefully and, if anyone remembered her enthusiasm for the synthetics, she was, by some sorcery, able to persuade them to forget. Her vocal support for the synth ban helped, as did the many speeches she made after the Romulan mission was ended. She busied herself outlining her vision of a new deal for smaller member worlds such as her own. Closer involvement in decision-making. More access to resources. These were trying times on the border, since the collapse of the Romulan Star Empire, and the Federation needed to look after its own. Quest faced no difficulty in being reelected to the Council and, in time, became the senior representative for Estelen. She did not hesitate to take on other jobs as well. The Federation Security Council was her ultimate aim, and who could doubt that she would succeed?

Admiral Bordson remained in his post for a few more years, but it was clear to those who knew him that his heart was no longer in it. There was some relief when Kirsten Clancy rose to the rank of admiral, and then to C-in-C. A number of officers found themselves reassigned in the weeks that followed the end of the mission. For some of them, this was a wrench; for others, less so—they were used to being sent where they were needed and turning themselves immediately to the task at hand. That was what Starfleet was all about, for them. A few—not enough—remained in post, on the small border worlds that had found themselves the new homes of thousands of desperate and sometimes hostile people. All along the old Neutral Zone, in fragile systems that stretched for light-years from the Qiris Sector to the Immian Sector, they found themselves trying to hold the thin line between structure and chaos. Some quit quietly. Why should they stay? They had been told, in no uncertain terms, that their work had no value. They left, and the buildings, half-done, crumbled, and with them the trust and the hope evaporated. A vacuum, into which less selfless and more grasping powers moved.

Then there were the worlds left behind. The worlds that had been waiting for salvation. Refugees, huddled into transit camps, looking up at skies for ships that were no longer coming. Shall we think about what must have happened to them? These lives that, as it turned out, counted for so little in the great scheme of things. Can we bear to imagine what came next? The slow death of hope and the sudden birth of despair—and at last, the violent, screaming end.

These were the true victims—but there were others. Geordi La Forge, perhaps; thinking of his lucky escape, thinking of the ones he had left behind. Sometimes it would catch up with him unawares. A simple thing might set him off; looking for a book or a tool; realizing that it had been in his quarters on Mars. He spent days thinking about how close that shave had been.

There was Zani, who knew that promises should not be made, and was therefore perhaps best equipped to cope when they were not kept. But there was also Elnor. How did one explain these things to a child? There was the crew of the *Verity*, that had set out so bravely, who found themselves leaderless, and torn from a mission to which they had given their all. And let us not forget Raffi Musiker, left suddenly without job or purpose, sidelined by her association with the man who walked away. Raffi, who had sacrificed a marriage—had sacrificed motherhood—to this task. Raffi, who could not make herself believe that the universe would be this cruel, this capricious, and went in search of some kind of explanation, no matter how outlandish, no matter how unlikely. Anything—god, please, *anything*—that would make sense of it all.

History had been made, yes, somehow; but history has its own agenda. And for those expelled from the courts and councils of the great, history can be very cruel.

Epilogue

La Barre, France

How do you find a home, when home is gone? How do you settle in a place when you wish to be elsewhere? Jean-Luc Picard dumped his bags in the hall and looked around what others might call the "family home" and felt dread fall upon him like a heavy cloak. *I am useless*, he thought. *I am without purpose.*

The day passed; so did the next, and the one after. The sun rose, and went overhead, and then set, as was its wont. Sometimes he noticed that the sunset was beautiful. Sometimes he did not. He was not entirely isolated. Messages came. There was one from Zani, asking him to remember them. He pushed it aside, and was ashamed as he did so, knowing how inexcusably he was breaking a promise. *I have been prevented from keeping it*, he thought bitterly. His mind would go back to that last conversation with Starfleet Command, and how little it meant to them in the end. A message came from Will and Deanna: *"You did the right thing."* Some consolation, he thought. But not much.

What does one do with empty hours? What does one do with enforced freedom? Picard took long walks. He beat the bounds of his estate, started to learn each centimeter of it, in the manner of his forebears. But even as he came to know each field, each blade of grass, each vine, he resented his presence here. As a boy, he had kept his eyes from the land, looking upward at the sky, at the stars, and had promised himself that he would go there. He had kept that promise . . . Once he had held whole star systems in the hollow of his hand. And yet, in the end, he had overreached, and had fallen ignominiously back to Earth, like burned Icarus. The stars were lost to him now. He had lost everything that he loved. He was exiled, and he could see no way back.

The days are long and quiet. They accumulate. There is no end to them. Picard walks the lanes around his fields. He broods. He writes—long, long books about great men and great deeds. Wine is made, and drunk. Winter comes, then spring, then harvest, then another deep cold winter. The cycle is endless. The huge clock ticks in the hall, eating time. His mind goes around in circles.

What shall I do, now?

Where do I go?

Who am I?

Beyond the window, he hears Laris and Zhaban muttering about him. Beside him, the dog—a kind gift from kind friends—catches his mood and whines. Picard reaches down, strokes the soft fur behind its ears. The dog, consoled, looks back up, with love. Picard smiles, despite all. He stands and walks to the door. The little creature trots loyally beside him.

"Come, Number One. We can't sit here forever. Let's find something to do."

ACKNOWLEDGMENTS

My heartfelt thanks to Kirsten Beyer for her friendship, and for making this project such a joy to work on from start to finish. It's a privilege serving with you.

Grateful thanks to Margaret Clark, Dayton Ward, and Scott Pearson for great ideas, sharp-eyed editing, and for knowing Trek so well. I'd be lost without you.

Huge props and thanks to my brilliant agent, Max Edwards, who works tirelessly on my behalf and always says things that make me feel better.

Most of all, my thanks and love to Matthew and Verity, my team, who patiently allowed me to disappear for most of the summer holiday to get this book written. I love you, guys.

ABOUT THE AUTHOR

UNA McCORMACK is the author of eight previous *Star Trek* novels: *The Lotus Flower* (part of *The Worlds of Star Trek: Deep Space Nine*), *Hollow Men*, *The Never-Ending Sacrifice*, *Brinkmanship*, *The Missing*, the *New York Times* bestseller *The Fall: The Crimson Shadow*, *Enigma Tales*, and *Discovery: The Way to the Stars*. She is also the author of four *Doctor Who* novels from BBC Books: *The King's Dragon, The Way Through the Woods, Royal Blood*, and *Molten Heart*. She has written numerous short stories and audio dramas. She lives in Cambridge, England, with her partner of many years, Matthew, and their daughter, Verity.